W9-BRS-429

"The Harte saga is as much a force of nature as a work of fiction . . . the issues at stake still compel readers after 25 years. Bradford understood early on readers' hunger for depictions of women who are strong and powerful and whose values embrace family. A quarter-century ago, Emma Harte crossed the no-woman's-land that once divided family and business, and now generations of readers consider her a role model in their own lives."   —*The Washington Post*

UNEXPECTED BLESSINGS

"Bradford gives her readers more of what she does best— strong, savvy female protagonists who relentlessly pursue great destinies, characters much like the author herself . . . well-written and full of emotion . . . completely riveting . . . the plot, while always complex, has suspenseful moments to keep the pace sharp . . . good reading . . . *Unexpected Blessings* clearly shows why Bradford is still the premier writer of family sagas."

—*Miami New Times*

"The exploits and adventures of Bradford's indomitable heroines continue to make for lusty escapist fiction in this robust fifth novel in the series."   —*Publishers Weekly*

"The enduring theme of family loyalty ennobles the Harte family saga and raises it to a heartwarming crescendo that longtime fans will appreciate. New readers will relish it as well."   —*Book Page*

MORE ACCLAIM FOLLOWS . . .

"Readers who loved *A Woman of Substance* will enjoy *Emma's Secret.*"
　　　　　　　　　　　　　　　　　　　　　—*Denver Post*

"In her 19th novel, the grande dame of mass-market fiction revisits her first heroine—the indomitable Emma Harte."
　　　　　　　　　　　　　　　　　—*New York Daily News*

"So many of us turn to novels like Barbara Taylor Bradford's latest, *Emma's Secret,* for our daily dose of amour."
　　　　　　　　　　　　　　　　　—*Woman's Day* magazine

"Promises to tantalize, mesmerize, and titillate readers of all ages. It has all the Bradford touches: strong and swift plot, hints of secrets about to be revealed . . . spellbinding . . . destined to fly off booksellers' racks and be passed around many book clubs. It is a darn good read." —*Roanoke Times*

"It will be . . . appreciated by those with an irresistible desire to follow the further adventures of the Harte clan."
　　　　　　　　　　　　　　　　　—*Publishers Weekly*

"Bradford's characters are so real, readers clamor to know them better."　　　　　　　—*USA Today Weekend* magazine

"[An] original story with new energy. Emma Harte is one of those characters . . . we never want to leave behind, and thank goodness Bradford has brought her back to us with a story worthy of this truly remarkable woman."
　　　　　　　　　　　　　　　　　—*Romantic Times,* "Top Pick"

A WOMAN OF SUBSTANCE

"An extravagant, absorbing novel of love, courage, ambition, war, death, and passion."   —*The New York Times*

"A long, satisfying novel of money, power, passion and revenge, set against the sweep of 20th century history."
—*Los Angeles Times*

"A wonderfully entertaining novel."   —*Denver Post*

VOICE OF THE HEART

"*Voice of the Heart* is the sort of book I cannot resist, indeed, I pray to find."   —*Washington Times* magazine

"It really keeps you turning the pages, wondering just why it is that two beautiful women who were once great friends are now sworn enemies."   —*Daily Express* (UK)

"A rare treat. We guarantee you will laugh and cry with the characters and that you won't be able to put it down."
—*Literary Guild* magazine

"Meant to be read in a peignoir on a chaise longue whilst nibbling scented chocolates."   —*Cosmopolitan*

"A rich tapestry of love and romance. The surprise ending is both poignant and fitting."   —*San Diego Union*

"Barbara Taylor Bradford is back with a new, vibrantly characterized leading lady and a glimpse into the dazzling world of the rich and powerful . . . [A] richly woven tale."
—*Working Woman*

"It is easy to want every item Bradford catalogues, easy to imagine wearing it, eating and drinking it, driving it, smelling like it . . . The geography of *Voice of the Heart* takes a reader to all the right places."   —*Los Angeles Times*

"A captivating work filled with glamour, intrigue, and ironic reversal . . . Richly textured, highly entertaining."
—*Booklist*

"Engrossing . . . Stunning."   —*Pittsburgh Press*

HOLD THE DREAM

"Readers who shared the trials and tribulations, and successes, of the indomitable Emma Harte in *A Woman of Substance* will find this sequel equally engrossing. Attractive, intelligent, and capable, Paula McGill Fairley proves a worthy successor to her grandmother's domain."   —*Booklist*

"Another instant bestseller. The men and women are all gorgeous, rich, well-dressed. There are luxurious descriptions in this perfect page-turner."   —*Philadelphia Inquirer*

"A deeply involving story of women of power and wealth and substance."   —*Publishers Weekly*

"Fascinating."   —*Houston Chronicle*

"A sweeping saga full of passion and intrigue . . . a gripping read." —*Hello* magazine

"A vibrantly characterized leading lady and a glimpse at the dazzling world of the rich and powerful. A richly woven tale." —*Working Woman*

"Barbara Taylor Bradford is the storyteller of substance." —*The Times* (London)

TO BE THE BEST

"A novel for everyone . . . A satisfying, lushly detailed saga." —*Rave Reviews*

"A compulsive read." —*Daily Mail* (London)

"Will keep you up 'til all hours reading just one more chapter before you can bear to turn out the bedside light." —*Prima* magazine

ACT OF WILL

"A master storyteller and character builder, Ms. Bradford again crafts another reader–holder novel . . . *Act of Will* is another winner." —*Pittsburgh Press*

"Pure gold—certain to be a runaway bestseller." —*Cosmopolitan*

"This novel continues the Bradford tradition of spirited romances peopled with memorable, self-made women . . . fetching." —*Booklist*

BY BARBARA TAYLOR BRADFORD

❧

THE EMMA HARTE SAGA

A Woman of Substance
Hold the Dream
To Be the Best
Emma's Secret
Unexpected Blessings
Just Rewards

❧

Voice of the Heart
Act of Will
The Women in His Life
Remember
Angel
Everything to Gain
Dangerous to Know
Love in Another Town
Her Own Rules
A Secret Affair
Power of a Woman
A Sudden Change of Heart
Where You Belong
The Triumph of Katie Byrne
Three Weeks in Paris

JUST REWARDS

∾

BARBARA TAYLOR BRADFORD

St. Martin's Paperbacks

This is a work of fiction. All of the characters, organizations and events portrayed in this novel are either products of the author's imagination or are used fictitiously.

JUST REWARDS

Copyright © 2006 by Beaji Enterprises, Inc.
Excerpt from *The Ravenscar Dynasty* copyright © 2006 by Beaji Enterprises, Inc.

Front cover dress by Anjolique Bridal, www.anjolique.com

ISBN: 0-312-98575-4
EAN: 9780312-98575-2

Printed in the United States of America

St. Martin's Press hardcover edition / January 2006
St. Martin's Paperbacks edition / October 2006

St. Martin's Paperbacks are published by St. Martin's Press, 175 Fifth Avenue, New York, NY 10010.

10 9 8 7 6 5 4 3 2 1

For Bob, with my love

CONTENTS

❧

THE THREE CLANS

∾

THE HARTES

(Shown in line of descent)

EMMA HARTE. Matriarch. Founder of the dynasty and business empire.

HER CHILDREN

EDWINA, Dowager Countess of Dunvale. Emma's daughter by Edwin Fairley. (Illegitimate.) First born.

CHRISTOPHER "KIT" LOWTHER. Emma's son by her first husband, Joe Lowther. Second born.

ROBIN AINSLEY. Emma's son by her second husband, Arthur Ainsley. Twin of Elizabeth. Third born.

ELIZABETH AINSLEY DEBOYNE. Emma's daughter by her second husband, Arthur Ainsley. Twin of Robin. Third born.

DAISY AINSLEY AMORY. Emma's daughter by Paul McGill. (Illegitimate.) Fourth born.

HER GRANDCHILDREN

ANTHONY STANDISH, Earl of Dunvale. Son of Edwina and Jeremy Standish, Earl and Countess of Dunvale.

SARAH LOWTHER PASCAL. Daughter of Kit and June Lowther.

OWEN HUGHES. Son of Robin Ainsley and Glynnis Hughes. (Illegitimate.)

JONATHAN AINSLEY. Son of Robin and Valerie Ainsley.

PAULA MCGILL HARTE AMORY FAIRLEY O'NEILL. Daughter of Daisy and David Amory. Sister of Philip.

PHILIP MCGILL HARTE AMORY. Son of Daisy and David Amory. Brother of Paula.

ALEXANDER BARKSTONE. Son of Elizabeth and Tony Barkstone. Brother of Emily, Amanda, and Francesca. (Deceased.)

EMILY BARKSTONE HARTE. Daughter of Elizabeth and Tony Barkstone. Sister of Alexander. Half sister of Amanda and Francesca.

AMANDA LINDE. Daughter of Elizabeth and her second husband, Derek Linde. Twin of Francesca, half sister of Emily and Alexander.

FRANCESCA LINDE WESTON. Daughter of Elizabeth and her second husband, Derek Linde. Twin of Amanda, half sister of Emily and Alexander.

EMMA'S GREAT-GRANDCHILDREN

TESSA FAIRLEY LONGDEN. Daughter of Paula and her first husband, Jim Fairley. Twin of Lorne. Half sister of Linnet, Emsie, and Desmond.

LORNE FAIRLEY. Son of Paula and her first husband, Jim Fairley. Twin of Tessa. Half brother of Linnet, Emsie, and Desmond.

LORD JEREMY STANDISH. Son of Anthony and Sally

Standish, Earl and Countess of Dunvale. Brother of Giles and India.

TOBY HARTE. Son of Emily and Winston Harte II. Brother of Gideon and Natalie.

GIDEON HARTE. Son of Emily and Winston Harte II. Brother of Toby and Natalie.

NATALIE HARTE. Daughter of Emily and Winston Harte II. Sister of Toby and Gideon.

HON. GILES STANDISH. Son of Anthony and Sally Standish, Earl and Countess of Dunvale. Brother of Jeremy and India.

LADY INDIA STANDISH. Daughter of Anthony and Sally Standish, Earl and Countess of Dunvale. Sister of Jeremy and Giles.

PATRICK O'NEILL. Son of Paula and her second husband, Shane O'Neill. Brother of Linnet, Emsie, and Desmond. (Deceased.)

LINNET O'NEILL. Daughter of Paula and her second husband, Shane O'Neill. Half sister of Tessa and Lorne. Sister of Emsie and Desmond.

CHLOE PASCAL. Daughter of Sarah and Yves Pascal.

FIONA MCGILL AMORY. Daughter of Philip McGill Amory and Madelana O'Shea Amory. (Deceased.)

EMMA "EMSIE" O'NEILL. Daughter of Paula and her second husband, Shane O'Neill. Half sister of Tessa and Lorne. Sister of Linnet and Desmond.

DESMOND O'NEILL. Son of Paula and her second husband, Shane O'Neill. Half brother of Tessa and Lorne. Brother of Linnet and Emsie.

EVAN HUGHES. Daughter of Owen and Marietta Hughes.

THE HARTES (continued)

Winston Harte. Emma's older brother and business partner. (Deceased.)

Randolph Harte. Son of Winston and Charlotte Harte. (Deceased.)

Winston Harte II. Son of Randolph and Georgina Harte. Brother of Sally and Vivienne.

Sally Harte Standish, Countess of Dunvale. Daughter of Randolph and Georgina Harte. Sister of Winston II and Vivienne.

Vivienne Harte Leslie. Daughter of Randolph and Georgina Harte. Sister of Winston II and Sally.

Toby Harte. Son of Winston II and Emily Harte. Brother of Gideon and Natalie.

Gideon Harte. Son of Winston II and Emily Harte. Brother of Toby and Natalie.

Natalie Harte. Daughter of Winston II and Emily Harte. Sister of Toby and Gideon.

Frank Harte. Emma's younger brother. (Deceased.)

Rosamund Harte. Daughter of Frank and Natalie Harte. Sister of Simon.

Simon Harte. Son of Frank and Natalie Harte. Brother of Rosamund.

THE O'NEILLS

Shane Patrick Desmond "Blackie" O'Neill. Founding father of the dynasty and business empire. (Deceased.)

Bryan O'Neill. Son of Blackie and Laura Spencer O'Neill.

Shane O'Neill. Son of Bryan and Geraldine O'Neill. Brother of Miranda and Laura.

MIRANDA O'NEILL JAMES. Daughter of Bryan and Geraldine O'Neill. Sister of Shane and Laura.

LAURA O'NEILL NETTLETON. Daughter of Bryan and Geraldine O'Neill. Sister of Shane and Miranda.

PATRICK O'NEILL. Son of Paula and Shane O'Neill. Brother of Linnet, Emsie, and Desmond. (Deceased.)

LINNET O'NEILL. Daughter of Shane and Paula O'Neill. Sister of Emsie and Desmond.

EMMA "EMSIE" O'NEILL. Daughter of Shane and Paula O'Neill. Sister of Desmond and Linnet.

DESMOND O'NEILL. Son of Shane and Paula O'Neill. Brother of Linnet and Emsie.

THE KALLINSKIS

DAVID KALLINSKI. Founding father of the dynasty and business empire. (Deceased.)

SIR RONALD KALLINSKI. Son of David and Rebecca Kallinski. (Deceased.)

MICHAEL KALLINSKI. Son of Ronald and Helen "Posy" Kallinski. Brother of Mark.

MARK KALLINSKI. Son of Ronald and Helen "Posy" Kallinski. Brother of Michael.

JULIAN KALLINSKI. Son of Michael Kallinski and his former wife, Valentine Kallinski. Brother of Arielle and Jessica.

ARIELLE KALLINSKI. Daughter of Michael Kallinski and his former wife, Valentine Kallinski. Sister of Julian and Jessica.

JESSICA KALLINSKI. Daughter of Michael Kallinski and his former wife, Valentine Kallinski. Sister of Julian and Arielle.

LONDON, 2002

The man stood in the doorway of the shop, huddled in a corner, sheltering from the icy wind. It was freezing on this bitter January morning, and he felt tempted to hurry off to the nearby Hyde Park Hotel for a cooked English breakfast.

Yet he was unable to tear himself away from this doorway, where he had always had a perfect view of the building opposite, one which he had for so long coveted as his own.

Leaning forward, he focused his eyes on the grand and impressive edifice across the road. It had been standing there for over eighty years, but it was untouched by the passage of time and impregnable. He thought of it as a bastion of prestige, privilege, and wealth, the center of that enormous, worldwide business empire created by his grandmother.

And it should have been his.

He believed he had been cheated. It had fallen into the hands of Paula O'Neill, who now thought of it as her own, when it was *his* by rights. But it wasn't; that idea sprang from his irrationality and jealousy. And that was the tragedy.

In the mid-1980s he had almost wrested the flagship Knightsbridge emporium and the provincial Harte stores away from Paula, when she had made a series of mistakes in a deal related to the stores. So flawed was her judgment that she had played right into his waiting hands.

Unfortunately, just as he reached out, had the stores almost in his grasp, he had been betrayed. As a consequence of this unexpected betrayal, Paula O'Neill had managed to outwit him. Curiously, losing had been the spur; he had created his own empire and was today a billionaire.

She had been his nemesis for years, but it was from this precise moment in time that he had become her sworn enemy, had vowed to wreak his revenge on her. And soon he would do that; he would finally triumph over her.

Abruptly, the man stepped forward, out of the doorway, his attention riveted on two young women who had hurried out of the store and were studying the windows fronting on Knightsbridge.

One of them was a redhead, and he knew her at once. She was Linnet O'Neill, Paula's daughter; however, she was now a Kallinski, after having married the Kallinski heir last month. His thoughts settled on the little church in Pennistone village where they had been married. How easily it would have burned to the ground, killing everyone in it, and his problems with the Hartes would have been solved forevermore.

For a moment the man was baffled, unable to pinpoint the other woman's identity. She was bundled up in a loden cape and long scarf, and her face was obscured. But then she turned, and he instantly recognized the distinctive chiseled profile.

His chest tightened, and a virulent anger surged through him as he gazed at Evan Hughes. She was his new nemesis, the American woman who had insinuated herself into the family and was about to become a Harte. He muttered an expletive. She was already a Harte, thanks in no small measure to his father's long-ago lust. And now she threatened everybody by her very existence, especially he himself. She, too, was now a target, along with Paula and her redheaded brat.

A knowing smile slid onto his handsome face; he stared hard at the two women for a very long moment before setting out in the direction of the hotel for breakfast. That self-satisfied smile remained intact as he turned up the collar of his expensive and impeccably tailored vicuña coat and increased his pace.

As he walked, he considered a plan he had recently formulated, one so devilishly clever it might have been devised by Machiavelli himself. It would surely help to bring about the fall of the house of Harte. He was convinced of this outcome.

Jonathan Ainsley laughed out loud. They were going to get their just rewards. He would see to that.

Part One

QUARTET

Envy slays itself by its own arrows.

— ANONYMOUS MEDIEVAL SAYING

I

Flurries of silvery snowflakes were blowing in the wind, sticking to the plate-glass windows of Harte's and on the faces of the two pretty young women gazing so intently into those windows.

Evan Hughes brought a gloved hand to her cheek and wiped the dampness away. Then she drew closer to Linnet O'Neill, shivering and hunching into her dark green loden cape, feeling the bite of the intense cold.

Instantly, Linnet glanced at Evan and exclaimed, "I'm so thoughtless, dragging you outside to look at our windows on a day like this! You're freezing. Come on, let's go inside. We've seen enough, actually." Linnet took hold of Evan's arm and hurried her toward one of the double doors leading into Harte's.

"I'm all right, honestly," Evan protested as she was propelled across the floor of the cosmetics department, adding irately, "I'm not a cream puff, you know. I'm not going to melt away."

"You've got guts of steel, I'm very well aware of that!" Linnet shot back. "It just became frightfully cold all of a sudden. And if you catch a cold, or get sick, Gideon will have my guts for garters."

Evan burst out laughing, as usual amused by Linnet's penchant for quaint sayings; she was frequently startled by the other girl's bluntness, as well as her pithiness. Evan considered her recently discovered cousin a unique person. She had never met anyone like her, and in this past year of working together, they had become the very best of friends.

Moving through the glamorous, eye-catching displays of cosmetics and perfumes, Evan felt her icy limbs beginning to thaw, and she loosened her scarf, opened her cape. Smoothing her hand over her bulging stomach, she confided, "I feel like a beached whale, Linny. I can't wait to give birth."

Linnet's expression was sympathetic. "I know. But just imagine, Evan, you're about to have twins. *Twins!* You've certainly given Tessa, India, and me pause for thought. We have a tendency to forget that twins run in this family. Grandy had twins, and so did Mummy the first time around, when she was married to Jim Fairley. It's only just struck *us* that we also might be candidates, have the same fate as you." Linnet smiled engagingly. "What do *you* think?"

"We share a lot of the same genes, I guess, so you're probably right."

"Julian's hoping so, and actually so am I. It makes life easier. Two children born together saves so much bother in the long run . . . an instant family and less time off work."

"Very well put," Evan responded softly, laughter filling her eyes. She couldn't help thinking that Linnet's inborn pragmatism inevitably came to the fore, but she admired her for being so down to earth.

By now the two women had arrived at a bank of elevators, and they stepped into one as soon as its doors slid open. Falling silent, they rode up to the management offices and hurried down the long corridor.

When they reached the alcove in the center, where the famous portrait of Emma Harte hung, the two of them automatically came to a standstill, looked at each other, smiled, and then briskly saluted their great-grandmother and moved on. It had become something of a ritual with them of late, whether they were together or alone. It signified their pride in being her progeny and working in the renowned store she had founded.

A few minutes later, settled comfortably in Evan's office, Linnet said, "So, give me your opinion about the windows."

"I have to agree with you, they are a bit outdated. Oh, they're beautiful, Linnet, of course. So well dressed. And they do evoke the kind of image we want for Harte's, but they could be a bit . . . *fresher*."

"Not enough pizzazz, perhaps?" Linnet suggested.

"Not pizzazz, that's not quite right for Harte's, is it?"

"I suppose not," Linnet agreed, sitting back in the chair, her eyes focused on Evan, whose opinion she valued.

Evan bit her lip, then shook her head. "I think the word I'm looking for is . . . *glamorous*. I'm talking about the fashion windows per se, Linnet, and they ought to be just a tad more eye-catching. Listen, they should say something to the customer . . . they should say, *Come in, try me on, buy me*."

Linnet nodded, her face lighting up. "That's true. You've just put your finger on it."

Evan said, "You've only recently come back from New York. You've seen the store windows there, and I believe you're now finding our windows somewhat flat." She raised a brow, and her pellucid gray-blue eyes rested on Linnet thoughtfully. When her cousin made no response, she asked, "Am I not correct?"

"I think you are. . . . But I'm not sure Mummy would agree."

"Have you discussed the windows with Paula?" Evan probed, sounding anxious.

"No, I haven't had a chance, and she and Dad are staying in Yorkshire this week, recovering from Christmas, the New Year, and all their entertaining. They're taking a week off, and they just want to potter around at Penni-stone Royal. They enjoy being at home with each other, doing what they've always done since they were kids growing up together." Linnet shook her head. "Anyway, I'm not going to say a word until she's back here at work. Actually, Evan, there are some other things I want to discuss with her, certain changes I believe we should make."

Evan sat up straighter but said nothing, merely raised a brow quizzically, her eyes full of questions.

"You look surprised," Linnet exclaimed, eyeing her carefully.

"I am. What kinds of changes do you have in mind?"

"I'll get to those in a minute, just let me say this first. As you well know, the fashion retrospective was a big success last summer. We gained lots of new customers, and we did terrifically well, but eventually sales dipped. What we need to do is keep our customers coming in, and we need to garner those new ones as well. I believe we're in a new age of retailing. We have to make shopping a unique experience, and offer other services."

"Obviously you've studied this carefully and come up with some fresh ideas," Evan ventured cautiously, wondering if Paula would permit any changes at the Knights-bridge store.

"I have," Linnet asserted. "For example, Harte's ought to have a day spa, a really beautiful spa offering every kind of treatment."

"That would be great!" Evan agreed swiftly and then thought to ask, "But where would you put it?"

Linnet grinned and explained, "I think one of those boring departments such as Mattresses would have to go. But seriously, we could carve out space. I know this store inside out, and I know we *could* do it."

"I guess it doesn't have to be a huge spa, just a unique one."

"That's it exactly. Evan, listen, don't you think we

ought to have more places to eat? Snack bars, for instance. Especially on the ground floor, near the Food Halls. We could feature shellfish, pizza, hot dogs, deli sandwiches, and pastas. The kind of fast food that's actually tasty. I'm sure they would appeal to people who work in Knightsbridge and the areas nearby, as well as our customers."

"That's a great suggestion," Evan agreed. "I can feel my mouth watering just at the thought. What I wouldn't give for a plate of oysters right now."

"And ice cream on top, I've no doubt," Linnet said, grinning at her. "Isn't that your favorite lunch these days?"

Evan shook her head. "Not quite, although I have had a few longings for some very strange food combinations."

Linnet leaned forward, her expression intense. "I'd appreciate any ideas *you* might have, Evan. You're always so creative, and I do think we really *have* to revamp the store. A little bit anyway."

Evan nodded. "I agree." She paused, hesitating, and then confided, "I did have an idea a while back. A floor devoted to brides. Called . . . Brides. Naturally we would feature bridal gowns, bridesmaids' dresses, page boy suits, and all those things. But we could also sell bridal shoes, jewelry, gifts for the bridesmaids, and even bridal lingerie. And there's another thing. In the States, wedding planners are very popular; we could offer that kind of service as well."

"Evan, I love it! And what about the Evan Hughes Bridal Collection? You know you love to design bridal gowns. How about it?"

Evan considered Linnet's words. "I think I'd enjoy that. I guess I've been itching to design again." Her enthusiasm was apparent. "Actually, the store has had inquiries about your wedding gown. There were lots of photographs in the newspapers, and women seemed taken with it."

"I don't blame them. You created something out of this

world. So, let's sell it to them," Linnet replied in a rush. At the same pace she continued, "Also, I think your idea for an entire floor for brides is inspirational. I'd really appreciate it if you could give me something on paper. As soon as possible."

"I've got a lot of stuff on my computer already. I'll print it out for you before I go to Yorkshire."

"Thanks, and when are you going to Pennistone Royal?"

"In three days. Gideon and I are driving up on Saturday. I'm glad. I'm already a bit panicky, to tell you the truth. I feel as if I'm going to give birth at any moment." She said this lightly, laughing, but she was genuinely concerned that this might happen, that the twins might be premature.

So was Linnet. Evan and Gideon had delayed getting married until January because her own big, splashy wedding to Julian had been long-planned for this past December. They hadn't wanted to compete. Pushing aside her worries, Linnet now also laughed and endeavored to reassure Evan. "You'll be fine, darling. Julian and I will be there for the weekend, so I can help with any last-minute details for the wedding."

"That's lovely, thanks for offering, but there's not much to do. It's only the family, after all."

"Your parents are coming over, though, aren't they?"

"Oh yes, and my sisters. My mother's already here; she arrived several days ago. And the others will be flying in next week. Robin's being wonderful, very kind, and he's invited my parents and sisters to stay at Lackland Priory."

"Well, that's nice of him, of course, but don't forget you've given him a new lease on life, Evan. Mummy says he's never looked better."

Linnet now pushed herself to her feet and picked up her coat. "I'd better go, I've loads of paperwork to catch up with. Thanks for listening, and for your input. It was just what I needed." She paused at the door, blew a kiss. "I'll see you later." Smiling, she was gone.

Evan gazed at the door, her face already clouding over.

She was fully aware that Linnet's nonchalance was assumed, that in fact she was worried about her mother's reaction to her ideas for the store. Although they were not particularly radical, Evan knew they would fall flat. As a newcomer, she saw Paula O'Neill from an entirely different viewpoint than did her daughters and India Standish, Paula's niece. Evan was aware that their boss was determined to keep Harte's in its traditional mode. What Linnet wanted to do wouldn't destroy Harte's image. Still, Paula would be upset. She was Emma Harte's granddaughter and heiress, and she never deviated from the rules set down by Emma. Having run Harte's in exactly the same way for well over thirty years, since before Emma's death, she wasn't likely to make any changes now.

There'll be trouble between them, Evan suddenly thought. Real trouble.

2

He could see her in the distance, riding on the escalator, obviously heading for the upper floors of the store. The bright red hair was a fiery halo around her face, impossible to miss, as was the sleek silhouette of her smartly tailored black suit, austere except for the touches of white at the collar and cuffs.

She was the spitting image of Emma Harte and knew it, because everyone had told her this for years. They had also told her how smart she was and canny, like her great-grandmother. Jack Figg, head of security at Harte's and an old family friend, suddenly wondered if anyone had ever told her that she, and only she in the family, had been lucky enough to inherit Emma's enormous *glamour* as well.

A small smile flickered on Jack's face as he stepped onto the escalator, and he acknowledged, somewhat ruefully, that he was prejudiced when it came to Linnet O'Neill. She was his favorite and always had been. To Jack she was the smartest of the younger generation in this family.

Then his thoughts swung to Linnet's cousin Gideon Harte, who was to marry Evan Hughes in ten days. Evan Hughes . . . now there was a name to conjure with. The newly found American relative. Quite a story that was. Sent to London a year ago by her dying British grandmother Glynnis Hughes to seek out Emma Harte, whom Evan quickly found out had been dead for thirty years. Evan stumbling into the midst of the Hartes, meeting Gideon that first day and falling under his spell . . . as he had fallen under hers. *Instantly*. Love at first sight was grand when it happened. Evan impressing Linnet enough to be hired to work at the store . . . Eventually causing Paula to delve into the past to uncover the truth about Evan's antecedents . . . Paula discovering that Evan was the granddaughter of her uncle Robin Ainsley, Emma's favorite son.

Everything was now out in the open; there were no more secrets, and with their typical generosity of spirit the entire family had welcomed Evan, made her feel at home amongst them. And later they had welcomed Evan's parents, Owen and Marietta Hughes, brought them into the clan without a murmur or a qualm.

But there was Jonathan Ainsley, Robin's son, to contend with. Jonathan's hatred had been focused on Paula for years, but he also loathed the rest of the family. Because of his dangerous games, Jack had Ainsley under surveillance at all times, wherever he was in the world. Jack needed to know *what* Ainsley was up to, *when* he was up to it, and most important, *where*.

Ainsley was currently in London, and this disturbed Jack. Evan and Gideon's marriage was uppermost in his mind. It was taking place on Saturday, January 19, in the little church in the village of Pennistone. Jack was convinced that Evan and her father were targets now, just as Paula and Linnet were. Linnet's resemblance to Emma must have been inflaming Ainsley no end, got his hackles up. And he must loathe Owen Hughes, his newly found half brother, albeit illegitimate. As for Evan, she was the grandchild Robin had always craved.

• • •

After walking around the top floor for a few minutes, Jack spotted Linnet in the auditorium. Pushing open the glass doors, he called out, "Linnet! Good morning."

As she swung around, a smile struck her face. She sped over to Jack and gave him a hug, then stepped back and said, "What a lovely surprise! And how did you know where to find me?"

He grinned. "I'm good at that, finding people, you know. Actually, I spotted you on the escalator and jumped on behind you. You're a sight for sore eyes, Beauty. I'm glad you're back. How was your honeymoon?"

"Brilliant. Barbados was hot. New York cold. And exciting. Julian and I had a great time, enjoyed both places. But it's nice to be home. And to see you."

Linnet had known Jack Figg all her life, and he was more like a favorite uncle than a colleague; now she tucked her arm through his in an intimate way, and together they walked to a grouping of chairs near the stage.

Linnet said, "I was going to phone you a little later, to talk about Evan and Gideon's wedding."

As they sat down, Jack told her, "Everything's in place, and the security will be as extensive as it was for your wedding last month. Truly, there's nothing to worry about."

Linnet nodded and leaned forward. "Mummy's staying in Yorkshire to have a rest. Ostensibly. But she felt she'd better be there to help Aunt Emily and Uncle Robin with the plans for the reception, since it'll be at Pennistone Royal. Mums could do it by herself, but the others *want* to be involved. Insist, actually. Robin because of Evan, and Emily because Gideon's her favorite child. Nothing's too good for him."

"Does anyone ever admit to having a favorite?" Jack asked, his gray eyes crinkling at the corners. "Especially in this family?"

Linnet laughed. "No. But they have them. And everyone loves Gid, you know that. He's unique."

Immediately Jack thought of Gideon's brother, Toby, whom he found highly competitive with his younger sibling. Toby was jealous. But Jack decided not to comment on this. He merely said, "True enough," and continued, "Your mother gave me Emily's guest list, and I received Gideon's a couple of days ago. It seems to me that family *only* have been invited."

"Yes, that's right."

There was a small silence.

Jack broke it finally, his voice grown more serious. "There's something I need to tell you, Linnet. . . . Jonathan Ainsley's back in London, I wanted you to know."

"*He* always manages to show up at the wrong time!" she cried, her voice rising an octave. And she was suddenly filled with apprehension. Her hand trembled as she straightened her collar.

"I have everything under control," Jack reassured her swiftly. "My people have him under constant surveillance, that's how we know he's back here." He refrained from telling her that Ainsley had been spotted that very morning watching the store from across the road. He went on, his voice as always calm and soothing. "I'm simply telling you this because I promised to keep you informed about him. I just want you to be *aware* . . . and on your guard, so to speak."

"I will be. Have you mentioned it to Gideon?" she asked, her voice worried, her face rigid, her green eyes still reflecting alarm.

"Not yet."

"Shall I say something to Evan?"

"No, don't. It could upset her, and, after all, she's very, very pregnant."

"She's holding her own, though. And the babies are not due until late February, early March. But it's probably better she doesn't know Ainsley's around. She and Gideon are going to stay at Pennistone Royal until the wedding. She can take it easy up there."

"And she'll certainly be safe there," he murmured in response. "That place is like Fort Knox these days."

"Thanks to you! And no doubt Gid's had you working on Beck House, ever since he bought it for Evan and himself. And the babies. Installing a security system, I bet."

"He has indeed, and I have," Jack answered, smiling. "It's a lovely old house, and they're both thrilled it came on the market when it did. Gideon especially, since his father owned it once."

"With Daddy when they were gay young blades," Linnet pointed out. "Gid told me it's almost ready for them to move in."

"I know. But getting back to the guest lists, do you think there might be any last-minute invitations? To non–family members?"

"I doubt it. You see, Jack, Evan hasn't really made any friends, I mean outside the family. She's been caught up with Gideon most of the time, and with India, Tessa, and me. Oh, wait a minute, there's that couple who own the hotel . . . George and Arlette Thomas. Her father's friends. I'm sure she would invite them, but—"

"She did," Jack cut in, "they're on Gideon's list."

"Then I can't think of anyone else."

Jack nodded. "As I said, there'll be plenty of security, but I do need your help with one thing, if you don't mind."

"Tell me."

"More than anyone else, *you* know every person who's going to attend the wedding. You would spot a stranger in a crowd, and instantly. Far quicker, certainly, than me. Or any of my people. And also, although I'm acquainted with every member of the family, I obviously can't be everywhere at once. So, here's what I want you to do . . . Keep your eyes peeled, make a mental note of everyone who's there, and tell me or one of my operatives if you see anyone you don't know. *Immediately*."

Linnet nodded. "I could wear a wire, or whatever you

call it. A mike and an earpiece. Like you did at my wedding."

Jack burst out laughing and sat back in the chair, amusement reflected in his eyes. There was no one quite like her . . . except for Emma when she was alive. She would have made exactly the kind of outrageous suggestion Linnet just had.

"Why are you laughing?" she asked, looking baffled.

"Because only you or your great-grandmother would have said that to me. My God, you're so like her."

"I'm glad I am. But getting back to the wedding, I *could* wear an earpiece and a mike, couldn't I, Jack? I mean, what's to stop me? Or who?"

"No one really, but don't you think it might alarm some members of the family? Like Great-Aunt Edwina, for instance."

"Oh come on, Jack, not Edwina! If she were to spot me with a mike on my lapel, she'd want one, too. You know she's the general in the family, taking charge at the drop of a hat. But she's a good egg."

"Indeed," he murmured, biting back a smile. There was no denying it, at times Linnet took his breath away, but he had no doubts about her whatsoever. She was brave and determined as well as smart, and one day she would be the one to run the Harte stores. She was a star.

"Jack, what about it?" she pressed. "Can I wear a mike?"

"It's not a bad idea at that, Linny," he replied at last, thinking: But wouldn't Paula balk at her daughter being miked up at a family wedding?

Almost as if she had read his mind, Linnet announced, "Mummy might object. If she knew. But she doesn't have to know. I'm sure I can hide the mike on my lapel, behind a large flower. And nobody would notice an earpiece. My hair's longer." As she spoke she fluffed out her auburn bob, staring at him pointedly, her green eyes intense.

"Your hair *is* longer," he murmured and stood up,

glancing at his watch. "Listen, I'll get back to you on that later in the day. Let me think it through. Basically, I don't believe it will be necessary. It is a small wedding, after all."

As Jack headed for the door, he turned and said, "Oh, there is one other thing. Your mother told me that all of the help at the reception are locals, who've been employed at Pennistone Royal in the past. Just scan them for me on the day, okay?"

She nodded and rose, walked over to him. "I'll mention it to Margaret this weekend, ascertain they're old hands. And of course I'll keep my eyes open at the reception. And so will Julian. He knows *everyone,* since we grew up there together." As she spoke of her husband, she filled with love for him; he was her childhood sweetheart, and she had always believed she would marry him.

"Thanks, Beauty."

Linnet fell in step with him, and just before they reached the door she touched his arm lightly. "Jack?"

"Yes?" He looked down at her questioningly.

"Do you really think Jonathan Ainsley might try to cause trouble? Do something slightly insane?"

"No, I don't think he will. He's too smart. On the other hand, I like to be one step ahead of the other guys. So I play it safe."

Linnet and Jack smiled at each other, and he left. Linnet watched him go down on the elevator, thinking what a relief it was to have him back, heading up Security. And then she wondered what Cousin Jonathan Ainsley was capable of—*really.* Anything. Even murder. She was convinced of that. She shivered. He was a sociopath who would stop at nothing to do them harm. Her mother had always said that, and Paula was rarely wrong. I've got to be on the alert at all times, Linnet told herself, and her face was grim as she went to look at the auditorium again.

3

Evan picked up a thick felt-tipped pen and in her bold, flowing handwriting wrote across the manila folder the word *Brides*. Then she pushed the folder to one side of the desk, smiling as she patted it almost lovingly. She had not realized how much work she had already done on the idea of creating a floor devoted to brides until she had gone into her computer an hour ago and printed everything out.

After reading all the pages written weeks ago, she knew she had a workable and comprehensive blueprint, and she was pleased. She hoped that Linnet would also be pleased. More than likely she would be. But what about Paula O'Neill? Would their boss really let them create a floor catering only to brides at the expense of other departments?

The question hung in the air for a moment. She had no answer. A sense that problems were brewing, a premonition of trouble still lingered in her mind. Very determinedly she endeavored to push this away, disinclined to ponder problems today. As Linnet would say, in her quaint way, there were better fish to fry.

Rising, Evan walked to the long worktable at the other side of her office. The table was covered with photo-

graphs of the house Gideon had bought in Yorkshire, and
she had an overwhelming desire to look at them again.

Sitting down, she stared at those she had laid out days
ago. Once more she experienced the familiar pleasure
and excitement that knowing this would be her home en-
gendered in her, as well as a genuine longing to be there
with Gideon and the twins. She could hardly wait to
move in, create a home, build a family with her beloved
Gideon. How she adored him.

As she shuffled through photographs of the grounds
and the exterior of the house, she thought of that Saturday morning last October, only three months ago, when
she had first seen the house.

Gideon had driven her over to the small, picturesque
village of West Tanfield, explaining on the way that he
wanted her to look at an old house with him. "It's a
house I've always liked, and it's on the market," he had
said. "My only worry is that it might be a bit ramshackle.
But we can walk through it and see how we feel about it,
can't we?"

Evan had immediately agreed, even though she was
surprised he wanted a house in Yorkshire when they both
lived and worked in London, especially since they could
stay with his parents or at Pennistone Royal whenever
they felt the need to escape the city. But then she had suddenly realized that he wanted a place of their own, especially for after the twins were born, because his
apartment in London, where they were currently living
together, would soon become rather cramped. The idea
of a house in the Dales now suddenly appealed to her,
and her excitement was fired.

On the drive over she learned that West Tanfield was
halfway between Pennistone Royal, the great stately
home which had been Emma's and was now Paula's, and
Allington Hall, his parents' family home, which had been
inherited from his grandfather Randolph Harte.

Just before they reached the village, Gideon had begun

to laugh softly and had confided that many years earlier his father and Shane O'Neill had owned the house they were about to see. Winston and Shane were the same age, the closest of friends since childhood, and had been at Oxford together. They had apparently bought the house as a property investment, intending to renovate it and then sell it for a vast profit.

Instead the two young bachelors had become so attached to the house while working on it that they had decided to move in themselves. It became their weekend retreat until Winston married Emily Barkstone, Gideon's mother. Shane had continued to live in the house for a year, but in the end he had felt lonely without his old sparring partner and finally told Winston he thought they ought to put the place on the market. Winston had agreed, and the house was snapped up almost immediately. In the ensuing years it had changed hands only once.

"Dad told me it was on the market," Gideon had gone on as he parked outside the house, which stood at the bottom of a small hill at the edge of the village. "He said that whatever its state, I shouldn't worry too much, because he and Shane had practically rebuilt it. Anyway, come on, darling, I have the key from the real estate office. Let's go and take a look at what might become our family home."

He had jumped out of the car and run around to the passenger side to help her alight, then led her to the black iron gate set in an ancient stone wall. It was quite a high wall, with lichen and moss growing between the stones, and many tall trees were visible above it.

"Beck House," she had read aloud when they stood in front of the gate. "I like the name, Gid."

He had merely smiled and led her through the gate, along the path to the house, at one moment confiding, "It's called Beck House because there's a little stream, a beck, running through the grounds."

The minute she saw it Evan was enchanted, smitten

actually, and she knew whatever its condition, she wanted to live there. It was positively beautiful.

Situated in a small dell, it was surrounded by sycamore trees and huge old oaks, which encircled the back. Elizabethan in origin, it was low and rambling, made of local stone. It had tall chimneys, leaded windows, and a half-timbered Tudor facade.

In her mind's eye, Evan had always had an image of what an English country house should look like, an image instilled in her by her grandmother Glynnis Hughes. And on that cool and sunny October morning, she had seen this image take shape in reality. When Gideon put the big old key in the lock of the front door, her excitement knew no bounds.

Evan knew she would never forget how she had felt when she stepped over the threshold and looked around the front hall. She was filled with joy, and she knew without any doubt that she and Gideon and their children were going to be happy here. The house had a good feeling.

She remembered that morning so well, walking through the big, empty rooms, empty of furniture but full of atmosphere and sunlight and dust motes rising in the shimmering air. She thought now of the enormous, old-fashioned kitchen with its dark-wood ceiling beams, mullioned windows, and huge stone hearth. It was a family kitchen, the core of the house, the kind every woman loves. To her relief, the reception rooms on the ground floor were spacious and well proportioned, while the upstairs bedrooms were cozy and intimate.

"It's the perfect house for a family," she had told Gideon. "It's just right for us, and it has a bit of family history as well, doesn't it?"

"Indeed it does," he had replied, his eyes full of laughter as he kissed her cheek, and asked, "Shall we buy it then?"

"Yes, please," she had answered, then wrinkled her nose. "If it isn't too ramshackle."

Gideon had laughed uproariously. "I don't think it's a bit ramshackle, actually, at least not the interiors. The outside woodwork needs a few coats of paint, and the stone wall needs repairing, but otherwise, I think it's rather . . . *a beauty*. Dad said the structure was solid, the bones good, and he was correct."

And so a decision was made in the middle of what would become their living room, and three weeks later the house was theirs.

Evan picked up some of the pictures and looked through them for the umpteenth time. The interiors had all been repaired and renovated, the walls and doors painted, the floors restored and polished, the chimneys swept by the local chimney sweep, and every window had been washed.

Beck House was ready. It awaited them. And next week, while they were in Yorkshire getting ready for their wedding, she and Gideon and his mother, Emily, were going to supervise the hanging of the draperies, the laying of the carpets and rugs, and the placement of the furniture. Many of the wood pieces, mostly antiques, had been gifts from Emily and Paula. Both women had hunted through their attics and come up with some really wonderful finds.

Evan had sent computer photographs of the best pieces to her father in New York, and he had sent her an e-mail almost immediately, telling her how good the furniture was in his opinion. All the pieces were Georgian, he was certain of that, and he had told her he couldn't wait to look them over when he arrived next week.

Evan sat back, reading his latest, loving e-mail, relieved and happy that their relationship was back on an even keel. It was as if there had never been a rift between them. She was glad he no longer seemed to mind that she was marrying a Harte. In the beginning, he had disliked the idea, and he had made his unhappiness very clear.

A light knock brought Evan's head up from the photographs, but before she could utter a word, Ruth Snelling, her new secretary, poked her blond head around the door.

"Do you need anything, Evan?" she asked in her breezy voice, with a bright smile. As usual, she was showing her concern for her boss, as solicitous of her as she had been from her first day of working at Harte's.

"I'm fine, thanks, Ruth. But perhaps you could get me a bottle of water, flat not fizzy, please?"

"No problem. I'll be back in a jiffy."

"Don't go, Ruth," Evan exclaimed. "I have something for Linnet. Do you mind dropping it off in her office?" As she spoke, Evan rose, moved slowly across the floor, picked up the manila folder, and held it out.

Still smiling, Ruth came and took it from her. "See you in a minute," she said as she disappeared, almost running out of the office.

Evan smiled to herself. The young woman was extremely efficient, and nothing was too much trouble for her. Things had been running smoothly since her arrival a few weeks ago, and Evan kept asking herself how she had ever managed without Ruth. I was always slightly behind the eight ball, that was the problem, Evan thought now as she sat down in her chair and glanced at her computer to see if she had any e-mails. There were none so far this morning, which pleased her. Work had begun to pall for her lately, and all she wanted now was to be settled in the peace and quiet of Pennistone Royal.

Paula had insisted she stay there until the wedding in ten days' time, and she was happy to do so. Evan felt at ease in that great house, where she had spent most weekends for the past year. It had been bought in the 1930s by her great-grandmother; she loved being there because she felt the presence of Emma Harte within its walls. Not only that but it was truly familiar by now. Everyone had made her feel at home, and Margaret, the housekeeper, never stopped fussing over her, was motherly and also protective of her these days.

Emily hadn't minded that she wasn't going to stay at Allington Hall and had insisted that she completely understood why Evan would want to be in such a familiar place as Pennistone Royal. Gideon's mother was one of the sweetest women Evan had ever met, and hilariously funny at times, frequently a bit blunt, just as Linnet was.

When Evan had mentioned this to Paula, she had laughed and nodded, her violet eyes twinkling. "They both take after Emma, I'm afraid. She was blunt, too, and Linnet, in particular, has inherited Emma's penchant for genuine pithiness. My grandmother always said what she meant, and so does Linnet."

"And what you see is what you get," Evan had replied, and the two of them had laughed knowingly.

Winston Harte, Gideon's father, was just as lovely as Emily. Both of them had made Evan feel special from the moment she started going out with Gideon. They had shown their approval of her as a wife for their son in countless ways. She couldn't have wished for nicer parents-in-law, or for a more lovely sister-in-law than Natalie, now back from Australia. She was pretty, and a charming girl, and they had taken to each other immediately.

The only person who seemed somewhat aloof was Gideon's brother, Toby. Linnet had once confided to her that Toby was inordinately jealous of Gideon. "And his marriage to the actress faltered almost immediately, so I guess his nose is now out of joint because Gid's got lovely you."

Not wanting to get into a long discussion about Toby for fear of seeming disloyal to Gideon, Evan had merely nodded; luckily, Linnet had suddenly realized she was late for a meeting and rushed off. The subject had never arisen again.

Pushing herself to her feet, Evan went back to the worktable, where she sat down and slowly began to look through the numerous photographs Gideon had taken of their wedding presents. Everyone had sent extraordinary gifts, which were not only costly but beautiful as well. As Gideon had said, with a chuckle, "We don't have to put any of these in the attic to be forgotten. We can use everything." She had agreed, also laughing.

"Hi there! How're you doin'?"

Evan sat up with a jerk, not having heard the door open. But she stared at it now in disbelief. Standing on the threshold was her twenty-three-year-old sister, Angharad. She was completely decked out in brilliant red, from her long cashmere muffler to her high-heeled leather boots. Not only that but she had dyed her hair, was now a platinum blonde.

Evan's jaw dropped, and it took her a moment to find her voice. "What are you doing here? I mean, Mom told me you weren't coming till next week."

"I decided to come early. I wanted to mosey around London before heading north."

Evan went over to her sister and kissed her cheek; her expression was warm as she went on, "Well, goodness, don't stand there, come in, come in."

Angharad did as Evan suggested, her eager brown eyes glancing around the room. "This office is *fab*. But then you always do manage to get a nice place to work, nicer than most people."

Ignoring this gibe, Evan murmured, "It's warm in here. You'd better hang your coat and scarf in the closet behind you." She padded across to the worktable, where she began to pick up some of the photographs, knowing it would be wiser to put them away before Angharad saw them. She was extremely nosy. But Evan was too late; her sister was heading her way. Turning away from the table, standing in front of it, Evan said, "Let's sit on the sofa over there; it's comfortable. And would you like something to drink? Tea? Coffee?"

Angharad shook her head, standing stock-still in the middle of the room, staring at Evan intently. After a moment she exclaimed, "I can't believe your size! *You're huge.*" She began to laugh, the laughter sounding brittle, and not at all warm. "You look as if you're about to give birth to baby elephants, not twin boys."

Wincing, Evan did not respond, and she found herself involuntarily putting both hands on her stomach, almost protectively. She recognized Angharad's tone only too well. It held that hint of envy which the younger woman had never been able to disguise, not even as a child. It was indicative of her need to put Evan down whenever she could. She had always been jealous.

Taking a deep breath, Evan now said softly, "I suppose you're staying at George's hotel with Mom."

"Yes. And Mom's coming over soon. To meet me here. We thought we could all have lunch together. What do you think?"

"Yes. Yes, of course." Evan swiftly agreed, although she was annoyed that her mother hadn't phoned first. She had a lot to do before the end of the day, and lunch had not been on her agenda. She wanted to fulfill her work schedule before taking maternity leave.

Stepping around her, Angharad was suddenly at the worktable, looking down at the photographs of Beck House, and within seconds she had zeroed in on the pictures of the furniture. "This is all Georgian," she remarked, her voice rising, her eyes scanning everything. Picking up one picture, she scrutinized it intently. Then, turning to Evan, she asked, "Where did this piece come from?"

"Out of the attics at Pennistone Royal. That's Emma Harte's former home. Now her granddaughter, my boss,

Paula O'Neill, lives there. Paula gave that sideboard to Gideon and me. It was a discard."

"*A discard.* Who would ever do that? It's a treasure. Have you had it evaluated?"

"No, we haven't. I was waiting for Dad. I sent him a set of the pictures. After all, he is one of the great experts on Georgian."

"I know that. I work with him, don't I? When did you send them?"

"Oh, three or four weeks ago now," Evan answered, staring at her sister.

"I wonder why he didn't show them to me." Angharad frowned, her mouth settling in a tight line.

"Maybe he glanced at them and put them away without thinking," Evan suggested, wondering herself why their father had not shown them to the daughter who worked alongside him in his antiques gallery in Connecticut. The daughter who was actually his protégée.

"Is this the house?" Angharad asked, leaning over the table, peering at the other set of photographs.

"Yes, that's it. Beck House it's called."

"Very nice. Very nice indeed," Angharad murmured without turning around, her interest captured by the pictures of the various rooms, as well as the other photos of the furniture Emily and Paula had unearthed and given to them.

After a while she straightened and turned away from the pictures. With a swift glance at Evan, her eyes cold, she said, "Well, you've done all right for yourself, haven't you? But then you usually do land on your feet, Evan. You had everyone wrapped around your little finger when you lived at home. Mom, Grandma Glynnis, and particularly Dad and Grandfather. You were always their favorite. Elayne was second. I came last."

"But it wasn't like that," Evan said softly. "You weren't last. No one was last . . . and I certainly didn't come first. Dad treated the three of us alike."

"That's a laugh. It's me you're talking to, Evan. Not Elayne. *Me.* I saw things very clearly. I was adopted, and therefore I was not *blood.* . . . I didn't have the *Hughes blood* running through my veins. Not like you. Oh no. You were the precious one, the peach darling."

"Oh, Angharad, please, don't be like this. Elayne is adopted, too, and Dad loves you both as much as he loves me," Evan exclaimed.

"Why do you always believe his spin?"

Evan shook her head and began to walk to her chair, suddenly feeling sick, needing to sit down. This was an old story. Angharad had been repeating it for years, convinced that she was the lowest of the low on the family totem pole. It had always annoyed their grandmother, this complaining and whining. Their father had simply ignored it, while their mother had tutted and cooed and embraced Angharad closer than ever, spoiling her in a way that made Elayne, the other adopted child, feel neglected.

"You're his princess!" Angharad cried. "The best, the smartest, the brightest, the most beautiful. You were always held up to us as the golden girl. If we didn't shine like you, we were going to be struck off his list. Or put on his shit list. Whichever you prefer."

"You're being really silly," Evan remonstrated, trying to remain calm. "It was never like that." Her protest fell on deaf ears.

"You're *still* the example. But you must know that by now. Evan the glorious one. The great-granddaughter of the famous Emma Harte. Talented and smart enough to get herself a top position at Harte's. Without batting an eyelash. So beautiful and bewitching she captures the Prince Charming of the Harte family. The super-good-looking, super-rich Gideon. And now she's fulfilled Gideon's desire to present his father with an heir. But golly gee whiz, not *one* heir. Oh no, not Evan. She's producing *two.* And his father's equally besotted with the great Evan, who's going to give him two instant grandsons."

"Please don't do this," Evan pleaded, her annoyance with her younger sister making her unexpectedly tense. It seemed to her that her anxiety was suddenly spiraling into a cloud that settled around her.

"*Do what?*" Angharad asked, her voice icy.

"Pick a fight like this. The way you did when we were little. Nobody wins in the end."

"I'm not doing any such thing," she shot back, her face flushing darkly. "I'm telling you the truth is all. And Elayne's as sick as I am of hearing about your damned wedding. Dad never stops talking about walking you down the aisle. Or talking about you. The bride of all brides."

"So why did you come?" Evan demanded, her indignation flaring. "If this is the way you feel, why didn't you boycott my wedding?"

"Mom wanted us here."

"Don't do me any favors," Evan shouted and took a step backward, one hand groping for the arm of the typing chair she favored. As her hand touched the arm, she went to sit, but the chair rolled away on its casters and she fell, crashing heavily onto the floor. Evan cried out and clutched her stomach.

Shocked, Angharad was unable to move. Swallowing hard, she asked in a whisper, "Are you all right? Evan? *Evan?* Are you all right?"

Evan moaned and brought her knees up, still holding her stomach. Her face was now chalk white, and she did not answer.

"Evan, please say something," Angharad begged and stepped closer to her. "Are you hurt?"

"I don't know," Evan responded faintly. "Go and look for my secretary . . . Ruth."

At that precise moment Ruth came into the office carrying a glass and a bottle of water, followed by Linnet and Marietta Hughes.

"Oh my God!" Marietta cried when she saw her

daughter sprawled on the floor, and, not heeding the others, she pushed past Ruth and Linnet.

"What's happened? My God, what's happened to you?" Marietta fell to her knees next to Evan, alarm racing through her.

"Call my doctor. I can't lose my babies, I can't," Evan groaned, tears sliding down her cheeks.

4

Gideon Harte pushed open the door of the waiting room at Queen Charlotte's in Chelsea, the hospital where Evan had been taken, and hurried into the room, his expression tense and worried.

Three pairs of female eyes instantly focused on him, and before he could say a word, Linnet rushed over to him. "Evan's all right, Gid!" she exclaimed, wanting to reassure him at once. "She's not hurt," she added, taking hold of his arm in a proprietary way.

"Thank God," he answered, a surge of relief rushing through him. "I've been insane with worry all the way here."

Marietta came to join them, and, leaning toward Gideon, she kissed his cheek. He put his arm around his future mother-in-law, a woman he genuinely liked, and asked, "What happened, Marietta? When Linnet rang me at the paper, she said you were in Evan's office when she had the accident." He stared at her, his green gaze penetrating.

"I wasn't in the room, Gideon," Marietta answered swiftly, shaking her head. "Evan was already on the floor when I arrived. I had no idea what had happened. I ran to her, of course, and when I was kneeling next to her, she said she'd had a fluky accident with the chair. She then asked me to call the doctor. Linnet, who was with me, did, and then we brought her here."

Gideon was frowning when he asked, "Did she fall out of the chair? Is that what you mean?"

"Not exactly. Evan told me she had reached behind her with one hand, pulled the chair toward her, and then sat down. Somehow the chair rolled away, and down she went on the floor. But she's fine, Gideon, just as Linnet said. The fall *scared* her more than anything else, I think."

"I understand. The nurse at reception told me the doctor's still with her. Why is that? Do you know, Marietta? Linnet?" He looked from one woman to the other.

"The doctor gave her a thorough examination when we arrived and came to tell us that she was not injured, that all was well. Then he went back to her room." Marietta shrugged lightly, shaking her head. "I'm not sure why, he didn't say."

"I hope he won't be too long," Gideon responded and then glanced across at the silent, blond young woman who was sitting in a corner. She was dressed entirely in red, which he thought somewhat flamboyant. He had never seen her before.

Marietta, noticing his curious glance, exclaimed, "How rude I'm being! I must introduce you to my youngest daughter, Angharad. Evan's sister."

On hearing her name, Angharad jumped to her feet and sped over. Thrusting out her hand, she said, "Hello, Gideon. It sure is great to meet *you*."

Gideon took an instant dislike to her. Unfortunately, he had no choice but to take hold of the outstretched hand. It was cold, icy, in fact, and he dropped it at once after giving it a swift shake. "How do you do?" he said, his manner reserved.

She looked him up and down in a brazen way.

He stared back, rapidly taking everything in. There was no question that she was pretty, with finely wrought features, perfect complexion, and large, dark brown eyes.

Yet Gideon found her curiously repellent; he took a step backward. His guard went up, and his gut instinct kicked in, warning him to be wary of this one.

It struck him that the platinum blond hair did nothing to lighten the darkness he sensed lived deep within her, and, in a flash of cold clarity, he saw her in his mind's eye as she really was, a small, dark, furtive creature, hiding in corners, peering through keyholes, forever seeking her own advantage. He was startled by these rather odd thoughts, yet he was convinced he was accurate in his assessment of Angharad Hughes. He sensed that wickedness dwelt in her, and this disturbed him.

Anxious to put distance between them, he strode across the floor, then turned, glanced at Linnet, his hand on the doorknob. "I'm going to talk to the nurse at reception. I must see Evan right away." As he jerked open the door, he found himself staring into the face of Charles Addney, Evan's obstetrician.

The doctor exclaimed, "There you are, Mr. Harte! I was just coming to fetch you. Let's go and see Miss Hughes, shall we?"

Gideon nodded and stepped out into the corridor, closing the door behind him. "I understand she's all right. She *is*, isn't she?"

"Absolutely. Except for a bruised coccyx. That's the tailbone. She went down rather hard, I'm afraid. But there's no real damage, and the babies are perfectly fine."

Gideon heaved a sigh of relief, then asked, "So I can take her home?"

The doctor paused and turned to face him. "There's no reason why you can't, but she must have bed rest for the remainder of the day. No harm's been done, but I do think she should start her maternity leave. Immediately."

"I couldn't agree more," Gideon responded as they began to walk along the corridor again. "I've been trying to persuade her to do that for several weeks now. We're going up to Yorkshire on Saturday, but perhaps we ought to leave tomorrow. Her problem is that she's a workaholic . . ." His voice trailed off.

"I know that, and I've just had a long talk with her about it. I told her to put her work on hold for the moment. I think you'll find she's now most amenable about leaving for Yorkshire tomorrow." Dr. Addney chuckled. "Although she did say she was going to take her laptop with her."

"Naturally!" Gideon exclaimed and laughed with him.

"Well, here we are," the doctor said, pausing at one of the doors.

Gideon entered and hurried over to the bed, relieved that Evan looked exactly the same as she had this morning, except somewhat paler. She was sitting up in the bed, surrounded by pillows, obviously none the worse for the fall.

"Gideon!" she exclaimed. "Don't look so upset! I'm all right." She beamed at him, her large, gray-blue eyes full of love for him.

"I've been so worried," he whispered as he bent over, put his arms around her, kissed her cheek, then stroked her dark head. "Actually, I was quite beside myself. I couldn't bear it if anything happened to you and the twins, Evan. I love you all so much."

"Nothing's going to happen to us, Gideon darling. The three of us are perfect. Truly. And I love you, too. So will the boys, once they . . . pop out."

Watching them, Charles Addney felt a flush of pleasure. How wonderful it was to see two people as much in love as they were. It did his heart good to know that they had managed to find each other in this dangerous and uncertain world. He closed the door quietly behind him and left them alone with their happiness in each other.

"How on earth did you manage to fall?" Gideon asked. He was sitting on the side of the bed, holding Evan's hand, gazing into that face he had come to know so intimately in the past year and now loved so much.

She shook her head, gave a small laugh. "I don't know, darling. Just clumsy, I suppose."

"Clumsy? You? *Never*. You're the most graceful person I know, have *ever* known, actually. Your mother said it was a fluky accident, so come on, tell me what *exactly* happened."

Evan pursed her lips together, her eyes narrowing slightly as she wondered how best to explain. She wasn't sure herself how she had managed to fall in the way she had. Clearing her throat, she explained, "I was standing by my desk, talking to Angharad . . . Oh, have you met her? She came to the hospital with Mom and Linnet." Her dark brows lifted questioningly.

"Yes, I've met her," he murmured, staring hard at her. "Are you saying she was in the room with you?"

"Oh yes, she'd come over to the store to see me. It was very unexpected, I didn't even know she was in England."

Gideon felt his hackles rising, and he sat up a little straighter, looking intently at Evan. "So, she was in the room. You were talking to her from behind the desk. And then *what*?"

"I reached behind me, pulled the chair toward me, the typing chair I use at my desk. I was quite sure it was right behind me, and I sat down. But it had rolled off to one side, and naturally I fell on the floor."

Gideon nodded but said nothing. He couldn't help wondering if Angharad had caused the accident. But how could she have? She was at the other side of the desk. Evan had just told him that. Nonetheless, he couldn't help thinking she was responsible in some way for Evan's nasty spill.

"When you fell, did she come to help you?" he wondered out loud.

"Yes, she came over to me, but she was really terrified, you know, that I might have badly injured myself, and so she just stood there, asking me if I was okay. I'd felt a stab of pain in my abdomen, so I brought my legs up, holding my stomach. Then Ruth appeared with the water I'd asked her to bring me earlier, and Mom and Linnet were with her. Mom ran over, got down on the floor next to me, and I told her to call the doctor."

Evan now lay back against the pillows, her expression one of bafflement as she murmured, "I just don't know how I could have been so careless, falling like that."

"You weren't careless, sweetheart. It's as you said it was, a freak accident. Thank God you didn't injure yourself. Now, let's get you dressed. Dr. Addney says I can take you home, but you have to rest all day. And tonight. We're going to Pennistone Royal tomorrow evening instead of on Saturday."

"But I—"

"No buts, Evan. I've made the decision. The doctor told me you should start maternity leave now. So I'm afraid it's no more Harte's, not until well after the twins are born."

"Oh, don't say that! I hope there'll be lots more Hartes. Well, one Harte in particular," Evan said, smiling at him.

"I certainly hope you're referring to me."

"Of course I am, silly. Who else do I love but you?"

Little things kept coming back to her, things she had forgotten long ago. And yet they had been significant when they happened. Now they were coming to the fore, clear and vivid as they took shape again. And each memory was shaped and defined by one thing, Angharad's jealousy and envy of her.

Evan lay under the duvet in the bedroom of Gideon's flat. *Their* bedroom now, since she had moved in with him. They had wanted to live together once she had become pregnant; this aside, Gideon's sister, Natalie, had returned from her sojourn in Sydney, and because it was her flat Evan was occupying, moving out had become mandatory.

"And why not live with me, your future husband?"

Gideon had asked, adding, "Come live with me and be my love, and we will all the pleasures prove."

"What lovely words."

"Yes. But they're not mine, Evan. They're Christopher Marlowe's, written in the sixteenth century. However, they truly *do* reflect my sentiments entirely."

And mine as well, she thought now, pulling the duvet up around her shoulders, making herself comfortable. Both Dr. Addney and Gideon had impressed upon her that she should rest all day and evening, and she knew they were correct. She was all right, no harm had been done, but she'd had a bit of a shock. Rest was the best medicine, just as they had said.

Angharad.

The name hung there, floating in midair before her eyes.

Evan had not failed to miss the distaste in Gideon's voice when he had mentioned her sister. And she completely understood why he had sounded that way. With the platinum blond hair and all that awful red clothing, she had looked flashy and a little bit cheap. Especially when contrasted with their mother, perfectly groomed and turned out in a mélange of soft beiges, and Linnet, in her smart black Chanel suit with its pristine white-satin collar and cuffs.

She couldn't help thinking that Angharad and Elayne had been adopted on the spur of the moment, after her mother had had the hysterectomy. Why hadn't they waited, her parents, let their emotional turmoil settle? Gran had always asked that, had been right as usual.

Once again, Evan cringed inside at the thought of all that dreadful red. Pretty though Angharad was, she had never looked worse than she did today. It was the hair as well; it did not suit her, was totally inappropriate. Her coming to the store dressed like that was embarrassing. And how mean-spirited she had been.

Then it came, a sudden flash of memory of a Christmas long ago. In Connecticut. She had been seven or thereabouts, Angharad around three and a half and very jealous of her, competitive even then. It was the Christmas that Evan's grandmother had given her a puppy, a beautiful chocolate brown Lab with unusual green eyes. They had named him Hudson, after the river.

"Gran, Gran, I can't find Hudson! He's disappeared," Evan wailed, worry ringing her face as she ran into the big family kitchen where her grandmother stood at the long oak table cooking for the holidays. Glynnis was making stuffing for the turkey, giblet gravy, applesauce, and all sorts of other good things to eat.

Glancing over her shoulder at Evan, she said, "I saw him trotting after Angharad a few minutes ago. Try the solarium, lovey. Perhaps you'll find them there, playing with his tennis ball."

Evan raced down the corridor in the direction of the solarium. When she came to the doorway, she was stunned to see Angharad pushing the puppy out into the snow and then locking the outside door.

"Angharad! What are you doing?" Evan shrieked, her shoes clattering against the terra-cotta flagstones as she flew into the solarium. "Hudson will die out there. It's too cold for a puppy. He's only nine weeks old!"

Evan pulled Angharad away from the door, glaring at her and exclaiming, "You're very bad. Bad." Frantically turning the lock, she ran outside, seeking the puppy. He was nowhere to be seen, and her eyes filled up with tears.

"Hudson, Hudson, where are you?" she shouted. He couldn't be far away, she thought desperately.

Angharad had come out and was standing on the steps of the solarium. "I'm not a bad girl," she yelled at Evan. "I hate that puppy. I hate you. It's the dog that's bad. It wee-weed in my room. So there, Miss Big Shot!" She went back inside, banged the solarium door, and locked it.

Evan paid no attention to her. She was far too intent on finding her puppy. Then she spotted the little paw prints in the snow and began to follow them, pulling her cardigan around her shoulders, shivering in the icy wind, regretting she had not stopped to get her coat.

It didn't take Evan long to find Hudson. The dog had sunk into a snowdrift against the terrace wall and was whimpering. Bending over the snowdrift, she almost fell into it herself as she reached down. Hudson was wet and cold, trembling with fright and still whimpering as she took hold of him and lifted him out.

"Little Hudsy, here I am. You're safe," Evan soothed. "I'll soon have you warm," she whispered against his wet hair, bundling him inside her cardigan. Holding him close to her body for extra warmth, she hurried back to the solarium.

Evan turned the knob, only to discover that the door had been locked by Angharad. The child stood on the other side of the French doors; she stuck out her tongue, then laughed.

"Open this door!" Evan demanded, banging on one of the glass panes.

"No, I won't." Angharad put her tongue out again, swung around, and ran away from the French doors.

Racing along the path, Evan went to the back door of the house, which led straight into the kitchen. Stumbling inside, she brought a blast of cold air with her, which made Glynnis swing around. She looked startled.

"You're going to catch your death of cold, my girl, going out without a coat in this weather," she chastised, then stopped when she saw that Evan had the puppy in her arms. She also noticed that the two of them were shivering.

"Goodness me, whatever happened to Hudson? He looks very wet," Glynnis exclaimed, frowning in concern. "Here, give him to me, Evan, I'll wrap him in this warm towel. As for you, lovey, take off that damp cardigan at once and stand in front of the fire. You'll be warm and dry in a jiffy."

"Yes, Gran," Evan said dutifully, handing over the puppy, then struggling out of her damp cardigan, which she laid on the hearth.

Once the puppy was dry and nestling in a bed of thick towels in his basket, Glynnis said, "Do you want to tell me what happened, Evan?"

Evan let out a long sigh. "I'm not a snitch."

"I know that. But how did the puppy get outside in the first place?"

"I found him in a snowdrift," Evan muttered, avoiding the question.

"Certainly Hudson can't open doors, so somebody must've put him outside, Evan. That's the obvious answer. Perhaps a little girl called Angharad, eh?"

Evan was silent.

"It *was* Angharad," Elayne announced, walking into the kitchen. "I saw her shoving Hudson out into the snow, Grandma." Elayne made a face. "She's always jealous of Evan, and me, too."

Glynnis nodded. "I understand. Well, please go and find her, Elayne, and bring her to me. *At once.*"

Elayne rushed off.

Glynnis looked pointedly at Evan. "I know you never want to confront her, but this time Angharad has gone too far."

When Evan was silent, Glynnis said, "You know that, don't you?"

"Yes, Gran."

Within minutes Elayne came back into the kitchen, pulling Angharad along by the hand. At five she was taller and stronger, so she was able to control the younger child, who was struggling and looked sullen.

When they came to a stop in front of Glynnis, she said in a quiet voice, "Angharad, what you did was a cruel thing, putting that defenseless little puppy out in the freezing cold. Hudson would have soon died in that snowdrift, there's no doubt about it. You've been a wicked girl. I don't often use such a strong word with you, even though you are frequently extremely naughty. However, this time you deserve it." Bending slightly, looking into the child's face, Glynnis said, "Now, explain why you did such a cruel thing."

"The dog wee-weed in my room," Angharad mumbled.

"*Oh really.* That's surprising, since you usually keep the door closed. Let's go upstairs, shall we? *All of us.*"

Glynnis, her face still grim, shepherded her three granddaughters up the front stairs and into the bedroom shared by Angharad and Elayne. "Now, show me where the puppy had an accident," she said.

Angharad hung back for a second, then ran to a small, damp spot visible on the light-colored carpet. She pointed to it. "There! It's there."

"That doesn't look like urine to me," Glynnis muttered, and, kneeling down, she sniffed the spot, then looked up at Angharad, her face grim again. She said, "This spot doesn't have a smell at all. I think it's water."

"Yes, it is, Grandma," Elayne told her. "She spilled it last night."

"I thought it was something like that," Glynnis replied, getting up. "And now you've resorted to fibbing, Angharad. Well, there's only one thing to do with a girl who lies. She's got to be left alone to think about what telling the truth means, how important it is. Girls who lie are not fit for decent company."

"I didn't lie!" Angharad cried, glaring at Elayne.

"I believe you did," Glynnis exclaimed, scrutinizing her intently. "And it's not the first time. You're to stay here in your room until your father and mother get back from New York with Grandpa. Then we'll see what happens."

She walked across the bedroom floor, beckoning to the other two girls. After ushering them out, Glynnis turned and looked at Angharad. "I'm not going to lock this door, but don't you dare come out."

Once they were back in the kitchen, Glynnis served

Evan and Elayne large bowls of chicken vegetable soup and small chicken sandwiches. They ate their lunch dutifully and in total silence, afraid to speak. And Glynnis didn't say a word either.

It was much later that afternoon, when she was playing with the puppy at one end of the kitchen, that Evan heard her grandmother talking to her mother. "There's something wicked in her, Marietta," Glynnis said. "Angharad is duplicitous, she tells lies, and she has a cruel streak." As Marietta began to protest, Glynnis went on firmly, "She was an abandoned child. . . . We know nothing about her genes. Now admit that's true, Marietta."

"I'm not denying it," Marietta finally answered in a low voice. "But she is pretty, and she can be very sweet, you know. Very loving."

"Yes, most certainly she can, when you're giving in to her, spoiling her," Glynnis pointed out.

Marietta did not answer.

Evan kept herself hidden, not wanting the two women to become aware of her presence.

As the memory slowly faded, Evan once again accepted that Angharad was just as envious and spiteful as she had always been. It struck Evan that her sister had come to the store today spoiling for a fight. And if they hadn't quarreled, she wouldn't have fallen, would she?

Evan shivered slightly and huddled deeper into the bedclothes. Then she filled with relief that she hadn't mentioned their quarrel to Gideon. She was certain he had already spotted something in Angharad which he didn't like. His tone of voice had given him away, and besides that he had great insight into people. Angharad would never find favor with him, of that Evan was convinced.

5

It's exquisite," India Standish said, looking at the diamond tiara resting on a square of black velvet laid on the dining room table at Niddersley House. "And I would love to wear it on my wedding day . . ." Her voice trailed off, and there was a moment's hesitation before she asked, "As long as you don't think it's too much, Grandma?"

"Do you mean too *grand*, India?" Edwina asked. The Dowager Countess of Dunvale gazed across the table at her only granddaughter and favorite grandchild.

"Well, yes, sort of," India admitted. "Is it a bit over the top?" She raised a blond brow questioningly, her silvery gray eyes focused on her grandmother. "I mean, for these days?"

Edwina did not answer for a moment. Instead she stared intently at the tiara, her head to one side, her eyes thoughtful. After a moment she murmured, "No, it's not too grand for today, nor was it ever, for any day, my dear. And it's certainly not very elaborate . . . just two bands of diamonds linked by interlocking circles of diamonds, with the large circle at the front holding a diamond star in a smaller circle."

Nodding, Edwina informed India, "It's Victorian, you know, and it belonged to Adele Fairley, my grandmother and your great-great-grandmother. That's why it occurred to me you might like to wear it on such an important day in your life. It's part of your family history."

India responded, "Yes, I understand, and it is beautiful, Gran. Perhaps I should try it on to see how it looks."

"Yes, why don't you do that?" Edwina motioned to the end wall. "There's a looking glass over there, and plenty of light from the windows on either side."

India rose, leaned over the table, and lifted the tiara with both hands. Moving across to the mirror, she placed the diamond circle on her head and stared at herself. She saw at once that Edwina was correct. Now that the tiara was on, it didn't look quite so grand after all, perhaps because of the cloud of hair around her face and the simple design. And it did suit her, no two ways about that; much to her surprise, it was also comfortable to wear. But would Dusty like her in it? He could be odd about things. She smiled, thinking how he had characterized her parents as aristocratic snobs when they weren't, not at all. But he had refused to meet them until very recently. Now he loved them, just as they did him. For a moment India attempted to visualize herself in her wedding veil and the tiara, and unexpectedly she liked the image floating in her head. And she knew Dusty would, too. She turned around and exclaimed, "What do you think, Gran?"

Edwina's answer was to beam at her. "It suits you, India, and it doesn't look . . . *over the top*, as you call it. Your veil will be held in place perfectly. Now, tell me, what is your wedding gown going to be like? You told me Evan was designing it."

"Yes, she is, and I've seen only the first sketches of it, but I love her design. We've chosen the fabric already, a pale ivory taffeta, light in weight, because the dress is going to be worn over an underskirt of layered net, for a very bouffant effect, like an old-fashioned ball gown. The bodice is tightly fitted, and there are big, puffy sleeves, slightly off the shoulder. Actually, it's Victorian in style,

Gran, now that I think about it. I've asked Evan to keep it
plain and understated, no embroidery."

"It sounds as if it will be lovely, my dear, and I feel sure
the tiara will be the perfect adornment, since it is Victorian, too. So, are you going to wear it on your wedding
day to please an old lady?"

India smiled at her grandmother, then turned again to
the mirror, gazing at herself for a split second. As she
swung back around to face Edwina, she exclaimed, "Yes,
Grandma, I'd love to wear your tiara, and thank you for
thinking of it."

Edwina returned India's smile with one equally loving.
"*Adele's* tiara, that's how I regard it. Would you like to
take it with you today? Or do you prefer to leave it here
for safekeeping?"

"I think I'd better do that, actually. You have that enormous safe, and I don't even have a small one in my flat.
Besides, it's only January, Gran. I'm not getting married
until June. So yes, it would be much safer here for the
next six months, I think."

"I understand." Edwina sat back in the chair and
watched India as she walked over to the dining table,
took off the tiara, and placed it on the black velvet,
thinking what a lovely young woman she had become.
She had the finely drawn aristocratic looks and pale
blond coloring of Adele Fairley, as did her cousin Tessa
Fairley; in fact, the two could easily be mistaken for sisters, and often were by strangers.

"Shall I put the tiara in its box, Grandma? Or do you
want Frome to do it?"

Edwina laughed. "You'd better do it, he's far too slow
these days. It'll take him half an hour to get the tiara in its
box, never mind into the safe. Old age creeping up, I'm
afraid."

India's mouth twitched with laughter. "You are funny,
Gran, the way you go on about Frome getting old. He
can't be more than fifty if he's a day."

"Fifty's about right," Edwina confirmed, still chuckling to herself. "But he's dreadfully slow lately. You know very well I'm much faster at everything, even though I am ninety-five."

"And quite remarkable!" India exclaimed.

"Imagine, Emma was only sixteen when I was born. She took me off to her cousin Freda's in Ripon to be brought up, at least when I was a baby—" Edwina stopped abruptly and sat there staring out the window, her eyes full of a curious yearning.

After a moment of watching her, India asked softly, "Are you all right, Grandmother?"

"Oh, yes, I am, India, I am. And I hope I remain so. At least until I see you well and truly married to Dusty." Pushing herself to her feet, she continued, "And shouldn't we be on our way to have lunch with him at Willows Hall?"

"Yes, we had better go," India agreed and put the tiara back in the worn, black-leather box where it belonged, then laid the black velvet cover over it. Closing the lid and fastening the small catch, India looked across at her grandmother and said, "Shall I put it in the safe?"

"*Absolutely*. It'll be quicker, as I just said, if you do it. Come along, my dear, I'll take you to the safe. And then we'll be off. It was nice of you to come and fetch me, India. I could've been driven over to Dusty's by Rupert, you know. He doesn't have much driving to do as it is."

"Oh, that's all right, Grandma. I wanted to come. To see you and spend a little extra time with you."

They crossed the hall together and went down a corridor toward the room where an enormous safe was housed. As she followed Edwina, India went on, "I think you'd better wear a warm coat, Grandma. It's bitterly cold today, and it could snow again."

"I will, my dear. I have a lovely quilted coat Paula got for me. From Harte's, of course."

As they drove to Follifoot, India thought about Dusty

Rhodes, the way she had fallen in love with him at first sight. She had made up her mind to marry him there and then. They had met at a cocktail party for young painters at the Artemis Gallery in Kensington and been drawn to each other at once. He'd taken her to supper at the Ivy later, and then back to his studio on the Embankment, where they had sipped herb tea and gone to bed. Instant sex. Instant love.

"Mr. Rhodes, I'm sorry to bother you, but there's a Mrs. Roebotham here. With Atlanta," Paddy Whitaker said from the doorway of the studio.

Dusty's head came up with a jerk, surprise flickering in his eyes. "*Atlanta?*"

"Yes, Mr. Rhodes," the house manager confirmed. "They're in the kitchen at the moment. Atlanta likes Angelina, as you well know."

Alarmed though he was by this altogether unexpected news, Russell Rhodes, one of the world's greatest artists, managed to keep his face neutral. Dusty, as he was commonly known, put the paintbrush down carefully, even though his stomach was suddenly churning; he managed to keep his movements totally controlled. His mind was racing. Obviously something happened to the child's grandmother. That was why Atlanta was here.

Turning away from the easel, Dusty asked, "What's the problem? Did Mrs. Roebotham say?"

"No, but she has a suitcase. It's Atlanta's. And the woman appears to be nervous and worried. However, she wouldn't say a word to me, Mr. Rhodes. She just repeated several times that she had to speak to you and only you."

"I understand. I'll come up to the house with you right away, Paddy." Moving across the studio swiftly, Dusty glanced at his watch and asked, "Is everything under control for lunch?"

Paddy, still framed in the doorway, nodded. "Angelina has finished setting the table in the dining room, and

Valetta's in the middle of cooking lunch. Everything smells delicious, as usual. I have the white wine cooling. *Pouilly Fumé*. No problems, at least not with lunch, sir."

"I'm sure not. Thanks, Paddy. By the way, you'd better make sure the dining room is warm. The countess feels the cold these days, so Lady India tells me."

"The fire's blazing up the hearth, and I turned the central heating on a while ago. Kept it low, though."

"That's fine." Dusty paused at the door and, doubting that he would be returning to his studio today, switched off all the lights. After grabbing his sheepskin coat from the wall peg, he locked the door and walked with Paddy to the beautiful Palladian house set at the top of the hill just a few yards away.

Once inside the house, Dusty murmured, "I'd better see Mrs. Roebotham before I greet Atlanta, find out what this is all about. Give me a couple of minutes to freshen up, then bring her to the library."

"I'll do that, sir. And in the meantime, I'll try to get her to have a cup of tea. She wouldn't have anything before. But perhaps she will now that she knows you'll be talking to her in a short while."

"That's a good idea," Dusty answered, and then he hurried across the marble entrance hall and into the spacious library. The first thing he did was go into the adjoining bathroom, where he washed the paint off his hands, splashed cold water on his face, and then ran a comb through his thick, black hair.

He stared at himself in the mirror, thinking, suddenly, that he looked tired. And also worried. Taking a deep breath, endeavoring to steady himself, he returned to the library, straightening his sweater as he went to his desk. Lifting the tweed jacket from the back of the desk chair, he slipped it on, then sat down at the desk, his mind in a turmoil.

Something must have happened to Molly Caldwell, Melinda's mother, he decided, or why would a stranger be here with his child? Unless it was Melinda who was in trouble and her mother had gone to the detox clinic to see her. But if that were the case, why hadn't Mrs. Caldwell phoned him? She usually did, wanting to keep him informed of everything that affected his child. She was a good woman.

Propping his elbows on the desk, Dusty dropped his head into his hands. Why today? he muttered under his breath. Why did it have to be *today* of all days? India was on her way to have lunch, bringing her grandmother, the Dowager Countess of Dunvale, and he wanted everything to go right.

But then Melinda Caldwell had spelled trouble from the day he met her, although he hadn't known it at the time. A top model, she had been young, fresh, beautiful, full of laughter and joy. He had fallen for her looks and gaiety. And then, soon after their meeting, she had rocketed to fame, became the face on every magazine cover. She had begun to earn big money, and it had all gone to her head. Within months she had fallen in with a fast crowd, had started breaking their dates. And he had soon discovered she was sleeping around. Recklessly. Then she had suddenly come back to him, contrite, loving, asking his forgiveness. They'd been together for two months when she became unusually violent, verbally abusive. Knowing he couldn't take it, and at his wit's end, he had left. Soon after, she had told him she was pregnant; there had been a DNA test after the baby was born, at his insistence. It was his child. Nevertheless, they hadn't been able to make it work. He exited Melinda's life promptly, but generously supported her and the baby.

Later, when Melinda had become fried on drugs, he had backed her mother, Molly Caldwell, who had taken Atlanta to live with her. And he had tried to help Melinda. But, very simply, she had not wanted help.

He sighed, lifted his head. Trouble he didn't want or need.

But there was no doubt in his mind that trouble was about to come and hit him smack in the face.

He braced himself. Everything was about to go wrong; his gut instinct told him that, and he trusted his instinct. Always had.

"Tell me about Emma, tell me about Grandy," India said as she drove down the driveway of Niddersley House and turned left onto the Knaresborough Road. "You promised you would ages ago, and you never have."

"There's so much to tell, I wouldn't know where to begin," Edwina murmured, settling herself in the car seat. "Do you like this car, India?" she then asked, changing the subject. "I gave it to your father, you know."

"Yes, he told me. And I love my Aston Martin." Giving her grandmother a quick look out of the corner of her eye, India asked, "Are you comfortable, Gran?"

"Very. Thank you for asking," Edwina answered, glancing out of the window.

"So, getting back to Emma Harte. Here's an idea, why don't I just ask you questions?"

"That's a very good idea, India. But surely you know a lot from your father. He was devoted to her."

"Oh yes, I do, and from Mummy as well. Daddy always says he was one of the Praetorian Guards."

Edwina chuckled merrily for a second or two. "He spoke the truth. He and Paula, Emily and her late brother, Sandy, and Winston felt it was their duty to surround and protect her in every way. I must admit, I did sometimes tease your father, asking him if he and the others were ever tempted to do away with her, as the original Roman Praetorian Guards had often had an urge to slay their leader." Edwina chuckled again.

India laughed with her grandmother and asked, "And what did my father say?"

"He was horrified that I could even countenance such

an idea. I'm afraid that my teasing fell flat. He and his cousins were utterly devoted to her."

"And you weren't, were you, Gran?" When Edwina did not answer, India pressed, "You were estranged from her for quite some time. I know that because Daddy told me."

A low sigh escaped Edwina, and she remained silent for a moment longer before saying, "Yes, it's true, I was. I became estranged from her just before I went off to finishing school in Switzerland, and we weren't very close for a number of years after that."

"Why? What happened?"

"It's such a long story, India dear, and I always get upset when I discuss it. I will tell you the details some other time, I promise. Let's just say, for now, that I was totally wrong. I was the one at fault, not my mother, and when I finally realized that, I tried to make amends. And we became devoted to each other at long last."

"You sound very regretful, Grandma," India said softly, sympathy echoing in her voice.

"I am, even to this day. I think what I regret most are the years I missed knowing her, being with her, when I was a young woman. I was married to your grandfather Jeremy, and living with him at Clonloughlin. I was so happy with him, and we were devoted to your father, our only child, and I didn't give a thought to my mother. Not for a very long time."

"My father told me that he went and sought her out, that he didn't even tell you."

"That's correct. And it was my uncle, Emma's brother Winston, who told me that the moment they met was memorable. He said it was instantaneous and absolute infatuation between Emma and Anthony." Turning to India, Edwina finished in a low voice, "I'm glad your father had the guts to defy me and went to meet his grandmother on his own. They remained close for the rest of her life, and they both benefited from the relationship."

"You said earlier that Emma sent you off to live in

Ripon with her cousin Freda. Was that one of the things that upset you?"

Again Edwina was silent, as if mulling over her answer, and when she spoke she found herself telling the truth. "No, not really. I was a baby, and I was given a lot of love, care, and attention, and it was a pretty, pastoral place to live. Freda was a loving young woman. I knew deep down, when I was older, that Emma had done the best thing for me. We were poor and she had to work hard to support us; she just couldn't look after me. Nor was there anyone in Armley who could. Yes, it was the right decision, even though later there were moments when I resented her for doing it. But I was far too young to understand all the ramifications. Later, I did."

"You know, Grandma, I really admire you. The way you admit your mistakes, take responsibility for things you did which you now regret. Most people can't do that . . . admit they've been wrong."

"Only too true, India," Edwina murmured, "and for you to understand that, at your age makes you a very smart young woman indeed. I'm proud of *you,* my dear. Now, enough of the past and Emma. Tell me about your plans."

"Just one more question, Gran, and then I'll stop," India pleaded. "I'll talk about my plans, and anything else you want to talk about."

"All right. One more question then. What is it?"

"Everyone says Linnet is Emma's clone. Is that true? You'd know better than any other member of the family."

"Oh yes, she's the spitting image of her, as Emma looked when I was growing up and living with her. But it's not only the looks, you know, Linnet is like her in other ways. It's in the genes, I suppose. She has inherited many of my mother's mannerisms; she even sounds like her at times. And quite aside from those things, her personality is similar to Emma's. Linnet can be brusque and blunt, just as my mother was, and she speaks her mind.

Very plainly. I've always said to Paula that with Linnet what you see is what you get, and Emma Harte was exactly the same way."

Edwina sat up straighter and looked at her granddaughter. "You might find this hard to believe, but sometimes when I'm with Linnet, I feel as if I'm a little girl again and actually with my mother. I fall into my memories, and I'm transported back in time. It's rather strange, I must admit."

"I suppose it is, but every time I pass that portrait of Emma in the store, I think I'm looking at Linnet, well, the woman Linnet will be when she's much older."

A fleeting smile touched Edwina's face, and after a moment she said, "Now come along, you promised to tell me your plans, yours and Dusty's. And what about his little girl? Will she come and live with you when you're married?"

"I don't think so, Grandma. . . . Dusty feels she should remain with Mrs. Caldwell, that's the child's grandmother. He doesn't want to uproot her to live at Willows Hall with us. Anyway, he always promised Melinda, that's the little girl's mother, that he wouldn't take Atlanta away from her."

"I understand his reasoning. And that's just as well, wouldn't you say? Surely she's better with her mother." As Edwina said this, she felt a surge of apprehension. She saw trouble on the horizon.

Part Two

TRIO

❧

The three clans stand together as one family.
Harte, O'Neill, and Kallinski against all foes.

—EMMA HARTE, *A Woman of Substance*

6

~

Linnet wished she could go up to the moors, but she knew it was impossible this morning. Snow had fallen during the night, and the line of hills along the horizon were topped with glistening white. She had to admit that it would be unbearably cold on the tops, as the locals called the highest parts of the moorland and the high fells that dropped down into the Dales. The snow would make them impossible to traverse, and then there was the wind. It was always blowing up there, even in the best of weather.

For as long as she could remember, Linnet had loved the moors above Pennistone Royal, the lovely, ancient house in Yorkshire where she had been born and which had belonged to her great-grandmother Emma Harte.

One day it would be hers. Her mother had told her that in great confidence. It was a big secret; no one else could know.

When she was still only a toddler, her mother had taken her up there to play amongst the heather and bracken, under a sky as blue as the tiny speedwells grow-ing in the fields below. The moors were Linnet's special place, her haven whenever something ailed her. Her mother had told her a long time ago that she had inherited Emma's love of them, certainly more than anyone else in the family.

"You're just like Grandy," Paula would often tell her, smiling indulgently. "Whenever you get a chance, you go rushing up there, especially when you're troubled or worried about something. That's exactly what your great-grandmother did for her entire life."

Linnet was beset by problems on this chilly Saturday morning, all manner of troubling thoughts jostling around in her head. Sighing, she walked down the gravel path toward the Rhododendron Walk and endeavored to sort her worries in the order of their importance.

Uppermost in her mind was Jonathan Ainsley. A short while ago, Jack Figg had phoned to tell her that Ainsley was now staying at his house in Thirsk, and his presence in the vicinity made her feel even more uneasy. Jack forever called him a loose cannon, and the idea that he might well be just that always put her on her guard.

Then there was the situation with Evan's family. Uncle Robin had invited them all to stay with him for the wedding, and this was now alarming Jack. He had voiced the thought that they would all be "sitting ducks" should Jonathan Ainsley decide to pay an unexpected visit to his father.

"But he can't shoot them dead," she had countered. "All he *can* do actually, Jack, is be very rude to them, and nasty to his father. Uncle Robin's used to that by now, I should think."

"Couldn't they be accommodated elsewhere for the duration of the wedding festivities?" Jack had asked, and she had then suggested he speak to her mother. "I suppose they could stay with us at Pennistone Royal," she had gone on swiftly, "or with Aunt Emily and Uncle Winston in Middleham. Allington Hall is big enough. But Mummy'll know best. Mind you, Uncle Robin won't like it if she interferes with his plans."

Jack had answered that Paula was head of the family

and he was going to call her the moment he hung up. And then he did just that, muttering, "And what *she* says *goes.*"

Linnet had nodded to herself as she replaced the receiver, thinking Jack was right.

Aside from Jonathan Ainsley, Paula's cousin and the family's bitterest enemy, Linnet was somewhat concerned about Evan. Fortunately she was all right, and there were no problems with the babies, but that fall still gave Linnet cause for worry.

Evan was the most nimble person she knew and moved with a unique elegance and grace. Linnet couldn't for the life of her understand how Evan had missed the seat of the chair, hit the floor the way she had. It both baffled and bothered her.

Evan and Gideon had arrived at Pennistone Royal on Thursday, and last night Linnet had spoken to Evan about her fall when she and Julian had arrived for supper with them.

Evan had laughed it off when Linnet had started to probe gently, so she had let the subject slide away without further comment. What truly disturbed Linnet was the remembrance, so clearly etched in her mind, of Angharad standing over Evan, looking down at her, doing nothing to help. There had been such an odd expression in Angharad's eyes that Linnet had done a double take, had given her a longer, harder stare, and been discomfited when she recognized that Evan's adopted sister was actually looking gleeful. Linnet had not missed the inherent spite in her, and she was enormously troubled by this young woman's sudden appearance on the scene.

Angharad Hughes had not been due to come to London until next week. *She* bears watching, Linnet now decided, shrugging further into her cape, increasing her pace down the hill. I wouldn't put anything past *her.*

When Linnet had arrived at Pennistone Royal last night, her mother had asked her to stay for the whole of the coming week so that she could help with Evan's wedding. "Evan can't possibly do much, darling," Paula had pointed out. "She's so very pregnant, and after that awful fall in her office, Emily and I don't think she should be exerting herself."

Immediately, Linnet had agreed to stay on. She and her mother were close and always had been, and whenever she could ease Paula's burdens, Linnet tried to do so.

Earlier in the week, Linnet had considered talking to her mother about making changes at the store in Knightsbridge, but now she realized this was hardly the right time for such a discussion. The wedding was distracting her mother as much as it was Aunt Emily, mother of the groom, who was undeniably her favorite child. So how could Linnet bring up old-fashioned windows that needed a fresh approach? Or explain the importance of having a spa or suggest the idea of devoting an entire floor to brides and weddings? Paula seemed set in her ways these days, much to Linnet's chagrin.

Put it on hold, she muttered to herself and continued on her way, heading closer to the walk. Her mother had created this over thirty-five years ago, for Emma Harte. The Rhododendron Walk at Temple Newsam, a stately home near Leeds, had been the inspiration, and Paula, inveterate gardener that she was, had copied it down to the last detail.

In the summer months it was extraordinary to behold, the glossy leaves of the rhododendron bushes alive with color from the giant flowers: white, lilac, and pale pink giving way to dark rose and purple. The flowery bower was breathtaking at that time of the year; now, in winter, the dark green leaves were speckled with frozen snowflakes and tiny icicles.

Linnet stopped and glanced up at the sky. It was forbidding, curdled and cold. The wind was beginning to blow the steel gray clouds away, and quite suddenly a weak sun was visible, a pale silver orb against the expanse of blue. She was used to the sudden changes in the weather in Yorkshire, especially in the Dales, where she had grown up. Rain was prevalent throughout the year; but apparently it wasn't going to be a wet, gloomy day after all, and this pleased Linnet.

Striding out, humming to herself, she began to enjoy her walk. But at the same time her busy mind was focusing once again on the Hughes family.

On the one hand, she was well aware that Uncle Robin would be upset and disappointed if Owen and his family didn't stay with him. Robin Ainsley had discovered a new lease on life through the advent of Evan Hughes and her father, Owen, his long-lost son by Glynnis Hughes. Certainly he looked better than he had for several years. On the other hand, the Hughes family presented problems all of a sudden, primarily because Jonathan Ainsley was in Yorkshire. There was no doubt in anyone's mind that he resented the very idea of a half brother in the shape of Owen Hughes.

Jack believed that Ainsley was dangerous, and Linnet had to pay attention to Jack because he had rarely if ever been wrong, especially when it came to their security.

Perhaps her mother would talk to Uncle Robin, make him understand his newfound family might be at risk with Jonathan floating around. Yet Robin Ainsley was a stubborn man, and full of confidence about his own judgment. He had been a Member of Parliament for years, and he was a lawyer as well, although he had never practiced. Still, he was an intelligent man, in fact, a brilliant man, as his career in government attested. Would he listen to Paula, his niece, daughter of his half sister Daisy, to whom he was close these days?

No, wait a minute, Linnet instructed herself. It had just struck her that the best person to tackle Robin was his other half sister, Edwina. They had been especially close throughout their long lives. "Hand in glove" was the way her mother had described them recently, pointing out to

Linnet that it was obviously Edwina who had helped to facilitate Robin's long affair with Glynnis.

That's it, Linnet told herself, and she came to a snap decision. She would telephone Great-Aunt Edwina the minute she got back and explain the situation. Paula might be head of the family, but Edwina was the eldest of them all at ninety-five. Furthermore, she still had all her marbles. Even more important, she had immense clout with Robin. To her he *would* listen, Linnet was convinced.

Glancing at her watch, she realized that Great-Aunt Edwina wouldn't be at Niddersley House now. When Linnet had spoken to India at the Leeds store yesterday, her cousin had told her she was taking Edwina for lunch at Dusty's house. At this moment India would be driving her grandmother to Willows Hall near Harrogate.

"Drat," Linnet muttered and pressed on along the walk, formulating a plan as she strode. She would phone Willows Hall after lunch and talk to Edwina then. And she had no doubt that Great-Aunt Edwina would be delighted to jump into the fray. She had always had the demeanor of a British general and loved to boss everyone, especially her siblings, around.

Julian Kallinski stood at the window of the bedroom at Pennistone Royal which he shared with Linnet, looking out across the lawns. They were covered in hoarfrost, and the skeletal branches of the trees were dripping long icicles, which looked like miniature stalactites. The whole scene resembled a painting in grisaille, the black and white tints strikingly beautiful against the backdrop of the pale sky. In the distance he could see Linnet coming down the Rhododendron Walk, bundled up in her favorite cape. It was bright red, and she was hard to miss, even from this distance. A smile struck his mouth, and his eyes brightened at the sight of his wife. *Wife*, he thought, *she's my wife*.

He suddenly wondered what he would have done if Linnet hadn't come to her senses, if she hadn't ended their silly estrangement. No, not *their* estrangement. *Hers,* actually, from *him.* He had never felt estranged from her, only puzzled by her odd behavior, and achingly vulnerable to her in so many ways.

After several months of their being apart, he had forced the issue, made her see him by not taking no for an answer. Fortunately, he had chosen the right moment, and she had come back to him willingly, lovingly. And during her emotional and physical capitulation to him, in the searing heat of their mutual passion, she had told him she loved him and only him, and she had finally agreed to become his wife.

But what if he hadn't become assertive because of his frustration, annoyance, and anger? What if none of those words had ever been said? By him and by her. How could he have continued his life without her by his side?

It would have been difficult, most certainly, even trying, because their families were so intertwined. He and she might have broken up, but they would have been constantly thrown together for the rest of their lives on special family occasions.

The three clans, Hartes, O'Neills, and Kallinskis, had been part of each other's daily lives for well over a century, since the day Emma Harte, Blackie O'Neill, and David Kallinski had met and become best friends in the early years of the twentieth century in Leeds. And they had remained friends until their deaths.

Exile, Julian thought. I would have had to exile myself. I would have had to leave England, go to New York and run the American end of Kallinski Industries. That would have been the only solution. And my life would have been empty and banal without *her,* without my lovely, red-haired Linnet by my side.

But he wasn't without her. They were married now

and had been for over five weeks, just as they had planned to be since their childhood . . . their dream of marital bliss together had come true in the end.

Smiling to himself, filled with happiness, Julian turned away from the window and went over to the desk in the corner. As he passed the old Queen Anne chest, he caught sight of their wedding picture in its silver frame. He paused, staring at it for a moment. It was the big family portrait with himself and Linnet in the center, and surrounding them were his parents, her parents, her grandmother Daisy, Great-Aunt Edwina, and the two grandfathers, O'Neill and Kallinski. And there were their siblings and cousins and the aunts and uncles. The three clans in full force.

Julian focused his attention on his grandfather Sir Ronald Kallinski, who had managed to stave off death in order to attend their wedding. But, sadly, he had died in his sleep three days later, just when Julian and Linnet had arrived in Barbados for their honeymoon.

His father and her parents, and Grandfather O'Neill in particular, had insisted they not come back to England for the funeral. "He wouldn't have wanted that, Jules," his father had said to him, using the diminutive of his name yet speaking in his firmest voice. "He was thrilled to see you and Linnet married, overjoyed to know the three clans were united in marriage. 'All mixed into a lovely stew,' he said to me at the reception. And he was finally able to let go. He died peacefully in his sleep, and he was a happy man. We'll bury him quietly, and I'll start planning his memorial service. You'll both be here for that."

Julian had told his father he wanted to help with the plans for the memorial, and Michael Kallinski had agreed that they would do it together. "Remember, he was in his nineties." His father had then added, "And he had a great life, a *big* life. He was ready to go, he was ill. And tired, really. But as I said, a happy man because of you two. So, enjoy your honeymoon, and good-bye."

Linnet had been loving, full of sympathy, and she had helped him to get through a few truly sorrowful days. Finally, after much discussion, they had taken the advice of their families and remained in Barbados.

Moving away from the chest, sitting down at the desk, Julian thought of the coming week. He was going to be at the Leeds office of Kallinski Industries, and he would greatly miss his grandfather's presence there. For the past six months or so, Sir Ronnie, as he was called by everyone, had made the Leeds offices his headquarters, since he was no longer fit enough to travel to London.

Naturally, his considerable influence was everywhere, from the wonderful Post-Impressionist art and the Barbara Hepworth sculptures in the lobby to the coolness of the upper floors. Sir Ronnie had insisted that the air-conditioning was turned on, no matter the time of year. He liked his working environment to be cool, which was why many of the women employees referred to Kallinski House as "the frozen North," and "Iceland."

Julian looked across at the door as it flew open, and his reflective expression was obscured by a bright smile. He jumped up.

There she was, his beautiful Linnet.

She hurried forward, smiling back at him, and when she came to a standstill, she wrapped her arms around him, held him close.

"Are you all right? You looked so sad when I came in," she whispered against his cheek.

"I'm fine, really. I was just remembering Grandfather."

"I know." Linnet drew away and stared up into his dark blue eyes, almost violet, like her mother's. "Don't forget what the Hartes have always said about a loved one who has died . . . *in my heart forever*."

"Yes," he murmured. "I remember that."

"And it's true, you know."

"Yes, Linnet, I think it is. I feel that Grandfather is in my heart forever. . . . That motto of your family is absolutely correct."

She smiled at him, touched his face with a fingertip. "You know something strange? Even though I never knew Emma, I feel *her* in my heart. Sometimes I think she's all around me, loving me, guiding me, watching over me." She put her head to one side. "Do you think that's silly, Jules?"

"Of course not. I certainly wouldn't be so arrogant as to dismiss such feelings. There's so much we don't know about this world, or the other . . . and I'm happy that you feel *she's* watching over *you*."

Linnet stood on tiptoe and kissed him on the lips, then asked, "Have you seen Gideon and Evan yet this morning?"

"Yes," Julian answered and led her over to the sofa near the window. "Let's sit for a minute. I've several things to tell you. First, Emily came over, and Gideon and I had coffee with her; then she took your mother off to Beck House in West Tanfield. Gideon is driving over there later with Evan, and he asked us to go to tea at the house and have a look around. How do you feel about that?"

"It's great! I'd love to see how far they've come in the decoration. So, does that mean we can have lunch alone? Just the two of us?"

"Not exactly," he answered, his eyes suddenly mischievous.

"Oh, who's here that I don't know about?"

"Your beloved brother Lorne."

"Oh goody! That's wonderful. Oh, sorry, Jules, about our tête-à-tête, you don't mind, do you?"

"Not at all, darling, I've always had a soft spot for Lorne. But, actually, that's not all of it. He's here with his twin and her French friend."

"Tessa and Jean-Claude are *here*?" Linnet sounded surprised.

"That's right, and Tessa says she's going to cook dinner for everyone, so we're in for a treat." He grinned. "She's making her specialty."

"Oh, God, not coq au vin."

"Oh no, she doesn't make that anymore, at least so she told me. We're going to have lamb stew."

Linnet began to chuckle. "Come on, let's go down to the kitchen and see what's going on. In the meantime, let me tell you about the call I had from Jack Figg just as I was leaving for my walk."

"Something important?"

"Just that the dreaded Jonathan Ainsley is staying at his house in Thirsk. Jack's a bit worried about that."

"I don't blame him," Julian muttered, following Linnet out of their bedroom. "That man's a menace. More than that, actually. I believe he's a genuine threat. I've never told you this, but he once beat Dad up when they were kids. Dad had to go to hospital, have stitches in his head."

"I knew about it, actually, Jules. Mummy told me a lot about Ainsley's violent behavior when he was growing up with them. He'll do something horrible to one of us, you'll see."

Julian's eyes narrowed. "I think I'm going to get you a driver who's a former policeman. You need protection."

Linnet did not answer.

7

～

Dusty jumped up from the desk and went to stand in front of the blazing fire. His face was taut as he stuck his hands in his pockets and warmed his back against the flames.

His mind had been racing ever since Paddy had announced the arrival of his little daughter with Mrs. Roebotham. The fact that the woman had brought a suitcase belonging to Atlanta meant only one thing: The child was coming to stay with him. Which, in turn, meant that it was Molly Caldwell who was out of action, not Melinda.

"This is Mrs. Roebotham," Paddy said, hurrying through the doorway, ushering the woman in at last.

Immediately, Dusty moved forward, exclaiming, "Hello, Mrs. Roebotham. *Hello!*" Drawing to a standstill in front of her, he stretched out his hand and smiled, adding, "I'm Russell Rhodes."

She took his hand and shook it, rather timidly he thought, and murmured in a subdued voice, "I'm pleased to meet you, Mr. Rhodes."

Paddy excused himself and disappeared while Dusty led the woman toward the fireplace. He knew everything about her the instant she entered the room, although he had never met her before. She looked about forty, was scrubbed to shining cleanliness, not a vestige of makeup on her face, neat and tidy in her appearance, her dark clothes plain, simple, but not cheap-looking in any way. Her luxuriant auburn hair was brushed back and formed into a sleek twist at the back of her head to reveal a slender, high-cheekboned face that was rather attractive, and she had light eyes, grayish blue, he thought. She was slim and wiry, and of medium height, and there was something about her that was arresting, a determination, perhaps, an honesty and straightforwardness. He knew immediately that she was a decent woman.

Leeds, he thought. Working-class Leeds. Same background as mine. No doubt grew up in a Victorian terrace house, just as I did. They had a lot in common, although he was quite sure she was not aware of that.

"Let's sit here, shall we, Mrs. Roebotham?" he said briskly.

"It's Gladys, everybody calls me Gladys, Mr. Rhodes," she said, sitting down where he had indicated, crossing her ankles, placing her hands in her lap on top of her bag.

"Very well, it's Gladys then. Now, would you like some refreshments? Tea? Coffee? Or something else? Something to eat, perhaps?"

"Nothing, but thanks ever so much. Cook made me a cup of tea when I got here, Mr. Rhodes."

He nodded his understanding and repressed the urge to tell her to call him Dusty. He knew that she wouldn't, that the mere suggestion would only embarrass her. She was probably overly impressed by this house, undoubtedly intimidated by his fame . . . the poor Leeds lad who'd made it big. The Yorkshire newspapers were his greatest boosters, always calling him a genius, giving him lavish accolades for his paintings.

As he took the seat opposite her, he asked, "What's happened to Molly Caldwell?"

"She's had a heart attack," Gladys answered calmly, but her hands were twisting together in her lap.

Dismay clutched at him. "How bad is she?" he asked, leaning forward, pinning his eyes on hers.

"It's serious, but her doctor is very hopeful," she murmured and tried, without much success, to give him a reassuring smile.

"When did it happen? This morning?"

"No. Yesterday afternoon. It was lucky I was there. I go three times a week to help her, and I was in the kitchen doing the ironing when she collapsed. I called Dr. Bloom immediately. It was him that sent the ambulance. She's in Leeds Infirmary, that's where they took her."

"And before that, before she went to hospital, she told you to bring Atlanta to me?" Dusty said.

"Oh, no, she was . . . Well, she was sort of out of it," Gladys explained. "I knew what I had to do, mind you, Mr. Rhodes. Bring Atlanta to you. Molly had drilled that into me. She said if ever she got sick or anything, I had to bring the little girl to you. Nobody else. Only to you. She kept an envelope in the kitchen drawer with your address and money for taxis in it."

"I'm glad she'd told you what to do in case of an emergency, Gladys. Very glad. And you did well. Thank you."

"I would have brought Atlanta to you last night. But it had turned seven by the time they took Molly to the hospital. Way past Atlanta's bedtime. I thought it best to stay the night at Molly's house, I didn't want to alarm the child. And so I brought her here today. I spoke to Leeds Infirmary this morning before coming here, and Molly's doing well."

Dusty nodded. "What else did the doctor tell you?"

"That her heart attack was not life threatening. Dr. Bloom thinks she'll be able to come home in a week."

"That's certainly good news," Dusty said, filling with sudden relief.

"By the way, she's in the ICU, under the care of a heart specialist, Mr. Rhodes. I shall go and visit her on my way back home, even if I can only wave to her," Gladys announced.

"That's very kind of you, and I'll go myself on Monday. By the way, this Dr. Bloom, is he in Meanwood?"

"Oh yes, he's our local doctor. He's been there years. And he's only three streets away from Molly, and not too far from me either. I've written his number down for you, Mr. Rhodes. I thought you might want to be in touch with him." As she spoke, she fumbled in her bag and brought out a piece of paper, handed it to him.

"Thanks, Gladys, thanks again for bringing Atlanta to me. Incidentally, how did you explain her grandmother's absence to her?" he asked, staring at the piece of paper, then putting it in his pocket.

"It was Atlanta who came to me in the kitchen. She said her grandmother had fallen down, had hurt her leg because she wasn't getting up. So when the ambulance arrived, I said they were taking Grandma to get her leg made better. She accepted that, and then when I told her I was bringing her to you today, she was so excited that was all she could think about," Gladys informed him.

Dusty stood up. "Thank you for all you've done. I'd best go and see Atlanta without any further delay. I thought it better to get the whole story from you before seeing my daughter. Now come with me to the kitchen, Gladys, and have some lunch. Then we'll arrange for a car to take you back to Leeds, to see Molly and later to your home."

"Oh, please, it's not necessary, honestly it isn't. I'll get off after I've said good-bye to Atlanta. She's a good little girl, you know, very grown up in so many ways, Mr. Rhodes."

"Yes, I know. She's a treasure," he said, escorting her out of the room. "I'm very grateful to you, Gladys, and I won't let you leave here without some food in you, and a car to take you wherever you want to go. And by the way, you'd better give me your phone number so that I have it handy."

She nodded. "Yes, I will. I don't live far from Mrs. Caldwell, just a couple of streets down." There was a moment's hesitation before she said softly, "Thanks for being so nice."

He smiled at her but said nothing and led her through the entrance foyer in the direction of the kitchen. He saw her looking around, staring at his paintings. But she didn't make any comment, and neither did he.

"Daddy! Daddy! Daddy!" Atlanta cried the moment she saw Dusty, dancing toward him on her tiptoes, her laughter echoing all around them. She was tall for three, and slender, "his little bean shoot" he called her, and had enormous grace of movement, much in evidence now.

As she came into his arms, there was no mistaking whose child she was, with her jet-black hair and light blue eyes. It always seemed to him that there was nothing of Melinda in her. After hugging her and kissing her cheek, he put her down on the floor and gave her a huge smile. "We're going to have a fun weekend together while Grandma gets her leg mended."

"Does it hurt her, Daddy?" Atlanta asked, staring up at him. Without waiting for his answer, she shook her head and said, "She didn't cry."

"No, I don't think it hurts, darling," he answered, and then, turning to Gladys, he said, "Please stay for something to eat, it's already twelve-thirty. You must be hungry."

Before Gladys could respond, Atlanta looked across at her and announced, "Valetta's made spaghetti, Gladys. It's got tomatoes in it."

"I don't think I can have lunch here, Atlanta, and—"

"Oh, please, please," Atlanta cut in, and looking at Dusty she went on, "Make Gladys stay, Daddy, please."

Dusty grinned, gazing down at Atlanta, and said, "I'm having lunch with your friend India, and then this afternoon she's going to take you out. So why don't you eat here in the kitchen, and Valetta will make some more of your favorite things, and then we'll all go for a drive?"

Atlanta nodded. "Can I go and see Indi? I like her."

"She hasn't arrived yet, but of course you can say hello to her. She's bringing *her* grandmother to see me."

"Oh. Is she like my grandma?" the child asked, staring up at her father.

Dusty bit back the laugh that rose in his throat and said, "No. I think she's quite different altogether. In fact, there's a big difference. But her grandma's as nice as yours."

"Oh goody." Atlanta ran to Gladys and took hold of her hand. "You'll like Indi. She's nice. She tells stories and reads to me."

"I know how much you like that. But I really think I have to go, lovey. I'll meet your friend India another time."

"*Oh*. Don't go, Gladys," the child beseeched, clinging to her hand.

"I have to visit your grandmother," Gladys explained, and then, becoming aware of the tears welling in Atlanta's eyes, she said, "Well, all right, I'll stay and have a snack with you." She managed a small chuckle, adding with a twinkle, "I'm getting a bit peckish."

"Like the birds!" Atlanta exclaimed, laughing. "That's what you always say. Peckish like the birds."

Dusty said, "Then it's settled. Come on, Gladys, and you too, Atlanta. You can both sit here at the table, and Valetta will bring plates of her delicious spaghetti, and whatever else you want. All right, Valetta?"

"That's fine, Mr. Rhodes," the cook said, laughter in her dark eyes. Waving her wooden spoon, she turned back to her pans, stirring the contents of one of them. "I'm almost ready to serve."

As Dusty was leading his child and Gladys Roebotham to the table at the far end of the large, family-style

kitchen, he heard a car on the gravel driveway. Kissing
the top of Atlanta's dark head, he murmured, "Drink
some of your water, darling, and I'll be back in a minute."

"Yes, Daddy," she answered dutifully, sitting in a chair.
She picked up the small glass of water and took a swallow. "Sipping like the ducks," she said, smiling at Gladys.

Dusty strode across the main entrance foyer, heading for
the front door, intent on greeting India and her grandmother on the steps. As he opened the door and went out
onto the terrace, he saw them coming slowly toward him.

He knew better than to go and escort them inside. The
Dowager Countess of Dunvale was something of a tartar,
with a very sharp tongue. She resisted any help from others, and he understood absolutely where she was coming
from. He admired her for her extraordinary stamina and
fortitude. After all, she was ninety-five and anything but
senile. Far be it from him to undermine her confidence in
herself.

India waved to him, and he waved back. He wondered
how she would react to the news that Atlanta was here for
a week at least. He would give her all the details as soon
as they were settled in the sitting room having their aperitif. Her grandmother liked a drink before lunch, and her
insistence on "a drop of sherry," as she put it, always tick-
led him. He would tell India about Molly Caldwell at
once, so there was no misunderstanding. Months ago she
had accused him of "lying by omission," and he had no
desire to have that accusation leveled at him again.

He knew that India liked the child as much as Atlanta
liked her, and her presence would not present any problems, as far as he could see. Angelina, the housekeeper,
and Valetta, the cook, would keep an eye on her while he
was painting during the morning, and he would spend
time in the afternoon with her. After all, since India ran
the northern stores, she would be at the Leeds store during the week, and she still lived at Pennistone Royal,

spending only the weekends with him here at Willows Hall. No, the child would not be intrusive on them or their relationship, he decided, and then it struck him that Gladys Roebotham could be very useful. It was obvious Atlanta was attached to her, and Gladys seemed to reciprocate the child's feelings. Perhaps she would consider spending part of the coming week here looking after Atlanta.

"Excuse me, Mr. Rhodes," Paddy said from the entrance foyer.

Dusty swung around to face the house manager. "Yes, Paddy?"

"I've put a decanter of amontillado in the sitting room, and I was wondering, is there anything else you need?"

"I don't think so, thanks very much. Lunch in about half an hour. Oh, and Paddy, order a car for Mrs. Roebotham, would you, please? It's to take her back home, with a stop off at Leeds Infirmary to see Mrs. Caldwell. And please tell her I'll be in to have a word with her in a few minutes."

"Right you are, sir," Paddy murmured and was gone on silent feet.

"Good morning, Countess," Dusty said a moment later as India and her grandmother finally came to a standstill in front of him.

"Good morning, Dusty, and *Countess* is far too formal. I do keep telling you that. You must call me Edwina."

"You know I can't," he replied, laughing. "That's not respectful."

She chuckled with him and then suggested, "Why not call me Great-Aunt Edwina? Or Grandmother. But perhaps you have a grandmother of your own?"

"No, she's dead." Turning to India, he smiled lovingly and kissed her cheek. "Hello, darling," he whispered against her hair before he ushered them both into the house.

Within several seconds he had Edwina settled comfortably in a chair near the fireplace, and India went and perched on the sofa, waiting for him as he poured their glasses and brought the sherry to them.

"Cheers, ladies," he said, lifting his glass, and sat down on the sofa next to India.

"Cheers," India answered, as did her grandmother.

Staring hard at Dusty, India now said, "You've got a peculiar expression on your face. What's the matter?"

He threw her a long, thoughtful look, realizing yet again how well she knew him, and in ways no one else ever had before.

Since his new tactic was to tell her everything upfront, he said, "It's Mrs. Caldwell. She had a heart attack late yesterday afternoon, and the woman who helps her brought Atlanta over here this morning."

"Oh, how dreadful!" India exclaimed. "I mean about the heart attack. How is Mrs. Caldwell's condition today?"

"Apparently it's serious but not life threatening. She'll be in hospital for about a week, and from what Mrs. Roebotham says, the prognosis is good. I'll call the doctor later; Atlanta's here to stay with me for a few days. Until her grandmother's better, actually."

India smiled at him. "Don't look so concerned, Dusty, she'll be fine with us, and I couldn't be happier. It's lovely to have her here for the weekend. We'll have some fun together. Where is she now?"

"Having lunch with Mrs. Roebotham in the kitchen, but she's really looking forward to seeing you later."

"So am I. And, Grandma, you'll get to meet Dusty's little girl. She's just adorable."

Edwina simply nodded and took a sip of sherry. No doubt Atlanta *was* adorable, and certainly India was genuine in her affection for the child, but Edwina couldn't help thinking that it was a good thing she was only three years old. And still malleable. There was no doubt in the older woman's mind that Dusty and India would end up raising his child. His former girlfriend was recovering from a serious drug addiction, and her mother obviously had a wonky heart. She might not live long; and who could answer for the daughter? Addictions were hard to kick.

8

Tessa Fairley stood in her room at Pennistone Royal, lost in thought. Of late, there were moments when she couldn't help wondering what the rest of her life was going to be like. What did the future hold in store? What was her destiny to be? She had no idea.

The one certainty, the one steadfast thing in her life, was her devotion to and love for her three-year-old daughter, Adele. Everything else was vague, up in the air, or out of her grasp, at least so it seemed to her lately.

Would she be made managing director of Harte Stores by her mother? Would she then run the stores herself, as she had always wanted to do? Or would her mother decide to make her joint managing director with her sister Linnet? Shared responsibilities had been bruited about in the past few months, startling and disappointing her, putting her on guard. That was something she had *never* wanted, sharing the top spot with her sister.

Conversely, would she abandon her career, ambitions, and dreams of being the new Emma Harte, and instead marry Jean-Claude Deléon?

She smiled inwardly. There was just one small problem in that regard: he had not asked her to marry him. But if he did propose, and if she accepted, there would be a vast upheaval in her life and that of her child. Since he lived and worked in Paris, she would have to move across the Channel and make a life with him there. Could she be happy in France?

Tessa almost laughed out loud. Of course she could. She was a dyed-in-the-wool Francophile, and she loved Paris, knew the City of Light as well as she knew London. Well, almost. Years before meeting Jean-Claude, she had been going to Paris on a regular basis, and Shane O'Neill, her stepfather, owned one of the most exclusive and deluxe hotels in the city. It was situated on the elegant Avenue Montaigne, off the Champs-Élysées.

Then there was Jean-Claude's small country estate, where he spent most weekends. Located outside Paris, near Fontainebleau, it was a picturesque country manor called Clos-Fleuri. On her first visit last summer, she had taken an instant liking to it, and she felt at home there, as if she truly belonged. Aside from the beautiful grounds and gardens, the house was lovely, full of charm, and when she was there she felt enveloped in quiet luxury and comfort. There was a peacefulness about it that she cherished.

All of these points aside, Tessa was deeply in love with Jean-Claude, and she had realized from the beginning of their affair that she could be happy with him *anywhere*.

Tessa had never known anyone like him. He was loving, warm, and kind to her, and he adored little Adele. Emotional considerations apart, he was a man she respected and admired. He had a vivid intelligence, was clever, street-smart, and brilliant in his work. Yet despite his superior intellect, he never made her feel inferior. They got on well and were great companions; she had never felt that way with her former husband, Mark Longden. He had always managed to put her down and beat up on her—verbally and physically.

Jean-Claude Deléon, one of the most famous men in France, if not indeed in the world, had fallen in love with her the minute he met her. And she with him. He called it

a *coup de foudre*. "We were struck by lightning," he sometimes said, smiling at her tenderly.

That had been last August. In the last five months,
they had managed to spend a great deal of time together
in Paris and London, at Clos-Fleuri, and here in Yorkshire at her mother's home. And during these months
they had grown closer, come to know each other most intimately on every level. It was so right, this affair of
theirs, and they both knew it.

But there was a problem, and it troubled her. What
would she *do* if she married him? She had always
worked. Hard work was bred in the bone of every Harte,
and she was no exception. She had been brought up to be
disciplined, dedicated, driven, and an achiever. Just as
the whole family had. So wouldn't she be bored if she
didn't have a job?

Naturally she would be bored. Bored silly. Especially
since Jean-Claude worked like a Trojan himself, writing
books, screenplays, theatrical plays, and articles for
newspapers and magazines. He filmed documentaries
and gave lectures. He was forever occupied.

And then there was his great fame in France. He was
the philosopher-king, the favorite of presidents and
politicians, and a member of the Parisian elite.

Fame had its own demands. She was well aware of
that; her brother Lorne, her beloved twin, was a famous
actor. Fame ate up his time, just as it ate Jean-Claude's.
There were personal appearances, press and publicity,
events to attend, and she knew it was all part of his work.

Tessa let out a heavy sigh and sat down in the chair at
her desk. There were so many questions bouncing
around in her head this morning, and no answers were
forthcoming.

She glanced at the mail on her desk, which she had
brought with her from London. After reading the letters
and e-mails, she put them back in their folder and
pushed it to the end of the desk, an old French *bureau*

plat she treasured. Then her eyes scanned the little sitting room which adjoined her bedroom. This intimate suite had been hers for as long as she could remember, and she loved its primrose yellow walls and yellow-and-red toile de Jouy documentary print at the windows. In this suite were displayed all her favorite possessions, decorative objects, books and paintings, which she had collected over the years. They helped to give the two rooms their attractive aspects and personality, bespoke her taste as well as personal preferences. It was distinctively her decor.

Glancing at her watch, Tessa suddenly realized she ought to go downstairs and find Jean-Claude and the others, offer them drinks before lunch. Her mother, who had gone to West Tanfield with Aunt Emily, had asked her to be the hostess in her absence.

Earlier, when she had talked to Margaret, the housekeeper had insisted on making lunch, because, as she put it, "You'll have your hands full doing dinner tonight, Miss Tessa." And so she had let the housekeeper take over. A short while ago, Margaret had come up to tell her about the menu. She was making hot leek-and-potato soup, a chicken pot pie, a cottage pie, and fish cakes for those who wanted lighter fare. There was green salad and a cheese platter, as well as fresh fruit.

Margaret had then thought to add, "And what about all this lamb stew, Miss Tessa? You've ordered far too much meat. Why, there's enough to feed an army, that there is!"

Tessa had quickly answered that there were a lot of bones in lamb shoulder and neck, and that everyone liked a stew the next day anyway, because it tasted even better.

Tutting to herself, Margaret had said no more, but she had looked annoyed as she stomped off to the kitchen. Perhaps she's mad at me because I've invaded her territory again, Tessa thought, then shrugged. She enjoyed cooking, and if she was in the kitchen, Margaret could have a night off. But she decided the housekeeper wouldn't see it that way.

Rising, Tessa now walked into her bedroom and took a sage green wool jacket out of the wardrobe. Slipping it on, she swung around and stood for a moment regarding the bed.

No one had ever shared *this* bed with her. None of her siblings when they were growing up, and certainly not Mark Longden. Whenever she and Mark had stayed at Pennistone Royal after their marriage, she had asked her mother to put them in the Blue-and-White Suite. On these occasions she had been able to use her own rooms as her private place, to be alone, to rest and work. The suite was her quiet haven during her marriage, as it had been from childhood. Her little yellow-and-red suite was sacrosanct. No one had ever been permitted to share it.

Until last night. When the house was still and everyone had gone to sleep, Jean-Claude had come to her bedroom at her invitation. He had slipped into the bed with her, taken her in his arms, and held her close. They had loved each other very tenderly, and it had pleased her that he was with her here. He was her one true love, her soul mate, the only man she wanted, and wherever she was she wanted him with her. So her private haven was opened to him willingly and with joy.

She never worried about the difference in their ages, but she was aware he did. He was over twenty years older, and it bothered him. Sometimes she chided him for that, told him not to be silly, and he would nod, and smile, and change the subject. She wanted to have another child, but only by him; she wanted it even if they weren't married. But whenever she thought of bringing it up, she lost her nerve. Perhaps this weekend she would mention it . . .

The buzzing phone interrupted her thoughts. "Hello?"

"*C'est moi, chérie,*" Jean-Claude said.

"How odd!" Tessa exclaimed. "I was just thinking about you."

He chuckled. "Nice things, I hope."

"Oh yes, very, very, very nice things."

"Are you coming downstairs, my Tess? I would like to talk to you about . . . something."

"I was just coming down to find you."

"I shall await you in the library."

"See you in a jiffy."

She hung up the phone, glanced at herself in the mirror, liking the sage green wool jacket with the cream sweater and matching cream wool pants. Invariably, Tessa wore light colors, knowing how well they suited her pale blond coloring, and she had discovered Jean-Claude preferred them to darker shades.

Hurrying across the bedroom, she went out into the corridor and down the wide, curving staircase, heading for the library, wondering what he wanted to talk to her about.

The great Stone Hall was empty, but a fire blazed up the chimney, and it was a warm and welcoming sight, as were the many large pots of gold, yellow, and bronze chrysanthemums and the white orchids. Her mother always had a lovely display of plants in the Stone Hall, following the tradition started by Emma many years before. Gardening was Paula's hobby, and many of the plants in the house were grown by her in the greenhouses; she liked to display them in all the rooms. And they gave everyone pleasure.

Tessa's high-heeled cream boots made a staccato sound as she crossed the Stone Hall and went into the library.

Jean-Claude swung around as she entered, and he hurried over to her, kissed her cheek.

His face was cold against hers, and she asked, "Did you go out for a walk after all?"

"*Mais oui, chérie*. I needed fresh air. And to clear my

head," he explained, and, taking hold of her hand, he led her down the long room. "Let's sit here, near the terrace windows," he murmured. Once they were seated, he stared into her face, his eyes searching, as if he were endeavoring to ascertain her mood.

"What is it?" Tessa instantly asked, frowning, staring back at him. "You look so intense. *Worried* even." Anxiety suddenly flared in her.

"No, not worried. Intense, perhaps. Tess, I am going to . . . get this out. Say it. I cannot encase it in fancy rhetoric."

She felt herself stiffening, and she gave him a harder, more probing stare. "Get what out? What do you mean? You sound as if you're going to tell me about something . . . unpleasant. About us, maybe?"

"*Non, non, chérie.* What I have to say is not about *us.* I have been given a big assignment. For a French television network, and I wanted to explain. . . . I will be out of Paris for a while, perhaps several weeks. Possibly a month. I hate to leave you for this period of time, Tessa, but it is an important assignment. I must take it."

Relief flooded through her, and she exclaimed, "That's fine, I understand." She laughed somewhat weakly and added, with a slight grimace, "I thought you were going to announce something quite awful, like you were finished with me. That it was over . . . that we were over."

Startled by her words, baffled at her lack of faith in him, he looked at her askance and said softly, "That will *never,* ever happen. You must not worry about such a thing. Which reminds me, I have this for you." As he spoke, he pulled a small leather box out of his pocket and handed it to her silently.

Tessa took the box, lifted the lid, and her eyes grew wide as she stared down at a glittering diamond engagement ring. "Jean-Claude!" she gasped, surprise echoing. "It's perfectly beautiful. Gorgeous. Oh, my God, Jean-Claude."

He beamed at her. "Do you like it?"

She nodded emphatically. "Of course. *I love it.* And I love *you!*"

He took the box away from her, took out the ring, and put it on her finger, noting that her hand trembled. He said, "Do you think I have to ask Shane for your hand in marriage? Or am I being a little old-fashioned?"

She laughed uproariously, filled with excitement and amused at this suggestion. "You don't have to ask him. Or Mummy. I am a divorced woman, after all. Well, not quite divorced. Yet."

"And will you be my wife, Tessa, once you are free?" he asked, his voice solemn, his face serious.

"Oh yes, Jean-Claude. Yes, very much *yes*," she cried.

He leaned closer, kissed her on the mouth, and told her, "You've just made me a happy man. A *very* happy man, my darling."

"And I'm a happy woman." She held out her hand, gazing at the ring. "It's just beautiful, Jean-Claude. Thank you so much."

"It's an old stone, I had it reset. It suits you." He smiled at her indulgently. "I think diamonds are your stones."

"And why not?" she asked gaily, and then sobering slightly, she added, "But you haven't told me where you're going. Where is your assignment taking you?"

"To Afghanistan."

She gaped at him, flabbergasted. For a split second words failed her, but after a moment she gasped, "Oh, no, not *there*. You're going to cover the war there. You could get hurt. Why, you could even get killed!"

"*Non, non. Jamais* . . . never. I will be fine. Remember, *chérie,* I have done this many times before. I am a war correspondent, Tessa. You must not forget that. I learned long ago not to take risks."

"But Jean-Claude, being a war correspondent is terribly *dangerous,* whatever you say," she protested.

"That I do not deny. However, I *am* experienced, and I

am not a hothead. I do not put myself in harm's way, and I have been there before when the Russians invaded Afghanistan. I know the terrain."

"I shall be frantic with worry," she cried, her face paler than usual, her eyes stricken. She began to tremble.

"I know that, but the time will pass quickly. It will be only a month. And thank God for cell phones. We can speak every day."

"Please don't go—"

He held up his hand. "My Tess, you know who I am, what I am all about. I must go. I do not have a choice in this matter. It is what I do. And you must learn to live with it." He sounded suddenly tough and very determined. His tone brooked no argument.

"You *have* to go? You really do?" she said in a low voice.

"I do."

"Then I *shall* have to learn to live with it," she answered and blinked rapidly as tears welled.

Jean-Claude noticed her tears at once and put his arms around her, held her close. "Nothing is going to happen to me. I promise," he reassured her. "I shall come back to you safely. We shall be married as soon as your divorce is final, and we will be together always."

Tessa did not answer. She was too choked up to say anything. As he held her closer, she silently prayed that he *would* be safe, that he *would* come back to her in one piece.

9

∾

I need to speak with you."

Lorne nodded, looking across at his twin sister from the window seat where he had so often sat as a child, here in the old playroom on the top floor of Pennistone Royal, underneath the attics.

Tessa stood near the ancient rocking horse, Gallant Lad, which had been ridden by their mother, aunts, uncles, and cousins before them. The vibrant red, green, yellow, and white paint was faded now, cracked and chipped, and the black mane had thinned with time, but oh, how that beloved horse had been ridden, hugged, patted, and enjoyed by so many Harte children.

Lorne waited patiently for her to speak; he was always patient with her and loving; they were the closest of friends, and he knew she was not the ogre so many of the family thought she was. Suddenly he noticed how pensive she looked, saw the worry flickering in her silvery gray eyes, so like his own, and he immediately thought of that bastard of an ex-husband of hers—well, soon to be *ex*—and he wondered if Mark Longden had been causing more trouble. Whenever he thought of him, Lorne saw red, wanted to find him and thrash him within an inch of his life. He had mistreated and abused Tessa in every way, and as far as Lorne was concerned, no punishment was too harsh for him. Blackguard, he thought, using a very old-fashioned word but one he believed most appropriate.

"Come on, tell me! Speak to me, Ancient One," he coaxed, using the name he had invented for her when they were children, when, at the tender age of five, she had announced to him that she was the elder twin by five minutes and therefore their mother's heir. Much to her chagrin, he had never let her forget that little child's boast.

Tessa smiled her special smile, the one she reserved for him, and giving the rocking horse a little push so that it began to move, she looked directly at Lorne and murmured, "Jean-Claude's going to Afghanistan. To cover the war for a French network."

"Is he really! That's great, he'll be in his element. He's such a brilliant war correspondent . . ." Lorne's voice faltered as he instantly noticed the pained look crossing her face, and quickly he added, "Oh, God, Tessa, how stupid I'm being. You're worried, of course, and who wouldn't be? Reporting a war is dangerous, I know that. But listen . . ." Lorne leaned forward, his expression intent as he swiftly went on. "He's been at this game for years. He knows what he's doing, he's a seasoned war correspondent and not a beginner, green behind the ears. Please try not to worry."

"Easy to say, brother of mine, hard to do." She shook her head slowly. "Very hard not to be on the verge of panic."

He nodded, compressed his lips, understanding exactly how she felt. "Knowing you, I suppose you told him how nervous you are about this."

"Yes, Lorne, I did. I asked him not to go."

"And?"

"He told me he had to, and that I would have to get used to it . . . more or less those words, anyway. He was adamant, so naturally I agreed with him." She lifted her slender shoulders in a light shrug. "What else could I say?"

"Nothing really," Lorne agreed. "In reality, you have no choice. You have to go along with him. He's a fifty-three-year-old man who's been doing what he wants all his life, especially when it comes to his career. That's who he is. His own man. I doubt he could be deterred once he'd made up his mind, not by you or me or anyone else. Look, it is his *forte*, after all."

"That's right, and he's good at it. And over the last few years he's become an expert on the Middle East, fanaticism, and militancy. He said to me only the other day that it's a political philosophy—waging war against the Western democracies, that is. He has the need to understand, to write about such things. That's one of the reasons he's excited about going to cover this war."

"I realize that. Actually, he's talked a lot to me about the Middle East, and especially in the last year. But listen, Tess, the news is good, and has been since December. The armed resistance of the Taliban at Tora Bora has come to an end, American forces destroyed the operations there, and Karzai has formed a new government. Things are better, most certainly, and let's not forget he *knows* the country, covered the last war there, when the Russians invaded."

"I know, he's told me bits about it, and anyway I read his book *Warriors*, and he covered it in that."

Tessa walked over to the window seat, and Lorne made room for her as he had always done when they were children. Leaning back against him, she murmured softly, "I'm so afraid he might get killed."

"He could get killed walking across the Champs-Élysées," Lorne answered. "It'll be all right," he went on quietly, putting his arms around her, wanting to calm and reassure her.

Tessa nodded, then sat up slightly, put her hand in her

pocket, and brought out the diamond engagement ring. Turning around to look up at her brother, she said, "We're engaged," and showed him the ring.

Lorne stared at it, then whistled, and his eyes twinkled as he exclaimed, "I'm thrilled. *Congratulations.* I couldn't be happier for you." He started to laugh then, looking at her with sudden amusement.

"What is it?" she asked, eyeing him intently, frowning.

"When I set the two of you up, I never guessed it would actually come to this . . . *a permanent relationship.*"

"I knew it!" Tessa cried, punching his arm. "Right from the beginning. I told Jean-Claude on our first date that I suspected you'd brought us together, and very specifically to have an affair."

"And aren't you glad I did?"

"You bet!" Smiling, she slid the ring on her finger and showed it to him again. "Look, Lorne."

"It's a bobby dazzler, and so are you!" he exclaimed, and then he added in a more sober tone, "He's a good man, Tess. True blue. And he's very good for you, just as you're so good for him. When do you plan to get married?"

"As soon as we can, and I'd really like it to be before June. I don't want to infringe on India's splashy wedding in Ireland."

"I agree. And can I hope to be best man?"

She grinned. "We haven't got that far. He only just gave me the ring this morning. But I'm sure he'll ask you."

Lorne nodded. "When does his assignment actually start?"

"In two weeks. He's going to Paris on Monday, but he'll fly directly from Paris to Yorkshire on Thursday. He says he's determined to attend one of our famous family weddings."

"Learning the ropes, eh?" Lorne teased.

"I suppose. Thanks, Lorne, for getting us together. It means the world to me that you did that for me, that you cared enough."

"Hey, come on, don't be a silly goose. Incidentally, why aren't you wearing the ring? Be careful you don't lose it, leaving it floating around in your pocket like that."

"I'll wear it tonight, after we've told Mummy and Dad. They don't know yet, since they're both out."

"Then we'll make it a celebration tonight."

"That's an idea. . . . Lorne?"

"Yes, what is it? You sound suddenly mournful."

"I'm worried about not having a job after I marry Jean-Claude. I've always worked. What I mean is, I'll have to give up Harte's."

Her twin gave her a long, thoughtful look, frowning, shaking his head. "Is it still that important to you, working at Harte's?"

"Yes. No. I don't know."

"You're thirty-two, darling, and you've had a lot of success at the stores. But let's not forget the rough ride you had with Mark Longden. A very bad marriage that gave you absolutely zilch."

"It gave me Adele."

"Yes, of course, and I know you love her, I know what she means to you. But you're a young woman, you should have happiness with a man, a fulfilled life. And how often do we find the right person? *The* one for us? I haven't yet. *But you have.* Jean-Claude is the perfect man for you, and you're going to be very busy being his wife and bringing up Adele. And what if you have a child, or indeed children, by him?"

"You're right, Lorne," she replied very quietly, looking into the distance.

"I know you, Tessa, and you're thinking about Linnet. About Linnet being the head of Harte's, and that kills you, doesn't it?"

Tessa stared at him. She said nothing, biting her lip.

Neither of them spoke for a while.

It was Lorne who finally said, "You've just got to get over this jealousy of yours. You've been rivals for years, and it only makes for bad blood between you. And upsets us all."

"I know . . . but she wants the top job desperately."

"And she'll probably get it. Face *that* now. You'll be living in Paris with your new husband. She'll be here, right on the spot. Of course Mummy's going to give it to her."

"I wish I could commute."

"Don't be so ridiculous! That wouldn't work. You'd better make up your mind to forget having the power at the stores and think of your marriage. I don't believe you can have both. And to my way of thinking, you'll be happier being Madame Jean-Claude Deléon than being the new Emma Harte. That role's for Linnet. Accept it."

Tessa stared at him. She did not respond.

"I would like to speak to the Countess of Dunvale, please, Paddy. I believe she's lunching there. This is Linnet O'Neill."

"Oh, hello, Miss O'Neill," Paddy Whitaker said pleasantly. "I'll put you through to the dining room."

"Oh, I don't want to disturb their lunch!"

"No, no, it's all right, they've finished. Just a moment please, Miss O'Neill."

It was India who picked up the phone in the dining room of Willows Hall and said, "Hello, Linnet, I hear you want to speak to Grandma."

"For a minute or two, India. I hope I'm not phoning at an inopportune time."

"No, no, it's fine. We've finished lunch, just waiting to have coffee. Let me get Grandma, she's talking to Dusty."

Linnet waited several minutes before she heard that famous sonorous voice. "Here I am, Linnet. To what do I owe this honor? A phone call from you is a rarity."

"Oh gosh, Great-Aunt Edwina, don't say *that*. You make me feel guilty."

"Don't be daft, and guilt's a terrible waste of time."

"Yes, Great-Aunt Edwina," Linnet responded and went

on quickly. "I need to talk to you about Uncle Robin and Evan's family, and it's urgent."

"Why? Is there something wrong?"

"No. But there could be. Is it at all possible for me to see you tomorrow? I could drive over."

"Today would be better, my dear. And if it's urgent, isn't it better we meet today? Or can you tell me about this problem on the phone?"

"I'd prefer to talk it out with you in person. I have an idea. Why don't you come to supper tonight? Tessa's cooking, she's making her famous lamb stew."

"It sounds delicious, but I'm not sure I could eat another big meal," Edwina protested, although she was now riddled with curiosity.

"You don't have to eat much, you know. You can pick, like the model girls do."

Edwina laughed. "Well, I am free this evening, and—"

"I could invite Robin, Great-Aunt, and we could kill two birds with one stone," Linnet cut in swiftly. "Please say you'll come. It's very important."

"What actually is it about?"

"It's too complicated to explain on the phone, but let's just say this. . . . I need *you* to talk some sense into *him*. About having the Hughes family stay with him. They can't."

"Why not?"

"Because Jonathan Ainsley's unexpectedly in Yorkshire, and he might cause trouble for everyone. Especially Owen Hughes. He's so angry and jealous of Owen. He sees him as a threat . . . because he's the half brother. And there's Robin's will."

"Ah yes, of course, Linnet, you are absolutely right." There was a little pause. Edwina took a deep breath and announced in her familiar, commanding voice, "I shall come tonight. And you must make sure Robin is there as well. You are correct, as usual. As your great-grandmother always was. Only I can talk some sense into my brother."

"Thanks for agreeing," Linnet said, her voice suddenly cheerful. "Shall I send somebody over to fetch you?"

"No, no, that's not necessary. I have my driver. Just tell me what time I should arrive, and I shall be there promptly."

"You'd better come before drinks. Is about six-thirty all right with you? Then we can have a chat before Uncle Robin arrives. Just the two of us. Oh, and it's a casual evening, Great-Aunt Edwina."

"I am never *casual,* my dear. I shall dress for dinner as usual."

"Could I have a word with you in private, Gladys?" Dusty said, walking across the kitchen to the small eating area where Gladys Roebotham was finishing lunch with Atlanta.

"Of course you can, Mr. Rhodes," Gladys responded, standing up and moving away from the small table. "I'll be back in three shakes of a lamb's tail," she said to the child, who laughed and clapped her hands with glee on hearing these words.

Dusty smiled lovingly at his daughter, and then, turning to Gladys, he said, "I haven't heard that expression in donkey's years. My mother used to say that." As he finished, he laughed when he saw Atlanta's face. It was a picture.

Gladys laughed with him and said, "It's funny the way these old-fashioned sayings always have a reference to animals in them. They certainly amuse Atlanta, she loves hearing them."

"Indeed she does." He guided Gladys across the kitchen and into a small hallway that led out to the back garden.

Gladys said, "What did you want to speak to me about, Mr. Rhodes?"

"I was wondering if you would be able to do a bit of babysitting for me, Gladys. You know, come over and look after Atlanta, if it's at all necessary? She seems very attached to you, and you're so good with her."

Immediately, a troubled look settled on Gladys's face, and she said slowly, "I'd love to do that, I really would, but it's a bit of a problem right now. I have a relative staying with me who's not been well, and I can't be away for too long during the day. I'm ever so sorry, Mr. Rhodes, I am that."

"I am too," Dusty responded, forcing a smile, filled with disappointment. Over lunch he had convinced himself that Gladys would be available and that she would solve a lot of problems for him.

Gladys saw the crushed look slide onto his face, and swiftly she said, "But perhaps I'll be able to do something to help later on. I mean, if Molly's still in hospital and Atlanta's out here with you."

"I'd appreciate it if that becomes the case, Gladys, I would indeed. I want to thank you again for looking after Atlanta, for being so responsible. Now let me take you back to the kitchen to finish lunch. And whenever you're ready, Paddy will call for the car. It only takes the driver five minutes to get here, and he'll take you anywhere you want to go."

"Thanks ever so much, Mr. Rhodes, you've been ever so nice. Any message for Mrs. Caldwell if I do get to visit her for a while?"

"Yes, of course. Tell her I'm wishing her better very quickly, and that she should have the hospital call if she needs anything. You can also tell her I'll be in to see her on Monday."

"That'll please her, it really will," Gladys replied, smiling up at him, thinking what a nice man he was, not at all the villain Melinda Caldwell had made him out to be. In fact he was a real gentleman.

IO

Paula sat at her grandmother's old desk in the upstairs parlor, making a list of things still to be done for the wedding, when a light tapping brought her head up with a start.

"Come in," she called, glancing at the door.

It flew open, and Margaret sallied in, carrying a laden tray and exclaiming, "Did you think I'd forgotten about your tea, Mrs. O'Neill?"

"No, Margaret, I didn't. You never forget anything," Paula answered, and, putting down her pen, she rose and went to the fireplace.

The housekeeper bustled over, put the tray on the coffee table, and then straightened. Looking across at Paula, who was now seated on the sofa, she murmured, "I made your favorite ginger biscuits, Miss Paula." As she spoke she dropped a piece of lemon in the china cup and asked, "Shall I pour the tea, or do you want to wait for Mr. O'Neill?"

"Oh, that's all right, Margaret, you can pour it," Paula answered, smiling at her. The housekeeper had grown up at Pennistone Royal, and the two women had known each other all their lives. Paula thought of Margaret as part of the family and never paid much attention to her odd moods and moments of familiarity. She said now,

"I'm so glad Tessa wanted to cook dinner, you can have a night off."

Margaret shook her head, said a little vehemently, "I've been pressed into service, so to speak, Mrs. O'Neill. Tessa needs a bit of help, that she does."

Frowning, Paula exclaimed, "What do you mean? She makes her lamb stew very quickly. Why does she need help?"

"I think you ought to know you're having a dinner party tonight, Miss Paula."

"I am?" Paula stared at the housekeeper in bafflement and disbelief.

Margaret nodded emphatically. "*Eighteen pounds* of lamb stew! That's what Tessa ordered from the butcher. It seems a lot to me, but when I questioned her about it, she said there're a loads of bones in neck and shoulder. Which is true, a' course."

"I know that," Paula answered a bit impatiently and asked, "But who's coming for dinner? Who are those I don't know about already?" She was curious more than alarmed.

"Miss Linnet's invited Mr. Robin and the countess, and Tessa told me that Emily and Winston are coming, and probably India and Mr. Rhodes."

"Good Lord! How many does that make altogether? About sixteen?"

"Seventeen," Margaret announced. "Grandfather O'Neill always has supper with you, doesn't he?"

"That's true. But we're used to that, aren't we? I've done the same for years. Invite loads of people. And perhaps Tessa didn't order too much lamb after all." Paula raised a brow, amused by Margaret's attitude.

"I usually reckon half a pound per person, because there're a lot of vegetables in the stew." The housekeeper gave Paula a smug smile, as always wanting the last word when it came to her domain. "She's gone overboard."

Paula nodded. "You're right as usual, Margaret. And

I'm so sorry you've been pressed into working when we'd agreed you could have the evening off. Perhaps I'd better come down and help."

"No, no, no, madam, it's not necessary!" Margaret exclaimed, reverting to formality again, her voice rising. "I'll help Miss Tessa flour the meat and sauté it, and the others are preparing the vegetables at this very moment."

"The others?" Paula raised a dark brow.

"Emsie's chopping onions. Mr. Julian's scraping carrots, and Lorne is peeling potatoes." A loving smile settled on her face as she mentioned him. "He's such a darling, Mr. Lorne is, and so obliging and helpful. There's nobody like Lorne. The woman that gets him is going to be fortunate indeed, a woman blessed."

Paula bit back a smile, endeavoring to keep her face straight. The whole family knew that Margaret had adored Lorne since his babyhood and he could do no wrong in her eyes. The fact that he was now a famous actor only added to his allure. Margaret was his biggest fan and spoiled him outrageously when he came home to stay. "Yes, Lorne *is* special," Paula finally murmured and at last let the smile slip onto her face. She added, "But you didn't mention Mr. Deléon. Or Linnet. Where are they?"

"Oh, Miss Linnet's on the phone doing business as usual, I think." Margaret beamed at Paula. "You know she's so like Mrs. Harte, open for business twenty-four hours a day, seven days a week. A right chip off the old block!"

Paula broke into laughter, then asked, "And Mr. Deléon?"

"He's sitting in the kitchen drinking coffee and talking to Miss Tessa, and looking very worshipful, I must say."

"And I suppose Adele is with Elvira?"

"Oh yes, Miss Paula. They're having tea in the nursery." Edging away from the fireplace, Margaret thought to add, "I don't mind helping Miss Tessa sauté the meat, you know. After all, she's been an apt pupil of mine, very apt."

"Indeed she has, Margaret. You've taught her everything she knows about cooking. Thank you for doing that. And you shouldn't mind too much when she invades your territory."

"I don't, Mrs. O'Neill. And I'll be enjoying her stew for supper, and so will Joe, since there'll be so much left over. Anyway, it's my recipe." With another smug smile and a nod, the housekeeper walked out.

A moment later Paula glanced at the bedroom door as it opened and her husband, Shane, sauntered in, laughing hilariously. "What a card she is these days, darling!" Still laughing, he joined his wife by the fire. "She can sound like a tyrant at times, and then quite suddenly she's all marshmallow. She moves from formality to casualness with such ease and in a way I've not seen or heard from anyone else."

"I don't pay too much attention, Shane," Paula replied, smiling at him lovingly. "I never know what she's going to call me . . . we all know that by now. And I don't care. She is part of the family, and her parents worked for Grandy all of their *lives.* She's like one of those devoted retainers of old, and she feels part of us, one of us. And let's remember, she did grow up with me; in fact, she's only about four years older than I am."

Shane nodded his understanding, reached for the pot, and poured himself a cup of tea. "But I think she's wrong about Winston and Emily coming to dinner. Winston didn't say anything to me about that when we had lunch today at the Drum and Monkey."

"Neither did Emily when we were working at Beck House. But Emily is rather besotted by Evan at the moment and, more important, with Evan's condition. . . . She can't wait for those babies to be born."

"But they're not going to be born tonight, are they?"

"Oh, Shane, don't tease, you know what I mean. She loves to be around Evan right now, and let's remember that Gideon is her favorite child."

"You'd better not let Toby and Natalie hear you say that," he warned, sipping his tea, reaching for a ginger biscuit.

"As if I would . . ." Paula paused, looked across at her husband thoughtfully, her violet eyes suddenly filled with puzzlement. Then she sat back on the sofa, shaking her head.

Shane, forever tuned in to her, said, "What is it? Come on, let's have it."

"Tessa said a funny thing the other day. She said that Toby's not her best friend anymore, that she never hears from him. Well, hardly ever. She sounds a bit sad, actually."

"Those two have been as thick as thieves since they were kids together, so I'm not surprised she's upset if he's pulled away from her. And yet that in itself is not surprising to me, Paula. They're both in the middle of divorces, and he's at a loose end, while she's involved with another man before her divorce has even come through. Personally, I think Toby's nose is out of joint. I always believed he was sweet on Tessa." When she remained silent, Shane pressed, "Didn't you?"

"Sometimes," Paula admitted and gave him a faint smile. "Although I'm not sure it would have worked, no, not at all. They're so much alike in so many ways."

Leaning forward across the coffee table, Paula continued, "I'm quite a fan of Jean-Claude's. I think she needs an older man, one who will give her love and support, but I don't think their romance will lead to marriage."

"Because of her career?" Shane suggested. When Paula said nothing in response, he let his eyes rest on her speculatively. "Come on, Paula, you know that's the reason. She's very ambitious, and she always has been. Tessa wants the top job at Harte's. She'll probably put it before Jean-Claude in the end."

"Everything you say is true, but I was thinking of *him*, of Jean-Claude. *He* might not want to get married, Shane."

"Your guess is as good as mine there, but I do know one thing. . . . Tessa may look fragile, even delicate, and in need of protection, but she has a streak of strength, even toughness in her, and she's not a Harte for nothing, you know."

"Yes, you're right, and I've noticed that she refers to herself as a Harte these days. It wasn't too long ago she insisted she was all Fairley. Quite a volte-face."

"I know, on the other—"

"Am I interrupting?" Linnet asked from the doorway, and, not waiting for her parents to answer, she hurried into the room. After kissing Paula on the cheek, she flopped down next to her father and hugged him. "I'll only be a few minutes," she went on. "I know how much you two lovebirds like to have this particular time to be alone together."

"It's all right," Shane answered, gazing at his daughter, his eyes full of love for her.

"I bet Margaret told you I've invited Great-Aunt Edwina and Uncle Robin to dinner—she's such a chatterbox," Linnet remarked.

"She mentioned it in passing," Paula replied. "I wasn't quite sure why you did it, though, unless you're simply being cordial."

"No, there's a reason, Mummy," Linnet admitted. "I need to speak privately to Edwina before Robin comes. You see, I've got to explain why she has to drill some sense into him."

"About what?" Paula asked.

"Having the Hughes family to stay at Lackland Priory during the wedding festivities. It won't work, and it could be very troublesome."

"Why is that?" Shane asked.

Paula experienced a flash of insight. *Jonathan,* she

thought. It's to do with him. Somehow. Dismay hit her like a punch in the chest. She sat very still, as always upset when she thought of her treacherous cousin, of his violent behavior when they were young.

Linnet explained, "Jack Figg called me this morning to tell me that Jonathan Ainsley has parked himself at his house in Thirsk. Jack believes he could easily pop over to see his father and run slap-bang into Owen Hughes. Jack says that kind of encounter could prove dangerous."

"By God, that's a possibility!" Shane interjected.

Paula made no comment.

"Didn't you speak to Jack, Mummy? He said he was going to phone you."

Paula shook her head. "I've been at Beck House all day with Aunt Emily. I guess my mobile was off. So Jack couldn't have reached me even if he'd tried. Anyway, Linnet, I could have talked to Uncle Robin quite easily. He does listen to me."

"But you've enough to do with all these wedding arrangements and the reception. I thought Edwina was definitely the best *other* person to convince him they should be put up somewhere else."

"I understand," Paula said.

"I wish I'd come over to Beck House this afternoon after all." Linnet shook her head. "But Julian and I had some other things we had to do. I could have explained then, couldn't I?"

"It doesn't matter, darling."

Shane said, "But where *would* they stay?"

"I thought they could go to Aunt Emily and Uncle Winston . . . after all, *their* son is marrying Owen's daughter. And there's lots of room at Allington Hall. The adoptees could stay there as well."

"*Adoptees,*" Shane spluttered, "that's a peculiar way to describe Evan's *sisters*, whom I assume you're referring to."

"*Adopted* sisters, Dad," Linnet corrected him.

"Do be careful how you describe them to other people,

Linnet," Paula cautioned. "You mustn't sound disrespect-ful."

Shane interjected, "You don't like them much by the sound of it. And I didn't know they were here *already*."

"They're not," Linnet said. "Well, one of them is. Ang-harad. I found her strange, Daddy."

"I see. Your mother's right, Linny, do be careful how you speak of these girls in public. And anyone else, for that matter."

"Yes, Dad." Looking across at her mother, Linnet now said, "I hope you don't mind me taking charge of this problem, Mummy."

"No, of course not."

"You're becoming a regular Margaret Thatcher, aren't you, Linnet?" Shane teased.

"All Yorkshire women are Margaret Thatchers in the making, Dad. Bossy and controlling. Surely you know that."

Shane laughed, shaking his head. "You're incorrigible!"

Paula looked from her husband to her daughter and smiled in amusement. She decided she wasn't going to give any thought to Jonathan Ainsley and the trouble he might make. At least not today. Nor did she want to deal with Robin. She said evenly, and with a certain sense of relief, "I'm sure Jack is correct about lodging them some-where else, Linnet, and thanks for taking charge. Since you've started the ball rolling, I'm going to let you con-tinue. Go ahead and deal with Edwina and Robin, and do so with my blessing."

"Oh thanks, Mums, I'm glad you agree. Well, I'd better go and change into something a little bit more suitable for dinner." Jumping up, she blew her parents a kiss and hur-ried off.

When they were alone, Shane said, "To me she seems more like Emma every day." He pushed himself to his feet, went and stood in front of the fireplace. "She's no-body's fool either."

Paula also got up, walked over to him, put her arms around him, and nestled her head against his chest. He was the love of her life; actually, he *was* her life. "I know she's smart and bright and quick, you don't have to tell *me* that. And yes, she is like Grandy. It's quite strange for me sometimes . . ." Paula paused and then quietly added, "I feel as if I'm listening to my grandmother speaking. It's as if Grandy has been reincarnated in my daughter."

"Perhaps she has," Shane responded, and mystic Celt that he was, he didn't think there was anything odd about his reply.

Paula murmured, "There's always the specter of Jonathan Ainsley hanging over our heads." Her voice trailed off, and she held on to him tighter, fear running through her.

"Let's not blow things out of proportion," Shane answered, wanting to soothe her worries. "He has a house here in Yorkshire, so obviously he's going to come and live in it from time to time."

"But why *now* all of a sudden, with another family wedding pending? He wants to make trouble, hurt someone, as he tried to do when Linnet and Julian got married last month."

"Oh, it's just a coincidence," Shane said swiftly. But he couldn't help wondering if he was wrong and Paula was right. Worry now shot through him, and he decided to speak to Winston later. These thoughts were interrupted by a knock on the door, and before either of them could answer, Tessa walked in, with Jean-Claude in her wake.

Shane and Paula quickly stood apart, and Paula said, "I hear you're making a wonderful lamb stew for dinner, darling." As she spoke she smiled, beckoned for them to come closer. "How are you, Jean-Claude?" she asked, moving toward him, her smile intact, her eyes warm.

Shane followed, extending his hand to the Frenchman. After greetings were exchanged, Tessa said, "I hope we're not interrupting."

"Not at all," Paula said. "Let's go and sit by the fire."

Once they were settled, Tessa looked at her mother and then at Shane, and said in an excited tone, "We've become engaged."

"This is just wonderful!" Paula exclaimed in surprise. But her face filled with warmth and love instantly. "Congratulations, Tessa . . . Jean-Claude."

"Thank you," Jean-Claude said and added, "I'm very glad to see you approve."

"I'll say we do!" Shane exclaimed. "Very much so. Congratulations."

Tessa beamed and then held out her hand to show them her diamond engagement ring.

"It's beautiful," Paula said, her happiness growing more apparent. Looking from Tessa to Jean-Claude, she went on, "I'm thrilled. It looks as if we've now got something wonderful to celebrate tonight. It's going to be a lovely dinner party with so many of the family coming. And I'd like to welcome you, welcome you to our family, Jean-Claude. It's wonderful that you are going to be part of us."

II

❦

The man took the key out of his pocket and inserted it in the lock of the back door. He turned it and smiled as the door opened easily. Stepping into the kitchen, he shut the door and glanced around.

It was late afternoon and the light was dim in the kitchen, but he resisted turning on the lights. Instead he went on into the front hall, took off his overcoat, hung it in the closet, and then walked through the various rooms on the ground floor.

There were moments when he wanted to laugh out loud as he moved through the space, surveying everything, chuckling with pleasure and pride in his own deviousness.

Paula O'Neill would have a heart attack if she knew he had a key to this house. But he did, it was in his hand; now he dropped it into his pocket, still smiling to himself. He had a key to the back door at Pennistone Royal as well. She would have a triple heart attack if she knew *that*. He guffawed aloud, his laughter echoing hollowly through the empty house.

How clever he had been all those years ago when he was a teenager. At that time he had had the keys copied for himself, and nobody, not even his canny grandmother, had been any the wiser. And nobody had ever changed the locks at Pennistone Royal. Or here at Heron's Nest in Scarborough.

Dumb, he said to himself. My cousins are indeed dumb. Paula O'Neill most especially. She ought to have known better. Locks should always be changed from time to time. Precautions always taken. Against people like him. Even Jack Figg was stupid. As if he didn't know that Figg had a tail on him. He laughed to himself. A tail was easy to lose.

The furniture in all the rooms was covered in sheets, the curtains partially drawn, and this gave the place a ghostly, eerie feeling. Yet this did not trouble him one iota. He did not believe in the supernatural, and, anyway, he had nerves of steel; nothing fazed him. Not ever.

As he went up the staircase, he noted yet again how neat the house was, thanks to the caretaker who came in once a week to check the heating system and pipes. Although the house was not used much by the family anymore, especially in the winter months, Paula O'Neill made sure it was in good condition. As some sort of ridiculous tribute to Emma Harte, no doubt, who had loved this house and favored it more than any of her other holiday homes.

As he walked into the bedroom that had been his as a boy, it never occurred to him that his cousin loved Heron's Nest as much as their grandmother had, and that it held many fond and sentimental memories for her. He knew little about sentiment.

Jonathan Ainsley opened the draperies and stood looking out the window at the gardens below and the sea beyond, stretching into infinity. Heron's Nest stood on a little promontory, and he had always thought his room had one of the best views in the house. He still did.

Under the pale sun, the sea was gleaming brightly this afternoon. It was smooth, hardly a ripple on the surface, and it had a grayish green patina that reminded him of the glaze-like surface of ancient jade. Automatically his hand went into his pocket, his long fingers curling around the piece of mutton-fat jade that he believed brought him good joss—good luck—because it had been blessed in a very special way by a beautiful and charismatic woman. Jasmine Wu-Jen. He thought of her now. He had missed her during this sojourn in Paris and London.

There had been times when he had thought of flying her in from Hong Kong, but invariably he changed his mind at the last minute. She wouldn't fit in here. She was too exotic. Too disturbing. Better she remained where she was. In her home high on the Peak above the teeming city he had always loved, a home he had given to her when she became his possession.

Turning away from the window for a moment, he let his eyes roam around the room, taking in all of the possessions from his youth. He had never removed them from here, preferring instead to let them stay intact on the bookshelves. Many of them were trifling things. Odd-looking or unusual pebbles and shells from the beach, an ancient miner's lamp made of brass, a small stuffed bird in a glass case, a big jar of multicolored marbles, and, in another glass case, an old Roman coin he had found on the moors above Scarborough, which as a teenager he had considered his most prized possession.

He still liked to walk across the moors and along the sea cliffs, as he had as a boy. He had loved history when he was growing up, and it had been easy for him to envision battles and skirmishes amongst the hills, conflicts at sea, those violent and bloody encounters that were part of the story of this island race he came from.

He turned back to the window and gazed out again, thinking of times past when there had been so much strife in this land, and often strife within families. Brother against brother, cousin against cousin. The royal houses of York and Lancaster in mortal combat, cousins warring with each other to gain the ultimate in power, the crown of England. That most glittering prize.

There's nothing new under the sun, he thought suddenly. I am prepared to do battle with Paula O'Neill to get what I want. It was no longer Harte's. He knew now that this would be an impossible undertaking. But he could still have his revenge on her by destroying those things she held dear. Her husband, Shane, long ago his friend . . . her children . . . and, of course, that little jewel, Adele Longden, her only grandchild.

He thought of Mark Longden with a rush of bitterness. What a waste of time he had been ultimately. No guts. Jonathan was convinced that it was Mark who had betrayed him last November by alerting Jack Figg that a gang of yobbos were going to rumble into Pennistone village to create havoc at the December wedding of Linnet O'Neill and Julian Kallinski. The scheme had almost worked; it would have if Mark had not lost his nerve.

The woman slowed her car as she came to the end of the main road and turned onto a patch of dirt, parking under an ancient tree. As she got out of her car and locked it, she glanced at the tree, so old its roots protruded like knotted fingers reaching out of the earth to grasp for life. It had hardly changed, had looked like this since her childhood, when she had first come here with her mother. It had always fascinated her.

Moving away from the car, crossing the main road, she saw that the area ahead was deserted this afternoon. But then, it was chilly and a sharp wind was blowing up from the sea; few people would venture out on a bitter day like this, not even the dog owners who were dedicated to their pets and made a walk along the cliffs a daily ritual.

As she finally came up onto the cliffs, the woman could see the house in the distance, standing on its little promontory, and she struck out toward it, striding briskly

along the path high above the North Sea. Below her the
waves foamed and frothed around the clusters of rocks,
but farther out it was calm and flat, glittering like glass in
the pale sunlight, a greenish gray reflecting the anthracite-
colored sky.

The path led directly to the back gate of the house,
and it would take her exactly nine minutes to walk there.
When she had been small, it had taken her double that
time as she trotted along next to her mother.

She was a tall woman, slender, with a mass of black,
curly hair tied back in a ponytail. Her eyes were the color
of coal under perfectly arched black brows; she had a
broad forehead, a sharply defined nose, and a long neck.
Although she was not beautiful in the classical sense, she
was attractive, very striking.

When she was a child, her friends had called her
Gypsy, because of her dusky complexion and jet-black
hair; her coloring resembled that of the Romany women
who traveled across the countryside from fair to fair, the
women who lived in gypsy caravans and told fortunes by
reading palms, looking into glass globes or at tea leaves.

But gypsy she was not. The woman was a mixture of
Irish and Scottish. Her mother had frequently told her
when she was growing up that she was a true Celt but
also a throwback to her Black Irish ancestors, who in turn
were descended from the sailors shipwrecked when the
Great Armada from Spain had foundered off the coast of
Ireland in Elizabethan times.

Matched to her striking looks were her striking
clothes—elegant, expensive, and colorful. No shrinking
violet, she usually selected vibrant colors, particularly in the
red–amethyst–purple–royal blue–violet spectrum, shades
that suited her and made her stand out wherever she
went.

This afternoon she was dressed entirely in purple,
from her belted purple wool coat with sheared beaver
collar and cuffs to purple leather boots over purple

trousers. Adding an extra dash of intense color were red woolen gloves and a red cashmere scarf, which was blowing about in the wind as she walked.

The woman's name was Priscilla Marney, and she had grown up in nearby Scarborough, although these days she lived in Harrogate, where she ran a successful business of her own creation.

She thought of that business as she strode out, worrying that she had left her small staff to cope without her on a busy Saturday. Still, she had not seen Jonathan the last time he was here in Yorkshire, and later she had bitterly regretted not making an effort to get together with him.

Yesterday, when he had phoned her out of the blue, he had been most persuasive, and she had given in immediately, unable to resist him, which was usually the case.

Jonathan Ainsley.

How long had they known each other? She pondered this for a moment or two.

It was something like forty years; that seemed impossible to her, but she knew it was true. She found herself frowning in surprise as she acknowledged this; she had, in fact, known him most of her life. How remarkable that was, now that she thought about it.

They had met as children when her mother had gone to work as a summer secretary to Emma Harte during those warm-weather months when Mrs. Harte lived at Heron's Nest. Once the school holidays began, Mrs. Harte brought her brood of grandchildren to stay at her holiday home in Scarborough. Here she trained them to look after themselves in every way possible.

"Emma's Boot Camp." That was what most of them called it, and each of them confided in her that their grandmother was tough, demanding, or overly stern with them. Each one had a different point of view, but they all loved Grandy, as they called her, and in the most unconditional way.

Priscilla had had a schoolgirl crush on Jonathan in

those days, and he had reciprocated her feelings, so much so she had lost her virginity to him when she was fourteen and he not much older. They had discovered sex together, and they had gone at it hammer and tongs; that was the way he described it, anyway. They thought they were wonderful.

In the ensuing years they saw each other off and on, and slept together off and on; he had been married to Arabella Sutton and divorced from her and had not married again; she had been married twice. Her first husband, Conner Mallone, had been killed by a bus in Manchester, where he had gone on business; she was separated from her second, Roger Duffield. At least at the moment.

Roger was currently begging her to take him back; she was resisting his overtures. She had not been happy with him, and she had recently come to believe she was better off on her own. Her daughter by Conner, Samantha, who was now in her twenties, agreed with her, was encouraging her to "be your own woman," as she put it.

Priscilla was well aware that there was no future with Jonathan, but old habits die hard, and she enjoyed meeting him in secret to have sex here at Heron's Nest, where they had first made love. It gave her a kick, and she was aware it turned him on. And there was another thing they both appreciated—the fact that theirs was the longest sexual relationship either of them had ever had with another person.

A few steps away from the house, Priscilla took out her mobile and dialed Jonathan's. He answered with a curt "Hello?"

"It's me. I'm only a moment away from the back gate."

"I just opened the kitchen door. I'm upstairs," he said and clicked off.

After stepping into the kitchen, Priscilla locked the door behind her and moved to the front hall. Here the light was dim, almost gloomy, but she did not dare put on a lamp. The caretaker lived not too far away, and Jonathan was constantly worried she would notice the lights if they were on in the house, which was locked up for the winter.

Taking a small flashlight out of her pocket, Priscilla turned it on and made her way up the winding staircase. When she reached the landing, she saw Jonathan hovering in the corridor, and a sunny smile broke across her face.

Smiling himself, he came to meet her, regarded her intently for a brief moment, and then pulled her into his arms and gave her a big bear hug. He clung to her for a moment or two, and she to him.

"It's great to see you, Pris darling, and you look wonderful." As he spoke he held her away from him and scrutinized her once again. It was true, she was in marvelous form, and beautifully groomed and dressed. He liked chic women.

"Thank you, and so do you, Jonny. Positively blooming. I've always told you Hong Kong agrees with you."

He made no response, took hold of her arm and led her down the corridor, asking, "You can have dinner with me later, can't you?"

"Oh, gosh, Jonny, I don't know—" She broke off, shaking her head. "My staff are all alone, and we're quite busy."

"Can't you give them a call?" He pushed open the door of his room and took her inside.

"Yes."

"Then do it now . . . so we can be relaxed about things," he said, eyeing her suggestively, then winking.

She did as he asked, using her mobile, and moments later was talking to her office. "Everything's under control, Priscilla," her assistant told her. "There's no reason for you to be here. We can manage."

When she gave Jonathan this news, a pleased expression leapt onto his face; he grinned at her and exclaimed, "And guess where I'm going to take you? The Grand Hotel in Scarborough."

"Good Lord! What kind of an idea is that? And how's
the food these days?" she asked, shaking her head.

"I don't know about the food. But who cares really? I
want to take you there for old times' sake. Remember
how we used to sneak down there for fancy teas? We
weren't supposed to go to the hotel alone, and it was
great breaking the rules, wasn't it?"

"Indeed it was, and especially when we came back and
broke even more rules here." She glanced at the bed, her
face flushing.

Jonathan followed the direction of her gaze, and a
knowing look crossed his face. "Anxious, are we?" he
asked, an amused glint in his eyes.

"I'm always anxious for you, just as you are for me,"
she replied in a low voice. "And why wouldn't we be? It's
been quite a while since we've seen each other." She
moved toward him, put her arms around him, brought
her face close to his, and kissed him on the mouth.

He responded most ardently and found himself instantly aroused, as he generally was with Priscilla. He
wondered if this reaction was because she was the first
woman he had ever had. It didn't matter, because he had
no time to ponder. None at all. He wanted her under him
on that narrow bed. He wanted to do all the things he had
done to her when they were teenagers, their hormones
roaring and so hot they had practically ripped each
other's clothes off.

As he had undressed her so many years ago, he did so
once more, helping her with her coat, her sweater, and
her boots. A few moments later he was shedding his own
clothes and joining her on the bed, where she was waiting
for him.

Stretching himself out alongside her, he leaned over
and kissed her cheek, held her close to him. After a while,
as his hand slid down to stroke her stomach, he whispered in her ear, "I remember how you flinched when I
did this for the first time." His hand rested between her

legs, and he began to touch her gently. "But I soon had you moaning, begging me not to stop, didn't I? As you will do in a moment, won't you, Prissy?"

"Oh, yes, yes, you know I will," she gasped as he continued to arouse her. Now he bent over her again and kissed her breast, sucked on it, and she found herself growing even more excited, the heat rising in her as passion flared. At one moment she thought, I'm in my fifties. How can I feel like this? So hot and wet and aching for him. Because I'm fourteen again, she suddenly thought, and opened her eyes and looked directly into his face as he got on top of her and brought her to him, his hands under her buttocks.

"Does this feel as good as it did when I was a mere lad?" he asked, gliding inside her.

"Oh, yes, Jonathan . . . yes . . ."

They sat in the bar of the Grand Hotel in Scarborough, sipping dry martinis and reminiscing about their youth. They didn't always have a chance to share a drink and dinner when they'd been together; they often had to rush off to keep other commitments. And so on this icy January Saturday evening, they were pleased they were able to have the luxury of a drink, a meal, and no pressure to leave each other after their intense and passionate lovemaking.

They spoke for a while about themselves, their unique relationship, and their lives in general, and then quite suddenly Priscilla said, "Your cousins were childhood sweethearts, and so were Shane and Paula."

Momentarily startled by this reference to the family, Jonathan said in a slightly bitter tone, "The Harte women always get what they want, no matter what that is." His mouth narrowed into a tight line, his eyes hardened.

Priscilla glanced at him quickly, frowning. "You sound odd, Jonny, what's the matter? Didn't you approve of Emily marrying her cousin Winston Harte?"

Not wanting to betray his true feelings to Priscilla, which he almost had, he forced a cheerful laugh, said in a steady voice, "It didn't matter to me, Pris, and actually that seems to be a family trait, doesn't it? Several of my cousins have married each other." He shrugged, and, making a tremendous effort, he smiled warmly, added in the nicest voice he could summon, "And fortunately they all seem happy enough. Grandy would be pleased if she knew."

"Talking of weddings, are you going to be at Gideon's next Saturday?" she asked curiously.

"Afraid not, old thing, I have to meet my French partner and his wife in Paris next weekend. Business takes up a lot of my time, you know. But I shall be returning to Yorkshire, and I was hoping there would be another chance for us to get together."

Her black eyes shone with happiness as she gazed back at him. "Oh, yes, Jonny, I'd love that. When are you returning?"

"On the Sunday night or Monday morning."

"Should we have a rendezvous at the house again?" she asked eagerly, gripping his hand. "I always love it when we're at Heron's Nest together . . . it's so exciting in the dark, taking chances because we never know if the caretaker will come by. But mostly it's delicious because of you and us and our youth. We recapture those days at Heron's Nest."

"I know exactly what you mean." He leaned into her, whispered against her hair, "And you're such a naughty girl, Pris, much naughtier and more experienced than you were then. . . . Oh, yes, a lovely naughty girl."

She felt herself blushing and said softly, "And you're very wicked. A wicked, wicked man, but I do love what you do to me."

Sitting up straighter, Jonathan murmured, "Let's not meet at the house next time. It is a bit dangerous, as you pointed out. And talking of houses, would you like to come to mine? In Thirsk? It's almost finished."

"Oh, that would be wonderful!" she gushed, a smile spreading across her face, which seemed to shine with eager anticipation.

"Then you shall come. On *Wednesday*. Let's make it Wednesday to be sure I'm back from France. Come early evening, and we'll have dinner after our little romp, and perhaps you'd like to stay the night?" A brow lifted, and he stared at her intently.

Priscilla sat back in the chair, returning his protracted gaze. She couldn't believe her luck; he was inviting her to his home, asking her to stay the night. This was a whole new twist in their relationship. Might it go even further? She stared at him greedily, taking everything in, his handsome face, those bright, intelligent eyes. And the clothes. So expertly tailored. That cashmere sports jacket and those dark, finely made gabardine slacks. Expensive, she thought. Everything about him is expensive. Big time. He was big time. He had a big life. Might she not share it with him?

"Well, Prissy, will you stay the night? Or can't you?"

"Jonny, of course I *can*! I'd love to. Absolutely *love* to."

"I'm sorry I can't make the wedding," he said unexpectedly. "But I won't be in Yorkshire, as I said. Anyway, I don't really like morning weddings, I prefer those that take place in the afternoon."

"Oh, but you've got it wrong, Jonathan. Gideon and Evan *are* getting married in the afternoon. At two o'clock."

"Gosh, how could I have made such a mistake? Still, I will be in Paris."

"And you'll miss the reception at Pennistone Royal," she pointed out. "That's a pity. And you'll miss the party after the lunch."

"That I will," he replied and smiled inwardly; now he knew for a fact that the reception and luncheon were to be held at his grandmother's pile of stones and not at his father's house. She knew a lot, Pris did. He must ply her with a few more drinks and lots of sex and see what else he could glean.

12

❧

Great-Aunt Edwina!" Linnet cried, rushing across the Stone Hall at the sight of the oldest and most important member of the Harte family. "Thank you for getting here so early."

As she came to a standstill in front of Edwina, Linnet grasped her hand and then leaned into her, kissed her on the cheek.

"I thought it would be a good idea to really get a head start, so that *we* could have that chat you suggested. *Alone,*" Edwina said, giving Linnet a long, knowing look.

Smiling, putting her hand under Edwina's elbow, Linnet escorted her to the fireplace, saying as she did, "You look wonderful in your trouser suit, Great-Aunt, and I love that bordeaux color. It really suits you."

Edwina, looking pleased, said, "Thank you, my dear. It happens to be the only casual thing I own other than a few jumpers . . . and you did say it was a casual evening."

"Yes, I did. And you look perfect. Now, would you like something to drink?"

"A drop of champagne, if you have some handy."

Linnet grinned at her and hurried over to the drinks table, exclaiming, "Of course we do. Pol Roger, how does that sound?"

"Very nice, thank you." Edwina had seated herself on a

chair near the fireplace, and now she turned around, focused her attention on Linnet, who was busy pouring the champagne. Neat and smart, Edwina thought, she always looks so well put together. Tonight Linnet was wearing a white silk shirt with long, full sleeves, black silk trousers, and a black wool cardigan draped over her shoulders. Several long strands of pearls hung around her neck. Fake, Edwina decided, but she knew the pearl earrings were the real thing, since she had given them to Linnet as a present just before her wedding. Yes, she was a very smart girl. In every way.

Linnet came back to the fireside carrying two flutes of champagne, and she handed one to Edwina. They clinked glasses, and Linnet sat down opposite her great-aunt.

After taking a sip of the champagne, Edwina said, "Now then, my dear, let's get to the point. What's all this about?"

"Basically it's about Jonathan Ainsley, as I told you on the phone. Jack Figg called me this morning to say that he's in Yorkshire. At his house in Thirsk. His sudden arrival just before Evan's wedding is making Jack nervous. Jack thinks Jonathan is a loose cannon out to make trouble."

"He may very well be," Edwina said, her eyes narrowing slightly, and then she pursed her lips before adding, "However, Jonathan's not going to do anything too foolish. He's a bully, and all bullies are cowards, don't you know?" She raised a brow quizzically.

"Yes, I do. Obviously he wouldn't do anything *himself*, because he *is* a coward. He'd hire somebody else to do it . . ." Linnet paused, took a deep breath, and plunged in, explaining in a serious voice, "Jack found out he was going to disrupt *my* wedding by sending in a bunch of yobbos. Who knows what they'd been instructed to do. I didn't know anything about it until later, of course. Jack hadn't wanted to frighten me."

"And Jack thinks Jonathan might try the same thing

next Saturday? Is that what you're saying?" Edwina asked, now sounding troubled.

"Perhaps not *that,* but he certainly believes Jonathan will more than likely go to see his father while he's here. And he'll run into Owen Hughes and his family if they're staying at Lackland Priory. That's what I wanted to explain, Great-Aunt Edwina. They can't be Uncle Robin's guests, the way he insists. They have to be housed somewhere else. In order to avoid a confrontation."

"I think you are right, Linnet," Edwina declared, and, giving her a very direct look, she continued, "Although I suppose all he could really do is be rude and rather nasty." She shook her head. "Never liked him. He was a strange boy, really, up to no good most of the time, and don't think my mother didn't know. Emma had his number all along; that's why she rearranged her will the way she did."

Linnet leaned forward, her intelligent green eyes fixed on Edwina. "What did Grandy actually think of him?"

"She said he was *treacherous,* and she was rarely wrong about people. So, let us come up with a plan of action before Robin arrives. Now, Linnet, if Lackland Priory is not a suitable place for Owen and his family to stay, what do you suggest? Where can they go?"

"Allington Hall. Emily and Winston will be happy to have them; after all, their son is marrying Owen's daughter. And if they can have only Owen and Marietta as their houseguests, the adoptees can stay with Robin. Or, come to think of it, Great-Aunt Edwina, why not with you at Niddersley?"

"Good Lord, Linnet, I don't know about that! And by *adoptees* I suppose you are referring to Evan's two sisters, who are apparently adopted."

"You're right, I am, and I must tell you something confidentially. . . . I didn't take to the one I met the other day. *Angharad.* She's the youngest. And a bit odd, in my opinion."

"Angharad. That's a mouthful of a name," Edwina muttered.

"It's a Welsh name."

"Oh, yes, I know." A smile suddenly illuminated Edwina's wrinkled face, and her wise old eyes became brighter. "Glynnis Hughes loved Welsh names. She was very Welsh, you know, very much into Celtic lore and all that kind of thing. I was close to her at one point in our lives. I liked her, and I suppose—" Edwina broke off, shook her head. "I suppose I was the one who helped to facilitate their love affair."

"I heard the story about Glynnis and Robin. About them never really giving each other up. Fifty years together. Evan told me the other day when I got back from New York. Quite romantic, wasn't it?"

Edwina nodded. "It was. Very. But fraught, and they ran a lot of risks, were almost caught out many times."

"They should have just divorced their spouses and married each other, that would have been the best thing," Linnet pronounced, sounding like Emma Harte, the great pragmatist.

"Glynnis didn't think like that, Linnet dear," Edwina confided. "She was the one who stayed the course, in relation to their marriages, that is. She made Robin stay with Valerie. You see, she didn't want him to ruin his political career."

"Would it really have been such a scandal? Could it have actually brought him down?" Linnet asked curiously.

"*Absolutely*. He would have had to resign his seat, leave Parliament."

"Gosh, that wouldn't happen today, would it? Politicians do all sorts of things and get away with it! They can practically commit murder, so to speak, without there being any repercussions."

"That's *now*. This was *then*. The fifties. People were not so permissive, or so forgiving either. The slightest thing could be interpreted as scandalous and cause great hurt. However, let us get back to the Hughes family today. I can't see why Emily wouldn't have them to stay. The whole of the Hughes family, I mean. But if there is any kind of problem, you know the young women can stay with me at Niddersley House."

"Thank you, Great-Aunt Edwina, you're a brick." Linnet sat back, sipping her champagne, relaxing slightly, and thinking about Angharad meeting Edwina. She had to swallow her laughter. Edwina would frighten the girl to death. Or would she? There was something about Evan's sister that puzzled Linnet; she couldn't quite put her finger on it, but a word suddenly jumped into her head. *Schemer.* Yes, that was it! She felt that the girl was not only manipulative but an opportunist and a dissembler. Perhaps even dishonest in relationships. I have to talk to Gideon about that, ask him what *he* thinks of Angharad Hughes, she thought. She had a feeling her cousin had not taken to Evan's sister.

Suddenly, hearing footsteps echoing at the other end of the Stone Hall, Linnet leaned forward and said to Edwina, "It's Uncle Robin, and he's very early." Putting down her glass, she got up, and again whispering, she said emphatically to her great-aunt, *"You've got to make him understand that they cannot stay with him."*

Edwina inclined her head, answered in a low voice, "I know what to say, my dear. Leave it to me."

"Uncle Robin! We're over here," Linnet exclaimed, hurrying forward to meet him, her face full of smiles, her eyes warm.

They came together in the middle of the Stone Hall, and after kissing Robin on the cheek, she asked, "What would you like? Scotch? Champagne?"

"Ah, yes, I wouldn't mind a bit of the bubbly. Thanks, Linny. And it's so nice to see you, and looking so well, you're positively blooming."

As Robin walked toward the fire, he called out, "Good evening, Edwina, I see you got here before me. As usual, the early bird catching the worm."

Linnet gave them a few minutes alone, pouring champagne in a crystal flute for her great-uncle. Robin Ainsley had been Emma's favorite son, just as he had always been Edwina's favorite brother. Edwina had usually tried to be on his side, to back him to the hilt, her mother had told her long ago when Paula had been recounting some of the family history. Linnet enjoyed hearing those stories, relishing them, and she was inordinately proud to be a Harte, and most especially to be Emma's clone, as the family said she was.

Putting the bottle of Pol Roger back in the silver ice bucket, Linnet carried the flute of champagne over to Robin, who was sitting on the large overstuffed sofa.

"Good health," Robin said, raising his glass first to Edwina and then to Linnet, smiling at them both.

"Good health," Linnet repeated.

"Down the hatch!" Edwina added in her sonorous voice and took a good swallow of the Pol Roger, thinking that she only ever drank this champagne here at Pennistone Royal.

Looking across at Robin, Edwina said slowly, "I'm trying to remember why our mother had such a fondness for Pol Roger. I could swear it had to do with her brother Frank."

"No, it had to do with Churchill," Robin corrected. "He was her great hero, and apparently his favorite champagne was Pol Roger. So it became hers."

"True, but not quite the whole story." Edwina threw her half brother a somewhat smug look and went on. "Her brother knew Winston Churchill. Remember, he was a journalist and was constantly writing about him even before Churchill became the P.M. It was because of him that Emma stocked Pol Roger. Her brother told her it was the only one Winston enjoyed. Frank liked it, too. I remember that."

"Got to hand it to you, Edwina, you recall everything. And you're correct about the Churchill story. Mother met him during the war, at some incredible bomb site with enormous damage, and she never let any of us forget he had shaken her hand and thanked her for her war effort."

"It's true. I was living in Ireland, but I heard the story from Uncle Winston."

The three of them fell silent for a second, and then Robin cleared his throat and said, "When you phoned to invite me to dinner, you said you wanted me to come early, Linnet. And I see Edwina is here early, too, so I can only deduce that you have some Harte business to discuss with us both."

"No. Hughes business, Uncle Robin. With you. I need to explain a situation that's developed, and then Edwina has something to say to you."

He leaned back against the pile of needlepoint cushions, looking from Linnet to Edwina, his expression nonplussed. When neither of them said anything, he turned to Linnet. "Well, come on then, let's have it. Tell me what's on your mind."

"Do you know where Jonathan is at the moment?"

Robin shook his head. "He *was* in London. I think he went back to Paris before returning to Hong Kong."

"He's in Yorkshire, Uncle Robin, at his new house in Thirsk."

It was obvious that Robin did not know this; he sat up straighter on the sofa, shaking his head. "I haven't heard a word from him. He usually calls at some point when he's in Yorkshire, even though we're not exactly close pals at the moment. How long has he been here?"

"Several days. Jack Figg phoned me this morning to tell me his whereabouts. He's worried, Uncle Robin. He thinks that Jonathan might get confrontational with Owen or Evan if he runs into them."

"He's not likely to do that, Linnet. *Really.*" Robin shook his head. "How on earth could he run into *them*?"

"At Lackland Priory. *Your house.* You're insisting the Hughes family stay with you, and Jonathan could easily stroll in unannounced to see you. Or perhaps he'll get wind that they're staying with you and come over, hell-bent on making trouble somehow. That's his nature."

"Oh, my dear, I do think you're letting your imagination run away with you. Jonathan is not a frequent visitor, I've told you that before. And especially now that he knows categorically his inheritance is perfectly safe. He doesn't feel the need to hover around me. As for a confrontation with Owen or Evan, he's got nothing to gain anymore, so why would he even bother?"

"Jealousy, envy, perversity, the desire to upset you," Linnet suggested pithily. "Or to get his own back at you for having the audacity to have another son. You name it, and I bet it would fit the bill and then some."

"I think you're exaggerating the situation, Linnet dear," he said again, shaking his head.

"Uncle Robin, have you forgotten that Evan was almost killed in a car crash? In a car that belonged to you? A car that was apparently tampered with. You might easily have been mourning your only grandchild at this time, a woman who's currently carrying your great-grandsons, instead of getting ready to celebrate her wedding a week today. Anyway, he's capable of doing bodily harm to one of us, or using a paid assailant. Mummy told me he once locked Emily in the cellar at Pennistone Royal and she was lost for hours. And so scared Grandy had to take her to the doctor. She had nightmares. I'd say he's still dangerous, Uncle Robin."

Robin bit his lip. He sat pondering, worry invading his face.

It was Edwina who spoke up resolutely. "You'd better *listen* to Linnet, Robin. She's making a lot of sense. *I* suspect Jonathan is up here because of Evan's wedding to

Gideon. I don't trust that son of yours. Never have. And neither did our mother; she thought he was a treacherous devil. As the eldest and head of the family, I must insist you change your plans about housing the Hughes family at Lackland Priory. They cannot be on your premises; at least they can't be your houseguests. That's tempting Providence. Jonathan would be over there in a flash, and the balloon would go up."

"How would he even know they were staying with me?"

"He'd know!" Linnet exclaimed. "I've always said he's got a spy in our camp, although no one ever really believes me."

"Not that awful secretary at the Leeds store?" Robin asked, staring at Linnet, horror written all over his face.

"No, not Eleanor, Uncle Robin, don't look so appalled. Jonathan's not going to marry her. That romance is long over. There's someone else, although I'm baffled about who it is. But as sure as God made little green apples, he's got someone giving him a lot of information about us."

"Can't Jack find out?" Edwina asked, her attention on Linnet for a split second.

"No, because we don't know exactly where to begin. And we've gone through all the possible suspects ages ago. But one day he or she will be revealed. In the meantime, Uncle Robin, Jonathan probably knows already that Owen and Marietta and the adoptees are coming to Yorkshire on Monday, and that they are to be your honored visitors."

"*Adoptees* is not a very nice way to describe those girls, Linnet," Robin muttered reprovingly. "Glynnis was very fond of them."

Edwina guffawed and exclaimed, "Like hell she was! She cared only about Evan, had eyes only for her biological granddaughter because she's part of you, and you know that very well. Let's not forget you don't have to keep up the pretense anymore, Robin. The whole family knows you were with Glynnis until the day she died.

Well, practically. Evan was no surprise to you. You knew all about her, and Owen you'd known since he was a child. Now listen to me, my dear." Edwina leaned closer and continued in a tone that forbade argument. "The Hughes family has to be lodged at Allington Hall with Emily and Winston, and if they don't have room for the two girls, Angharad and Elayne can come and stay with me at Niddersley. And that's the end of it."

"Oh, but Edwina, I was so looking forward to being with Owen. Don't forget, I've been deprived of him all of my life . . . my son by the only woman I ever loved—"

"Oh, don't be such a sentimental old fool!" Edwina snapped, although not unkindly. "You can pop over to Allington Hall to see Owen whenever you want, and once the wedding is over and Jonathan has returned to Hong Kong, you can visit with Owen as much as you wish. Furthermore, you can go and stay with him in America after he returns there. There's nothing to stop you."

"Oh, I don't think I'm well enough to go tripping off to New York," Robin protested.

"You look spry enough to me," Edwina asserted and patted his hand. "Let us do the best we can to get Evan married to Gideon without the proverbial hitch. Once they are safely married and installed at Beck House, you can do whatever you want with Owen. My main concern is for that granddaughter of yours. She's the only one you've got to continue your family line, and don't you forget *that*."

"All right," Robin replied in a meek voice. "I expect you're right, Edwina. I can't ever remember you being wrong, except for the years when you cut Mother out of your life. But everything you say tonight is true. Evan is of the utmost importance. We must, *I* must, consider her first."

"Thank you, Robin," Edwina murmured, falling back against the chair, looking exceedingly relieved.

Linnet smiled at him, also relaxing, for the first time that day.

Edwina sat in splendor, looking every inch the countess, smiling warmly and greeting everyone with her special brand of charm and graciousness.

Finally they had all arrived, and she leaned back in her chair near the fireplace, sipping from her glass of champagne and observing the scene being enacted before her in the Stone Hall.

Tonight this room looked as wonderful as it had in her mother's day, filled as it was with chrysanthemum plants and white orchids, the fire blazing up the hearth, the candlelight flickering, and the softly shaded lamps giving off a warm glow. How welcoming it was.

There was a faint buzz of conversation as everyone moved around to spend a few minutes talking to each other. It was a most cordial and convivial atmosphere, and this pleased Edwina. My mother would be proud, she suddenly thought. Most of those present tonight are her progeny, and they *are* rather special, even if I do say so myself.

She focused momentarily on Tessa, and then Lorne. The twins were also part Fairley, and it was the Fairley looks they had inherited. They had the pale complexion, silvery eyes, and blond hair of the famous beauty Adele Fairley, mother of Edwin, who had been Edwina's father and for whom she was named.

Edwina's eyes moved on to the Frenchman, and she wondered where *that* affair was going. Would he propose to Tessa? She hoped so. The best thing that could happen to Tessa would be to marry him.

Edwina liked the charismatic and brilliant Jean-Claude and knew without a shadow of a doubt that he would be a stable and loving partner, and a good influence on her great-niece. And how beautiful she looked tonight, the ethereal Tessa. She was wearing a pair of narrow-cut pants, a camisole, and a narrow coat, which came to her knees and was somewhat in the style of the Indian Nehru jacket. The outfit was made of silver-gray taffeta, and with it she wore silver-gray Tahitian pearls and earrings. She's just perfection, Edwina thought, and she hardly looks as if she's been cooking half the day. But she had made the entire dinner, Linnet had told her that earlier.

Edwina's glance moved on, this time settled on Bryan O'Neill, who stood talking with his son, Shane. She was pleased Bryan was looking so well after his bout with bronchitis. Now, fully recovered, he seemed as strong as ever. Tall, broad-shouldered, silver-haired, not to mention silver-tongued, he was the spitting image of his father, Blackie O'Neill.

For a split second the decades slipped away and she fell down into the past, thinking of Blackie with affection. He had been her mother's dearest friend until the day he died. And he had been very good to her when she was a young girl, even when she treated him badly.

Edwina sighed, thinking how unfair she had been to Blackie, who had loved her like his own. For a while, after she had obtained her birth certificate, she had believed he was indeed her father, because his name was on the certificate. But as it turned out, Edwin Fairley had been her father. Blackie had merely lent his name.

A good man, Blackie O'Neill, Edwina mused, and his son Bryan is a good man. Good Lord, Bryan must be at least eighty-five! He certainly doesn't look it.

For a long moment her eyes rested on Shane, Black Irish like his father and grandfather, and another good man. Her mother had once said when he was young that he had an intense glamour, and he still possessed that glamour.

Shane was the best. He had always been there for Paula, even when she was a child. He was her rock. Ed-

wina recalled how upset she had been when trouble had
broken out between Paula and Jim Fairley, and their marriage had gone awry. At the time, she had put most of the
blame on Paula, but it hadn't been her fault. It had been
Jim's in reality. He was a Fairley through and through and
had inherited Adele's vanity as well as her drinking problems. He'd had to fight alcoholism, just as Adele and his
uncle Gerald Fairley had. Genes, Edwina thought, it's all
in the genes. There's simply no escaping that.

Emma had permitted Paula to marry Jim Fairley despite her better judgment, and because she was a fair
woman who had no intention of blaming the sins of the
grandfather on the grandson. But Emma had always said
it wouldn't work, and it hadn't. Jim had been the wrong
man for Paula; also, deep down, she had been in love
with Shane, even though she had not realized that for a
long time.

But then one day, after Jim had been killed in an avalanche in Chamonix, Paula had finally married Shane
and lived the life of a contented woman at last. Her happiness with Shane was manifest in everything she did,
and Edwina knew she was one woman in the world who
was at peace with herself.

No sooner had this thought entered her mind than
Paula hove into view, came to stand next to Shane, link-
ing her arm through his, leaning against him. He looked
down at her and smiled and drew her into him in the
most intimate way.

As always, Paula was elegant, wearing an ankle-length
dress of amethyst cashmere and matching suede boots. It
was a color that echoed those unique violet eyes, her
most striking feature.

Edwina leaned forward slightly, peering at her niece.
She looks exhausted, Edwina thought. And pale. She
doesn't look like her normal energetic self. Is she ill? Or is
she worried? Perhaps about the dratted Jonathan Ainsley?
Yes, maybe it was just worry, not ill health. No, she's not

ill. She couldn't be. The Hartes are a robust lot, and we all live to a great age . . .

"A penny for your thoughts, Great-Aunt Edwina," Lorne said, drawing close. "And how about a refill?"

"Oh, I don't know about that, Lorne darling, I don't want to get tipsy."

He laughed, his light eyes twinkling mischievously as he took her crystal flute and hurried over to the drinks table. Edwina watched him go, thinking it was about time *he* got married, too.

Within seconds Lorne was back at her side, handing her the glass. He touched his to hers and murmured, "Cheers."

She smiled at him over the rim, exclaimed, "Down the hatch," and took a long swallow.

"So, a penny for your thoughts, Great-Aunt."

"Actually, I was thinking about your mother," Edwina admitted. "She doesn't look like her usual self, Lorne. Or is that my imagination?"

"No, it's not, I agree with you," he responded, placing his arm along the chair back, bending over her. In a low-ered voice, Lorne went on. "I think Mum's under the weather, and I've thought that for a while now, actually. She seems somehow slightly . . . *depleted,* that's the only word I can come up with. I've asked her, and Dad as well, if there's anything wrong, and they've both denied it. In fact, they seemed truly dumbfounded that I even asked such a question."

"Could she be worrying about Jonathan Ainsley being in Yorkshire?" Edwina suggested, looking at him keenly.

"You know what, I think everyone around here tends to exaggerate about *him.* I think he's more of a specter hovering than an actual threat. But to answer your ques-tion, yes, I think she does worry about him."

Edwina nodded and then exclaimed, "Oh, there's the lovely Jack. Linnet didn't tell me he was coming to sup-per. He's a favorite of mine, Lorne."

"He's everybody's favorite," Lorne answered with a laugh. "Especially the ladies. I think I'll have to borrow a few tricks from his book."

"I'm sure you're just as popular as he is," Edwina chided and went on, "I see Emsie over there, but where's Desmond?"

"He's at boarding school, Great-Aunt Edwina."

"Oh, yes, of course he is, and your mother is beckoning to you," Edwina said. "Goodness me, she looks as if she's about to make an important announcement."

When Paula made her way across the Stone Hall, heading for the staircase, everyone present knew that she had something special to say to them. All family announcements were made from these steps; it was a tradition which had begun with Emma.

Shane was behind her, and as she beckoned to Lorne, her son patted Edwina's arm and hurried to join his mother and stepfather. Linnet and Emsie were also walking over to the staircase and took up positions near their parents and brother.

"We have some wonderful news!" Paula began, reaching for Shane's hand, drawing closer to him. "Shane and I are happy to tell you all that Tessa has become engaged to Jean-Claude!" As Paula finished speaking, Tessa and Jean-Claude walked over to the stairs and stood smiling at the group as everyone called out congratulations.

Shane exclaimed over the din, "Let's raise our glasses to Tessa and Jean-Claude, and wish them much happiness in their life together."

Everyone did as Shane asked, and once the toasting was over, Tessa came forward a few steps, bringing Jean-Claude with her. "Thank you all so much. If you're surprised about this sudden announcement, then I must tell you that I am, too! It was just before lunch *today* that Jean-Claude asked me to marry him, and I must admit I was taken aback. But only *momentarily,* and I said yes to him. *Immediately.*" Turning to look at Jean-Claude, still clinging to his hand, Tessa continued, "I think I'm the luckiest woman alive to have you."

Jean-Claude put his arm around her, brought her closer to him, and kissed her cheek, then, looking around at the group of family members, he said, "I thank you for your good wishes. And I'm the lucky one!" Turning to Paula and Shane, he added, "And I promise you both I shall treasure Tessa, take care of her always. I want you both to know she's safe with me."

"Yes, we *do* know that," Paula answered as Shane stepped forward to shake Jean-Claude's hand.

After that there was a lot of hugging and kissing. Linnet, Emsie, and Lorne were in the forefront, enveloping Tessa in their arms, and then they went to Jean-Claude to shake his hand. And the others all crowded around, kissing Tessa, offering their congratulations and best wishes to her and Jean-Claude.

It was Tessa who finally said, "Thanks, all of you, but I'm afraid I must now dash off to the kitchen—or we won't have any dinner tonight!"

"I shall accompany you, *chérie*," Jean-Claude said.

"No, no, I can manage, and Margaret's there to help me. Besides, Jean-Claude, you'd better stay and get to know my family . . . those that are here tonight at least. I dread to tell you how big it *really* is!"

Bryan O'Neill walked slowly across the floor, making for his favorite grandchild. *Linnet.*

When she saw him, she gave Lorne an apologetic smile and hurried over to her grandfather. "I can see you're looking for me, Grandpops. Do you need anything?"

"Only a few more years on this earth, so that I can bounce *your* babies on my knee," he murmured and took hold of her arm, led her to a far corner of the Stone Hall. Together they sat down, and Bryan, leaning forward, said, "She may not let her ambitions go to waste just because she is marrying Jean-Claude. Knowing Tessa the way I do,

I'm sure she thinks she can live in Paris *and* London, somehow commute in order to head up Harte's. She's always wanted the top job, Linnet, you know that."

"I do, Grandfather, and you're right, Tessa may well think she can run things from Paris. But let's not forget, Mummy's still the boss, and she has absolutely no intention of retiring. She's only in her early fifties for goodness' sake."

Bryan smiled, and took her hand in his. "Such small, capable hands," he murmured. "Just like Emma's. I remember her hands very well; she took care of me when I was a baby and a toddler with those hands. But then you know all that. Watch your step, Linnet, and keep your eyes peeled . . . as sweet and lovely as Tessa is being to you at the moment, she is still your archrival. Don't ever forget that."

"I won't, I promise, Gramps. We all know she's the way she is because she's the firstborn, the eldest."

"True. But that was never Emma's way of passing on power. The person best equipped to do the job got it. And I'm sure your mother thinks the same thing; after all, she was trained by Emma Harte."

Linnet nodded, leaned forward. "I've got some good ideas for bringing the store into the present. It needs a whole new approach, and I want to talk to Mummy about a few changes once the wedding is over."

"Yes. But please wait awhile, Linnet," Bryan replied quietly. "She's had a lot of pressure on her since well before Christmas. Just take it easy for the moment. All right?"

"Yes. Oh, Gramps, there's Evan looking for us. Come on, let's go and see what she wants. She seems a bit concerned."

"And she looks to me as if she's about to give birth any minute," Bryan muttered, half to himself. "Do you think she can last until after the wedding?"

Linnet burst out laughing. "She'll just have to, won't she?"

Bryan simply smiled, made no further comment as they crossed the Stone Hall to the spot where Evan had suddenly paused. She was beckoning them. His eyes went across the room to Robin Ainsley, who was about to become a great-grandfather. That can't please Jonathan very much, Bryan thought, and wondered whether the black sheep of the family was planning anything diabolical for next Saturday. He prayed to God he was not.

Evan said, when they came to a stop, "I got a bit out of breath and had to pause for a moment. Anyway, Great-Aunt Edwina wants a word with you, Linnet, if you could please come over to her."

"Of course. But is she all right?"

"Oh, yes, she's perfectly fine. She says to tell you she's had a brain wave."

Laughing, Linnet glided across to Edwina, whose face lit up when she saw Linnet moving in her direction.

"What's your brain wave, Great-Aunt?" Linnet was asking her a moment later, crouching down next to the chair.

Drawing Linnet closer, Edwina said, "I think I've solved the problem of that wretched Jonathan Ainsley. Gideon and Evan must *elope*. And right away."

"Not a bad idea," Linnet said, although she knew it wouldn't work because of Evan's condition. The babies could be premature and she decided to say this to Edwina, who was looking like the cat that had swallowed the canary.

"Oh, yes, you're right. I'd forgotten that part. Drat. Mmmmm. Well, they should have eloped a long time ago. If they had, everyone wouldn't be worried about Jonathan pulling a stunt next Saturday."

Linnet didn't answer. She'd just had a brain wave of her own. "I'll be back in a jiffy, Great-Aunt Edwina," she murmured and went in search of Jack Figg, bursting to confide her idea to him. It was brilliant; never had she been more certain of anything.

• • •

Linnet found Jack talking with Julian, and the two men welcomed her enthusiastically. Her husband put his arm around her and drew her closer to them while Jack gave her a huge smile.

"Looking more beautiful than ever tonight, I see, Beauty," he told her, and, turning to Julian, he added, "*You're* one lucky chap, I can tell you!"

"Oh, I know that," Julian answered, grinning at the older man, whom he'd known most of his life.

Linnet said, "Thanks, Jack, for your lovely compliment. But listen, I've just had a brainstorm. Let's move over there, away from everyone, so I can tell you both."

Jack nodded, and the three of them slid toward the library door where they could be alone, leaving the others grouped in the vicinity of the fireside.

"We'd better not go into the library," Linnet cautioned, "we'll be missed. Let's just stand here. What I have to say won't take a minute."

"I'm all ears," Julian murmured.

Jack said, "Okay, kid, shoot."

"A few minutes ago Great-Aunt Edwina suddenly said Gideon and Evan should elope. To avoid any trouble the ghastly J.A. might bring down on them. I explained to her that it was too late, that they couldn't go rushing off to Gretna Green, or anywhere else for that matter. And of course she understood." Linnet paused, looked from Julian to Jack, and said, "And then I had a sudden flash of . . . *inspiration.*"

"So tell us then," Julian urged.

In a low voice she explained the plan that had evolved in her head in the last few minutes, her attention riveted on Jack Figg.

When she had finished, Jack nodded, his face reflective; after a moment he asked, "Are you sure they'll do what you want?"

"I don't know, Jack, to be honest. But Gideon and I

have been best friends all of our lives, and I think he'll see the sense of it."

"Let's hope so," Jack said, and a cheerful smile suddenly slid onto his face. "You're a clever lass, Linnet. Very clever."

"She is indeed," her husband agreed. "And knowing Gideon, I'm sure he'll go along, and he'll talk the others into it."

"Let's go back and join the group," Linnet murmured, edging toward the center of the Stone Hall. "We'll get together tomorrow, Jack, and discuss it. You are staying the night, aren't you?"

"Your mother and father insisted," he said and then explained, "They didn't want me driving if I'd had a few drinks."

"And you have to do that. You have to toast Tessa's engagement to Jean-Claude," Linnet replied succinctly.

"Yes, indeed. And that's another story in the making," Jack announced, looking from Linnet to Julian, his eyes narrowing.

Julian grinned, a knowing look in *his* eyes.

Linnet said nothing. Her face was as inscrutable as Emma Harte's had often been when it was wiser to conceal innermost thoughts and feelings. A still tongue and a wise head—that had been Emma's motto, and it was Linnet's also.

13

~

There was no question in Dusty's mind that Molly Caldwell was a very sick woman, much worse than Gladys Roebotham had indicated on Saturday.

Now, on Monday afternoon, he stood next to her bed in the ICU of Leeds Infirmary, forcing a smile onto his face as she looked up at him, her dark brown eyes locked on his. She was extremely pale and strung up to tubes, but the nurse had removed the one from her mouth so she could speak.

"But you can only stay a couple of minutes," the nurse had warned as she slipped out of the room, leaving them alone.

"Atlanta?" Molly whispered and looked as if she was about to say something else.

He held up his hand and said in a gentle voice, "Don't exert yourself, Molly, please. Let me do the talking. . . . Atlanta's all right. She's with me, safe and sound at Willows Hall. Gladys brought her over to me, as you instructed."

Molly's brown eyes lit up, and she blinked, said in a parched voice, "She's a good woman. Is Atlanta . . . asking for me?"

"Yes, she is, to be truthful. But Gladys dreamed up a story that you'd hurt your leg, so we're sticking to that. She thinks you're getting your leg mended, and that you'll soon be home. And you will be, Molly. I spoke to your doctor this morning, and he's very positive about you making a full recovery."

A faint smile touched her mouth, and in a low, almost inaudible voice, she said, "Melinda must never have her, Dusty. *Never.*" There was a short pause as Molly appeared to struggle for breath, and then she whispered, *"Promise me."*

Startled though he was by this demand, he said swiftly, "Of course I promise. Melinda's not really capable of looking after her, even though she is apparently getting better in the detox clinic."

Ignoring this comment, Molly continued, "Atlanta must be with you at all costs. . . . *You* must bring her up."

For a split second he searched her face, and then he nodded and, endeavoring to reassure her, said, "I *will* bring her up, I promise, and she'll be with me at the house until she goes to boarding school. I'll look after her until she's grown up. But listen, you'll be doing that, love, you'll be out of here in a few days, recuperating at home with Atlanta. I'll hire a nurse to look after you, and any other help you need."

Molly made no answer, she simply gazed up at him for a long moment, her eyes suddenly filling with tears.

At once he became alarmed. The last thing he wanted was for her to grow agitated or upset. Rest and quiet was what she needed, the doctor had told him that.

"Molly, don't fret, love. I'll take care of you and Atlanta, and Melinda as well."

"She doesn't deserve you," Molly muttered, "and she mustn't have the child."

Dusty stared down at Molly Caldwell, not only startled again by her words but also perturbed. She had sounded annoyed, even angry, and was obviously displeased with her daughter. Taking hold of Molly's hand, he squeezed it and said, "I'll come to see you tomorrow, love."

She gave him a faint smile, and her trust and belief in him shone in her dark eyes.

In the corridor, Dusty paused, took a deep breath, and leaned against the wall. He was worried about Molly. His gut instinct told him that she was truly ill, that she might be plagued with heart trouble for the rest of her life. Although her physician had told him she would be able to go home in a week, Dusty wasn't at all sure about this now. She looked drained, depleted, not at all like herself.

But then she'd had a heart attack on Friday, he reminded himself. Of course she wasn't herself. Pulling himself together, he glanced around, wondering if he should ask to see the heart surgeon, Mr. William Larchmont, the heart specialist who was in charge of Molly's case. It had always struck him as strange that surgeons in different branches of medicine were called mister rather than doctor. Could Larchmont add anything? Dusty doubted it. And Dr. Bloom had been noncommittal earlier that morning, when Dusty had telephoned him at his office in Meanwood. "She'll pull through. She'll be all right" was all he had said.

Shrugging into his sheepskin coat, Dusty strode across the foyer, nodded to the nurse at the reception desk, and took the elevator down to the ground floor. Crossing the lobby, he pushed through the glass doors and went out into the street; instantly, he regretted that he had sent Paddy Whitaker and the car back to Harrogate. The weather had changed in the hour he had been at Leeds General Infirmary, and for the worse.

It was a raw afternoon, bone-chilling cold, the air layered with that awful northern dampness that seemed to infiltrate the entire body. He lifted his head, stared at the sky, saw that it was the color of lead, hard and unmoving, without a single cloud to give it life. It hangs there like a shroud, he thought, and shivered involuntarily, pulled up the collar of the coat, stuck his hands in his pockets as he strode out, moving as quickly as he could without actually running.

Leeds had never been his favorite place. This tough, bustling, and bleak industrial city had always intimidated him when he was growing up, and he had been glad to leave when he won a scholarship to the Royal College of Art in London. Funnily enough, he had immediately settled into his digs in Belsize Park, on the fringe of Hampstead, and in London he had never felt any kind of intimidation. Because he was older then? Was that the reason? He wasn't sure. No, of course he knew the reason. London was a beautiful city architecturally, and beauty of any kind had always thrilled him, brought to him enormous joy, expectation, hope for the future. His future.

He pushed these thoughts away, wondering where to go for a hot drink; he had time to waste before he went to Harte's to collect India. They would drive back to Willows Hall together, and she would stay the night. He knew how much she liked Atlanta, and the child liked her, but he was reluctant about encouraging them to bond. He did not want to burden India with a child who was not hers, yet she constantly protested that Atlanta was not a burden.

He must strive to believe India, understand her better. It was this lack of understanding on his part that had created their problems. She was a good person, bright and intelligent, a smart young woman, and, oh, how he loved her. Loved her beauty, her sexuality, her manners. And the way she handled herself so perfectly normally with everyone, whether she was talking to the cook, the housekeeper, Atlanta, himself, or her grandmother, the Dowager Countess. She treated all in exactly the same way.

A smile crossed his face, obliterating his scowls. He had a soft spot for India's grandmother Edwina. She was quite a card, undoubtedly her own woman, and certainly a bit of a martinet. Yet she was kind, thoughtful, and it was she who· had managed to ease and eventually obliterate his discomfort about India's parents being titled aristocrats.

"This is all nonsense, balderdash. In your head," she had begun one evening and stopped when he held up his hand in a peremptory way.

"Listen!" he exclaimed, "I'm not ashamed of my background, or where I come from. I'm a working-class boy from the suburbs of Leeds. I've never pretended to be anything else. And I'm proud of that, proud of what I've made of myself. I'm not in the least impressed with titles or aristocrats, I think that kind of attitude is . . . *nonsense, balderdash,* to use your own words."

"I understand. So what's it all about then?" Edwina had demanded, peering at him across his dinner table at Willows Hall, the Palladian mansion he was inordinately proud of. His stately home.

"I guess I associate aristocrats and titles with a bygone age. With snobbery and class injustices in the past. Centuries of them, actually. This is Cool Britannia now, not Rule Britannia. Talent talks to everyone, from Tony Blair to the average man. That's how it is in this *new* century."

Edwina understood him perfectly; most of his words sprang from his upbringing, even though he might not admit that. Whatever he believed, his background got in the way—well, at least a little bit. She told him her thoughts very bluntly, and he listened patiently.

"Perhaps you're right," he said when she'd finished, no longer concerned, or interested in fact. "Let's move on."

Edwina, Countess of Dunvale, firstborn child of Emma Harte, was not having any of that. Instead she said, "Listen to me now, my young friend. My mother, Emma Harte, was born a poor girl in a mill village on the Yorkshire moors. When she discovered she was pregnant, she came to Leeds, where she was helped by her old friend Blackie O'Neill, at that time a navvy on the Leeds canals and a bricklayer, and by Abraham Kallinski, a Jewish clothing manufacturer and a refugee from the pogroms in Russia. I was that child she was carrying when she was no more than sixteen herself, and I was born illegitimate. Edwin Fairley had made her pregnant; he was the son of Squire Fairley of Fairley Hall, where she had worked as a maid. When I was only six months old, my mother packed me off to live with her cousin Freda in Ripon, so that she could work, make money, lots of it, and so protect me. Emma said money made you safe, that it was power, and she was right. It's always been that way, hasn't it?

"Eventually, I was sent to boarding school, a very good one, and later I completed my education at a finishing school in Switzerland. At that time I returned to London, where I became a debutante, because by then my mother was a successful woman. *The* Emma Harte. And she had the money and standing in society to bring me out. I met Jeremy Standish, the Earl of Dunvale, almost at once, and he fell in love with me. Head over heels, that was the way he put it. And so we were married. We had one son, Anthony, who is India's father. If there were any aristocrats around, Dusty, they were all Dunvales, not Hartes, I can assure you of that."

She laughed then, and he laughed with her, and he sat back in the chair, scrutinizing her carefully, wondering if she had loved the earl the way he had loved her. And then, much to his surprise, he asked her, point-blank, and she answered him without a minute's hesitation.

"I adored him, Dusty. Jeremy was my ideal. You know, I worshiped him in a sense. Wrong to do that perhaps, but I did. He was older than I was, over twenty years older, and I think that's one of the reasons I loved him so much. There were moments, when I was a young woman, that I truly felt the need for a father figure, and Jeremy was very protective, indulgent, kind, and in a way rather fatherly. Don't misunderstand me, it was a love match, very much so, and we had an extremely sexual marriage.

We were mad for each other; in fact, I was always surprised we never had any more children. We were always making love."

Her blunt words threw him for a moment; it seemed ludicrous that this lady of ninety-five years was talking to him about sex. Then he looked at her intently yet again with those penetrating artist's eyes of his, and he saw at once beyond the wrinkles, the great age, saw her as he knew she must have been. *A great beauty.* He knew without question that she had looked exactly like India did today.

As he walked on, ruminating to himself, he suddenly wondered whether he should stop off at Harte's, have a cup of tea in the restaurant, then decided against it. Instead he went into the first coffee shop he spotted.

Dusty slid into a booth, ordered a pot of tea, leaned into the corner, waiting for the waitress to return with his order.

Within seconds he became conscious of his dreary surroundings, was assailed by a mixture of old, familiar smells, troubling smells associated with his youth: burnt pans, cabbage on the boil, bacon frying, a whiff of gas from a leaking ring, and overall a faint odor of dampness, of wet washing. And decay. Poverty. Mean streets.

He could not bear it. Too many unhappy memories rushed at him, and he leapt to his feet with such energy, the waitresses all turned to stare at him. Without a word he threw five pounds on the table and rushed out, not looking back. Gagging.

He struck out in the direction of City Square, walking rapidly, breathing deeply, blocking out the past, the childhood days that brought such pain. Remembering was a burden.

What a relief it was to be outside, damp and bitter cold as it was.

In no time at all, Dusty was crossing the road, hurrying into City Square. When he came to the statues in the center, he paused, stood looking, thinking how banal they appeared to him now. When he was a child, they had seemed magnificent, looming high above him. Now they were scaled down to size in his eyes.

The scantily clad nymphs who stood on plinths holding up torches which became electric lights at night seemed utterly ridiculous as companions to the statue in the center of the square. Edward, the Black Prince, in his armor, seated on a black horse, beloved son of Edward III, a warrior like his father, one of England's greatest kings. Why were the nymphs there at all?

Dusty was unaware of the sudden icy wind blowing up as he stood there staring; he was momentarily mesmerized by that statue, which he had thought so magnificent when he was a little boy.

Time shattered.

The present fell away.

The past was all there was left.

Memories flooded him, memories long ago shut off. Now he lived within them . . . here in the city of his birth.

"Who's the man on the horse, Dad?" Dusty asked, staring up at his father, tugging at his hand when Will Rhodes did not immediately respond.

Looking down at his boy, his only child, his adored son, Will smiled and said in his usual gentle way, "That's a statue of Edward, the Black Prince. A brave prince he was, too."

"Why's he called the Black Prince then?"

"Because of his black armor. At least, I thinks that's the reason, Russell."

"It's a right big horse, in't it, Dad?"

"Aye, lad, it is, and black as coal."

*   *   *

Coal.

Black dust.

Black dust inhaled for years.

Silicosis.

Death.

Dusty turned away from the statue of Edward, the Black Prince, on his coal-black horse, and crossed the main road to the Queen's Hotel.

He was thinking of his father as he walked. Will Rhodes had been a miner, had gone down the pits in Castleford for years. All his life really; he had been a pit lad when he was very young.

And it was the pits that had killed him. His lungs had been destroyed by the work he did to support his little family—his lovely wife, Alice, and his beloved boy, Russell. The boy who would never go down the pits. Will would never allow that. Never. The boy who would be an artist. A great artist. The boy whose talent "shone like the brightest moon in midsummer," that was the way his father always put it.

His father had died young. Only forty. Amazing he had lasted that long.

Dusty had known when his father was going to die. It was because of his strange manner, what he had said to him. It was a kind of . . . *premonition.* "Take care of your mam, lad. Take care of my Alice." Will had seemed perfectly well when he said that, out of the blue, but he must have known death was knocking on his door. He was dead and gone within the month.

Silicosis. That was the cause of death. Black dust had stolen the life out of Will Rhodes. A man far too young to die.

Dusty swallowed hard as he approached the hotel. He always got a lump in his throat when he thought of his father. He had loved him so much, but he had never told Will that, which was something he had regretted ever since. You must always tell those you love that you *do* love them. He never had. Never told anyone. Until he had finally said it to India Standish. His fiancée, soon to be his wife. In June. In Ireland. At Clonloughlin. Lady India Standish, the girl of his dreams.

The moment he set foot in the lobby of the hotel, which was the best in Leeds, they surrounded him respectfully. They all wanted to help him, to please him. He was their hero, the local boy made good. Bloody good. Famous. Rich. A celebrity. Whatever that meant.

He smiled and thanked them, was scrupulously polite, and managed to get himself into the lounge, where he took off his sheepskin coat.

The waiter came immediately, took his order for a pot of tea, and departed. Dusty settled himself on the sofa, glancing around as he did. He hadn't been inside the hotel for years, and he noticed at once that it had been refurbished. The surroundings were pleasant, comfortable, tasteful, and there was a welcoming warmth in the lounge. Dusty began to thaw out, and he realized how chilled he had become standing in City Square, although he had been too lost in memories to notice it then.

The past was immutable. It was always there. You carried it around with you. Some people referred to it as baggage; he did not. The past was the sum total of himself. It made him who he was.

Dusty's thoughts went back to his father.

He had been sixteen when Will had died. It was just after he had started to attend Leeds College of Art; his father had seen that happen, at least, and he had been proud. "No pits for you, my lad," Will had said, full of smiles after Dusty's first day at the college. "You're going somewhere, aye, you are that." And his mother, always quick on the draw, had exclaimed, "Yes, he is. To the Royal College of Art in London. When he's eighteen."

Dusty remembered now, so very clearly, the huge, proud smile on his father's face, the unexpected sparkle in those deep blue eyes. He had inherited his father's eyes and his dark hair, but there the resemblance stopped. Dusty was much broader than his father had been, and he had a craggy, almost rough-hewn face, while Will Rhodes had been slightly built, thin, with refined, almost delicate features. Dusty took after his mother's side of the family, was built like her twin brothers, Ron and Ray, who had his type of muscular torso, wide shoulders, and smoldering good looks.

Leaning back against the sofa, Dusty closed his eyes for a moment, and captured behind his lids the image of his father's face.

Will was smiling; he was happy because his only child had won a scholarship to Leeds College of Art, and in Will's considered estimation, and Alice's, there was no reason why their brilliantly talented son wouldn't win yet another scholarship to the Royal College of Art in London. And he had done so. But his father was dead and buried by then.

The rattling of china brought Dusty up with a start, and he nodded to the waiter when asked if the tea should be poured, then thanked him as the cup was passed.

Sipping the tea, finding it refreshing, Dusty suddenly wondered if people who knew they were dying tried to warn loved ones, those who would be left behind to grieve. Or *prepare* them, if not exactly warn them.

His father had instructed him to look after his mother a month before he had passed on. And Gram, his father's mother, had done the same thing only a year later. Unexpectedly, she had told Dusty he must never forget who he was, where he came from, and what he was all about. "And always stay close to your mam, lad. Be there for her, take care of her. She's the bravest, the kindest woman I've ever known. Don't you ever forget that, Russell. Stand by her."

Did people get a feeling they were soon to die? He did not know. But his mother had known, certainly she had, because she had told him. "I'm dying, Dusty," she had murmured ten years ago, and on seeing him turn pale, falter as he walked across the sitting room toward her, she had smiled bravely and said, "It can't be helped, love. It's the cancer. It eats away at you, and I'm getting weaker. It's better you know; then I don't have to pretend with you."

He had gone to sit with her on the sofa, taking her hand in his, staring into her gentle face, and as he had looked into her soft, gray-blue eyes, he had choked up. She had been his rock all his life; she had worked and slaved so that he could go to college in London. Even though he had won the coveted scholarship, there were all those extras to pay for, and even though he had a weekend job, he still needed money. And his mother provided it without a murmur. God knows how she had done it. But, thank God, he had been a success almost immediately after leaving college, and he had been able to give her the comforts and luxuries she deserved once he was established. Eventually he had bought her a small house in Leeds, insisted she stop working, and she had repaid him with her obvious happiness at her newfound financial security. Most of all, she was proud of him, and it pleased him that he had succeeded in fulfilling her dreams for him.

"You're the best, Dusty," she had said to him for years, her eyes full of love. "And never forget who you are. You're the best-loved son of Alice and Will Rhodes. And remember, you have it all. Talent, intelligence, and Looks with a capital *L*. Let's not forget your handsome looks, Dusty. They're important in this world, and don't let anyone convince you otherwise."

He *had* remembered all the things they had told him: Will, Gram, and his mother. It was their love and devotion, their self-sacrifice that had put him where he stood today. That and their belief in him, their belief in his talent. That talent sometimes baffled him. He did not know where it came from, and there were times when he shook his head, marveling at it. It was the essence of him. That he *had* come to understand.

He was forty-two, a mature man. Well, most of the time. He was about to marry; he must make *her* happy. He must be a good husband. And he must trust her, trust her judgment and her good sense. Ever since she had come back to him, after their painful quarrel and separation, he had managed to do that. He had even told her he loved her . . . a first for him.

There was the child. His and Melinda's. Molly had made him promise to bring her up. She had warned him—was that the right word?—not to let Melinda have her. Because of Melinda's drug abuse? Or for some other reason?

Molly had been preparing him. *For her death.*

She knew she was going to die, just as his father, his grandmother, and his mother had known. They had prepared him. So it wouldn't be too much of a shock when it happened. But it was always a shock when someone you loved died, even if you were expecting it.

Molly Caldwell was going to die. She knew it. And now, so did he.

Dusty leaned against the sofa cushions, taking a deep breath. A wave of sadness enveloped him, and he felt his throat closing with emotion. Molly Caldwell had been a good mother, and a good grandmother, and she hadn't deserved to suffer the way she had because of her daughter. Melinda had led her a merry dance over the years . . .

Dusty sat upright with a start. If Molly did die, there would be Melinda to contend with. She wouldn't allow him to have custody of Atlanta. She would want the child for herself, to use as a weapon against him. That was the way she was made. He thought of Tessa Fairley and her battles with her ex-husband, Mark Longden. Was he going to go through the same thing?

Probably, he answered himself. But there was always a

way to solve problems of this nature. Money talks. And
Melinda did not have a savory reputation these days.
Drunk. Drugged. In and out of many beds. In and out of
detox clinics. Unfit mother? Unquestionably.

Dusty sat quietly for another half hour, thinking of all
the worst possibilities he might have to contend with. As
he ruminated, one thing became crystal clear. He must
confide in India tonight, explain his feelings about this
situation, about his past with Melinda. And he must
speak to her about his childhood. She had always wanted
to know more about those early years, and he would
never tell her.

Tonight he would. He owed her that. She was going to
be his wife. There should be no secrets.

14

The clock in the church tower began to strike.

Inside the church, the noise was deafening. Startled from her reverie, Evan sat up with a jerk. The din continued for a few seconds longer, and then, much to her relief, all was quiet, the interior of the church peaceful once more.

Evan settled back against the wooden pew, waiting for Gideon and the others to return. They had left her off at the church and driven around to the vicarage to see the vicar. She knew they would arrive at any moment; in the meantime, she was enjoying her sojourn alone. The church had a beautiful altar, and the three stained-glass windows set high above it were quite something to behold. Their jewel colors were stunning, and they sparkled brightly in the sunlight, creating rainbow reflections against the pale stone walls, which were nine hundred years old, dating back to Norman times. She knew the church was considered a local treasure.

Glancing around, Evan filled with happiness. Yesterday, the florists had worked all day and into the evening, under the supervision of Paula and Emily, creating the loveliest of flower arrangements for her wedding. The church was brimming with them. Alcoves, corners, the altar steps, and the windowsills were aglow with white and pink orchids; banks of white and pink carnations filled the air with their sweet perfume, while tall white lilies and evergreens added a seasonal touch. The setting took her breath away. Paula and her future mother-in-law, Emily, had done her proud.

Settling back, relaxing, Evan let her thoughts momentarily stray to her great-grandmother Emma Harte. It was she who had kept this Norman church in good repair over the years, and had arranged for central heating to be installed. "You'll be warm," Gideon had told her the other evening, knowing how much she suffered from the icy weather lately.

This morning she was cozy in her ankle-length, pale gray overcoat, worn with matching trousers and a sweater. She was in good form, although she did feel a bit top-heavy. For this reason she would be relieved when the babies were born. She couldn't wait to see her twin boys, and neither could their father.

Evan smiled to herself, thinking of her genes, his genes. Twins ran in the Harte family, and seemingly she was carrying on the tradition.

Evan wondered if it would snow today. Wiggs, the head gardener at Pennistone Royal, had announced that snow would fall this weekend. There was nothing more picturesque than a winter wedding in the snow, especially in the countryside, which became a white and glistening wonderland. Her mother agreed with her about that.

Zeroing in on her mother, Evan thought about their conversation on Wednesday. In the afternoon a troubled Marietta had come to her. Something had happened that morning which had worried her so much she had felt compelled to confide in her daughter. As her mother had recounted the story, Evan had filled with unease herself.

It seemed that Marietta had driven down to Pennistone village with Angharad that morning, wanting to buy a few small things at the village newsagent's shop.

"We were minding our own business, selecting postcards and a few other items, when a handsome man walked in," Marietta had explained. "He started going through magazines on the rack. Then suddenly Angharad caught his eye, and I couldn't believe it! They were instantly chatting away as if they knew each other well. I'm sure Angharad was flirting with him. I was angry about her vulgar behavior with a total stranger, so I paid, and we both left the shop. I had taken only a few steps when I realized I'd left my glasses in the library area, so I went back. As I was entering the shop, I heard the woman behind the counter addressing the man as *Mr. Ainsley.* I was shocked, Evan. I grabbed my glasses and fled."

At this point, her mother had paused for a moment, looking at Evan with concern, and then she had asked, "Could it have been *Jonathan,* do you think?"

"More than likely," Evan had replied quietly, her unease increasing. "There is no *other* Mr. Ainsley. Except for Robin."

Evan remembered now the genuine dismay she had experienced as she answered her mother. How unfortunate that it was Angharad, of all people, who had met Jonathan Ainsley. She was not only a flirt but impulsive, and she had slept around indiscriminately since she'd been fourteen. Evan couldn't wait for the wedding festivities to be over, for her family to go back to London, then on to New York. She loved her parents and Elayne, but long ago she had become extremely cautious, even wary of Angharad. Furthermore, she knew that Gideon couldn't stand Angharad and that Linnet held her at arm's length. But on Wednesday afternoon, wanting to put her mother at ease, to reassure her, Evan had gone on in a steady, level voice, "I'm sure Angharad and Jonathan won't run into each other again, Mom. Truly. That's highly unlikely."

Marietta had agreed, looking relieved.

Evan, however, had worried so much about this

strange encounter that she had finally told Gideon about it. Later that evening, when Linnet returned from a visit to the Harrogate store, they had confided in her.

Linnet had listened alertly, instantly looking troubled herself. "I'll let Jack know immediately. There's the possibility that Ainsley knew very well who Angharad was. They might not have met by accident at all, you know. It could have been arranged to look like one, though. By Ainsley. He's a sneaky chap, Jack says, and somebody's feeding him information, of that I'm certain. And listen, aren't you glad you agreed to go along with my plan?"

They had both said yes in unison. Linnet's Plan with a capital *P*, that was what she called it, and it was already in operation. Evan felt at ease this morning, and all because of Linnet O'Neill, who was the smartest woman she knew, except for Paula.

There was a sound behind her, and Evan glanced over her shoulder. She saw Linnet, Julian, and Gideon coming into the church along with the vicar of Pennistone Royal village, the Reverend Henry Thorpe, and she waved, her face lighting up.

It was the good-looking young vicar who led the way to the pew where Evan was sitting. She stood up and smiled as he greeted her warmly and shook her hand. They chatted for a moment, until Gideon said in a low but firm voice, "Could we get things started, please, Vicar?"

"Absolutely, Gideon. That's why we're here."

And so in that peaceful, ancient church filled to overflowing with flowers and early morning sunlight, with only the vicar and two other people present as witnesses, Evan Hughes was married to Gideon Harte. It was exactly eight-fifteen on Saturday morning when they pledged their troth to each other with clearly spoken words and gold wedding rings.

This wedding ceremony, conducted in absolute secrecy hours before it was due to take place, had been Linnet's brain wave a week ago. And it was Linnet who had insisted on the necessity for secrecy. "Nobody can know," she had pointed out to Jack.

Nevertheless, he had been stubborn about Paula being informed. "She *has* to know," he had said emphatically. "And so do Shane, Emily, and Winston. The four of them control the clans. They'll keep their mouths shut, that I can guarantee. But they *must* be in the picture. However, I agree with you, Linnet, no one else should be told. Not even Evan's parents or Robin can know. They'll be told after the event. Everyone in the family will be told then."

Linnet had nodded, had pointed out, "No one can be present except me and Julian as witnesses. The wedding has to be so low-key it will go unnoticed."

And that was the way it was.

After the simple ceremony, the four of them followed the vicar into the vestry to sign the church register. Once that had been done, they all thanked the clergyman for his cooperation in Linnet's plan.

When they left the church, Jack was waiting outside with several of his operatives, and he came forward to congratulate the bride and groom. A moment later he was ushering Gideon and Evan toward his Land Rover, along with Linnet and Julian. Once they were settled, he went back to the vicar, who was standing on the church steps.

"Thank you, Reverend Thorpe. We couldn't have done it without you."

The vicar grinned. "Not if you wanted it to be legal, you couldn't," he quipped. "I was happy to be of help, and I'll see everyone later at the reception."

With a smile and a nod, Jack hurried back to his car and drove out of the sleepy, deserted village. He was relieved that nothing had gone amiss, that Gideon and Evan were now well and truly married to each other. That was all he had been concerned about, making sure there was a wedding without a hitch.

There was an air of secrecy at Pennistone Royal when they got back. On the way there from the church, Gideon had called Paula on his mobile and exclaimed, "It's done! We're married! And no one is any the wiser." So when they arrived at the house no more than ten minutes later, Paula and Shane came rushing out to greet them.

Paula kissed Evan and Gideon, and so did Shane, and then they congratulated them. Paula led the way back inside, heading for the breakfast room, and she explained, "Margaret has prepared breakfast for the seven of us, but she doesn't know where you've been. No one does." Glancing at her daughter, she said with a warm and loving smile, "I'm glad you had that brain wave of yours, Linnet, and that you put your plan into action. You're a clever girl."

"Thanks, Mummy, but I do feel a bit awful. I've deprived Evan of her beautiful wedding." As she spoke, she looked across at her cousin and offered an apologetic smile.

"I don't feel a bit deprived!" Evan exclaimed. "I feel privileged to be a member of this family, and anyway, it *was* a beautiful wedding, with you and Julian there to stand up for Gideon and me."

Gideon said, "She's right, you know, Linny. The main thing is that we *are* married, and because of your plan Evan's not a target. Thank God."

They all seated themselves at the round table in the bay window of the breakfast room, and within seconds Margaret was bustling around serving ham and scrambled eggs, toast and large pots of tea and coffee, along with dishes of marmalade and butter.

Once Margaret had retreated, Jack said quietly to Paula and Shane, "The village was half asleep and completely deserted. I spoke to the vicar as you requested,

Paula, and he's going to phone a few key villagers later, tell them the wedding was private, held earlier today because of Evan's condition. He's also arranging for the Women's Institute to give a special tea party in the church hall tomorrow, to make up for their disappointment. You know how much they enjoy a Harte wedding."

"That's nice of him," Shane said. "It might be a good idea to send down a few cases of bubbly for their party. What do you think, Paula?"

"It's a very good thought, darling. I'll have Joe run it over to the vicarage tomorrow morning."

Gideon looked at Paula and grinned. "I bet you had a hard time keeping my father and mother away from this little breakfast, didn't you?"

Paula began to laugh. "In a way, yes. Emily, in particular, wanted to be here to greet you and Evan. But to be honest, in the end she understood that it would be kinder to stay at Allington Hall with Evan's parents. The only alternative was to bring them along, and I felt it would be better if we kept this really simple. Evan can rest later and get ready for the reception without pressure from any of us. And as soon as I phone Emily, she will tell Evan's parents about your early ceremony."

"And besides," Shane interjected, "we have our work cut out for us. Once breakfast is over, Paula and I have to phone a lot of family members, Gideon, to tell them to come to the house at three rather than go to church for a two o'clock ceremony that's not going to take place."

"Are you going to explain the early morning marriage in the same way?" Julian asked, looking from Paula to Shane.

"Indeed we are, Jules," Shane replied. It's the most logical thing to do. Evan's looking more pregnant than ever, and why wouldn't we all be worried that the twins might be born premature? I think everyone will buy our story."

"And if they don't, too bad," Linnet announced. "Anyway, to tell them the real reason serves no purpose. It will make us all look a bit paranoid."

"You *are* paranoid," Lorne said from the doorway and strolled in, looking debonair in a white turtleneck sweater and jodhpurs. Smiling hugely at them all, he added, "I assume you were making a reference to Jonathan Ainsley when you brought up the word *paranoid*, Linnet. I think you all pay too much attention to him, give him too much credence. I think he's a specter rather than a threat."

"Perhaps you're right," Linnet answered, smiling at her brother. "But it just so happens that he did attempt to disrupt my marriage to Julian last month. Tell him, Jack."

Jack Figg nodded, focusing on Lorne, who had pulled up a chair and sat down next to Shane. Jack began to explain. "My operatives and I thwarted a band of yobbos who were about to come down into Pennistone village and start trouble. Serious harm to the church and everyone in it was fortunately averted."

"How did you find out?" Lorne asked, raising a blond brow.

"We got it from the horse's mouth, so to speak," Jack murmured. "From someone who was involved. But I prefer not to say who."

Gideon leaned across the table and asked Paula and Shane, "Do you want me to make some phone calls for you? I agree that Evan should rest for a few hours, since it's going to be a long day, and into the evening. But I'm totally free."

"Not anymore you're not," Linnet teased. "You're very much taken."

"Yes, I am, and it's great," Gideon replied, smiling from ear to ear.

15

The fruitwood casket, scrolled with silver, had stood on the Queen Anne chest for Paula's entire life. Many times in the past she had asked her grandmother where the key was, and Emma had always told her it was lost. The casket had been intriguing to everyone, because Emma would never explain what was in it, if anything.

But not anymore. Not only did it have its silver key in its silver escutcheon but the entire family knew what the mystery box had contained. Letters from Glynnis Hughes, Evan's grandmother, written in the fifties to Emma Harte here at Pennistone Royal. And it was the letters which had solved Evan's identity. Once Paula had found the key and opened the casket, she had discovered that Robin Ainsley, Emma's favorite son, had been the father of Glynnis's child, Owen Hughes, and Evan was therefore Emma's great-granddaughter from America.

With Evan on her mind, Paula walked across the upstairs parlor and into her bedroom, her eyes focused on the casket. Lifting it down, she carried it back to her oval Georgian desk near the window in the parlor and smoothed her hand across the lid. On it was a small silver plaque; it was engraved with the initials E.H., which stood for Emma Harte. But they could also stand for Evan

Harte, and perhaps, more than to anyone else in the family, this lovely old box should belong to Evan.

I'm going to give it to her, Paula decided, lifting the lid, looking at the faded, red-velvet lining. It was empty, since Paula had given Glynnis's letters to Emma tied with blue ribbon to Evan last year. And she must also have the diamond star, Paula suddenly thought; it will match the diamond star earrings Emily has given her for a wedding present.

Smiling to herself, almost laughing, Paula stood up and hurried back into her bedroom, opened the wooden jewelry box which stood on her dressing table, and took out the Victorian star brooch. It was very old, too; it had been given to Emma Harte by Arthur Ainsley's mother when Emma married Arthur in the 1920s, along with a pair of matching diamond earrings. Paula was laughing to herself because she was thinking of her cousin Emily, who years ago had asked Emma if she could borrow "those old diamond earrings of yours, Grandy." Grandy had shaken her head and said, "I didn't know diamonds got old, Emily, but of course you can borrow them." Later, Emma had given the earrings to Emily, because her mother, Elizabeth, had been an Ainsley.

Evan was also part Ainsley, through Robin, so she should have the brooch which belonged with the earrings, Paula thought, and everything would be neat and tidy that way. She had no trouble remembering how much her grandmother liked to keep things straight in her head, in her business, and in her life. Neat and tidy, Emma had called it.

The sound of the door opening and Lorne calling, "Mother, are you here?" brought Paula hurrying out into the parlor, the brooch still in her hand.

"Darling, what is it?" she asked, staring at her eldest son.

"Can we talk for a few minutes?" Lorne said, joining her near the fireplace, sitting down on a sofa.

"But of course we can. You sound anxious, Lorne. Is everything all right with you?"

"It is, Mums, yes. Except that I worry a lot about *you* these days, you've seemed so tired lately."

"I have been, actually, Lorne. Since before Christmas. But now this wedding is finally happening today, I'm sure I'm going to be much better. It's been a worry."

"Because of that bloody cousin of yours?"

"Only partially. There's been a lot to organize with Emily. She so wanted Gideon's marriage to be perfect, and in a way she was cheated this morning. I feel sorry for her in that sense."

"Because she didn't see Evan walking down the aisle? Standing at the altar with Gideon? Is that what you mean?"

"Yes, I do. But she saw the need for the secret ceremony, immediately it was suggested, and the reception is going to be both beautiful and glamorous. I told her she'll see Evan and Gideon go onto the floor for the first dance, and she knows that will take the place of her being at the actual ceremony."

Lorne shook his head, looking across at his mother, and said, in the quietest of voices, "Do you really think Ainsley is dangerous?"

"I'm afraid I do . . . through other people acting on his behalf. He would never be caught red-handed, he's far too smart for that. Let's not forget that he is a Harte, whatever else he is."

"Too bad," Lorne muttered and went on, "Jack told me a short while ago to watch myself at all times. That I could well be a target because I'm your son, and also that I'm an *easy target* because I'm so damned visible as an actor."

"You must listen to Jack," Paula exclaimed, her voice rising an octave. "He's right. Maybe you should have a bodyguard; a lot of famous actors and actresses do, as you well know."

"Not for me, Mums, thanks for the suggestion anyway. I'll keep my eyes open and watch my step, as Jack has cautioned me to do. But Ainsley can't disrupt the reception, that's a foregone conclusion. There's so much security here at Pennistone Royal, a fly couldn't get in." He grinned. Then his eyes went to the diamond brooch and he asked, "What's that you're holding? The famous Ainsley pin?"

Paula smiled. "I'm going to give it to Evan today, since she is a descendant of Arthur Ainsley, and Emily's given her the matching earrings, the ones Grandy gave *her* years ago. They belong with the brooch, it's a matched set. And now it's going to be complete again."

"That's nice of you and Emily, passing down family heirlooms. A rather charming tradition, actually. Anyway, I also came up to ask you what the drill is for this afternoon now that everything's going to take place here."

"Nothing has changed, Lorne. At three o'clock, instead of arriving in the Peach Drawing Room from church, Evan and Gideon will arrive from . . . upstairs." She laughed as she said this; her sense of humor never failed her.

Lorne laughed with Paula and nodded. "Then there will be the champagne reception in the Peach and Gray Drawing Rooms, and after that the late lunch at four-thirty in the Stone Hall. Once lunch is over there'll be dancing, and revels."

"That's correct, darling, and actually, now that they're married, I feel much more relaxed. I'm going to enjoy myself. I feel as if a heavy load has been lifted off my shoulders, Lorne."

"I'm glad, Mother. You worry too much, and all the time. Now I'm going to go off and cadge a sandwich from Margaret, eat it in the kitchen, and then skedaddle, have a rest, and get into my dark blue suit. I'll be downstairs early in case I'm needed."

"You'll be the handsomest man there, my darling."

"Except for Dad," Lorne said, pushing himself to his

feet and walking across to the door. Before leaving, he glanced back at his mother. "Is there anything you need help with?"

"Not really, Lorne, but thanks for asking."

"All you have to do is yell if you need me."

"Oh, there is one thing. Will you make sure Desmond's well turned out, please? He always used to look so smart, but lately he's seemed . . . a bit disheveled."

"All the kids are these days, but I'll go and give him the once-over later," Lorne promised and closed the door softly behind him.

Paula continued to sit on the sofa for a moment, thinking of Lorne and how lucky she was. Her son had never given her a moment of worry. Ever. He was almost too good to everyone, and she frequently worried that he might be taken advantage of, especially by women. Sighing, she stood up and went to the desk, put the brooch in the fruitwood casket, and closed the lid. Later she would find the little velvet box for it and take these gifts to Evan's room, with a note telling her their history in the Harte family.

"You know you can wheedle anything out of me, luvey," Margaret said, smiling up at her favorite, who lolled against the big window in the kitchen, looking impossibly handsome. "We're very busy in here, as you can see, but I'll make you a chicken sandwich. Mind you, my lad, you'll have to eat it somewhere else, this 'ere kitchen's teeming with the caterer's staff. Still, I'm glad your mother is having the lunch catered. It would've been too much for me."

"Yes, it would, Margaret, my darling," Lorne answered, leaning forward, kissing her on the forehead. "You've got to take care of yourself. Sometimes I think you work far too hard."

Margaret grinned at him. "That's the curse of this family, Lorne. Your great-grandmother set the standards

around 'ere, you knows, and because she was a work addict, or whatever you call it, she expected everyone else to
be just like her. She was a bit of a slave driver, Emma was."

Lorne burst out laughing and then swung around when
he heard his name. He found himself staring into the face
of the caterer, whom he had known all his life. "Hello,
Prissy!" he exclaimed, smiling hugely at Priscilla Marney,
who often did the catering for his mother's big parties and
receptions. "How're you? And how's Samantha?"

"She's great, and so am I. And you look wonderful,
Lorne." Shifting slightly on her feet, she continued, "I
can't wait to see your next film."

"It'll be out in a few months, and in March I start re-
hearsals for a play in the West End."

"When it opens, we'll come and see it. Sam and I are
your biggest fans," Priscilla said.

Lorne smiled at her, noticing in a glance that her appearance was much toned down. Usually Prissy wore
flamboyant clothes in brilliant purples and red. There
was a theatricality about her that he appreciated, being an
actor; with her gypsy coloring and height, he thought she
was a striking-looking woman. However, she was low-
key today. Her wild black hair was pulled back into a neat
chignon, and she wore a businesslike black trouser suit
and white shirt.

Lorne said, "If you get in touch with me when the play
opens, I'll make sure you have house seats, Priscilla."

"Thanks, Lorne, that's very nice of you." She glanced
at the clock on the kitchen wall. "Isn't it getting late?
Shouldn't you be changing? You're due at the church
soon, you know."

"I'd better go," Lorne replied, edging away, not wanting
to be drawn into a discussion. He was certain the caterer
knew nothing about the secret ceremony this morning.
He himself hadn't been aware of it until he had joined his
parents and the others for breakfast.

Margaret, bustling over, put a plate in his hands. "Get

on with you, my lad," she said, "and enjoy your chicken sandwich. See you later." She almost pushed him out of the kitchen.

Lorne went striding down the corridor in the direction of the breakfast room. His mother believed Margaret knew nothing about the secret wedding ceremony, but he was not so sure. He thought his mother often underestimated the housekeeper. The way Margaret had moved him on when Priscilla started talking about the time told him a lot. Not that it mattered if Priscilla Marney knew; she would know at three o'clock anyway. And she'd been working for the family for years. Everyone liked Prissy, and she was the best caterer in Yorkshire.

The breakfast room had one occupant, Lorne's half brother, Desmond, who was sitting at the table eating a bowl of fruit salad.

"Hey, Des, where've you been all morning? I haven't seen you around," Lorne said, walking in and sitting down next to him.

Desmond groaned. "Doing my homework. Dad's been on my back about it."

"Need any help?"

"No, but thanks anyway for offering. I suppose we've got to get all dressed up for the wedding. What a *bore.*"

Lorne began to laugh, and after a moment he said, "What does it matter, Des, really? Wearing a suit and tie for a couple of hours is no great hardship. Anyway, it's only an ordinary suit today, not a morning suit, thank goodness. I hate having to get into a top hat and tails, which most weddings require."

"Oh, God, so do I!" he exclaimed. "Mums wants me to wear my new navy blue suit. What're you wearing, Lorne?"

"A navy blue suit; that's what our mother wants us both to wear. And Dad and Grandpops, too."

Desmond made a face. "I wish I didn't have to go. I *hate* weddings!"

"I know what you mean. Lots of family and all that stuff, and usually lots of quarrels and fights as well. It is a bore, in a sense, you're right. But think about this. You got home from boarding school for the weekend because of it."

"True," Desmond said and had the good grace to smile at his brother, whom he adored. He went on, "Haven't you got a new girl yet, Lorne?" As he spoke a dark brow lifted quizzically, and then Desmond, Black Irish to the core, began to grin cheekily. "I bet Mum is forever on *your* back about settling down."

"You're right, she is. On the other hand, Desmond, I can't settle down when I don't have a woman in my life."

His brother nodded, then, leaning forward, he asked, "Can I stick with you at the wedding, Lorne? I always get eaten alive by the aunts and female cousins if I'm not careful."

Lorne began to laugh again, and he was still laughing as the two of them finished lunch. That had been his fate when he'd been Desmond's age; he understood exactly how his brother felt.

The man parked on top of the hill, close to a clump of trees. He knew that from the village the car would be hidden by the trees; it was also a good vantage point. He was able to see the main street without being seen himself. Climbing out of the car, he found a pack of cigarettes in his jacket pocket, stuck one in his mouth, and cupped his hand around it as he flicked his lighter.

Leaning against the hood, he inhaled, enjoying his smoke and the early afternoon sunshine. As he stared down into Pennistone Royal village, he was struck by the absence of cars. There were always lots of cars at a posh wedding. Glancing at his watch, pursing his lips, he wondered if the wedding party was running late or if all the cars had been parked in the yard next to the pub. The problem was he couldn't see the pub yard from here. The Duck and Drake was out of his line of vision.

He nodded. The wedding was no doubt in progress; everyone was inside, listening to the vicar do his stuff. He grinned, maliciously. Any moment they would all have a rude awakening. He grinned again.

This thought had hardly entered his brain, the grin hardly touched his mouth, when the bomb he had planted during the night blew up. Exactly on time. The explosion was so loud he thought his eardrums would burst; smoke filled the air, along with slabs of stone and bricks and other debris.

The man swung around, not waiting to see any more. He slid into his car, turned on the ignition, and drove over the hill and down the other side, racing toward Ripon. Mission accomplished, he muttered and laughed out loud.

Jack Figg opened the door of the Peach Drawing Room at Pennistone Royal and stood for a moment regarding the room. It was his favorite spot in this great and ancient house, and now, as he glanced around, he marveled that it had not changed much in over fifty years.

At this moment it was empty, since the family were all upstairs getting dressed and no guests had arrived for the reception. Jack glanced at his watch and saw that it was just ten minutes to two. Over an hour to go before the reception began, far too soon for anyone to come yet.

Slowly, he walked across the floor to the white marble fireplace. The peach silk walls held a golden glow as shafts of winter sunlight filtered through the many tall windows, filling the room with a soft, hazy light. He had always thought this was the loveliest of all the rooms, with its peach-and-cream color scheme, elegant Regency furniture, and exquisite Impressionist paintings.

Standing in front of the fireplace, he looked up at the

Sisley landscape which Emma had hung there over fifty years ago, then moved on, his eyes taking in the other two Sisleys and the two Monets which graced the walls. These five paintings would always hang there. Emma had decreed that in her will.

Jack noticed that Paula had changed nothing; she simply refurbished things as they became worn or shabby and therefore remained true to Emma's original decor.

There were flowers everywhere. Several tall crystal vases were filled with lilies, imported lilac, and branches of mimosa; porcelain bowls held carnations and tulips, and Paula's signature orchids were displayed in wonderful china tubs. But no roses. That was Emma's old rule, and Paula abided by it.

His thoughts centered on Paula as he moved over to one of the windows and stood staring out at the terrace and snow-covered gardens beyond. She had looked exhausted lately, but earlier today, when he had walked around the Stone Hall with her, helping her put the place cards on the tables, she had seemed better. For one thing, she appeared more relaxed and lighter in spirit. It was because of the secret ceremony at eight-fifteen this morning, he was positive.

She worried herself to death about Jonathan Ainsley. Jack was well aware of this, and he wished there was something he could do to alleviate her worries. But he was helpless. Unless, of course, he went out and killed Ainsley. Then she would be at peace. But naturally that was impossible. Jack decided he had to find a way to stop the man in his tracks; there had to be something he could do.

Jack had been part of this family for years; he thought of it as his own in so many ways, and certainly they thought of him as one of theirs. Because of his love and affection for them, he wanted to ease their burdens whenever he could, especially Paula's, since he had been close to her for years.

A sigh escaped his lips. He had to do something to

help her immediately. More security would be a good idea; he was going to talk to Lorne about hiring a driver who was an ex-policeman. That way Lorne would have proper protection. He was a famous actor, a Harte even though his name was Fairley, young and good-looking. And therefore a perfect target. Jack had said that to Lorne already. But he must make his own moves and provide protection, because Jack knew that Lorne wouldn't.

As he turned and walked back toward the double doors, Linnet suddenly appeared and waved to him. "I've come for my stuff," she said as she hurried toward him.

Jack nodded, put his hand in his pocket, and brought out a large envelope.

Drawing to a standstill, she took the envelope from him. "It's the mike and the earpiece?"

"Yes. Make sure the mike doesn't get muffled by the flower you plan to wear on your lapel," he said. "And you must hook the mike pad onto your waistband, then put the wire of the mike into it." As he spoke he turned around, lifted up his jacket, and showed her how the pad was attached to his waistband at the back of his trousers. "Okay?"

"Yes, I understand everything. I understand about the earpiece, too."

"What will you be wearing, Linnet?" he asked.

"A long skirt with a top, and a full-length silk coat. I chose that outfit because of all this stuff," she explained, indicating the envelope.

"Good girl. There's nobody like you, Linnet."

"I hope not," she shot back. Eyeing him appraisingly, she added, "You look very smart, Jack, very smart indeed."

"Thanks for the compliment. Where's Julian?"

"Upstairs in our bedroom, getting changed, and I'd better go up myself, get into my clothes. I promised Evan I'd help her." Linnet looked at the carriage clock on the mantelpiece and said, "Goodness, it's well past two already! I'd better hurry."

"Right, Beauty—" Jack broke off as his mobile rang. Pulling it out of his pocket, he said, "Hello?"

"Jack, it's Pete."

His operative sounded tense, upset. Jack exclaimed, "What's wrong?"

"The west wall of Pennistone Royal church just blew out."

"Oh, my God!"

Jack kept his voice low, but Linnet had heard his exclamation and seen his stricken face. She remained perfectly still as he stayed on the phone, listening intently.

Pete went on, "Somebody put explosives there, or a small bomb. People would've been killed, Jack, if they'd been in the church."

"I realize that. Have you informed the village police?"

"The vicar did."

"Are you all right, Pete? I know you're parked across from the church."

"I'm fine. So is Chuck, who's down the street."

"Where's Al?"

"On the riverbank . . . looking for yobbos. But there are none in sight."

"Where's the vicar, do you know?"

"He's standing a few feet away from me, examining the damage. He's with the sexton. Do you want to speak to him?"

"Yes, put him on."

"Right away."

A moment later the Reverend Henry Thorpe said, "What's going on, Mr. Figg? Do you know?"

"No, I don't, Reverend Thorpe, but I suspect it might be the work of somebody who's disgruntled with the family. And fortunately no one was hurt."

"Fortunately. And what do you want me to do?"

"I understand the police are there. Once they've done a thorough search of the church to make sure there's . . . nothing else *amiss*, the mess should be cleaned up and the hole covered with planks or boards, and tarpaulins. To keep the animals out."

"I'll see it's done."

"Could you put somebody else in charge, Vicar?" Jack now asked. "I do think it will look strange if you're not up here at three o'clock to attend the wedding reception."

"Of course I'll be there. I understand I must be present."

"Vicar?"

"Yes, Mr. Figg?"

"I think it might be more discreet, and certainly wiser, if this incident wasn't mentioned at the reception. It would be very disturbing to Mrs. O'Neill. Not to mention upsetting to the bride and groom if they thought they'd been targets."

"I understand, and I won't say a thing. However, the explosion was quite loud, and there are a few villagers hanging around, as we speak. What shall I tell them?"

"Nothing. Say you don't know what happened. Be vague. Act baffled. The less said the better."

"I'd better deal with Sergeant Lyons. He's in charge. I don't think I'll mention anything about *disgruntlement,* if you know what I mean."

"I certainly do, Vicar. And I think that's smart. I'll see you shortly. In the meantime, there are a number of my security men in the village. If you put Pete back on, I'll tell him to help you in any way he can. And remember, not a word about this when you get here."

"You don't have to worry about me, Mr. Figg," the vicar said firmly. "I'm giving the phone to Pete."

A moment later Pete said, "I'm on, Jack. I think it might have been a bomb. One which was probably planted during the night and triggered about ten past two."

"Sounds right to me, Pete. The church would have been full of Hartes at that time if we hadn't made the other plan. Stick close to the police, let them know you're there to help if they need you. I'm sure they won't. Just stay in touch."

"I will."

Jack closed down his mobile and looked at Linnet, who had remained glued to his side. He said softly, "The west wall of Pennistone Royal church blew out. Nobody's been hurt, but you will have gathered *that,* I'm sure. Pete, one of my operatives who's down there, thinks the bomb was planted during the night and triggered when the wedding was supposed to be starting. Around ten minutes past two."

Linnet had turned very pale, and she whispered vehemently, "It had to be Ainsley. There's no other explanation."

"But we can never prove it. And the police are not going to find any real evidence, only the remnants of the bomb. Trust me on that."

"What can we do?"

"Nothing, Linnet," Jack answered quietly, shaking his head. "The police will examine everything, check out the church to make sure it's safe, write up a report. Anyway, nothing else will happen at the church or in the village, rest assured of that."

"But Ainsley might still attempt to hurt Evan and Gideon."

"Not right now, he won't. He'll lay low. It's more than likely he'll leave Yorkshire, go back to Paris or Hong Kong. He's smart enough to realize that we've got our ears to the ground. He'll be very aware that we suspect him."

"That's what Mummy always says. We can't tell her about the bomb in the church, Jack." She stared at him, worry in her eyes.

"You're damned right we can't! Let's keep this as quiet as we can until tomorrow. Okay?"

Linnet nodded, biting her lip.

"You still look extremely pale, Beauty. And worried. You're going to have to put on that Emma Harte *face of inscrutability* before you come to the reception. And by the way, for God's sake don't say anything to Evan and Gideon."

"I wouldn't dream of it! I'm not stupid, Jack. But if it's all right, I will mention it to Julian."

"That's fine, but tell him not a word to anyone. We don't want to spoil their wedding reception, do we?"

"Never. I ruined their wedding by insisting on the secret ceremony."

"You saved their lives, Linnet," Jack murmured, his expression serious. "Never forget that."

16

～

Gideon Harte was furious. Angry words flew to his tongue, but before he could utter one of them he caught sight of his mother's face, saw the warning look on it, one he knew of old. He endeavored to swallow his anger, stepped closer to Evan; her fingers reached for his, and he held her hand tightly, loving her so much.

As he sought the appropriate words to address Owen Hughes, his wife saved him the trouble.

Evan said, "Dad, *please*. Don't go on like this. We're all as disappointed as you. But Gid and I are *married* now, and that's that."

"But we could have been there! Should have been there! We're your parents. Why didn't you invite us to come this morning?"

Ignoring the question, she said in a slightly weary voice, "After my fall, I've been a bit nervous, and the doctor cautioned me to take everything at a slower pace, so—"

"I didn't know you fell! Why wasn't I told?"

Again she avoided answering. "Listen to me, Dad. Gideon and I decided at the last minute to play it safe. A small wedding, no guests, just two witnesses. *No excitement. No fuss.* We knew we would celebrate at the reception here at Pennistone Royal, where I can go to bed if I'm feeling queasy or tired."

Gideon glanced at his father-in-law, saw the disgruntled look settling on his face, and thought: *the whining bugger.* He's thinking of himself, not of Evan. Gideon had long been aware that Owen Hughes didn't think much of the Hartes, and that he wasn't particularly impressed to have discovered he himself was one. He probably didn't like any of them. He was a man who was selfish to the extreme, and Gideon's sympathies lay very much with Marietta. He looked across at her now, and she gave him a faint, apologetic smile and shrugged lightly. He saw the discomfort in her eyes; she was sensitive, like Evan.

Owen said, "Well, I must admit I *am* disappointed—"

"I know that, Dad," Evan exclaimed, showing her irritation. "So is Mom. And also Emily and Winston. But *they* understand."

Marietta went across the sitting room, took hold of her husband's arm. "You're being a bit silly, Owen. The important thing is that Evan and Gideon are now married. You can have the enjoyment of taking your daughter into the reception . . . and to the strains of the wedding march. Just let it go now. *Please.*"

Owen gave her a strange look but made no response, simply tried to shake her hand off his arm. The odd couple, Gideon thought.

Winston now took charge, growing as impatient as Evan and his son. After glancing at Gideon, he turned to Owen. "I think it's a good idea if we leave the ladies to their own devices, give Evan a chance to get dressed."

Owen nodded and said to Evan, "I'll send Elayne and Angharad up to help you, honey."

"No, no! I don't want them!" Evan exclaimed without thinking and then, softening her voice, explained, "I have Mom and Emily, and that's fine. Truly, Dad, I don't need anybody else."

"But it's traditional for the sisters of the bride to help."

"I don't want them, Dad, and I'm not a normal bride.

And right now I can't stand people hovering over me, fussing."

"As you wish," he said in a clipped tone and headed for the door, looking more put out than ever.

Winston smiled lovingly at Evan, squeezed her shoulder as he walked past her. "See you downstairs, sweetheart. And whenever *you're* ready. Do take your time. People have been invited to stay through the evening, you know; there's no rush for you to make an appearance."

"Thank you, Winston," she replied, smiling at her father-in-law, a man she had grown to love, respect, and admire. He was so kind to her, the most considerate person she had ever known.

Gideon said, "I'll join you in a minute, Dad," and, turning, he looked at Evan and murmured, "Come on, darling, let's go into the bedroom for a moment, I want to talk to you."

Once they were alone in the adjoining bedroom of the Green Suite, Gideon put his arms around Evan and held her close. "Don't let your father upset you," he whispered against her hair. "He'll get over it."

"I know he will, and I'm not *upset* . . . just annoyed with him."

"Let it go, Evan, don't be annoyed with anybody. It's our wedding day. I'm so lucky . . ." He held her away, stared into her face. Never had he seen her look as delicate as she did today; there was a fragility about her that suddenly worried him. He noticed how pale she was, and her skin was almost translucent. He saw a small blue vein throbbing on her temple, and her mouth trembled slightly, made her seem childlike, very vulnerable. His heart clenched. He couldn't bear it when she was upset and cursed her father under his breath.

He bent into her, kissed her forehead. "I'm so lucky, the luckiest man alive. I love you very much, Evan, and I promise once again to love and protect you all the days of your life."

"Oh, Gideon, Gid darling . . . I promise the same." Gently, lovingly, she touched his cheek. "I'm all right, honestly I am, and I'm so glad we took Linnet's advice and got married without a fuss. I know it was because of our anxiety about Jonathan, but it *was* a wise move in reality because I do keep feeling queasy . . . I have all morning. I was glad to have a rest after breakfast."

"But you just said you were all right! Are you sure you don't need the doctor?" Worry clouded his face, and he peered at her intently.

"No, of course I don't. The queasy feeling comes and goes, and I promise you I'm not about to drop the twins in your lap." She smiled at him. "But too much fuss or excitement does get to me, I guess."

"Then take it easy, as Dad said you should. Don't hurry, get dressed leisurely. Do you need me to get anything for you?"

She shook her head. "I'm going to do my makeup, and then Mom and Emily can help me into my clothes."

"Come on then." He led her across the room to the kidney-shaped dressing table in the bay window. Once she was seated on the stool, he kissed the top of her head. "I'll tell our mothers to come in, shall I?"

Swiveling to face him, Evan said softly, "Not for fifteen minutes. I need to collect myself, do my hair as well as the makeup." She grinned up at him. "Just a little peace and quiet for a while, Gid."

He nodded, passed his hand over her hair. "Your wish is my command, madam." With a smile and a wink he crossed the room, paused at the door and blew her a kiss, then went out.

The moment he stepped back into the sitting room of the suite, Marietta said, "Is Evan feeling ill?"

"No, not really. A little queasy, she said, but she's fine actually. Please don't worry."

"I could've killed her father. He just doesn't know when to shut up." Marietta shook her head, her expression one of exasperation.

"He did go on a bit," Gideon agreed, smiling warmly at Marietta, a woman he genuinely liked. "But Evan didn't pay too much heed to him. She's rather preoccupied with getting herself ready for the reception, amongst other things, like preparing for twins . . . et cetera, et cetera."

His mother smiled. "Yes, we're all a little preoccupied with the soon-to-arrive additions to the family, Gid. And so we must just excuse Owen for flogging a dead horse. And after all, he *is* disappointed."

"Not more than you, Dad, and Marietta," Gideon couldn't help pointing out. "But you're right, Mother, let's not hold a grudge. Evan needs a while to do her hair and makeup; she wants to be alone. As soon as she's ready for you both, she'll invite you in. Okay?"

"Very okay," Emily answered. "And later we'll all meet up in the library. The flowers for the men's buttonholes are on a card table in there. White carnations. And there are sprays of orchids for the bride's attendants. But I'm sure Linnet's got that in hand."

"I'll see to it that the men have flowers in their buttonholes. Linnet can look after the ladies. And by the way, you both look smashing, Mum . . . Marietta. Very elegant indeed."

"Thanks, Gideon," Marietta responded, very much appreciating her son-in-law, a man of great quality in her opinion. Evan was lucky, luckier than anyone she knew, because she had married the man of her dreams. And who cared when and how they got married, as long as they were happy together and committed to each other? What a fool Owen was at times; she suspected he felt overshadowed by the Harte family. Inadequate perhaps? She wasn't sure of that, but she did know he was ready to go home as soon as possible after this weekend. She was planning on staying; after all, it wasn't every day that a woman became a grandmother to twins.

Emily glided over to her son and took hold of his arm, led him to the window. "She's not upset, is she?"

"No, Ma, she's not. *Annoyed*, though. I told her not to be. After all, it's our wedding day, and I don't want anything to mar it."

"It won't, my darling." Wanting to get off the subject of Owen once she knew Evan was fine, Emily remarked, "I'm glad you think I look elegant. Evan created my outfit. Isn't she a clever girl?"

Gideon agreed, then, noticing the design, he commented, "It looks like an antique tapestry. Is it?"

"Indeed it is! Evan discovered it in the attics here. Grandy must have bought it years ago, intending to have something made and never did."

Emily now stepped away from her son, slowly turned around so that he could get the full benefit of the design on the back of the coat. The tapestry was grayish blue overall, the actual design woven in red and violet, soft yellows, pale orange, and sage green. The evening coat was trimmed around the edges with a narrow border of brown fox, and the cuffs were also made of fox.

"It's the lady and the unicorn," Gideon exclaimed. "And the cut is superb, Ma. Did Evan make your dress as well?"

"Yes. I asked for something very simple in pale gray, and she came up with this long silk sheath." Emily laughed, her eyes dancing. "It's like a lovely, long sweater, so easy to wear."

"I'm afraid I wasn't so lucky," Marietta murmured. "Evan didn't design my outfit. I only wish she had."

"But you do look lovely!" Emily exclaimed. "Only a blonde like you can wear those soft golds and browns. And I'm glad for your sake you chose palazzo pants and a long jacket, Marietta. Even with central heating and blazing fires, Pennistone Royal tends to be drafty in winter."

"Well, ladies, I'd better be on my way," Gideon announced. "Dad'll be wondering where I am. Also, I want to have a word with Jack Figg. I'll see you both later."

As soon as the door closed behind Gideon, Marietta said quietly, "I'm sorry Owen's been difficult, Emily—"

"Marietta, please don't apologize!" Emily exclaimed, cutting in. "He's disappointed because he didn't get to walk his daughter down the aisle. You know what fathers are like."

Marietta inclined her head, went and stood near the fireplace, staring into the flames. She remained quiet, a reflective look settling on her face. Emily suddenly realized she was still feeling embarrassed by her husband's rather silly behavior and instantly decided that silence was the best way to handle the situation. Any comments she could make would only upset Marietta more.

Emily walked across the green-and-white sitting room and stood looking in the elaborate, gilt-framed mirror over the Georgian chest. She liked the way she looked today, was pleased with her new haircut and the honey-blond shade concocted by her hairdresser.

Emily was a typical Harte—blond, green-eyed, and fair of complexion, but the bright blond hair of her youth had deepened in the last few years, and there were now strands of silver in her tresses. The solution had been this warm honey tone, which, she now decided, was rather flattering.

"I think Evan's been so lucky, having met and married Gideon," Marietta suddenly announced, startling Emily out of her reverie.

She swung around to stare at the other woman and nodded. "Gideon's lucky, too," Emily replied. "Evan's a lovely young woman, and we all took to her right from the start."

A thoughtful look slid onto Marietta's face, and she seemed about to say something, then hesitated.

Emily watched her, waiting for a moment before saying, "Is there something you want to tell me, Marietta? You look a bit troubled."

"No, I'm not, but Owen . . . well, he's been going on at me about Gideon and Evan being related, being cousins. It doesn't matter to me, but I need to shut him up. So . . . well, I was wondering . . . could you explain . . ." Her voice trailed off helplessly.

"It's perfectly legal in this country to marry your cousin, you know. Even first cousins can marry," Emily told her. "But as a matter of fact, Evan and Gideon are *not* first cousins. They're second cousins. Here's how the lines of descent evolved, Marietta. Emma Harte, my grandmother, had a brother Winston. We call him Winston the First in the family." She laughed and went on. "Winston the First had a son whom he named Randolph, and Randolph had a son whom he named Winston, after his father. *That* Winston, Winston Harte the Second, is my husband . . . Gideon's father." Emily stared hard at Marietta and asked, "You do understand that line, right?"

"Yes, of course."

"Now, to Evan. Her great-grandmother is Emma Harte, because of Emma's son Robin Ainsley. As you know, it was Robin who had an affair with Glynnis, your mother-in-law, during the war years, and made her pregnant."

"I understand that, too, but Evan said something about Emma being Gideon's great-grandmother. She would be his great-great-aunt, wouldn't she?"

"She's both," Emily answered. "Through his great-grandfather, Winston the First, Emma *is* Gideon's great-great-aunt. But she is also Gideon's great-grandmother, because Emma was *my* grandmother."

"However do you keep it straight?" Marietta asked, laughing. "I'm sure I couldn't."

"Yes, you could, if you'd grown up with it, as we all have. But there's nothing to worry about, you know, as far as the twins are concerned. They'll be perfectly all right;

there won't be any genetic defects because Evan and Gideon are related."

"Oh, I know that, and anyway, Evan had all the tests and everything's normal. It's just that—" She stopped, shook her head. "Owen is a worrywart." There was a small pause, and then she confided, "He drives me crazy at times."

"I can well imagine," Emily blurted out sympathetically and could've bitten her tongue off. A small flush crept onto her neck.

Marietta burst out laughing, then confided further, "That's why I'm glad he's going to go back to the States after the weekend! But I'm staying on. I want to be here for the birth of my grandchildren."

Emily smiled at Marietta warmly and walked across the floor, took hold of her arm in an affectionate way. She murmured, "I'm so happy you're going to be here for the arrival of the twins, and I just want you to know you are welcome to stay with us at Allington Hall whenever you wish."

For a split second Marietta was taken aback, then she said, "That's so kind of you, thank you very much. Evan told me yesterday that she and Gideon are not moving to Beck House until after the twins are born. She explained there were a lot of things still unfinished."

"That's right," Emily replied, nodding. "Anyway, in my opinion Evan's better off in London until the weather's better. I don't know why the two of them thought they could trot up here to Beck House every weekend. Evan seems to suffer from the cold, just like my grandmother did. Emma was always complaining that she was freezing to death. And it's a lot colder up here than it is in the south. Mind you, I expect they'll come up some weekends and stay at Pennistone Royal while things are being finished at Beck House. Winston's volunteered to help them."

"Yes, he would, he's such a nice man."

Emily merely smiled.

Marietta said, "You grew up with him, didn't you?"

"I did indeed, and I was madly in love with him by the time I was sixteen. But he hardly noticed me. He was off with Shane, chasing the girls. My heart was always breaking because of that."

"So how did you two finally get together?"

"It was at the christening of Tessa and Lorne at Fairley Church, over thirty years ago now. Gosh, so *long* . . . how time flies. A bit of a problem arose that day about Shane, and my grandmother gave me the third degree about it, and Winston, too. Afterward, we went for a walk, commiserating with each other. And I can't tell you how it came about, but he suddenly kissed me. And *wow*! That was that!" Emily shook her head. "I couldn't believe it, couldn't believe we were suddenly in each other's arms. And we have been ever since."

"That's such a lovely story," Marietta murmured and swiftly turned away, a sudden sorrow washing over her face.

Emily said, "Are you all right?"

"Oh, yes, I was just remembering . . . something similar that happened to me long ago. But it didn't have your happy ending."

"I'm sorry. Do you want to talk about it?"

"I don't know—*perhaps*. Well, yes, why not?" Marietta sat down on the sofa as she spoke, and Emily joined her, listened attentively while Marietta confided one of the saddest stories she had ever heard.

She wanted them to leave—her father and her sisters.

Her mother was staying on for the birth of the twins, and this was fine with Evan. Her mother was comforting, soothing, and always loving. Her father and her sisters were irritants.

Well, no, not Elayne, who was as quiet as a mouse, sweet and simple and as adoring as she had always been. But Angharad was a dangerous presence.

As for her father, he was difficult and grudging these days, prone to temperamental outbursts if he didn't like something. His first complaint was about Allington Hall. He was put out because it was a racing stable, one of the finest in England and forever busy, teeming with horses, stable boys and girls, other helpers, and jockeys. She loved the bustle at Allington Hall, especially during their week, when everything was flying at full speed, and she also shared Gideon's pride and excitement when one of their horses had a big win.

Her father found the whole atmosphere distasteful, the stable staff a nuisance, and he had told her so the first time he had gone over there to meet her future in-laws, last September. And so she had not been surprised at his annoyance when he discovered he and Marietta were staying there for the period of the wedding, instead of at Lackland Priory with Robin.

Evan had endeavored to placate him, explaining, "Listen, Dad, Jonathan's back in Yorkshire, and everyone feels it's wiser for you and Mom to make Allington Hall your base. You see, if Jonathan should come over to visit his father and bump into you, there could be a lot of unpleasantness."

"So what! I can handle that, handle him," her father had blustered, and she had simply turned away, adding that the decision had already been made. She pointed out she could do nothing about it, and neither could he, unless he preferred to stay at a hotel in Harrogate. "It's up to you," she had added.

At one point, trying to engage his interest, she had told him some of the history of the stables, how they had been founded by Gideon's grandfather Randolph Harte, who had become one of the most famous trainers and breeders in England. It was Randolph who had been in

charge of Blackie O'Neill's string of racehorses, which
were stabled there, including the renowned mare Emerald Bow. This was the horse which Emma Harte had
given to Blackie as a gift, and Randolph had specially
trained her to run in the Grand National at Aintree. It was
the greatest steeplechase in the world, a difficult course,
with some hazardous obstacles, including the famed
Beecher's Brook, which had to be jumped twice during
the race.

When Emerald Bow won the Grand National the year
she was run, the three clans had been exultant, proud of
the courageous young mare who had sailed over the difficult brook twice with the greatest of ease, winning the
steeplechase and proving herself to be the best.

Now that Randolph Harte was dead, the stables were
in the hands of the Colonel, as he was known. Colonel
Humphrey Swale, formerly of the British army, was an
extraordinary trainer who had worked with Randolph in
the last years of his life and been handpicked by him to
take over one day.

Winston, Toby, and Gideon loved the stables as much
as Randolph had, but since they were occupied with the
day-to-day running of the family-owned newspapers and
television network, they were happy to leave the stables
in the capable hands of the Colonel, who had maintained
the success and profitability of Randolph's years.

Evan remembered now how she had led her father
into the study at Allington Hall one afternoon last week.
It was her favorite room, a charming spot with dark green
walls, green tartan carpet, comfy, worn-leather sofas and
armchairs, and a collection of fine country antiques. Taking pride of place in the study were the many gleaming
cups and colorful ribbons which proclaimed the stables
to be one of the finest in Yorkshire, indeed in England.
But he had shown no interest at all in the room, its decor,
the Stubbs paintings, the antiques, or the trophies, had
merely muttered that horses and horse racing bored him.

Evan let out a deep sigh, thinking how much her father had changed lately. Or perhaps he hadn't. Perhaps she simply saw him through different eyes these days, perhaps clearer eyes . . . and how he did annoy her at times.

Sitting up straighter on the stool, she pushed this thought away at once, remembering Gideon's earlier words. He was right. It was their wedding day, and she should not be annoyed with anyone. It should be a day of happiness and joy. After all, it was the most important day of her life; she wasn't going to spoil it for herself. Nor was she going to permit her father or Angharad to spoil it.

Leaning forward, Evan stared at her image in the mirror. She was pale, washed out, needed to make herself look pretty for her husband. And so, armed with foundations, powders, blushes, and eye makeup, she set to work bringing color and life to her face. Then she brushed the dark cloud of hair away from her face and forehead, took it back and around her ears, coaxed it into a soft, sleek pageboy.

A few moments later she stood up, went to open the door into the sitting room, announced to her mother and mother-in-law, "Mom, Emily, I'm ready. Can you help me into my dress, please?"

The two women jumped up and hurried to join her, and both exclaimed, almost in unison, "You look beautiful!"

Within seconds Evan was stepping into her gown and being zipped up, and then she slowly turned around to show Marietta and Emily the overall effect of her special creation. They gasped in surprise.

The gown was cut in the French Empire style, which had been favored by Empress Josephine. It had a square neck, a very high waistline, and long, narrow sleeves. The dress was created from several layers of chiffon, and these fell away from under the bustline, the fullness cleverly camouflaging her pregnancy.

The design was lovely, but it was the color that

stunned. It was not one color in actuality but various shades of blue to green, each one ombréed into the next, deep pavonian blue shading into pale sky blue, the sky blue changing to turquoise, the turquoise ombréed into the palest of greens. The effect was sensational.

As Evan turned again, very slowly, the chiffon drifted around her in an eye-catching mélange of sea colors, and Emily said softly, "It's like that wonderful beaded cocktail dress of Grandy's, Evan, the one Linnet and you used in the fashion retrospective last year. It inspired you, didn't it?"

"Yes it did, Emily," she acknowledged and smiled. "I just loved the colors of that gown, and I was lucky when I stumbled onto this ombréed blue chiffon at the Renaud Brantes fabric showroom. *Very lucky,* I thought."

"It's exceptional, Evan," Marietta said, "all the colors of the sea." Her voice was low, almost inaudible, and she continued to stare at her daughter almost in awe, thinking how beautiful Evan truly looked, and then Marietta suddenly exclaimed, "But it's also the colors found in a peacock's tail, isn't it?"

"Why, yes it is," Emily said, and Evan nodded in agreement.

"Don't you have a coat?" Marietta then asked, suddenly worried.

"Yes, I do." Evan walked across to the armoire, opened the door, and took the coat off the hanger. "It's made of the same chiffon, three layers," Evan explained and handed it to her mother. "If you can hold it for me, Mom, please."

Marietta did as she asked, and Evan slipped into the floor-length coat, then turned toward the cheval mirror and settled it on her shoulders properly. It was a simple design, with a full swing back and straight panels at the front; the collar, cuffs, and edges were trimmed with a rolled band of bugle beads, which reiterated all the shades of blue and green in the gown.

"Honey, it's just lovely," Marietta murmured, "but I do hope you'll be warm enough. Emily says the house is drafty."

"I'll be fine," Evan reassured her mother. "Actually, it's silk chiffon, which is quite warm when it's layered. Now, all I need are Emily's diamond earrings and Paula's diamond star pin, and I'm ready."

"*Your* earrings, *your* pin," Emily corrected. She moved across the room, leaned closer to Evan, and kissed her on the cheek. "You are indeed the most beautiful bride, Evan, and I'm happy and proud to have you as my new daughter."

17

ℰ

Nettled by what he perceived as his daughter's extreme
indifference to him, and still feeling slighted because he
had not been invited to the early morning wedding ceremony, Owen Hughes meandered into the Stone Hall
looking unhappy, even morose.

As he glanced around, he forgot about his displeasure
for a moment, impressed by the beauty of the hall this afternoon. It had been transformed in the last few hours.
He had to give Paula and Emily their due. No two ways
about it, the Stone Hall was looking fantastic, had a fairy-
tale feeling.

Paula's pride and joy were her glass houses where she
grew her orchids, many of which were exotic and rare.
She had given him a tour the other day, and he had been
amazed by the extent of her collection and the variety of
the hundreds of plants.

Now some sixty or so of these orchids in glazed cream
ceramic pots graced the Stone Hall. There were snow-
white orchids, white orchids tinged with pink or with
deep pink centers, all kinds of pink orchids, solid in
color, or speckled or veined with white; mixtures of these
were grouped on the mantelpieces, and on chests and tables placed around the hall; or stood in corners on special
wooden stands of different heights. Others were used as

centerpieces on the round tables which had been set out
for the wedding luncheon.

The latter were covered with floor-length pink silk
cloths; there were pink silk cushions on the small gold
chairs, which were trimmed with large pink satin bows.
These tables and chairs were grouped around a small
dance floor, which had been put down in the middle of
the Stone Hall, near the fireplace. Already lamps had
been turned on, a huge fire blazed in the tall stone
hearth, and overall the scene was lovely, had a welcoming
warmth to it.

It pleased Owen that Paula and Emily had created this
setting for Evan, and he felt a lifting of his bellicose
mood. As he moved amongst the tables, heading for the
library, he noticed that his place card was on one of the
large tables. He saw at once that he was seated between
Emily and Paula, and this cheered him even more. It was
a place of honor, befitting the father of the bride.

Marietta had been seated between Robin, his father,
and Shane. That would please her; she liked both men,
particularly Shane O'Neill, with whom she flirted outrageously he had noticed, much to his chagrin.

Owen frowned as he moved on, thinking of the way
Marietta had brushed aside his complaints this morning.
She hadn't seemed to care that Evan had gone off and
married Gideon without asking them to be present. But
then that was just like Marietta these days . . . she was
something else. How she had changed, how independent
she had become. It was the inheritance; her aunt's will
had made her a rich woman, given her a new lease on life
and certainly a wholly different attitude. It was an attitude he didn't particularly like. Because she was child-
less, her Aunt Dottie had left Marietta everything, her
apartment in California, all of her money and invest-
ments. It was the aunt who had even convinced her to go
to a new doctor before she'd died.

It irritated him that his wife was staying on in London,

that he hadn't been able to persuade her to leave with him next week. She fully intended to remain in England for the birth of the twins, who were not due until the end of February, or early March. So be it, he thought, and then paused as he heard his name being called.

Owen swung around, found himself almost, but not quite, face-to-face with Priscilla Marney, the caterer, whom he had met earlier in the week.

He smiled at her. "Hello, Miss Marney."

"Good afternoon, Mr. Hughes. And you must call me Priscilla, or better, Prissy, as everyone does. Can I get you anything? Would you like a drink, perhaps? The waiters will be coming out in fifteen to twenty minutes, but I can go to the kitchen, bring you a glass of wine."

"No, no, Priscilla, but thanks anyway. I was just strolling through, admiring the Stone Hall."

"It's charming, isn't it? Paula and Emily have done a great job."

"Yes indeed," he said, wondering why she called them by their first names.

As if reading his thoughts, Prissy said, "That must sound rude to you, my use of their Christian names, but—"

"Oh, no, it doesn't," he cut in swiftly, smiling at her. He liked her.

"You see, we all grew up together. My mother was Mrs. Harte's summer secretary when she was at Heron's Nest, her seaside house in Scarborough. She always had her grandchildren to stay: Paula and Philip; Emily and her brother, Sandy, who's dead now; Sarah and Jonathan, and her great-nephew Winston. And Shane always came, too, and sometimes Michael Kallinski. Anyway, we all played together, shared our summers when we were youngsters."

"It must have been a lot of fun."

"It was. We were great chums." A faint smile played across her mouth as she added, "Paula and Emily have been good to me, using my catering service."

"You're good at what you do, Priscilla, the dinner was terrific the other night. Very good indeed."

"Thank you, that's kind of you to say so."

"So you know my half brother, Jonathan . . ." He let the sentence slide away, not wanting to probe too much.

"Oh, yes, we're great friends." Immediately Priscilla knew she'd said too much and quickly corrected herself. "What I mean is, we *were* good friends, a long time ago. I haven't seen him in years." She always felt the need to protect Jonny and their special relationship; he had warned her not to let anyone in the family know about them. Or anyone else, for that matter. And she would never let Jonny down. She thought of their date for next Wednesday, and a little thrill ran through her. "Well, I must be off, Mr. Hughes!" she exclaimed. "I've got my hands full today."

"I understand. And call me Owen," he said to her retreating figure.

Elayne Hughes stood in the grand, very formal dining room at Pennistone Royal, where all of the wedding presents were on show, laid out on the long mahogany dining table, and on other tables set up for this purpose. She was staring at the picture she had painted herself as a wedding present for Evan and Gideon, studying it really.

It was displayed in a prominent place, propped up on an easel which stood on top of a Georgian chest. She nodded, liking it even more than she had when she had finished it. She had chosen to paint a spot Evan knew, a field near the family farm in Kent, Connecticut, golden corn blowing in the breeze, set against the dark green Litchfield Hills, a bright blue sky filled with puffball white clouds floating high above, and, in one corner, three red barns and two gray silos, so very typical of the area where they had grown up. She was glad now that she had had the painting framed; somehow, the ornate, gilded frame made all the difference, gave the painting a sense of substance, even of importance, and this pleased her.

Elayne knew that Evan and Gideon loved it, especially Evan, since it was a reminder of home for her. *Home.* No, Connecticut wasn't home anymore, not for Evan. Yorkshire was her home now. And London, of course, where her beloved Harte's store stood in Knightsbridge. Elayne had the feeling that Evan had come into her own skin *here,* in this beautiful county, in this extraordinary and quite magnificent house. She was happy for Evan, who had always been special, and so loving and protective of her when she was growing up. Unlike Angharad. Their younger sister had been mean-spirited, constantly playing pranks on them both, telling lies about them to their grandmother Glynnis, and getting them into trouble with their mother. Deep down, Elayne disliked Angharad intensely, although she tried not to show it. Angharad was not the kind of person she had any desire to upset.

Stepping away from the painting, Elayne moved slowly around the table, admiring the other gifts. Their parents had given Evan and Gideon a beautiful silver tea service, Georgian naturally, since their father was an expert on everything from the Georgian period. Leaning closer, peering at the card propped up against the silver teapot, Elayne saw that Angharad's name was on it as well. So their sister hadn't wanted to give Evan a separate gift after all. How typical of her. Elayne knew she was jealous of Evan, and of her; Angharad thought they had been forever favored, usually referred to herself as "the low girl on the totem pole." How ridiculous she was at times. And how ridiculous she looked with her dyed, platinum blond hair, all that heavy makeup, and such gaudy clothes.

At least today Angharad was dressed elegantly, since she was wearing her bridesmaid outfit. Evan had designed it, a simple, floor-length A-line gown with a tight

bodice and long sleeves. It had a high-standing collar at
the sides and back, somewhat like a half ruff, and the
style and cut of the gown were Elizabethan. Made of an
expensive moiré taffeta, pearl gray in color, it was worn
over a stiffened petticoat, which made the skirt stand out
properly. Angharad looked good in the gown, but then
they all did. She and Natalie, Gideon's sister, and Emsie
were the other grown-up bridesmaids, while Adele,
Tessa's little daughter, was the flower girl. She had the
same gown in miniature; Elayne thought she looked
adorable, and the soft gray suited them all.

The wedding present from Robin, Evan's grandfather
and Gideon's great-uncle, was spectacular, a huge, red
leather box lined in black velvet, and holding twenty
chased silver wine goblets. Instantly, Elayne thought of
Jonathan. Angharad was convinced he would be at the
wedding, was itching to meet him again after having run
into him in the newspaper shop in the village. But he
wouldn't be there. He wasn't invited because he was the
black sheep of the family and Paula's bitter enemy. Evan
had confided this to Elayne the other day. But Elayne
hadn't repeated it to Angharad. Why would she break a
confidence? Anyway, let Angharad look for him and be
disappointed; he was old enough to be her father. Her sister had apparently flirted with him in the shop. She was
more than ridiculous, she was crazy. Not to mention
promiscuous.

"There you are," Owen exclaimed from the doorway.
"I've been looking all over for you, honey."

Elayne swung around and broke into smiles. "Dad,
you look wonderful. So handsome in your blue suit with
your white carnation. Come see my painting, so well displayed. Doesn't it look great?"

"It sure does, Ellie," he responded, smiling back as he
walked toward her, thinking she cut quite a swath in the
gray gown with her dark hair and large blue eyes. People
who didn't know she was adopted often said how much

she resembled him, and actually she did. Marietta once remarked that they'd grown to look alike, but he thought that was a stupid thing to say. How could you grow to look like someone?

Coming to a standstill, he gazed at the painting for a long moment, then nodded. "It's one of your best," he said at last, beaming at her.

"Dad! Dad, have you seen Mom?" Angharad cried, rushing into the dining room. "Your father's looking for her." She hurried toward Owen and Elayne, almost stumbling over herself, looking flushed, a little flustered.

"Calm down, Angharad!" Owen was startled by her headlong swoop toward them and went on, "She can't have gone very far. Maybe she's still upstairs with Evan."

"Oh, by the way, why weren't we allowed to help our sister dress?" Angharad demanded, her search for Marietta suddenly forgotten. "It's traditional that the bride's sisters help her get ready for her wedding."

"I know. But circumstances are not quite normal, are they?" Owen replied. "Evan is very heavily pregnant. She doesn't feel too well, and she's awfully big."

Angharad nodded, smiled, and said spitefully, "Like she's going to drop four infant whales and not twin babies."

Owen ignored this comment, but Elayne couldn't stop herself from exclaiming, "Why are you always so bitchy about Evan? You're mean and ungrateful. She's never been anything but nice to you all of your life, and all you want to do is make nasty comments."

"Tut-tut, Elayne, don't lose your temper on her wedding day. She'd be so put out, would think you're vulgar, now that she's become such a snob."

"No, she hasn't," Elayne shot back. "She hasn't changed at all, and you know it."

"Girls, no quarreling, please. Not today. And especially not here. And why does my father want to see your mother?" Owen asked Angharad, staring at her.

"How the hell do I know?" she snapped. "He said something about wanting to be seated near you at the luncheon, wanted her to check."

"Oh. I see. I don't believe he can be, actually. He's seated next to Marietta. I noticed his place card when I walked through the Stone Hall. Please go and tell him that, honey, and we'll be with you in a second. I just want to take a look at the other gifts. I hadn't realized they were on display until Gideon told me."

"Okay, but hurry up. I don't want to get stuck with Robin."

Owen watched her retreating figure, asking himself why it was he was beginning to distrust her. Elayne's correct, she's bitchy, he thought. And that's not all. She's devious, just as my mother used to say. Glynnis was right, as usual.

The moment she walked into the library, Linnet knew that Jack had told Shane about the explosion at the church. She was close to her father and she knew his every expression. He was disturbed, she could tell that. He stood with Jack and Winston at the fireplace.

Hurrying to join them, she lost no time in asking, "Jack told you about the church, didn't he, Daddy?"

Shane looked at her and inclined his head. "He did, Linnet, and I can only say thank God for your foresight. Because of your brain wave to change the time of the ceremony, no one was killed."

"It was all Jonathan's doing. But we'll never prove it," Linnet answered. "More's the pity."

"That's absolutely true," Shane agreed. "However, I don't think we have to worry about Jonathan at the moment. He achieved what he set out to do . . . which was to upset us all, make us apprehensive."

Linnet stared at her father. "But he meant to kill us, didn't he?"

"That's the general idea, I think. Nevertheless, he has the satisfaction of knowing he's truly thrown us, and I'm certain that this gives him a degree of pleasure. Upsetting the Hartes has become his favorite hobby."

"He won't be back for a while," Jack volunteered, staring at Linnet.

"You mean he's not in Yorkshire?" Linnet asked, frowning, her green eyes suddenly filled with puzzlement.

"He's back in London. I think he'll stay put, or at least he won't come back up to Yorkshire. He might go to Paris, of course." Jack shook his head and went on. "I have a bit of surprising news for you, Linnet. He had a visitor yesterday morning before he left."

"Who?" she asked, her eyes narrowing as she searched Jack's face.

He threw her a knowing look.

"Not *Angharad*? Don't tell me she had the nerve to go over to Thirsk to see him?"

"She did indeed."

"When did you find that out?"

"A short while ago. Yesterday, the operative tailing Jonathan saw a woman in a head scarf and dark glasses visit him at his home, and he made a note of the number plate on her car. He checked it out later in the day. Then, when he heard about the explosion at the church, he thought he'd better tell me about her. The car is registered to Winston." As he spoke, he glanced at Winston, who nodded.

"So she borrowed your car, is that it?" Linnet said.

"One of the stable cars, actually, Linnet," Winston answered. "Apparently she phoned Emily from Edwina's, asked if she could come over, borrow a car to go sightseeing. Emily said of course she could. It was Edwina's driver who dropped her off at Allington Hall."

"Well, well, well. She doesn't waste any time, does she?" Linnet muttered. "The odds are she'll see him in

London . . . if *he's* interested, that is. What do you think? The three of you know him." Her eyes roamed over Jack, her father, and Winston, held their collective gaze.

"He'll see her, if only to pump her for information," Jack announced, sounding positive.

"Or he could be interested in her as a woman," Winston suggested.

"That's true," Shane muttered. "He harbors a weakness for women, always has, and the younger the better."

"You'd better have her watched, Jack," Linnet exclaimed.

"I'd already thought of *that,* Beauty. It's done."

Shane took a step forward, put his arm around his daughter, and pulled her closer. "Don't worry, darling, at least not this weekend. Jonathan Ainsley's out of the way, and I'm positive nothing else is going to happen."

"Sometimes things happen when he's *not around.* Usually most of the time, wouldn't you say, Dad?"

"True," Shane murmured, hugging her tighter. "However, as I pointed out a moment ago, he's thrown a spanner in the works, and that's enough for him."

"Oh, Daddy, I hope so."

She sounded so forlorn, she who was always cheerful, upbeat, and stoical, that Shane looked down at her, put his hand under her chin. Staring into her upturned face, he said, "Come on, get it together, Linnet. You're a Harte and an O'Neill, and you're married to a Kallinski. *You* are the embodiment of the three clans. You've got to play that role today. Nothing less will do, my darling. You must be the very best of all of us."

She nodded, took a deep breath.

Leaning down, Shane kissed her forehead. "That's my girl . . . *our* girl."

"This is it, chaps," Winston said, straightening to his full height. "Here come the troops, the bridesmaids, the ushers, and the bridegroom as well."

"I'd better go and help the girls with their sprays."

Linnet gave her father a huge smile and glided across the library.

"Hello, Adele darling," she said, when she spotted the three-year-old. "You look so pretty."

"Thank you, Auntie Linnet," the child responded. "Mumma says I'm going to carry a nosegay."

"That's right, sweetheart, and here it is." Linnet put the miniature bouquet in her niece's hands and kissed the top of her silver-blond head.

Angharad sidled over to Linnet, holding the spray of small green orchids, and asked, "Where exactly am I supposed to pin this?" Her voice was so shrill Adele drew closer to Linnet, looking a little afraid. Linnet took hold of her hand.

"Just below your shoulder, on the left side." Linnet indicated her own spray, which was already pinned to the lapel of her jacket. "A bit higher than mine, though."

Angharad nodded, glanced around, and exclaimed, "Oh, there's a mirror on the wall there. Come on, Elayne." They rushed across the room.

Emsie came over to her sister and whispered in Linnet's ear, "That adoptee is definitely gross."

"Shhh. Someone might hear you, and you'll catch it."

"You started it," Emsie shot back and then grinned at Linnet and asked, "How do I look?"

Linnet couldn't help laughing. "You've become awfully conscious of your appearance these days, Emsie, my lass. You who never cared at all, were always in the tack room grooming the horses. What's going on?"

"I made a decision," Emsie announced and looked over her shoulder at Natalie, Gideon's sister. "I'm going to work on one of our newspapers like Natty does."

"Are you now?" Linnet raised a brow and said teasingly, "I always understood you were going to be a jockey."

"I never said *that*!" the seventeen-year-old protested, flushing. "And you know it."

Linnet merely smiled and said to Natalie, "Pick your spray, dear one, and I'll pin it on for you. Yours, too, Emsie, if you bring it."

Natalie hurried to Linnet and hugged her. These two were great friends; they had bonded as children, and they actually looked more like sisters than like cousins. Natalie Harte had inherited Emma's red hair, just as Linnet had, along with her green eyes and pretty complexion.

Stepping away from Linnet, Natalie said, "I suppose Mummy is with Evan and Marietta."

"Yes, they're upstairs. They'll come down about two forty-five. I thought we could get one or two photographs of the bride and groom, with the bridesmaids and groomsmen, before we all go into the reception. What do you think?"

"The three photographers are all set up, Linnet, just the way you wanted. I have one in the Cream-and-Gold Drawing Room, and another in the Gray Sitting Room. I kept the Peach Drawing Room free for the reception, as you said. The third photographer has a setup ready in the Garden Room. This way, everyone can move from one room to the next, and with the setup more or less in place, the photographs will be done quickly."

"Thanks for organizing this for me, Natalie, I really appreciate it."

Natalie was staring hard at Linnet and didn't say a word for a moment. Then in a low voice she hissed, "Are you wearing an earpiece and mike?"

"Keep your voice down. Yes, I am, so I can stay in touch with Jack."

"I see. But *why*?" Natalie probed, riddled with curiosity.

"To make sure everything's running smoothly, that's all," Linnet fibbed and turned to Emsie. "Just look at you, Emsie, you are a silly goose, you've got the orchid practically upside down. Come here, let me fix it."

"Oh, there's Great-Aunt Edwina and Uncle Robin!"

Natalie said suddenly, sounding excited. Handing her orchid to Linnet, she asked, "Can you do me first, please, so I can go to Edwina? I just adore her, and she does need looking after."

"Like the Earl of Warwick in his armor astride his destrier needed looking after," Linnet scoffed. "She could be Warwick's second in command, in fact. She looks as if she's about to lead a charge into the Lancastrian hordes."

Emsie giggled, and it took Natalie a lot of self-control to keep her face straight. Linnet could be very amusing at times.

"Gosh, she's coming this way," Emsie muttered. "Quick, Linnet, get my orchid on." Emsie looked down when she felt a tug on her dress and frowned. "What's wrong, Adele?"

"Where's Mumma?"

"I think she went with Grandma to the Stone Hall." Taking hold of the child's hand firmly, she added, "We'll go and find her in a second."

Adele smiled up at her, clinging to her hand. "All right, Emsie."

Edwina said, "Ah, Adele, my darling girl, you look a picture today, you do indeed. A very pretty picture."

"Thank you, Great-Aunt Edwina. So do you."

Edwina chuckled at this unexpected comment. "Out of the mouths of babes and sucklings," she murmured and turning added, "Good afternoon, ladies. And you are both so fair and charming in your lovely frocks. And you, Linnet, should always wear pale blue."

"As you must always wear purple, Great-Aunt," Linnet answered.

He felt like part of them, and they thought of him as family, yet he was the outsider.

Jack Figg was well aware of this, but it did not trouble

him one iota. He cared about them all in different ways, loved some more than others; in a sense, they were his only family now, with all of his blood relatives dead and buried.

It was just before three o'clock, and he stood in the Gray Sitting Room watching in amusement as his two favorite redheads, Linnet and Natalie, bustled like sergeant majors, lining up the family for the big wedding portrait the photographer was impatiently waiting to take.

His eyes followed the two young women alertly, and as he noticed how skillfully they moved people around, he realized that what they were working out had a lot to do with the color coordination of the clothes. They both held clipboards and kept conferring with each other, stepping back and viewing the group as a whole.

How clever. Somebody, more than likely Evan, with her eye for clothes and her color sense, had created a color plan for the wedding, especially the photographs. As he continued to watch with great interest, he saw this plan take shape. Brilliant, he thought. Just brilliant.

All of the male members of the family were wearing dark navy business suits, white shirts, and pale blue ties. Each man had a white carnation in his buttonhole, just as Jack did, and of course he was dressed in a navy blue suit, too. He had been told to wear that color.

The four adult bridesmaids, Natalie, Emsie, Elayne, and Angharad, were beautiful in their long, pearl gray taffeta gowns; little Adele wore the same dress in miniature and was enchanting. The grown-up girls had green orchids pinned on their left shoulders; Adele carried a bouquet of the same green orchids.

Linnet was dressed in a pale blue silk suit with a long, well-tailored coat and long skirt, while her sister Tessa was in a pale bluish gray caftan, which had blue beading around the neck. Their cousin India had chosen a long Nehru-style tunic and narrow pants made of heavy silk that was the same bluish gray as Tessa's caftan.

Snap, he thought. Navy for the men; gray for the bridesmaids; pale blue or bluish gray for these three. Color coordination indeed.

Jack's eyes scanned the other women. Paula, his great favorite, wore a long, violet-colored velvet coat and a violet chiffon gown underneath; Emily had chosen a tapestry coat predominantly grayish blue, with small touches of soft color; while the mother of the bride, Marietta, was in gold brocade over dark brown silk.

Glancing along the rows, he found another touch of gold brocade, this time worn by Elizabeth, Emma Harte's second daughter, while Daisy, her daughter by Paul McGill, was dressed in a splashy magenta shade.

Great-Aunt Edwina, the eldest of Emma's daughters, wore her favorite deep purple. Jack smiled broadly. God bless her, he thought, she just keeps on plowing the seas like a great old battleship. He adored Edwina, whom he considered the greatest character he had ever known.

Finally, he found another pool of rich purple and gold. Sally, Countess of Dunvale, India's mother, wore a long, gold brocade coat over wide palazzo pants of gold-colored silk, and her sister, Vivienne, had chosen a purple cut-velvet coat and dress that echoed Edwina's deep purple.

What it boils down to is a mixture of dark navy, pearl gray, and grayish blue, Jack decided, with strong color from the violet, purple, and magenta, these shades balanced by the gold brocade.

And at the center of this rather simple color plan stood the bride, in her shimmering blue-on-blue ombréed chiffon that reflected all the shades in the sea. How beautiful she was. Jack couldn't help smiling wryly to himself. He, the most conventional of red-blooded heterosexuals, had certainly learned a lot from Emma Harte. More than he'd realized until today!

The family portrait is going to be spectacular, Jack thought, silently congratulating Evan for her foresight. She must have guided the women in their choices of color, even been insistent, perhaps.

Seemingly all was completed. Linnet and Natalie took their own places, and the relieved photographer got ready to start shooting film when Shane stepped forward.

"No, no! Stop! Wait a minute," he cried, looking at the photographer, then he shifted his gaze, zeroed in on Jack. "What are you doing down there, Jack? You're supposed to be up here with us. We need you for this shot in particular."

"But I—"

"No buts, Jack. *You're family.* Come up here and stand with me and Paula."

Jack did as he was told, unable to utter a word. He was overcome with emotion.

Much later, when the reception was in full swing, Angharad wandered amongst the guests, looking for Jonathan Ainsley. She was fascinated by him, expected him to be present, but he was not. She was bitterly disappointed.

He was the best-looking man she had met in a long time, and so tasty; she really fancied him. Of course, he was much older, but she did not care about that. Age did not matter, only sexual attraction was important. And money. Her mind swung to Evan, whom she could see out of the corner of her eye. Jealousy spiraled, and Angharad suddenly hoped things would go wrong for her. Perhaps there would be problems with the birth; or perhaps the twins would be ugly. She didn't care what it was, as long as it was bad. She wished disasters on her sister—well, her adopted sister. Evan had always had everything, and that just wasn't fair. Ugly babies and a bad marriage,

Angharad thought, throwing Evan a spiteful look, pouring silent curses on the other woman.

Only Linnet noticed the malevolent look on Angharad's face, and she shriveled inside, turned away filled with an unexpected sense of foreboding.

Part Three

DUO

❧

Fortune is not satisfied with inflicting one calamity.

—Publilius Syrus, Maxim 274

18

〜

Linnet was so excited she picked up the phone and dialed Evan's home number without a second thought, wanting to convey her pleasure immediately.

After numerous rings, just when she was about to hang up, Evan was saying hello.

"It's Linnet!" she cried, "and I can't get over your sketches for the wedding gowns. They're fantastic! Whenever did you design *fifty* dresses? When did you find the time?"

Evan chuckled. "I'm thrilled you like them, Linnet. I designed at least twelve of them for you. When I was creating your wedding gown last year. But we decided to go with the Tudor princess look in the end, so I just put the rest away. The others I've created over the past few years, in my spare time. I liked most of them, so I kept them. I did throw a few away, the ones I thought weren't very good."

"You didn't! That's a crime. Please keep everything you design in the future, and let *me* be the judge. You're far too critical of yourself."

"I promise I won't ditch a thing, not even a rough sketch. How's that?"

"Just great, and thanks for sending your portfolio over to the store. I do appreciate it, and I hope we can start putting a few of the designs in the works very soon. For all those June weddings that will be coming up."

"Of course we can. I'll send you an e-mail about some of the seamstresses I've used, and which designs I think they'll handle best. How's that?"

"So you can't come to the store? Is that what you're saying?" Linnet asked quietly. "Not even to discuss the gowns with me?"

"Oh, Linnet, I wish I could. But Dr. Addney has simply forbidden it," Evan murmured, at once understanding Linnet's disappointment and need for her to be at Harte's. "He says I have to stay at home and rest, not exert myself in any way, or get myself agitated or stressed out. But listen, you can come over to the apartment, can't you? We could look at the sketches here, make our plans, choose the seamstresses."

"What a great idea, but unfortunately I'm really jammed today."

"That's all right. We'll do it later in the week. Whenever. . . . Actually, Mom's here, she's going to go with me to meet Emily at that apartment in Belgrave Square. The one which belongs to her friend Lavinia Constable, who's off to Los Angeles. I think Gid might have mentioned it to you?"

"Yes, he did. The other day. And isn't it a funny coincidence that it's near Emma's house in the square?"

"That's the best part, being so close to Paula and Shane. As far as the flat is concerned, it's only a rental for a year, Linnet. But the great thing is that it has been renovated. It's brand-new, and *unfurnished*. So we could use our own things. Gid's really excited, he's seen it already. If I like it, then it's a done deal, because he thinks it would be perfect for us, if only on a temporary basis."

"Since Gid likes it, I'm sure *you* will, and if it's halfway decent, rent it for the year. You can't continue to live in Gideon's bachelor flat once the twins come, you'll be cramped to death."

"I know. I thought we'd be able to furnish the apartment quickly, maybe find a lot of the things we need at Harte's."

"You will, and I'll help you. So will Emily. We'll make it livable for you, at least."

"We'll have to hurry," Evan said, laughing.

"You do feel okay, don't you?" Linnet asked, concerned.

"I'm great, honestly, and I'm sure I'll deliver in late February, early March, which is when I'm supposed to." There was a moment's hesitation before Evan continued. "I'm so sorry you have only India to help you at the moment. I know how tough it can be at the store. When is Tessa coming back from Paris?"

"In a few days, once Jean-Claude goes off to Afghanistan. He wanted her to spend some time with him at his home. Did she tell you she's going to meet his son?"

"No, she didn't. But that's nice, and it's a good idea, don't you think? Now that they're engaged."

"Yes," Linnet agreed and added softly, "My mother told me last night that Tessa's divorce should be through at the end of this week. So they can get married fairly soon."

There was a silence.

Linnet said, "Have I lost you, Evan?"

"No, I'm here," she answered. "I was just startled to hear that bit of news. Will Tessa be leaving Harte's, moving to Paris?" Her voice was low, almost conspiratorial.

"I don't know anything . . ." Linnet left her sentence unfinished and then cleared her throat. "I don't think she's said a word to Paula." The other line began to shrill, and Linnet exclaimed, "Let's talk later today, Evan. I've got to take this."

"I'll call you after I've seen the flat," Evan responded and hung up.

Linnet pressed the other button. "Hello? Linnet O'Neill."

"It's India," her cousin said. "Have you got a moment?"

"Yes, of course. Is something wrong, India? You sound strange."

"I think I've got a problem, well, a sort of *developing* problem."

"Here or at the Leeds store? Or is it personal?"

"Personal," India announced and then sighed. "Mrs. Caldwell, that's the grandmother of Dusty's child, if you remember, has taken a turn for the worse. I just got off the phone with Dusty, and he posed a very difficult question. I didn't know how to answer him. I need your advice, Linnet. Can I come along to your office?"

"Absolutely. I'm free right now."

Several seconds later India walked into Linnet's office, came over to her desk, sat down, and blew her cousin a kiss. "Sorry to dump on you at ten o'clock in the morning, but I simply don't have the answer for Dusty. I'm a bit baffled."

Leaning over the desk, focusing on India, Linnet suggested, "Tell me what it is, let's go from there."

"Dusty thinks Molly Caldwell's going to die. Soon. He's had a premonition about it for over a week now, he says, and his dilemma is what to do about taking the child to see her grandmother. Should he? Or would it be better if he didn't?"

"Wow, that's a tough one."

"Don't tell me. I've wrestled with it for the last hour."

Linnet sat back in her chair, a reflective look settling on her face. She closed her eyes, concentrated for a few moments; then she snapped her eyes open, sat up, and said to India, "Let's just analyze it . . . let's bring it down to our own personal level. For example, if Paula were dying, would we tell Tessa to take Adele to see her grandmother?"

India bit her lip, shook her head. "I don't know."

"Okay, look at it this way. If Great-Aunt Edwina, your grandmother, were dying, and if you had a child of your own, and your child had been close to Edwina, what would you do?"

"I think I'd take her. For Edwina's sake as well as the child's."

"I feel the same way. And after all, India, Atlanta doesn't have to be *told* her grandmother is dying, now, does she?"

"No, she doesn't," India agreed. "I have a feeling Dusty's concerned about Molly's condition, how she looks, whether she's hooked up to tubes. He doesn't want Atlanta to be frightened. And I also have a feeling he thinks perhaps Atlanta should remember her grandmother the way she was the last time they saw each other."

"Do you want to go back to Yorkshire? Help Dusty with this?"

"Yes, I think it would please him, make it easier for everyone, in a sense. On the other hand, it's Thursday, and I've only been back here for three days and a bit. My desk is piled high."

"I know, so was mine. Do you have anything truly pressing, India?"

"Not really. But I should follow up on some of the clothes and accessories we ordered for spring. Then again, I suppose a day won't make too much difference. I could leave tomorrow morning, early, and meet Dusty in Leeds."

"Is it pressing? Is Mrs. Caldwell actually at death's door?"

"Not exactly, as far as I know. However, the woman who helps her told Dusty that Molly was getting weaker, and also fretting about Atlanta."

"Then go today. Go now, India," Linnet said. "You can be in Leeds in several hours. Why waste time? Tempt Providence? I think it's awfully important that the child sees her grandmother again, and is given a proper explanation about why she's in hospital. Also, I think it's important for Molly Caldwell to see her granddaughter, so she can die in peace. And you should be with Dusty, as his fiancée."

"I'd planned to go with him if he did decide to take Atlanta to see Molly."

"I believe that to be very fitting, compassionate," Linnet said, in a soft voice. "We must always be kind to people."

"Yes. And thanks, Linnet, for helping me to help Dusty make a decision," India answered, the faint Irish lilt echoing in her melodious voice. She gave her cousin a little smile. "I know he'll go along with whatever I suggest."

After India had left, Linnet began to collect Evan's sketches from her worktable. She put them carefully into the portfolio, thinking about India's upcoming wedding. Evan had designed a beautiful crinoline gown of ivory taffeta for her. Edwardian in style. How talented she was.

A long, very heavy sigh escaped as Linnet tied the string on the portfolio, put it at the back of her worktable, and returned to her desk.

She sat staring into space for a few minutes, thinking about Dusty Rhodes and the problem he would face when Molly Caldwell did die. She now knew quite a lot about Melinda Caldwell; Gideon had made it his business to find out as much as he could in order to protect India.

The woman was dangerous, no question about it. She was a drug addict, could be violent, and apparently she was difficult to deal with. There was no way she would give up custody of her child, Linnet was quite certain of that. And so was Great-Aunt Edwina, who had worried aloud about India to Linnet during the wedding festivities at Pennistone Royal this past weekend.

"It will be a replay of the Mark Longden situation with Tessa," Edwina had pronounced dourly. "Just you wait and see. Dusty's in for a lot of trouble, mark my words."

"What can we do?" Linnet had probed as she guided Edwina away from her sisters, with whom she had been standing—Elizabeth, Emily's mother, and Daisy, Paula's mother and Linnet's grandmother. They both had big ears, were consistently curious about the entire family, and loved intrigue and gossip. In fact, it often struck Linnet that they thrived on it.

Edwina, not one to miss a trick, had given Linnet an amused glance and said, "Yes, better to find a quiet corner to chat. My siblings are very nosy."

Linnet had laughed, taken Edwina to the other end of the Stone Hall, and her great-aunt had gone on. "I shall advise Dusty to get a top-notch solicitor to handle the situation. Maybe we can avoid a court case if he has the right firm. Better use the one Emma and Paula have always used. Mmm, that's a good idea. And then there's *money*. That might well be the answer." All this had been said in a decisive tone, and Edwina's dour mood had lightened as she spoke.

"Money isn't always the best currency, though," Linnet had answered succinctly.

Edwina had given her an admiring look. "Spoken like a true Harte, dear Linnet. And I must tell you this while I think of it. I rely on you to stand by India, in your very clever and daring way. Just in case I'm not around, that is."

"Are you going somewhere, Edwina?" Linnet had asked swiftly, addressing her by her first name, as she often did everyone in the family.

Edwina had laughed heartily. "No, I'm not planning any trips. But you never know, I might just pop my clogs, even though that would be such a nuisance. I've so much to do at the moment, so many engagements."

Linnet had thrown her arms around her great-aunt, hugging her tightly, laughing with her, once again thinking how extraordinary she was.

And Edwina's right, Linnet now thought. Dusty must have the best law firm behind him. She made up her mind to talk to Paula later today about it, get her mother to introduce him to the solicitors she used, Crawford, Creighton, Phipps, and whatever. They were big time. And that was the kind of lawyer Dusty would need to deal with Melinda if the occasion arose.

No sooner had this thought entered her head than the phone rang. When she picked it up and said,

"Hello? Linnet O'Neill here," it was her mother who spoke.

"Good morning, Linnet dear," Paula said. "Are you very busy at the moment?"

"No, Mummy, I've just been going over some really gorgeous sketches for wedding gowns, Evan's designs. I'd love to show them to you if you've got a minute." It had suddenly struck her that this might be a wonderful opportunity to broach the idea of a floor devoted to brides.

"I'd love to see them, but not now. We have a problem. A very serious problem. Could you come to my office?"

"You mean *now*?"

"At once, Linnet."

"What's wrong?" she asked, her voice rising.

"Just come to my office, Linnet, *please*."

"Right away, Mummy." Linnet dropped the receiver in the cradle, jumped up, and went out. As she left the outer office, she told her secretary where she was going and headed for the chief executive's suite, almost running down the corridor.

Her mind was racing as she pushed open the door of her mother's domain and said to Jonelle, one of her secretaries, "The boss lady sent for me."

Jonelle smiled at her. "Go right in, Linnet."

Stepping into the spacious and beautiful room which had been Emma's office from the day the store opened until her death, Linnet went cold when she saw Jack Figg sitting next to her mother. Paula was perched on the edge of the sofa, looking the epitome of elegance in her well-tailored black suit, but also very tense, taut.

Apprehension flooded Linnet, but she swallowed it back as she walked toward them, saying, "Mummy . . . Jack . . . what's going on?"

"Hello, Linnet," Jack said, sounding a bit weary. His voice was gruff. He had dark rings under his eyes, which were bloodshot.

She stared at her mother, an auburn brow lifting quizzically.

Paula stared back, smiled at her somewhat falteringly, and patted the sofa. "Come and sit with me, darling. Jack has some news. News I regard as rather bad, if not, indeed, disastrous."

Without responding, Linnet did as she was bidden. She was eaten up with curiosity.

"Would you fill Linnet in, please, Jack?" Paula said, sighing.

He nodded, but for a moment he didn't say anything. He sat gazing at the two women, mother and daughter, heirs of Emma Harte, who had always worn her uniform both literally and figuratively. Today mother and daughter were both dressed in the same kind of smart black suit Emma had favored, obviously couture, and worn with white shirts. Both in high heels. But no jewelry except for pearls on their ears, watches on their wrists, and plain gold wedding bands on the appropriate fingers. Just like Emma. Her style down to the last detail. Intelligent, brilliant women. Kind and loving women. He couldn't bear it if anything happened to either of them. He cursed silently, frustrated and boiling inside.

Taking a deep breath, Jack now focused on Linnet and said calmly, "I have excellent reasons to believe Angharad Hughes has hooked up with Jonathan Ainsley."

Linnet nodded. "I'm not going to say I'm surprised, Jack, because I'm not. We had a discussion about this very thing the day of the wedding."

"We did indeed."

"What have you found out?" Linnet asked, feeling a sudden tension in her chest.

"As you know, Angharad went to see him on Friday morning at his house in Thirsk. What happened at that meeting we've no way of knowing, but she was there for about thirty minutes, no longer. Some time later that day,

Ainsley went to London. Angharad was at the wedding, as we all know, but she left Yorkshire first thing on Monday morning. She took the early train to King's Cross and checked in at the hotel owned by George Thomas, her father's old friend."

"And her father and mother returned to London on Tuesday, along with their daughter Elayne," Linnet pointed out. "I believe Owen Hughes and Elayne left for New York yesterday. Isn't that so?"

"It is," Jack replied, nodding. "Marietta is still at the hotel. She's staying until Evan gives birth; she told me that at the reception. I'm sure everyone knows this."

"We do. And she's with Evan at this moment." Linnet glanced at her watch. "I believe they are on their way to view an apartment in Belgrave Square, which was arranged by Emily."

"That's right," Paula volunteered. "Emily's old friend Lavinia Constable just did the place up only to get a marvelous job offer to do the sets for an important movie in Los Angeles. She's gone away for a year."

"So we know the whereabouts of *all* the Hugheses," Jack said acidly, "including Angharad."

"Is she in London with *him*?" Linnet probed.

"She's actually in Paris. But then, so is he," Jack answered, throwing her a pointed look. "One of my London operatives was tracking her from the moment she stepped off the train at King's Cross. We know everything she did on Monday. She checked into the Thomases' hotel off Cadogan Square, then went to the hairdresser's around the corner, later spent an hour or so shopping at Harvey Nichols. That evening, she went to Jonathan Ainsley's apartment in Grosvenor Square around seven and stayed until ten-thirty. Obviously having dinner, or whatever. She went back to see him at his apartment on Tuesday afternoon for an hour only. That night she had dinner with her parents, and George and Arlette Thomas, at the hotel. Elayne was present as well. Angharad went shopping again on Wednesday afternoon, ate alone with her mother on Wednesday evening, and flew to Paris this morning. Very early. When she arrived, she checked into the George V Hotel. My Paris operatives have her under permanent surveillance now."

"So J.A. was already in Paris, eh?"

"He was, Linnet. He flew in on a private jet early Wednesday morning. He's been ensconced in his flat on Avenue Foch ever since."

"Something's going on between them, that's patently obvious," Linnet now ventured. "I think they must have planned to meet in London when she saw him at Thirsk on Friday. They made a date, probably because he couldn't spend any time with her then."

"*Correct!*" Jack agreed. "He had just stowed away his luggage in the car and was ready to leave the house when she drove up. But she didn't stay that long, as I said, half an hour maybe."

Paula interjected, "What transpired between them, whatever it was, made them want to see each other again. They clicked in some way, that's what I think. He was rushing up to London, and she knew she was going back there, so they made a date. And during their encounters in London, he decided to invite her to Paris, and she probably was thrilled to go." Pausing, Paula stared hard at Jack. "That's the way I see it, anyway. Don't you?"

"I think you've pretty much got it right, Paula." Jack glanced at Linnet and then back at Paula. "I must pose a question to you both. Is it personal? Is it a sexual liaison? Or is he using her to get information about Evan and Gideon? Or about Owen and Marietta? Or the entire Harte family? What's *he* up to, in other words?"

"Maybe it's both—business and pleasure," Linnet muttered. "Certainly she could be very useful to him. It's like having a spy right in the bosom of our family. And Owen's. Don't forget, he hates *all* of us." Linnet leaned back against the cushions. Angharad was such a gross, gushing, vulgar woman, Linnet couldn't bear her. Nor could Tessa and India. Angharad had tried, during the short time she was in Yorkshire, to make friends with them, ingratiate herself, to infiltrate their little group, but without success. Even Evan had distanced herself from Angharad. Linnet was well aware that Natalie and Emsie had also been turned off, fled whenever they saw Angharad on the horizon.

Paula said, "She's *useful* to him. *Dangerous* to us, Jack. Let's face it, she knows everything that's going on in her own family, and also ours probably. Because Evan and Marietta are in constant contact. And no doubt there's a lot of chitchat passing back and forth, there usually is in families."

"Mummy, Evan doesn't like Angharad! She confided in me. She's not close to her, never was, in fact, not even when they were children. If you want my opinion, Evan actually *hates* her. I know it's a strong word to use, but I think she does. Gideon can't abide her either. I know he blames her for Evan's fall. He told me."

"Does Gideon think she pushed Evan? Something like that?" Paula asked, her eyes narrowing.

"No, because Evan says Angharad never touched her. However, Gid believes she managed to get Evan so worked up, so agitated that she missed the chair. He is *convinced* that if Evan had been alone in her office, the accident wouldn't have occurred. He has this idea—that somehow Angharad goaded Evan, yes, that's what he believes, even if we don't."

"So, as far as we know, those two dangerous people have become cohorts . . . but for what reason?" Jack wondered out loud. "We must find that out. *How? Who can help us?*" He sat back on the sofa, rubbing his chin with one hand, looking thoughtful.

"I would say there is only one person. *Marietta,*" Paula pointed out. "Neither of her sisters likes Angharad, apparently, so there's only the mother left. That's the one person Angharad would confide in anyway."

"Don't you think, under these circumstances, she might be wary of talking to her mother? Anyway, she'd never admit to plotting something diabolical with Jonathan Ainsley. Would she?" Linnet asked.

"Damn right she wouldn't!" Jack exclaimed. "But you have a point, Paula, about Marietta. Angharad would more than likely see her, especially if she were having an affair with Ainsley. She just might want to boast she's snagged him, because she undoubtedly sees him as a catch." Jack jumped up, walked over to the window, stood looking down at the busy traffic in Knightsbridge. But he was oblivious to everything; his mind was working in the strange ways it often did as he tried to envision what Angharad would do. What would motivate her to boast to her mother? Spite? Jealousy of Evan? Dead-on, he thought.

After a few seconds, he swung to face Paula and Linnet. "Listen to me. She *won't* confide in Marietta if Ainsley's plotting something bad. She probably *will* confide in her mother if she's having an affair with him. She won't be able to resist doing so. She'll feel more competitive with Evan than ever."

"So what do *we* do?" Linnet asked. "In the meantime?"

"Get Marietta on our side," Paula suggested, a dark eyebrow lifting.

Jack smiled for the first time that morning. "I don't think that will be very hard, do you, Paula? All we have to do is explain the situation to Marietta, tell her that Evan and the twins might be in serious danger. I don't think she'd want anything to happen to her biological daughter and her first grandchildren, do you?"

Paula shook her head. "No woman would take that risk."

Linnet said, "Marietta has to be told how *dangerous*

Angharad actually is if she's hooked in with J.A. And then
she'll help us, I'm sure. Perhaps she knows Angharad has
gone to Paris, and maybe she'll go over, too. To visit her."

"Only Marietta can get to the bottom of the situation,"
Jack murmured. "We *must* find out what's going on."

"Evan and Gideon have to be told about Angharad and
Jonathan. They can't be left in the dark," Paula interjected. "Maybe we can invite them for drinks this evening, and Marietta as well."

Linnet nodded. She did not trust herself to speak. She
suddenly had such a dreadful foreboding of trouble
ahead.

19

❧

Linnet and Jack left the executive suite, and Paula turned to her work, taking a manila folder off the top of a pile at one end of her desk.

She attempted to study the first page of the current balance sheet but found it hard to concentrate. Images of Jonathan Ainsley intruded. A sudden thought occurred to her, and she sat up straighter; her mind had unexpectedly focused on her cousin Sarah. She used to be close to Ainsley but was now more inclined to take the family's side. And wasn't she a better judge of his current situation than Marietta Hughes? The latter would have to rely on her daughter, but would the girl *really* tell her mother the truth? And what if she didn't actually know the truth? There were a variety of elements involved here, and in Paula's opinion, Angharad Hughes was no match for Jonathan Ainsley. Evil though he might be, he was a brilliant man, and a past master of dissimulation.

To her way of thinking, Sarah Lowther Pascal, whom Paula truly believed was now on the side of the family, was the one person who would see everything as it really was. Sarah had convinced Paula last year that she was opposed to their cousin because she had come to understand how dangerous Jonathan was, and that he fully intended to do the Hartes harm if he could.

Reaching for the small red book that contained all of the family phone numbers, Paula found Sarah's direct line at her Paris office and punched in the numbers.

Sarah answered within seconds, and Paula said, "Hello, Sarah, it's Paula."

"Paula, hello!" Sarah exclaimed. "How are you?" Her mellifluous voice was very warm.

"I'm fine. We were all sorry you couldn't make it to the wedding, especially Emily, but we understood your problems. How is your daughter doing? Is Chloe feeling better?"

"Yes, she is, thanks for asking. Bed rest and the right antibiotics seem to be doing the trick against her viral bronchitis. She really wasn't well enough to come to Yorkshire, and frankly I just didn't want to leave her. Also, Yves was snowed under. He's preparing a new exhibition, and he always gets so involved himself with the mounting of it. Anyway, I'm sure it was a lovely wedding, and everything went well."

"It did, thanks to Linnet." Paula took a deep breath and plunged in, told Sarah about the secret early morning ceremony, then gave her details of the explosion. "Thank God nobody was hurt, because there was nobody in the church," Paula finished.

Sarah, aghast, cried, "But he's gone mad! Why on earth is he so determined to hurt the family? It just doesn't make sense."

"It's because of the past, Sarah. He feels cheated of what he thinks is rightfully his. That will never change. He's *obsessed*."

"Our grandmother did what she thought was right, what she believed to be the best. It had nothing to do with you or me or anyone else. None of her children or grandchildren were involved in the making of her will. Why can't he get that through his head?"

"I don't know, and quite frankly I think he's delusional," Paula responded. "He's sick in the head as far as

I'm concerned. And he's being grossly unfair. He still gets his dividends from Harte Enterprises, as we all do, Emily sees to that. He has the trust fund Grandy made for him, and he's a talented businessman who's made millions for himself because of Emma's legacy to him. So why this vendetta?"

"You said it yourself, Paula . . . he's sick."

"And a loose cannon. Jack Figg has absolute proof he's hooked up with Evan's sister. Angharad Hughes. Apparently she ran into him in the newsagent's shop in Pennistone Royal village, and according to Evan's mother, who was there, they kind of . . . flirted with each other. Since then Angharad has visited him at his house in Thirsk, has met him twice in London. And now they're both in Paris. They flew separately, and she's staying at the George V, but she's there because of him, no two ways about that in my mind, and Jack's also."

There was silence at the other end of the phone, and then Sarah said, "So *that's* who it is."

"What do you mean?"

"He phoned me early this morning, suggested dinner on Saturday. He said he wanted me to meet a protégée of his. I wasn't sure what he meant by *protégée*, but anyway, I put him off because Yves is so busy with the exhibition."

"Could you go? Would you go? For me? For the family, Sarah? We simply need to know if he's using her, pumping her for information in order to get to us. Or is it simply a middle-aged man's lust for a much younger woman? A twenty-three-year-old platinum blond with a pretty face and sexy body."

"Twenty-three. Good God, he's cradle snatching!"

"That he is . . . if it's a sexual involvement. But it might be all business. Linnet believes Angharad is one of those women who is hungry for everything. Men, money, the good life. It's possible he has a business arrangement with her. She's rather envious of Evan; there's no love lost there from what Linnet has told me. Nothing like envy, is there?"

"Only jealousy perhaps," Sarah murmured, thinking unexpectedly of Shane and how much she had loved him once, and how jealous she had been of Paula long, long ago.

Paula said, "So, Sarah, what do you say? Will you consider going to dinner with him on Saturday? Just to make an assessment of their relationship?"

"I'll not only consider it, I'll do it!" Sarah exclaimed with sudden vehemence. "I need to know for myself what he's up to."

Tessa was happy that they had come to Clos-Fleuri after spending three days in Paris. She had grown to love Jean-Claude's lovely old country house, and it was the perfect place for Adele to roam around in, with so many odd nooks and crannies. Elvira liked it here, too, and enjoyed tramping around the grounds with Adele in tow.

Now, as she sat at the dressing table in her bedroom, putting on makeup, Tessa thought about the next few days. Jean-Claude's only child was coming to spend the weekend with them before Jean-Claude flew off to fulfill his assignment in Afghanistan and she returned to London.

Tessa was looking forward to meeting Philippe Deléon. He was thirty-one and an artist who lived in the South of France, not married and something of a loner. He was a talented painter, according to his father, and was finally beginning to get the recognition he deserved. She had spoken to him several times on the phone, and he sounded nice. She found herself wanting him to like her. Jean-Claude had chuckled when she had said this to him yesterday, and he had answered, "*Mon Dieu, chérie,* how could he not like you? Please, do not worry so much." After that there had been no further discussion about Jean-Claude's son. Tessa knew he had been brought up by his mother in a little town called Beaulieu-sur-Mer, between Nice and Monte Carlo, visiting his father in Paris during the school holidays.

Picking up a comb, Tessa ran it through her silver-blond hair and then walked over to the armoire. Within seconds she was dressed in a white silk blouse, white wool trousers, and a white cashmere jacket with hand-embroidered front panels. Stepping into high-heeled beige suede shoes, she walked over to the window, parted the draperies, and looked out.

It was a very clear night, with a huge full moon floating low in the ink-black sky. It cast a silver sheen across the frost-covered lawns and the bare trees, skeletal in the moonlight. Bereft, she thought, the garden looks bereft and very eerie in this light. An involuntary shiver ran through her as she lingered, staring at the ghostly landscape. Then she stepped away quickly, letting the drapery fall from her hands, and returned to the dressing table; after spraying herself with perfume, she put on pearl earrings and slipped her engagement ring onto her finger. Looking at it for a moment, she thought of Jean-Claude and his impending trip to Afghanistan.

How it worried her, this assignment covering the war. All she could think about were guns and destruction and death. She dared not let him know how concerned she was because it would upset him, and that was the last thing she wished to do. She wanted him to go off with a clear head; she did not want him worrying about her while he was away—he needed to be totally concentrated on what he had to do—but she did have her moments when panic overwhelmed her. She had had so many losses in her life, and she could not bear another one.

Jim Fairley, her father, taken from her when she was just a toddler. Killed in an avalanche in Chamonix; David Amory, her grandfather, who was also killed in the avalanche. And then there was her half brother, Patrick, such a dear sweet boy, who had died of a rare blood disease when only in his teens. And even the failure of her marriage to Mark Longden was a loss in a sense, because to her any kind of failure was a loss.

A sigh escaped her, and she bit her lower lip nervously. She must be strong and courageous, and hold positive thoughts, keep a cool demeanor. Nothing was going to happen to Jean-Claude. He would be away for only a month at the most, and he was an experienced war correspondent, used to dodging bullets. He had told her that he never took risks, that he wore a flak jacket, as did most journalists and war photographers, and that he had every intention of staying alive . . . so that he could come back and marry her.

Marriage. The word bounced around in her head. She wasn't even divorced yet from Mark Longden, and she was engaged to another man and prepared to start a new marriage, a new life with him. But she was sure of Jean-Claude, knew full well how much he loved her, just as she loved him with all her heart. And she knew that this time the marriage would work, because of who Jean-Claude was, what he was as a man. Brilliant, a writer and philosopher of no mean repute, he was also kind, loving, generous, compassionate, and strong of heart. And he had a loving soul, a gentle soul.

Mark Longden had been *killing* her soul, destroying her spirit, just as he had hurt her physically. And she was relieved that he was gone from her life. He was now in Australia, thanks to the extraordinary deal her mother had made with his lawyers, and he could not come back to England for a very long time. Not if he wanted to keep the money Paula had given him in the divorce settlement.

And within the next couple of weeks her divorce would be final, and she could marry Jean-Claude whenever she wished. He was anxious for them to marry as soon as possible, and her inclination was the same. The thought of being with him permanently now filled her with a rush of happiness, and she swung away from the dressing table, hurried across her bedroom, which served as a dressing room in actuality. Gliding through the open door into Jean-Claude's bedroom, which she shared with him, she glanced around.

At this exact moment he came hurrying out of his own dressing room, struggling into a tweed sports jacket. His face lit up at the sight of her, and he exclaimed, "Tessa, you look beautiful, *chérie*."

"*Merci beaucoup, monsieur.*" As he came to a stop in front of her, she leaned forward, kissed his cheek, added, "I'm going to see what Adele is doing."

Jean-Claude laughed, his warm brown eyes sparkling. "A moment ago she was sitting in the kitchen with Elvira."

Smiling, Tessa began to edge out of the room. "I'll just pop downstairs and see her," she said and went on, "She must be feeling tired, she's had such a busy day for a small child."

"I'll join you in a few minutes," Jean-Claude murmured, walking over to the small desk in a corner of the room. "I have a business call to make, but it won't take long."

Adele was almost four, and she had sprung up in the last few weeks, looked rather tall for her age. With her exquisite little face, silvery gray eyes, and pale blond hair, she was the spitting image of her mother, a beautiful child who was sweet-natured and docile.

Everyone fell in love with her, and Lourdes, Jean-Claude's cook, was no exception. For this long weekend in the country, and with several houseguests, she had traveled from the house in Paris to do the cooking, and Hakim had accompanied her. Although Gérard was the houseman at Clos-Fleuri, Jean-Claude had decided extra help was necessary, and Hakim had been a willing volunteer.

When Tessa walked into the wonderful, old-fashioned family kitchen, Adele was eating a light supper and talking to Elvira in the most animated way. Tessa noticed at once that Lourdes and Hakim were looking on, their affection for her child written across their smiling faces. It pleased her so much that Jean-Claude's staff had fallen in love with Adele the first time they met her. All of them, both in Paris and here, had made the child feel comfortable, welcomed her warmly. And Adele had responded in kind. Not all of them spoke English, but a few gentle words in French had been significant, and somehow Adele had known they were saying nice things to her by their tone of voice and expressions.

"Mumma!" Adele cried when she saw Tessa coming across the kitchen, and she made to jump down from the table. But Elvira put a restraining hand on her arm. "You have to finish your supper, Adele," the nanny said softly.

Tessa came to a standstill at the big, family-size table, nodding to Hakim and Lourdes as she did, and then sitting down next to Adele. "Hello, darling. What did you have for supper tonight?"

"Fish, Mumma, a little itty-bitty fish with mashed potatoes and *petits pois* . . . that means peas."

Tessa smiled. "I know, and so you are learning French, are you?"

Adele nodded. "Lourdes is teaching me the name of . . . food. It's a beginning, she said, and *pommes de terre,* that's potatoes. *Viande,* that's meat, and I told you about peas, and then there's *crème caramel,* that's a custard, and *lait*—"

"Is milk," Elvira cut in, adding, "Come along, Adele, please finish your supper like a good girl."

"Oh, I've finished, thank you." Turning to her mother, she said, "*You're* not having fish tonight, you're having *viande.* Lamb. Jean-Claude likes lamb, Lourdes told me that. Where is Jean-Claude, Mumma?"

"Right here, *ma petite,*" he announced from the doorway and came into the kitchen. He rested a loving hand on Adele's head when he reached her, bent down and kissed it, then took a seat next to Tessa. Looking across at

Hakim, who was filling an ice bucket, he asked, "Has my son arrived yet?"

"Fifteen minutes ago, monsieur. Gérard took his suitcase upstairs."

"Bien," Jean-Claude said, and then, putting an arm around Adele, he asked, "Now, *mon petit chou à la crème,* how was dinner?"

"Very nice. *Merci.*" She smiled up at him.

He smiled back, and, gazing at Tessa lovingly, he said, "So she's learning French. I think that is charming."

"When can I meet Philippe?" Adele now asked, peering into Jean-Claude's face.

"Soon, I think. I'm sure he will come down in fifteen minutes or so. To join us for an aperitif before dinner."

"Oh, goodie! He's going to be my big brother, Mumma said so."

"Of course he is. . . . Your mother spoke the truth."

Adele slipped off the chair, planted her feet on the floor. Elvira said firmly, in a quiet tone, "But you've not had any dessert."

"Thank you, but I don't want any, Elvira." Reaching for Jean-Claude's hand, the child went on, "Can we go to the little room? So I can watch my *Cinderella* tape? Please, Jean-Claude."

"And why not?" he replied, rising, winking at Tessa, and taking Adele's hand firmly in his.

The child swung her head and exclaimed in her little girl's voice, "Thank you, Lourdes . . . *merci beaucoup.*" And then she and Jean-Claude left the kitchen.

20

❧

Whatever they said about him, no one could accuse him of not being thorough. He had been trained by Emma Harte to be just that, and she had instilled in him the absolute need to pay attention to details and, most important, to leave nothing to chance.

His thoroughness had now brought him to this desk at six-thirty in the evening, where he sat down and opened the black-leather binder that held all of the information he had garnered about the Hughes family. From the moment Evan Hughes had been pronounced one of the great-granddaughters of Emma Harte, Jonathan Ainsley had employed a team of American and British investigators to provide him with everything he needed to know about each and every member of her family. Cover all your bases, that was *his* motto.

His eyes settled on the name ANGHARAD HUGHES, and he scanned the page, which told him a few things about her. Twenty-three years old. An abandoned baby who had been adopted by Marietta and Owen Hughes when she was only a few months old. Reasonably well educated. An expert in Georgian antiques, trained by her father. Considered wild in her teenage years. Sexually attractive to men of all ages. *Well, he knew that, didn't he?* Beautiful. *He was very well aware of this, also.* Not very close to her sisters, Evan and Elayne; something of a loner, in fact. Closer to her mother than to Owen Hughes. Never really a favorite of her grandmother Glynnis Hughes. Et cetera, et cetera.

Jonathan sighed and closed the binder. He had had all this information for months; obviously nothing new had come up on her, or any of the other family members. And certainly the things he truly needed to know would never appear in a dossier.

Why was she pursuing him?

What did she want from him?

Had she been planted by the Hartes to spy on him for them?

He had voiced one of those questions in London. "What do you want from me?" he'd asked the night she had come for drinks with him at his flat in Grosvenor Square.

"Nothing," she had replied. "Just to see you. I sure thought you were the most handsome guy I'd ever seen when we bumped into each other in the village shop. But I told you that when I came to your home in Thirsk." She had shrugged and added, "I guess I thought you were flirting with me. I kind of . . . well, you know . . . fancied you." She had shrugged again and eyed him in the most suggestive way, and he had thought, Bedroom eyes, she has bedroom eyes, and wondered where that very old-fashioned expression had been dredged up from. And later that evening she had made quite sure he understood that she was available, ready, willing, and able . . . and planning to stay on in Europe for a while. As long as he wanted, in fact.

He had been certain that he could have taken her to bed there and then; in fact, he was very well aware that was what she wanted. But as attracted as he had been to her, he paid attention to the small voice in his head that warned him to be cautious. The last thing he needed was a woman in his bed who was running back to the Hartes, to report to them about his sex life, his life in general, his business, his associates, and anything else she might manage to glean if she were around him for any length of time.

And so he had sent her packing that night, seen her the next afternoon for tea at the flat, and, against his better judgment, he had asked her to join him in Paris.

She had jumped at the invitation, and from the look on her face he had understood that she would jump through hoops for him . . . in bed. He wondered what else she would do for him if he asked her nicely.

As he leaned back against the chair, Jonathan's eyes drifted around the library, his favorite room in the apartment on the Avenue Foch. It was elegant without being pretentious, and it was sumptuously comfortable. Designed by one of Paris's leading interior designers, the library was paneled in bleached oak, furnished with priceless antiques, such as two handsome Louis XV chests and a beautiful standing clock by Le Roy, which were balanced by comfortable sofas and deep armchairs upholstered in dark red velvet. The carpet was Savonnerie, and the paintings on the walls were from the Impressionist period, two were Degas ballet dancers, while an extraordinary Sisley hung over the carved antique fireplace. Whenever he looked at the latter, he thought of his grandmother's Sisleys, which hung at Pennistone Royal, and smiled smugly. His was so much better, one of Sisley's finest works, and a true prize, something to cherish.

As his thoughts settled on Pennistone Royal, his face changed; an angry glint settled in his eyes. This time they had outwitted him. The bomb had blown out the west wall of the church, but it had been empty. Next time those bloody Hartes would not be so lucky. He'd get them yet, do them harm no matter what. Plans were hatching in his head.

Rising, he walked over to the fireplace and stood with his back to the logs burning brightly in the grate, shaking off his anger, his thoughts focusing again on Angharad Hughes. He had invited her for drinks, and then dinner this evening, but he had no intention of taking her out to one of his favorite haunts. He couldn't possibly permit himself to be seen with her in public.

She was a beautiful young woman, underneath all that muck she put on her face. But the hair was ghastly. Nonetheless, he had wanted, no, needed, to see her again, to explore the *possibilities* . . . of her, to take her to bed, if only this once. *Tonight.* He knew there would be no argument from her. But he had to be sure she was on the level, was merely interested in a relationship with him, not on some kind of mission to gather information.

He would assess her yet again when she arrived for drinks and make up his mind. Then he would have dinner with her at the apartment, whatever his final decision, and send her back to the George V if necessary, but only after he had enjoyed her company in his bedroom.

There was a knock on the door, and his houseman, Gaston, came in and stood discreetly in the doorway. "Marie-Claire wishes to know if you would like caviar with the aperitifs, Monsieur Ainsley?"

Jonathan shook his head. "Not this evening, Gaston, *merci.*"

The houseman nodded and withdrew, closing the door behind him as he returned to the servants' quarters of the spacious apartment.

Jonathan was not crazy about caviar, disliking the strong fishy taste, and he certainly didn't want Angharad Hughes tasting and smelling of it. The last time he had eaten it was with Priscilla, on one of their hot dates in Scarborough, and the taste had lingered for too long.

Priscilla Marney. Of course. She could help him make the right assessment about the Hughes girl. Prissy had catered the wedding reception last week. And she was observant. She could enlighten him, but without knowing she was doing so. Prissy was jealous of other women, and also put out with him at the moment for canceling their rendezvous in Thirsk. It was meant to have been yesterday. But if he phoned her now, and sweet-talked her, made her think he was unhappy not to have seen her, he might be able to glean a few useful tidbits.

Returning to the French *bureau plat,* he sat down, picked up the receiver, and dialed her number in Harrogate. She answered within seconds, and he said softly, "Hello, Prissy darling. It's Jonathan."

"Yes, I know," she responded, her tone not revealing her mood to him.

"I'm calling to tell you how much I'm missing you at this very moment, sweetie. I'd really been looking forward to seeing you yesterday, having you all to myself at the house in Thirsk."

"So had I," she replied, still not softening.

"I know you're upset with me, Prissy, but you mustn't be. I'm going to make it up to you, I promise. I will definitely be back in Yorkshire next week, and that's why I'm calling now. I want you to come to the house in Thirsk, spend the day with me and the night, as we'd planned to do yesterday."

When she did not respond, Jonathan said in a soft, throaty voice, "You know I can't resist you, darling girl, and I must see you before I go to Hong Kong. Please say yes. You'd make me so happy." He hoped he sounded appealing and sincere.

"All right," she answered slowly, almost reluctantly. "But you haven't said *when* next week, Jonny. I hope I can make it."

"I was thinking of next Thursday. A week today. I'll fly in early to Yeadon, so we can meet for lunch, and then we'll have the afternoon and the evening together. How about it, sweetie? Come on, say yes, Priscilla. You know how I feel about you."

It seemed to him that he felt the lifting of her cool, somewhat begrudging mood flowing down the telephone lines. "Oh, that's wonderful, Jonny! Yes, that's a really good day for me. And I'm missing *you,* aching to see you.

I was so looking forward to our little rendezvous, I really was, and I felt truly deflated yesterday, bloody let down, if you want the truth."

"Don't be. Look what's in store for you . . . for us. Together at Thirsk. No staff. Just the two of us, having a long, sexy day and night together. . . . Think of *that,* Prissy."

"Oh, Jonny, yes, yes, it'll be great!"

"My God, Prissy, you sound so loving and sexy, I wish you were here with me now . . . what I would do with you . . ."

"Oh, Jonny," she moaned. "*I* wish I were there, too."

"I think we'd better change the subject," he replied, suddenly laughing, pleased he had won her over. He could get her to eat out of his hand. "Tell me what happened at the wedding. You weren't very forthcoming the other day."

"Oh, I know, forgive me. But I was very upset when you canceled our date."

"So how did it go? What did I miss?"

"Well, you certainly missed the fireworks, if I can call it that. Linnet changed the time of the wedding. The two of them—Gideon and Evan—were married in a secret ceremony at eight-fifteen in the morning."

"Oh, really! Why was that?" He made himself sound surprised.

"Evan hasn't been feeling well. The twins are due in late February or the first of March. She looks awfully ready to give birth to me and to everyone else. Anyway, she hadn't been up to snuff, and the early ceremony was just a precaution actually. According to Margaret. Everyone was worried that the excitement of the ceremony with all the family in attendance might cause problems for Evan."

"I see," he said. "But what about the reception?"

"Oh, it went very well, and I must say everyone was turned out in their Sunday best. You'd have enjoyed it, Jonny, being with your cousins and your father."

"Yes, I'm sure I would," he answered in a very neutral tone. "And you saw my father, did you?" he probed, wanting to bring in the Hughes family.

"Yes, he was very handsome. Marietta Hughes was looking after him, she was wonderful with him."

"And what about her adopted daughters, Pris? What are they like? Evan's sisters? Are they as beautiful as she is?"

"Not really. Elayne is rather nice, a brunette, she's the middle one, but the youngest, Angharad, is just awful."

"Oh dear, is she the ugly sister then?"

"Not ugly ugly," Priscilla answered, sounding as if she disliked Angharad. "But cheap-looking. She has this horrendous hair, sort of spiky and dyed platinum. A cute face, I suppose, but she wears tons of makeup. She's got a wonderful figure, mind you, Jonny. And she acts sort of sexy. For a moment I thought Lorne might go for her, but I was mistaken. He couldn't stand her actually. Do you know, nobody can."

"And why is that?" he asked, his interest fired on.

"I don't know. I didn't really get to chat with her. I was very busy, you know. But later, when I was having a cup of tea with Margaret in the kitchen, she told me that none of the Harte girls like her at all. She's tried to make friends with them, but they shun her, *really shun her*. Margaret says Evan can't stand her. Neither can Gideon." Priscilla took a deep breath, and, lowering her voice, she confided, "I heard on the grapevine that Gideon blames her for Evan's accident."

"Really! Is that so? But actually, I didn't know Evan had had an accident." This was true; Jonathan's hand gripped the phone. "Do tell me."

"Apparently Evan fell in her office before coming to Yorkshire for the wedding. She missed her chair and hit the floor. She had to go to hospital because everyone was certain there was going to be a miscarriage. Or problems at any rate."

"But why would Gideon Harte think it was the sister's fault?"

"Because she visited Evan at the store unexpectedly, and they had a row. I *heard* they all believe she went there to pick a quarrel, actually. To upset Evan. Margaret heard Marietta saying to Emily that Angharad has always been envious of Evan, and never more than now. Because of Gideon, the Hartes, and all of that stuff."

"Oh dear, don't tell me there's trouble at t'mill," he murmured, using one of their favorite Yorkshire expressions.

"That's not just possible, it's a *probability*!" Priscilla announced. "Evan's father and sister have gone back to New York, but then I'm sure your father told you they'd left sooner than expected."

"Of course," Jonathan said. It was not his father who had kept him so well-informed. However, he had no intention of letting Priscilla know this. He asked, "And what about the awful sister? Where is she?"

"She's in London with her mother, but I don't think she's all that welcome as far as Evan and Gideon are concerned. Wiggs, the gardener, told me that Gideon wants her to return to the States as well. Oh, and by the way, Jonny, here's a bit of news. Tessa became engaged to the French writer."

"Oh, yes, so I'd heard," he exclaimed, chuckling, recognizing that what Angharad had said about some members of the family was absolutely true. "I'm really sorry I missed the wedding," he hurried on. "Just think, *we* might have sneaked a few hours together over the weekend."

"Oh, Jonny, don't tease me so . . . you're getting me all hot and bothered."

"Now, now, Priscilla, be a good girl until next week."

Her answer was a long sigh.

"I'll call you on Monday, darling," he murmured, and they hung up.

Jonathan rose, walked over to the fireplace, and stood

looking at his Sisley. That smug smile played around his mouth; he was not really seeing the painting, though, only Angharad Hughes. In his mind's eye. So they didn't like her, eh? None of them, or so it seemed. Perhaps she was the genuine thing after all. Just a hot little girl on the make, looking for a rich older man to be her sugar daddy. Well, why not? He wouldn't object to that.

He experienced a little rush of excitement. He couldn't wait for her to arrive now. He wanted to study her once again, question her, get her views of the Hughes family and the Hartes. It might be very telling, and certainly interesting. His best champagne would loosen her tongue no doubt. But then again, she sounded like a girl after his own heart; she might even be very useful to him, especially if he asked the right questions. That was always the key, wasn't it? Asking the right questions. That way you usually got the right answers.

When, an hour later, Angharad Hughes walked into the library, Jonathan was pleasantly surprised. On the few occasions he had seen her, she had been badly dressed. But tonight she looked quite stylish in a black wool dress, very high-heeled black shoes worn with lacy black stockings. The stockings were all wrong, and the dress was cut far too low, but what an improvement. She had made an effort for him, or so it appeared.

He rose from the chair, moved across the floor to greet her as Gaston showed her in and then swiftly departed.

"Hi!" she said as they met in the middle of the room.

"It's nice to see you again," he replied in a neutral voice, stretching out his hand.

She took it in hers, shook it, and then moved closer, stood on tiptoe, and kissed him on the cheek. "That's what *I* feel like doing!" she exclaimed, eyeing him flirtatiously. "I expect you think I'm forward, don't you?"

"Not really," he said, allowing a smile to surface. "A little bold perhaps, but certainly a girl who knows what she wants." Drawing her toward the fireplace, he went on, "I hope you like champagne, or do you want something else?"

"I want a lot of things, but sure, the champagne is fine for now." As she spoke, Angharad took a seat on the large, overstuffed sofa and patted the cushion next to her. "Why don't you sit here?"

Preferring to keep his distance for the moment, Jonathan shook his head. "I'm going to sit opposite you . . . so I can look at you, my dear."

"And do you like what you see, then?"

"I like the way you're dressed this evening, Angharad. You look quite elegant."

"I know that's what you like, elegance, stylishness. I'm not too sure of myself with clothes. You'll have to help me. You will, won't you? Teach me, I mean?"

"About clothes?"

She gave him a long, appraising look, and said, "Yes, what did you think I meant?"

He was wondering how to reply, whether to lead her on or not, when the door opened to admit Gaston. The houseman placed the tray he was carrying on a table set up for that purpose, and, after popping the cork, he poured the Dom Pérignon into crystal champagne flutes, brought them over to the fireplace on a silver tray.

"*Merci*, Gaston," Jonathan said. "I'll ring when I need you."

"*Oui, monsieur.*"

Once they were alone again, Jonathan stood up, went over to the sofa, and touched his glass to Angharad's. "Happy days!" he said, immediately stepping back and sitting down in the chair again.

"And happy nights!" she said, winking at him.

It took all of his self-control to keep his face straight, and he remembered how he had thought her a little tease the day she had appeared unannounced at his house in Thirsk. She had displayed the same suggestive characteristics then, said similarly cheeky things. Well, she *was* only twenty-three. Was this the way the young behaved these days? He thought of Jasmine Wu-Jen and her superb elegance and sophistication, and shoved the thought to one side. He did not want to be burdened with *those* memories tonight.

Angharad said, "I told you in London, I was real disappointed you didn't come to the wedding. I was looking all over for you. Why didn't you come?"

"Unfortunately, I had an emergency in London." He frowned. "I thought I told you that on Monday, when you came for drinks."

"You didn't say *emergency,* you said you had a pressing appointment. Was it with a woman?"

"That's none of your business."

"I know. But was it?"

He shook his head, slightly annoyed, and then found himself saying, much to his surprise, "No, it wasn't, it was business."

"That's great," she answered, crossing her legs, smiling at him, then taking a sip of the champagne. She eyed him over the glass, slightly parting her lips as they lingered on the rim. "If you'd been at the wedding, I was going to get you into a quiet place, just so I could . . . you know, get close to you . . . maybe even smooched with you. Would you have . . . kissed me back?"

Startled by the question, he lifted his glass, took a sip from it, settled in the chair, regarding her thoughtfully. She had the most extraordinary legs, long and shapely, and the tight-fitting dress revealed voluptuous breasts and a beautiful figure. She moved suddenly, pushed herself deeper into the cushions on the sofa, and immediately her skirt rode up; he caught his breath as he realized she was not wearing underwear, at least not much.

Jonathan stood, walked over to the table and poured himself another glass of champagne, returned to his chair, asking as he did, "Was it a nice wedding? Did you enjoy it?"

"No, I didn't!" She said this sharply, sat up a bit straighter, smoothed her skirt.

Her expression had instantly changed, he noticed. Her face was tight, tense, and there was an unexpected hardness in her dark brown eyes. "Because I wasn't there, is that the reason?" he probed, wanting to lead her on, discover her true feelings.

"No, not really. I was *disappointed* you weren't there, but I knew I'd see you in London. You said you'd have me over for drinks. I didn't enjoy the wedding because . . . *nobody cared about me.* My parents were caught up in Evan. Elayne was being mean to me, and everyone else was cold and . . . uppity. Snobs, all of them."

"So that's what you think about my family, is it?" he asked, his eyes narrowing.

"*You* think it, too, don't you?" she shot back swiftly.

He was silent, staring at her with growing interest.

She said, "I've heard whispers about you. I've heard that you're the black sheep. Are you?"

A slow smile spread across his lean, handsome face, and his bluish gray eyes twinkled. "I've heard that rumor, too, Angharad, but it doesn't do to listen to rumors, you know."

She laughed, leaned back against the cushions once more, and he caught a glimpse of a red garter belt as her skirt rose; then he quickly glanced away.

"I hope you *are* the black sheep. I love black sheep," she said.

"Do you now?" He put his glass down and leaned forward, his eyes riveted on hers. "And why is that?"

Laughing quietly, Angharad pushed herself up, stared back at him. Provocatively, her tongue came out, and she licked her lower lip, said very softly, "Because I'm the black sheep in *my* family. Well, they don't call me *that*, but they've always said I'm . . . a bad girl."

"And are you, my dear?"

"What do you think? Sure I am, and I love it, love being a bad girl up to her wicked games."

"And what are those?" he demanded in a low, amused tone, a blondish brow lifting questioningly.

She patted the cushion. "Come on over, I'll whisper in your ear. Better still, I'll show you."

Since he had decided to take her to bed tonight, Jonathan saw no reason why he shouldn't start the proceedings a little earlier than planned, so he went to join her on the sofa.

Immediately, she took hold of his hand and brought his palm to her mouth, licking it, then letting it go. Gazing up at him, she leaned closer and whispered, "On Monday night you asked me what I want from you. I never said. Shall I tell you now?"

He nodded, intrigued. He also realized she had enormous sexuality; it seemed to him that sex emanated from her, and when she said nothing, he pressed, "So tell me, what *do* you want from me?"

There was a little silence; finally she said, "*Everything.* That's what I want. *You.* All of you. And you can have all of me. I'll even give up the other men for you."

His bright, intelligent eyes, now brimming with shrewdness and calculation, roamed over her, and he said softly, "Would you give up *everybody* for me?"

She gaped at him, not understanding. "I have nobody else to give up, only my boyfriends. Who do you mean?" Unexpectedly, the answer came to her at once, and she cried, "*Them.* Do you mean them? My father and mother, my sisters?"

He nodded, his eyes not leaving her face.

She began to laugh before shaking her head and explaining, "They don't mean anything to me. They gave *me* up a long time ago. Besides, they've only ever been interested in Evan. She's the biological child. I'm the adoptee."

"*Adoptee.* That's a strange way to describe yourself, Angharad."

"That's Linnet's name for me, for *us.* She calls me and Elayne the adoptees. I heard her say it."

"That's not nice, but rather typical of the Hartes, I must admit. And how do you feel, Angharad?"

"I couldn't care less."

"What I meant was, do you feel like an adoptee?"

"I've always felt like an adopted girl. It doesn't matter, though. I'm my own woman, I have been for as long as I can remember. I said to hell with them a long time ago."

"I understand . . ." His voice trailed off. She was gazing at him with such intensity, and there was such a look of yearning on her face, he was quite startled. For a moment she was utterly vulnerable.

Angharad said in a low voice, "In the village shop . . . I wanted to grab hold of you and kiss you. Did you feel like that?"

"I was certainly attracted to you. Didn't you notice that I flirted with you a little?" He smiled faintly, remembering.

"I did." Leaning against him, she kissed him on the mouth.

He was taken by surprise but found himself kissing her back, not resisting as her tongue slipped into his mouth and her hand slid onto his crotch. Although she was exciting him, he took hold of her hand, lifted it off, and then drew away from her. "Let's not rush this," he murmured.

Without saying a word, Angharad swung her legs across his lap, took hold of his hand, and lifted her skirt. "Feel how much I want you," she whispered.

21

❧

The child carried the small bouquet of flowers in one hand and held on to her father's hand with the other. Together they walked down the corridor which led to Molly Caldwell's room at Leeds Infirmary.

"Is Grandma going to come home with us, Daddy?" Atlanta asked anxiously, looking up at Dusty. "Is her leg better?"

"I think it is, yes," he responded in a low voice, smiling, wanting to be reassuring. "Still, she might need a bit more rest, sweetheart."

The little girl nodded her head, made no comment, and a moment later they were standing outside Molly's room. Bending down, Dusty explained, "We can't stay long, you know, we mustn't tire Grandma. But guess what. I've got a surprise for you."

"A surprise? What is it?" she asked excitedly.

"If I tell you now, it won't be a surprise," he teased.

"Please, Daddy," Atlanta beseeched, her blue eyes looking soulful in her heart-shaped face.

"I'll tell you half of it now, okay?"

She smiled at him beguilingly and nodded.

"India's coming to lunch with us after we've visited with Grandma."

A huge smile illuminated her face, and she squeezed his hand. "I'm glad Indi's coming with us! What's the rest of the surprise?"

"Oh, no, Miss Nosey Parker, you'll have to wait for that," he declared and knocked on the door lightly, turned the knob, and walked in, saying quietly, "Here we are, Molly."

Molly Caldwell lit up at the sight of Dusty and her granddaughter in the doorway. "Come in, come in," she exclaimed, her weary face a picture of sudden happiness, her eyes shining.

Letting go of her father's hand, Atlanta half ran, half skipped across the room, and when she got to the bed she thrust the flowers at Molly. "These are for you, Grandma."

"Aren't you a little love," Molly said, her eyes settling on Atlanta's face as she searched for signs of change. She found nothing untoward. Atlanta looked perfectly beautiful, her cheeks pink and healthy, her blue eyes as bright as bluebells, and her hair a shining mop of dark curls.

"You're such a pretty girl, darling. My pretty girl." Leaning forward, she kissed Atlanta's cheek and brought the child closer so that she could embrace her, then said, "We'd best put the flowers in water, don't you think?"

"Good idea," Dusty agreed, closing the door and walking over to the bed. "Perhaps I should give them to one of the nurses?"

"Yes, you should."

Dusty bent and kissed Molly on the cheek, his eyes quickly scanning her face as he tried to ascertain how she was. "How do you feel?" he asked.

"Much, much better indeed. They've been wonderful to me here, I'll be on my feet in no time." Leaning back against the pillows, she continued, "Would you take the flowers now, please, Dusty, so that they can be put in water? And thank you for bringing them, they're beautiful."

He simply smiled at her, saying nothing, took the flowers from her and went in search of a nurse and a vase.

Atlanta moved nearer to her grandmother and took hold of her hand, which rested on top of the sheet. "I'm glad your leg's better. Did it hurt, Grandma?" she asked, her head to one side, a questioning look on her face.

Molly shook her head. "Not really, darling, just a little bit."

Atlanta continued to gaze at Molly, her eyes solemn, her voice serious when she said, "You didn't cry when you fell down . . . you were brave."

"Mmmm" was all Molly could say. She was suddenly choked up with emotion. She loved her granddaughter more than anything in this world, wished she could live to see her grow to womanhood. But she knew that was not to be. Swallowing and blinking back the incipient tears, Molly said, "And have you enjoyed staying at Willows Hall with Daddy?"

"Oh, yes, Valetta's nice, and so is Paddy, and Angelina. But I miss you, Grandma. Come home." As she spoke, her voice quavered slightly and her eyes grew large in her delicate face.

"I will, as soon as I can, but in the meantime I think it's nice for you to visit with your father." Molly tightened her grip on the child's hand and gently pulled her forward so that their faces were almost cheek to cheek.

Against Atlanta's hair, she said softly, "I want to tell you something about your father, Atlanta. He's such a *good* man, kind and gentle, but also very strong and dependable and trustworthy." Molly paused, leaned away, and studied her granddaughter. "Oh, I do hope you understand what I'm saying, lovey," she murmured. "But you're so young." Bringing a smile to her face, Molly added in a stronger voice, "Your father loves you very much, wants only the best for you. Remember that. Always listen to him and do what he says."

Atlanta blinked, drew even closer to her grandmother, kissed her cheek. Her voice was a whisper when she said, "I love my daddy." Looking suddenly sad, the child touched Molly's cheek. Molly caught her hand, kissed it, wondering what would happen when she was gone. But Dusty wouldn't let her down; she had confidence in him. He would withstand all pressure from Melinda, she was certain of that.

Atlanta asked, "Can you come and live at Willows Hall, Grandma? And Gladys? Can she come, too?"

"Perhaps. It would be lovely, all of us together, wouldn't it?"

Atlanta nodded, her face lighting up. "And Indi, too. She's nice, Grandma! We're having lunch, do you want to come?"

"I'd love to, but I just told you, I have to stay in hospital for a while. When I come home, we'll have that lunch, *a special lunch,* just the three of us. You and India and me."

"I wish you could come home now," Atlanta persisted, her face as solemn as her voice was plaintive.

The door suddenly opened, interrupting them. Dusty was standing there, a big smile on his face. "I found the other half of your surprise, Bean Shoot," he exclaimed, and he stepped aside to reveal Gladys, who was hovering immediately behind him. "Look who's here!"

"Gladys!" Atlanta cried and ran to hug her friend. Gladys hugged her back. Then, releasing Atlanta after planting a big kiss on her cheek, she went over to Molly.

"Hello, Gladys dear, thanks for coming."

"It's good to see you looking so much better," Gladys answered, meaning every word. Molly had improved in the last few days. "And I'm sorry I couldn't come yesterday, but I was seeing Gertrude off. To Canada."

"Oh, she's gone, has she?"

"Yes. She's fully recovered, and we've mended all of our fences."

Molly murmured, "Doesn't do for sisters to quarrel. I'm glad all is right again."

"Right as rain."

"It was India's idea actually," Dusty said, pulling a chair up to the bed and sitting down in it. "She thought that you and I would have a few minutes alone to chat if I sent Gladys with Atlanta to pick her up at the store."

"That was clever, and I *am* glad to have you to myself for a few minutes," Molly replied, leaning back against the pillows. "I'm so happy you brought Atlanta, Dusty. I've been longing to see her." She gave him the benefit of a warm smile and added, "And she's doing so well with you, but then she always has. She's happy to be with you, and she loves India, from what she says."

"*You* haven't said if you're coming to the wedding, Molly. It would please us both so much if you would. I'll arrange everything for you, make it as easy as possible . . . the travel, all that."

There was a small silence.

Molly stared at him; her face was unreadable.

Dusty swallowed, held his breath, waiting for her response. He wouldn't have even brought this matter up a few days ago, since he had believed her to be at death's door. But she looked so much better today he had been taken by surprise; since arriving this morning he'd decided that maybe she wasn't in danger of dying after all, at least not yet.

Clearing her throat, Molly finally said, "You know I'll come if I can. It pleases me that you've found the right woman to share your life with. It also comforts me that Atlanta will have a mother when I'm no longer here to look after her. Remember, Melinda can never have her, Dusty. I told you that when I first came into Leeds Infirmary."

"Yes, you did, but don't you think Melinda would fight me? I don't believe she would let me have custody of Atlanta without a struggle."

"What you say is true. On the other hand, if you have a good solicitor, I think you would win, perhaps without even having to go into court." A sudden sadness swept across Molly's face, and she sighed heavily as she thought of her only child, a young woman lost to her, lost to everyone. A ruined life, a wasted life, she thought; then, getting a grip on herself, she said in a voice laden with sorrow, "You wouldn't find it difficult to prove she's an unfit mother, and that is exactly what you must do if . . . I die. When I die, I mean."

"Because of the drugs, the drinking?" Dusty began and then stopped, shaking his head. "You don't think the detox clinic is working, do you?"

"Perhaps it is, for the moment. But I know her only too well, and I know she'll soon be up to her old ways. She has the wrong friends, Dusty, as you well know, and she goes right back to them every time she's clean. It's only a matter of days before she's hooked on drugs yet again." Molly fell silent for a moment before she finished. "She's my daughter, and I love her, but I can't help her, I don't think anyone can. And so I must think of her child instead, my granddaughter, *your* child, Dusty. *What's best for Atlanta,* that's all I can think about these days. You have to promise me again that you will fight to gain *sole* custody of Atlanta."

"I promised you before, and I reiterate that promise," Dusty reassured her. "I'm fully aware that Melinda is a lost cause. If only I could help her—I've tried, Molly."

"Nobody could have tried harder, and you've been wonderful to her, and to your child. And to me as well, and for that I am ever so grateful." Leaning forward, Molly now took hold of his hand and held on to it tightly. "I want to impress something on you, Dusty, something you must never forget. Atlanta would be in mortal danger if she lived with her mother. Melinda is neglectful, irresponsible, selfish, and undisciplined. And uncontrollable when she's drunk or doped up. Please don't ever let that innocent child be alone with her mother *ever*—" Molly's voice broke, and she began to weep.

Dusty put his arms around her, held her close, wanting to give her a measure of peace, to make her understand that he *understood* all that Melinda was. Molly's words had been stark in their honesty. He would never forget them, as she had no doubt intended.

"Please don't upset yourself so, Molly, you know you can rely on me," he said, stroking her back, continuing to hold her in his arms.

After a few minutes, Molly's weeping became quieter, and eventually it abated. With an effort, she pulled away from him and looked up into his face. "I'm sorry," she whispered. "I didn't mean to break down like that, Dusty. It's just that I worry about Atlanta all the time; she's so vulnerable, so defenseless."

"But she has me, and I will never let anything happen to her."

Molly nodded, reached for a tissue on the bedside table, and dried her eyes. "I trust you implicitly, and please forgive my tears."

"There's nothing to forgive." Wanting to change the subject, to cheer her up, Dusty said, "When I spoke to Gladys last night, asked her to join us here today, she told me that she would be available to help me out, do a bit of babysitting. That was good news."

"The best," Molly agreed. "Now that her sister has gone back to Canada, and as long as I'm in the infirmary, she's available. She loves Atlanta, and the child is happy with her, she's used to being with Gladys. They get on well."

"That's the impression I got," Dusty replied. "You haven't told me what the doctors say, Molly. How are you, actually?"

"Dr. Bloom's a bit noncommittal; he doesn't say much," she answered. "But then he's my general practitioner, and he put me in the hands of a heart surgeon, as you know. As far as he's concerned, I'm on the mend. He's a good man, Mr. Larchmont. That's my news."

Dusty felt a lessening of the tension in him. "What great news it is! I'm thankful you're going to get better, Molly. To tell you the honest truth, I've been worried to death about you."

"I know. But it'll be all right. I'll be all right. You'll see."

It did Molly Caldwell's heart good to see her granddaughter interacting so well with India Standish. The young woman who was going to marry Dusty Rhodes was beautiful in a delicate, cool blond way. But her looks were not all that important to the older woman. What pleased Molly, and gave her such reassurance, was the gentleness and kindness she detected in India. That she loved Atlanta was patently obvious, and the feeling was undoubtedly mutual.

Her mood was one of optimism and relief. Gladys and Atlanta had returned with India, and suddenly her little hospital room seemed crowded, especially since Dusty's presence was so potent. For a moment she studied him surreptitiously, endeavoring to see him objectively.

That he was handsome there was no question; his dark good looks were strong and somewhat rough-hewn, as if he had been carved from some great and ancient boulder dragged down from the moors. Heathcliff, she suddenly thought, he has the look of Heathcliff the way Emily Brontë envisioned him. Grandly masculine, carved from granite in great strokes, a thing of nature, mythic, powerful, gypsy dark. It was the eyes of course that bespoke his lightness, his spirituality, his sensitive nature. A blue deeper than the speedwells that grew in the fields below the moors, bluer than the sky that soared above; they were a supernatural blue, uniquely his.

And then there was his talent. A gift from God. Talent such as his was rare, sublime, transporting in its beauty. Molly Caldwell had always admired artistic talent, whatever field the artist had chosen. Yet she especially loved the visual arts, and Dusty's paintings had stunned and be-

guiled her long before she met him, before he had known
Melinda and fathered her granddaughter.

There was no hope for her own child, not anymore.
Melinda was on a journey of self-destruction, a journey
she had embarked upon long before Dusty Rhodes had
strolled casually by and fallen, momentarily, into her sexual trap. He had been wise to move rapidly out and on,
Molly understood that. He was a man with a purpose in
life, a talent he needed to use, great ambition to fulfill.
And so he had wasted little time with the demented
woman Melinda had become.

It was only later, when he had discovered there was to
be a baby, his baby, that he had done the correct thing,
done an about-face and come back to Melinda. But he
had not remained long in that maddening circus of dys-
function, populated with her crazy and crazed friends.
Instead he had moved on again, knowing he must save
himself, accepting with the best will in the world that he
could not save her.

Dusty had been a good father, diligent, responsible,
caring, and loving. He must have Atlanta, she said to herself silently as she watched him now, holding her granddaughter on his knee, turning to talk to India. There was
so much love in his eyes for them both. It brought a flush
of genuine happiness to Molly's face, and she looked intently at Gladys, who nodded, understanding exactly
what she was feeling, also recognizing that this room, at
this moment, was full of unconditional love.

22

～

Linnet knew the moment she walked into Paula's office that her mother was annoyed with her. So sure was she of this that she hurried forward, exclaiming, "Hello, Mummy," and sat down in the chair opposite her, determined to jump-start the conversation before Paula had a chance to say anything.

"Good morning, Linnet," Paula replied, looking up from the papers spread out on her desk. "I understand—"

"Oh, Mummy, I'm sorry to interrupt, but before we get into a discussion about the Easter Fashion Week, I just want to explain something." As she spoke, Linnet took a sheet of paper out of a folder, continuing, "I've written you a memo about a plan I have. I just finished it this morning, and I want you to have it now." Linnet leaned across the desk and handed the memo to Paula.

"Thank you." Paula scanned it swiftly and said, "Well, I'm relieved to have something on paper. Your father mentioned to me a short while ago that he had spoken earlier to Bonnadell Enloe, and she told him in passing you'd been making inquiries about her spas. Do you have an idea about opening one of her spas here at the store? Is that why you called her?"

Leaning forward, her expression eager, Linnet exclaimed, "Yes, I do! That's what my memo is about."

"But where would we put a spa?" Paula asked, her voice rising.

"Where the hairdressing salon is now. It's really quite large and—"

"And where will the hair salon go? There's no other available space," Paula cut in, sounding exasperated and annoyed.

"I explain that in the memo, but very frankly, I don't think we need a hair salon anymore. Business has been awfully slack lately. In my opinion, that space would be better utilized as a spa."

Paula sat back in her chair, staring at her daughter in disbelief. "What makes you think a spa will do any better than the hairdressing salon?" she demanded in a cold tone.

"Women love spas. Especially young women who work hard. They enjoy relaxing at a day spa, having a massage, a facial, pedicure, manicure, and other special treatments. I think we'd have a big success if we opened one."

"Do you really?" Paula shot back, still sounding sharp. "And have you considered the cost of remodeling the space? It will be enormous."

"But it won't," Linnet countered. "Once the hair salon equipment is removed, like the banquettes, hair dryers, and sinks, we'll be left with a large empty space. All we have to do is build wooden cubicles, little enclosed areas for the massages and treatments. I've got it all planned out, and I believe that an Enloe spa would work in the store just as well as they all work in Dad's hotels around the world."

"I don't know about this, Linnet. I think it will be a lot more costly to remodel that space than you do. Furthermore, I'm not sure you're right about getting rid of the hair salon. And who's going to run the spa if we build one? The store? Or the Enloe Company?"

"I'm not sure. I hadn't quite figured that out. But it might be simpler for us if we did use the Enloe Company. That's why I put a call in to Bonnadell on Friday." Linnet gave a little laugh. "She didn't waste much time in telling Dad, did she?"

"No, she didn't. She spoke with him early this morning about something else, but your call came up. Anyway, for what it's worth, I think she's very interested in the idea of a spa at Harte's of Knightsbridge, but—"

"Oh, Mummy, that's great!"

"But that doesn't mean that *I am*, Linnet," Paula pressed on. "I will have to give this considerable thought. I'm not sure you're correct, you know. And if the Enloe Company are running the spa, how are we going to make money, tell me that. What's in it for Harte's? I really think you have to do a great deal of research on this—"

The shrilling of the phone brought Paula up short, and she picked up her private line. "Paula O'Neill here."

"Hello, Paula, it's Sarah. Sorry I couldn't phone you earlier. I had some meetings with two of my suppliers, and they went on longer than I expected. Anyway, here I am, reporting in as promised."

"I'm assuming you and Yves had dinner with our cousin on Saturday."

"No, Paula, we didn't. But only because Jonathan asked to change the date to Sunday evening. Of course I agreed, because I'd promised you I'd do it, and as it turned out, Sunday was far better for Yves. So . . . we met him at the Relais Plaza in the Plaza Athénée last night." There was a pause at the other end of the line, and Sarah sneezed, then said, "Sorry about that," and went on. "We met for drinks and dinner and—"

"Was the girl in question with him? Or was it his protégée, so called," Paula interrupted, anxious and now growing impatient to know.

"It was Angharad Hughes, she's his protégée, and do I have a story for you!"

"I can't wait to hear everything. But would you mind if I put you on the speakerphone? I have Linnet here with me . . . Linnet, say hello to Sarah."

Taking the phone from her mother, Linnet said, "Hello, Auntie Sarah. Thanks for helping with this. Mummy's been so worried about J.A. And upset, especially about the church being damaged."

"I can well imagine, Linnet. Jonathan's become more than troublesome. Well, I hope we get to see you when you next come to Paris. Now, may I speak with your mother, please?"

"Here she is." Linnet handed the phone back to Paula.

"So, Sarah, tell me the story. And may I put you on the speaker?"

"*Absolutely*. No problem. So here goes. It was definitely Angharad Hughes who accompanied him, but a very different Angharad Hughes than *you* could ever *imagine,* I'm quite certain of that."

"What on earth do you mean?" Paula asked.

"I think I'd better begin at the beginning," Sarah announced, her lovely speaking voice echoing around Paula's private office. "Early on Friday morning I had a call from Jonathan, asking if he could change the dinner date to Sunday. After I'd agreed, he said he needed a favor. When I asked him what that was, he explained he wanted my advice about women's hairdressers, also where to buy elegant women's clothes. When I suggested couture houses such as Pierre Balmain, Valentino, and Givenchy, he said he didn't have time to wait for pieces to be made to measure. He needed the clothes at once."

Sarah paused for a split second, and Linnet exclaimed, "Don't tell me he got her all dressed up in couture! *Not Angharad.* What a laugh that is. She's such a strange looking girl, a bit cheap-looking actually."

"I know what you mean," Sarah continued. "Anyway, I agreed to make an appointment with a good hairdresser, either Carita or Alexandre, and told him I would take him to Madame Valencia, the woman who makes some of my clothes. She has an atelier on Avenue Montaigne and usually has a small selection of elegant, handmade pieces in stock. He told me the young woman was of medium height and a size eight. Like you, I was very anxious to find out what their relationship was. I got there early and picked out a few things. When he arrived with Angharad, she was lathered in rather heavy makeup and, oh, dear, that frightful platinum blond hair. I couldn't believe my eyes."

"So he bought her some chic clothes and did a make-over on her, is that what you're saying, Sarah?" Paula asked, instantly understanding that if Jonathan Ainsley was going to all that trouble, he was embarking on a special relationship with Angharad. If he was treating her merely as a one-night stand, he wouldn't be buying her stylish clothes. She said this to Sarah, who agreed. "He's spent *real* money on her."

"I'm very curious," Linnet interjected. "What did he select for her?"

"A tailored gray flannel skirt suit, which I'd pulled out for him to look at. The jacket had a feeling of Givenchy to it, and there was a silk camisole, which also fit her. He spotted a gray wool overcoat, trimmed down the front with chinchilla. That was another choice, along with a plain black day dress and a cashmere overcoat, as well as a black velvet cocktail suit," Sarah finished, then added, "That was about it, except for accessories."

"And how did she look in the clothes?" Linnet asked. "I mean, the clothes didn't change her *looks*, did they?"

"No, of course they didn't," Sarah replied. "But they fitted her well, and suited her. After buying gray and black shoes, bags to match, and gloves at Madame Valencia's accessory boutique, Jonathan took her off to Carita to have her hair done."

"Just finish up about her appearance," Paula requested. "What did she wear on Sunday night, and how did she look? Why were you so taken aback?"

"She looked absolutely stunning. I hardly recognized her, to be honest," Sarah confided, and then she rushed on. "She was wearing the gray flannel suit, gray overcoat, and the gray accessories. But that wasn't the point. What stunned me was her hair. It had been dyed a lovely russet brown and had a few blond highlights. All that heavy makeup had disappeared, too. She looked very fresh-faced, with a lot of emphasis on her eyes, well-applied makeup. But just a light dusting of powder and pale pink lipstick."

"How very interesting," Paula murmured thoughtfully. "It appears that he is extremely taken with her, wouldn't you say, Sarah?"

"Yes, indeed. Very frankly, he has transformed her, well, at least her appearance. Yves thought she had the look of a young Audrey Hepburn, and, to be honest, so did I. By the way, she was wearing pearl-and-diamond earrings which looked real, but they could have been fake."

"To my way of thinking," Paula remarked, "this kind of attention means he's sleeping with her and plans on keeping her around. At least for a while. But is it merely a personal relationship, or do you think he is using her as a conduit to us through her mother? *That* is the crucial question."

"It's hard for me to say whether she's supplying him with information about the Hartes," Sarah answered swiftly. "But I will hazard a guess. . . . I believe it to be more of a *sexual liaison* than anything else."

"What brings you to that belief?" Paula asked, even though she trusted Sarah's judgment.

"Angharad's hugely besotted by him, hangs on his every word, clings to him. At least she did on Sunday evening," Sarah explained. "As for Jonathan, he can't take his eyes off her, nor can he keep his hands off her. The lust, the passion were patently obvious, not only to me but to Yves as well. My husband, by the way, thought she oozed sex appeal." Sarah finished with a small, dry laugh of amusement.

"I'm hoping it *is* a sexual affair and nothing else," Paula informed Sarah, her voice suddenly brisk. "She's too close for comfort as far as Evan and Gideon are concerned."

"Yes, I know," Sarah answered quietly. "But if this is any consolation, I think he might actually be falling for her. *Hard*. I haven't seen him act like this since the days of Arabella Sutton."

"What makes you say that?" Paula asked, her tone still businesslike and crisp.

"The look in his eyes, the expression on his face, the way he's somewhat . . . *solicitous* of Angharad. He was very much in love with Arabella Sutton, and when it all blew up, he was devastated. Truly, he was, Paula. I know because I got him through that awful period. He's never loved a woman since. Oh, he's had plenty, that I know only too well, since I've usually had to entertain them. But this one, well, it could be the real thing, just as it was with Arabella. If you'll excuse the expression, Angharad's sexually entrapped him, that's what Yves said when we got home. And Yves has a lot of insight into our cousin."

"I see." There was a moment's silence, and then Paula asked, "Are you planning to see them again?"

"Oh, yes, since I promised to help you determine the situation. I invited them to dinner later this week. Jonathan's going to let me know, but he did murmur something about taking off for Hong Kong. I must tell you, Paula, Angharad looked crushed when he said this, and Jonathan quickly added that he wanted to show her the sights. So he's obviously hooked."

"For the moment," Linnet remarked pithily. "But we can't leave things to chance, Mummy." All of her attention was now focused on Paula as she added, "Evan and Gideon have to be informed of this development at once, and so does Marietta. In fact, the entire Hughes family has to know. They have to be warned not to give Angharad any information about Evan's movements, or any of our movements for that matter."

"You're absolutely right," Paula responded, nodding. "And what's your opinion, Sarah?"

"The same as Linnet's. They should be warned to keep her at arm's length."

"I think she ought to be ostracized by the family, cut off completely," Linnet suddenly announced in a tough voice. "As a matter of fact, I'm going to see that this happens. And immediately. We can't afford any slipups here."

"That might not be necessary," Paula pointed out. "It could be that her family will do that without any encouragement from you."

"True," Linnet conceded, although she didn't entirely agree with her mother's assessment of the Hughes family.

After thanking Sarah and asking her to continue to socialize with Jonathan, Paula hung up, switched off the speakerphone, and stared across the desk at Linnet. "I know you'll talk to Evan and Gid, but what about Marietta? Are you sure you want to break this news to her, or should I do it?"

"Oh, Mummy, don't bother, you've so much on your plate, I'll talk to her later today. I think I have to do it in person actually, don't you?"

"That would be nicer."

"I like Marietta, she's a lovely woman, and I think she's going to be horrified when she hears about Angharad's behavior."

"Very disloyal." Paula shook her head. "But then I've gained the impression that Angharad's not on such good terms with anyone."

"No, she's not. Leave it to me. And by the way, what do you think of Sarah's opinions about the situation?"

"She's always been very intelligent and sharp-eyed. So I tend to trust her judgment. And I am certain she *is* on our side. She thinks Jonathan is dangerous. Sarah's been turned off him for some time now and stays in touch with him only to help me."

"You do really believe that, don't you, Mummy?"

"Yes, I do, Linnet. I trust Sarah all the way. You see, she wants very much to be part of the family. She'll do anything she can to get back into my good graces."

Linnet nodded. "Okay. Anyway, about the spa idea, will you consider it?"

"I'll *think* about it. But I'm not sure you're right about closing down the hair salon." Paula's voice trailed off. Her head was buzzing, and she suddenly felt tired out, yet the clock on her desk told her it was only eleven o'clock. Taking a deep breath, she went on slowly, "Do the research I need, Linnet, and then we'll talk again."

"I'll have it for you in a few days, Mummy. In the meantime, did you call me in to talk about the Fashion Week at Easter? Or the spa idea?"

"The spa, actually. I was curious after your father mentioned you'd been talking to Bonnadell Enloe."

"I see."

Leaning across her desk, Paula said in a warmer tone, "There's another thing, Linny. Don't you think you have your hands full at the moment? Evan's on maternity leave for three months, and Tessa's now engaged to Jean-Claude. Eventually she will leave Harte's, you know."

"I wouldn't count on that!" Linnet cried, sitting up straighter. "She'll want to have the top job and commute from Paris to London, you'll see."

Paula sat back, staring at her daughter, but she made no comment. She had a strange feeling that Linnet was correct; Tessa had not yet given up on the idea of taking over as head of Harte's one day. After all, she had considered herself the Dauphine since childhood. But what of Jean-Claude? Wouldn't he object? Or, maybe he wouldn't. Perhaps he liked the idea of a young wife with modern ideas and a career.

"Is something wrong? You have a funny look on your face, Mums," Linnet said with a frown.

"No, I'm fine," Paula reassured her. "I was just thinking

about Tessa. Perhaps you're right, maybe she will want to . . . cling on. However, I'm not retiring. Nor do I plan to for a very long time. You should all remember that."

"I'm sorry I'm late," Marietta apologized as Evan greeted her in the entrance hall of Gideon's flat.

"It doesn't matter, Mom, I was just making lists of the everyday things we're going to need for the new apartment. Kitchen stuff and all that."

Mother and daughter hugged, and then Marietta took off her topcoat, hung it in the hall closet, and followed Evan into the sitting room, explaining, "The estate agent delayed me."

"Real estate agent?" Evan repeated, looking at her mother, her lovely, bluish gray eyes full of questions.

Marietta took a seat opposite her in the sitting room and explained, "That's one of the reasons I wanted to see you today, to tell you something. I'm going to take an apartment here, Evan. Not only because of you and my grandchildren but because I love London, and I realized I want to spend part of the year here."

"Oh, Mom, I think that's just great! And it'll be wonderful to have you and Dad here, getting to know the twins. I bet he's real excited. And Robin must be thrilled as well."

At first Marietta didn't respond. She simply sat, staring at Evan blankly, wondering how to break the news to her, hoping she wouldn't be upset when she understood how things really were.

"*Mom*. What is it? You're looking peculiar."

"I'm just wondering how to explain to you that your father won't be spending much time in London, Evan."

"Oh, you mean because of his business, the shops?"

Taking a deep breath, Marietta said, "I'm leaving your father. We're separating."

Evan leaned back against the cushions on the sofa, gaping at her mother. For a split second she was rendered speechless, and then she said, "Oh, my God, why didn't you tell me before?"

"Because I didn't want to upset you when you were about to get married, and also because of your pregnancy. It was bad enough that you had the fall in the office, all Angharad's fault, I'm positive of that. She's worse than she ever was . . ." Marietta paused, shook her head. "Your grandmother used to say we didn't know anything about her, what kind of people she came from, and Glynnis was right. She used to say it's all in the genes, and again she was correct. Angharad was a foundling, left on the doorstep of the church."

"Mom, please don't digress. Tell me about you and Dad. Why *are* you splitting up?"

"Goodness, Evan, how can you ask that? You and I talked about my marriage last year. You know very well it hasn't worked in years. And less now than ever."

"Since your aunt left you everything? That's part of it, isn't it?" Evan suggested, gazing at her mother intently. *"Isn't it?"* she pressed.

"Not as far as your father's concerned, no. It doesn't matter to him that my aunt left me her entire estate and made me quite wealthy. He's not interested in the money; he's doing very well himself these days."

"But surely he's sort of put out. Kind of . . . ticked off? Because you're now independent and can do what you want. In a way, her money has set you free."

Marietta nodded and looked into the distance for a moment. And as she thought of all that had happened between her and Owen, a shadow fell across her face. For a moment she was unable to speak. All she could think about was the past, and the past was immutable. *That* she *had* come to understand in the last few years. You could never escape the past. Not ever, no matter how hard you tried.

Watching her acutely, Evan recognized that her mother was wrestling with something, and she decided not to probe. Better to wait for her mother to tell her what she wanted to tell her in her own time. And so Evan kept still on the sofa, her hands resting lightly on her stomach, as if protecting her boys. She couldn't wait for them to be born now; she longed to hold them in her arms, and longed for her body to be back to normal. There were times, like right now, when Evan felt like a beached whale.

Marietta suddenly sat up and said, "Our marriage went wrong a long time ago, Evan, when you were small. I left your father at that time. Eventually I came back for many reasons, mostly because of you. But it was only to discover that he—"

"Had taken me for himself," Evan said, cutting her mother off. "And that's why you adopted Elayne and then Angharad, isn't it? Because you wanted girls of your own. And you wanted a family."

"Yes, that's true. We discussed this, you and I, last summer. Adopting the girls was Glynnis's idea. She loved me and she loved her son and she loved you . . . we were all so important to her. And so she begged Owen to take me back, and eventually he did, but—"

The telephone jangled, interrupting Marietta. "I'll get it, don't move," she instructed, jumping up. "Harte residence," she said, smiling across at her daughter as she spoke.

"Is that you, Marietta?"

"Yes, it is, Linnet."

"Hello! And I'm so glad you're there. I need to see you and Evan about something. Can I come over? Take you both to lunch? Or better still, I can bring a picnic lunch over from Harte's."

"Let me just ask Evan what her plans are, Linnet. Hold on a moment, please." Covering the receiver, Marietta looked over at her daughter. "Obviously you know it's Linnet. She wants to take us out to lunch, or bring a picnic lunch over; she says she needs to speak to us both. So which do you prefer? Or do you have a doctor's appointment or anything?"

"No, Mom, I'm free all day, and I think I'd prefer a picnic lunch, wouldn't you?"

"Why not, it'll be lovely." Marietta now spoke to Linnet at the other end of the phone, saying, "It's fine for you to come over. Evan says she'd love a picnic lunch, and so would I. What time should we expect you?"

"In about thirty minutes, if that's all right."

"Yes, I'm sure it is. See you later." Replacing the receiver, Marietta returned to the chair. "What can I do, Evan? She's coming in thirty minutes. Shall I set the table?"

"Yes, let's do that, Mom. But did Linnet say why she's coming over?"

"No. She just said she needed to talk to us both."

"I see." Evan sat quietly, her heart sinking. Then she looked at her mother, her eyes narrowing, and asked softly, "Where is Angharad? Do you know?"

"No, I don't, not really. She said she was going to go to the South of France, perhaps via Paris," Marietta replied.

"I see."

Marietta gave Evan a probing glance. "Why do you look like that?"

"Like what, Mom?"

"Come on, Evan, don't play dumb. You know very well how you're looking . . . like someone who knows what this is all about but isn't going to say. *Conspiratorial*, that's how you look."

"Don't be silly!" Evan cried, shaking her head. "How could I know why Linnet's coming to talk to us? But I do have an imagination, and I suspect it could be about the dreaded Jonathan."

"Oh, God, no, not that." Marietta turned pale.

"Well, maybe not," Evan said quickly, not wanting to alarm her mother. "Listen, let's not speculate. Let's get back to Dad and your marriage. How did he take it, I mean when you told him?"

"With his usual indifference," Marietta murmured, slowly standing up. "I'm going to set the table for lunch, Evan. I'd prefer to drop the matter of my separation for the moment. We can discuss it after lunch, when we're alone again."

"All right," Evan agreed, pushing herself to her feet. "I'll hold you to that, you know."

"I don't doubt," Marietta muttered.

23

~

Marietta opened the door, and Linnet came breezing into the apartment as if she didn't have a care in the world, carrying several large Harte's shopping bags, exclaiming, "Hello! Here I am with lunch. Hot vegetable soup, mixed finger sandwiches, and fruit. I hope it tempts you."

"It sounds yummy," Marietta answered, taking some of the bags from her. "Let's put all of this in the kitchen. Do you think I should reheat the soup?"

"The containers keep it fairly hot, but why not?" Linnet followed Marietta, helped to take the food out of the bags, then returned to the hall and hung up her topcoat.

A moment later Evan came out of the bedroom, hurried into the sitting room, and greeted Linnet warmly. "What a nice surprise, Linny, you coming over today." Dropping her voice, she then asked, "Is this about Jonathan Ainsley? Or Angharad?"

"Both. But let's have lunch first. This news can wait."

"All right," Evan answered, knowing better than to argue. "Can I get you anything?"

"Not right now, thanks. I'll just have water with lunch. Where do you want us to eat? In the kitchen or in here?"

"I think it's easier in the kitchen, don't you?" Evan said. Linnet nodded, and together they went to join Marietta in the next room.

Within minutes Marietta was serving the soup as Linnet told Evan about the meeting with her mother regarding the day spa. "And I think with a little luck she'll go along with it," Linnet finished.

"Oh, I do hope so. It'll be great to have a spa, won't it? I'd certainly make use of it, and so would you."

Linnet began to laugh. "Let's not forget, it's for the customers, not us."

Evan laughed with her and went on. "When are you going to break the news about the floor devoted to brides? Soon, I hope."

"Yes, very soon. Later this week, in fact. I'm just finishing up the various memos. Then I'm going to jump in the deep end and give them all to her, along with my plan for the next couple of years. I hope that Mummy sees what I see, and that she will share my vision."

"Do you mean you're going to mention the cafés in the Food Halls as well as everything else?" Evan asked, experiencing a flicker of apprehension. "Like the deli and the cheese bar?"

"Well, yes, I am. I'm doing memos on *everything*. I think it's easier to comprehend a plan when it's down on paper. Anyway, my mother's always liked memos, you know."

Marietta was listening with great interest, and when there was a break in the conversation, she said, "I certainly like the sound of a floor devoted to brides, that's a great idea, and so is the spa. I've become addicted to *them* in the last year. They're so pampering, relaxing."

Evan glanced at her mother, then, turning to Linnet, she said, "By the way, my mother's going to take an apartment here. She's planning to spend part of the year in London."

"That'll be lovely. After all, you're going to have grandchildren growing up here. And where's the flat? Or haven't you found one yet?" Linnet asked. She liked Marietta, was interested in her plans.

"I have. It's just off Sloane Street, and I think it would work well for me. I'd love you both to see it." Marietta stood, picked up two of the empty bowls, and carried them to the sink; Linnet followed with hers, and a moment later the two women were putting the rest of the food on the kitchen table.

"How about a cup of tea?" Marietta asked, filling the kettle and plugging it in.

Evan shook her head.

Linnet said, "I think I'd like a cup after all. Thank you, Marietta." She sat down, took a cucumber sandwich, and bit into it. Evan followed suit, and they ate in silence. In fact, silence reigned even after Marietta had joined them at the table; all three of them concentrated on lunch, not wanting to embark on what might prove to be a difficult and disturbing conversation.

Once lunch was over and the dishes cleared away, it was Evan who broke the silence. "All right, Linnet, give us the bad news," she prompted. "Because it's bad, isn't it?" She held her breath as she waited for Linnet to answer.

"*Peculiar*," Linnet replied, then carefully told them about the conversation Paula had had with Sarah earlier that morning, not missing one detail.

The two women were startled to hear that Angharad was with Jonathan in Paris, but it was Marietta who was the most disturbed. She had blanched when Linnet embarked on the story, and now she looked as if she was about to burst into tears. Evan appeared calmer, and she discovered she was not all that surprised to learn that Angharad had hooked up with Jonathan; it had seemed a probability to her ever since her mother had relayed the story of their odd encounter in the village store.

"I had a horrible sinking feeling that something like this would happen," Evan remarked, looking from one woman to the other. She gave her mother a long, piercing glance. "Glynnis once said something to me about bad seed in reference to Angharad, and she was quite prophetic, don't you think, Mom?"

Marietta could only nod.

"She's not only promiscuous and greedy but selfish and careless, and far too casual about her life. Not to mention utterly disloyal," Evan said in a cold voice. "My God, she'd sell us all out for a hot night in bed with Ainsley and a few glittering toys."

"Lots of nights in bed with him, and lots of glittering toys," Linnet corrected. "But that's her business. I'd like to discuss *my* business with *you*."

Evan nodded but made no comment.

It was Marietta who exclaimed, "How could she do this? Get involved with the man who is the family's deadly enemy. It's unbelievable!"

"Did she know that?" Linnet wondered out loud. "Did she realize he was the enemy?"

"Sure she did!" Evan cried, her anger suddenly coming to the surface. "She's heard us discuss Jonathan, heard us complain how troublesome and dangerous he is. But she doesn't care, because she doesn't care about us. She never has. There's something oddly detached about her, and that dates back to our childhood. She was a nasty kid, and she hasn't changed. Talk about self-involved, she takes the prize."

Marietta suddenly exclaimed, "She has now become *our enemy*."

"Indeed she has," Linnet agreed, "and that's what I want to talk to you about, Marietta . . . Evan." Leaning forward, pinning her eyes on them, she continued. "We know what Angharad's up to, in the sense that we know she's after *him*, and she's also after his *money*. You've made that clear. She wants bed, board, and bling. But what is *he* after? My mother is worried that J.A. sees her as a conduit to the Hartes, and especially to you, Evan, and also Gideon. She's part of your family, your sister, and it would be so easy for her to find out everything about your life, your movements, your plans."

"Oh, no, not from me she won't!" Evan shook her head vehemently. "She's been off my list for quite a while now. I don't want anything to do with her, not ever again."

"And neither do I," Marietta announced, pulling herself up in her chair, endeavoring to bring her swimming senses together. "Angharad has gone over to the other side, and therefore I shall cut her out of my life."

"I'm glad to hear that." Linnet offered Marietta a warm smile, reached out and touched her hand resting on the kitchen table. "I'm sorry she's betrayed *you*, all of you, but now that she has shown her true colors, you can't have anything to do with her. None of you—"

"But I just said that," Marietta cut in.

"I know. However, what about Owen and Elayne? Where would they stand if they knew? Where *will* they stand when they *do* know?"

"Next to us," Evan answered. "We'll be standing side by side. Elayne, for sure, knows she's a . . . *bitch*."

"That's true," Marietta concurred. "And Owen understands what she is. I don't believe we have to worry about him or Elayne."

"But they must be told," Linnet pointed out. "They must know she's with Jonathan Ainsley, must know everything I've told you today. Will you call Owen, Marietta? Or do you want me to do it?"

Marietta hesitated.

Evan said, "I'll call Dad."

"No." Marietta shook her head. "I'll do it."

"*Mom*, please. I think that's a bad idea."

"You know what . . . I should call him," Linnet now interjected. "If I call, there will be more of an *impact*."

"Probably," Marietta murmured.

Evan nodded.

"Then it's settled. I'll phone him later today at the shop

in Connecticut, and I'll explain that Angharad has to be totally ostracized." Linnet paused, took a drink of water, and added, "Of course, there is just the possibility that she's not a conduit to us, and that J.A. has truly fallen for her, is interested only in *her,* just as Sarah believes."

"Let's not take any chances," Marietta remarked. "Angharad has always been jealous of Evan, seen herself as the neglected child. She got it into her head years ago that we favored Evan and Elayne, and she would often accuse me of holding Evan up as the shining example of excellence, showing Evan off as the star, as she put it. And nothing could be further from the truth."

"She's bitter," Evan said in a subdued voice, feeling cold and uneasy.

"You know, Marietta, Angharad is not likely to be in touch with Evan, but she may well phone *you* from Paris. After all, you're her mother."

Marietta shook her head. "No, she won't, Linnet."

"Doesn't she stay in touch?"

"Not really."

"She might call you to boast, though," Evan suggested.

"Oh, definitely," Marietta said. "If she's got something worthwhile to boast about."

"About Angharad," Marietta began, when they were finally alone. "What I wanted to say, Evan, is that—"

"Please, Mom, I don't want to talk about Angharad. Or Jonathan Ainsley," Evan interrupted. "Not right now. I'm much more interested in talking about your separation from Dad."

Marietta walked across the sitting room and sat down in the large armchair near the fireplace. After a moment, she said, "There's not much more to tell. Your father and I have separated, and that's that. As I told you, he seemed indifferent, as if he couldn't care less."

"I don't mean now, Mom, I mean years ago. *Earlier.* Before Linnet arrived, you told me you had left my father when I was little. Why?"

Marietta leaned back in the chair, crossed her legs, stared into the distance, as if looking at times past. In a sense, that was what she *was* doing. "I want to be honest with you," she answered finally. "As honest as I can possibly be, Evan. I owe you that. Things were not all that great between us when you were small, but that wasn't the real reason I left your father then."

"So why did you?" Evan probed, anxious to understand at last about her parents' marriage. Lately it had baffled her.

"Because I . . . I fell in love with another man."

Evan stared at Marietta, momentarily startled, and then, recovering herself swiftly, she asked, "Who was he? Tell me about him."

"His name was Val Timball, and we'd known him in London, your father and I. He was an artist and set designer, very talented, mostly working in the theater in the West End. He came to New York to do the sets for a Broadway show, and we saw a lot of him. During the months he was living in Manhattan, something happened between us—we fell in love with each other. He'd always had a yen for me, and I was very unhappy with your father by then. Val and I became involved, very heavily. When he went back to London, he begged me to go with him. He wanted me to get a divorce and marry him. I couldn't do it, Evan. I realized I couldn't leave you."

"But you just said you left Dad."

"I did go to London, yes. But only because Val became very ill. His sister Solange told me he was begging to see me, so I went, intending to spend only a few days. But I loved him so much I had to stay with him. And he needed me. I told your father I had left him because I wanted to be with Val, and he went crazy. He flew over immediately, made a helluva stink, and stormed out again without really listening to me or trying to understand. He vowed to divorce me for adultery. His behavior antagonized me more than ever."

"And you stayed with Val for how long, Mom?"

"Only a few weeks. You see, as it turned out, Val was dying. He had a rare form of leukemia." Marietta's voice quavered, and she stopped, took a deep breath.

After a moment she began again, speaking softly. "It was impossible for me to leave him to die alone. Not when we loved each other the way we did. But he didn't last long, not even a month. I felt my whole world had fallen apart that summer. Val was dead. Your father was determined to divorce me. And he'd vowed that I would never see you again. That he wouldn't allow it."

Stunned for a moment, Evan sat waiting for Marietta to continue, as she knew her mother eventually would.

"It was your grandmother who intervened. She was furious with your father, told him that he was being immature, that he was lacking in compassion," Marietta explained. "She talked us both into getting back with each other. He didn't really want to, and in a way, neither did I. Because by then I understood we couldn't really be happy." Marietta sighed heavily and shook her head. "I did go back to him, but only because of you. I wanted to bring you up, love you, be a good mother."

"He took me away from you, though, didn't he? Isn't that the best way to describe what happened?"

"Yes. It was kind of a retaliation, I think."

"Is that when your depression started?"

Marietta nodded, and her face became taut with tension as she continued to talk. "It just came over me one day. I couldn't get out of bed. I had very dark feelings all of a sudden. I didn't understand what was happening to me. At first, I thought I was sad because of Val's death." She shook her head vehemently. "It was awful. I lived in a dark world. Then suddenly the depression lifted, and I was fine. Six months would go by, and then something would trigger the depression again, and I'd stay in bed afraid of everything, of everyone. Terrified, actually. Eventually, of course, I saw a doctor, got help, medicine."

"I remember how you gradually seemed to get better, Mom, when I was growing up. But I also remember how you'd suddenly be ill again, and seemingly for no reason."

"I might still be like that if it weren't for my Aunt Dottie, God bless her. She's the one who sent me to a new doctor last year, told me to get a life. And—"

"That's what you're doing," Evan interrupted. "Good for you, Mom! You have a *right* to be happy. And so does Dad. Maybe he'll be better off alone, too."

"I think he will, Evan. And I bear him no ill will, you know."

"I realize that. It's not your nature. Do you want to talk some more about your depression?" Evan now asked, looking at her mother intently. "I'm happy to listen if it helps."

"Perhaps another day, honey. I'm worried about Jonathan Ainsley at this moment. Do you think he'll try to hurt you and Gideon, Evan?"

"Not at the moment. I think he's too busy with Angharad. And by the way, Mom, I tend to go along with Sarah Pascal. I think that J.A. has fallen hard for Angharad and that he's not trying to get information out of her about us." Evan suddenly began to laugh. "He might even be suspicious of *her*! He might believe she's been sent to spy on him by us. Wouldn't that be a laugh?"

"I suppose so," Marietta concurred, although without much enthusiasm. "I can't help worrying about you, worrying about your safety."

"Everything's going to be all right. We've lots of security, in every possible way, even though you might not be aware of it."

"Do you mean bodyguards, that kind of thing?"

"Yes, I do. I'm fully protected at all times, as are all the Hartes. Try to relax, Mom. Jonathan's not going to win, he's not going to get the better of us."

"Isn't there anything the family can do about him interfering in your lives?" Marietta asked.

"I'm afraid not, Mom. You see, he himself never does anything. He employs others to do his dirty work, and even then it's impossible to prove," Evan pointed out.

"Perhaps he'll get his comeuppance," Marietta muttered, thinking out loud. She gave Evan a knowing look as she added, "Perhaps Angharad will be his downfall. With a little luck."

Later, after Marietta had left, Evan lay on the sofa in front of the fire, half dozing and thinking about her mother's life. It hadn't been very happy for the most part; in fact, it had been quite hard at times. But then life was never easy, it never had been actually, not for anyone. And for some it could even be catastrophic.

Evan was glad her mother had found her way out of that awful maze of depression and loneliness, and she understood perfectly well why Marietta wanted to live in London now. A new beginning, a fresh start, Evan thought suddenly. This is a wonderful chance of renewal for her: a new apartment, in a town she knows and loves, the great expectation of being a grandmother, of watching the boys grow, of being with me, having me to herself without Dad's interference.

As she dozed off, a smile settled on Evan's face. She was truly glad her mother was going to be here in England part of the year, and she would do her best to help her be happy, make Marietta part of their lives, give her the daughter's love she had been cheated of so long ago.

And she would try not to be angry with her father for too long, even though she was at this moment.

24

❧

Linnet sat staring at the latest sales sheets, for a moment thinking she had misread them. But as she scanned them a second time, she saw that the figures were as bad as she thought. Every department on the three Fashion Floors which were under her aegis had done badly.

It's not possible, she muttered. She realized with a sinking feeling that sales for last week had been very poor, if not disastrous.

Leaning back in her chair, she frowned, wondering why her mother had not mentioned these figures to her. Paula got the sales sheets several days ahead of Linnet; but then perhaps her mother hadn't had a chance to study them either. She herself had been busy preparing all those memos for Paula, and Paula appeared to have been overly preoccupied with that loose cannon Jonathan Ainsley.

It seemed to Linnet that her mother was speaking to Sarah in Paris almost every day, and to what purpose? she wondered. All Paula heard from Sarah was that Jonathan was obviously besotted by Angharad, and vice versa.

It pleased Linnet that these two schemers were caught up with each other, entwined figuratively and physically. Thus enraptured, they would leave the rest of the family alone, she believed. And hoped. At least for the moment.

Gideon tended to agree with her. They had met for a drink the day after she'd had lunch with Evan and Marietta, and Gideon had confided his feelings to her. Because they had grown up together and were best friends, there were no holds barred, and he had poured out his genuine fears. "She's evil," he had said. "I saw the wickedness in Angharad the afternoon I met her at the hospital, after Evan had that fall. I still blame that woman for Evan's accident. I think she got Evan very upset. We have to wait and see what happens next." He had smiled knowingly, added, "I do believe Ainsley has met his match. I think Angharad Hughes is a real piece of work. She'll lead him a merry dance."

Linnet sighed, then looked down at the figures once more. They loomed up. Damnation, she muttered. Things were much worse than she had realized regarding Fashion sales.

Her memos to Paula, which she'd worked on for days, were about bringing the London store into the twenty-first century, and these figures now told her how important this was. Actually, it was vital.

Every aspect of the store needed overhauling. All the windows required a new look, the displays on the various floors had to be glamorized, and in general merchandise had to measure up to the new age they were living in. She had understood this for a long time, if the truth be known, but visiting Harte's in New York, and other department stores in that city, had brought it home with a vengeance.

She believed Harte's in London was beginning to lose its cachet. Oh, it was still elegant, a landmark actually, and world famous, but to her way of thinking it had become a trifle staid, especially for the current generation of shoppers.

Linnet was smart enough to know that the latest sales figures for her Fashion Floors didn't spell disaster for Harte's, but at the same time she understood that they were indicative of a trend. If something really drastic wasn't done, the retailing company might, within the coming year, be on a downward slide. She knew Harte's wasn't losing money. At least not yet, she muttered. But she also was aware that this could happen if innovative ideas were not put to work.

Jumping up, she went over to her worktable, picked up the *Financial Times,* which she had dropped there when she had come in that morning. Rustling through its pink pages, she finally came to the stock prices, scanned the pages until she found Harte's. Nodding, she let out a small sigh of relief. The shares were stable, even up a little.

Although she was reassured, Linnet knew she had to pursue her plan no matter what. She suddenly felt more determined than ever to force through her ideas, *most* if not all of them. Somehow she had to find the means to convince her mother that they could not remain sitting here in what Linnet called "the doldrums." Her mother lived in the past, caught up with the regime of Emma Harte and Grandy's memory.

Seating herself at the desk, she picked up the phone and dialed India, who was working at the Leeds store this week.

India answered her private line immediately. "India Standish here."

"It's Linnet, India. How are you? How's Dusty? Oh, and little Atlanta?"

"They're both great, thanks. But how're you? You sound tense, Linny," India replied in her soft way, the hint of a brogue behind the lilting voice.

"I am a bit anxious. Listen, I just got around to looking at this past week's sales figures for the Fashion Floors, and they're awful. Actually, India, they're *appalling.* I don't mind telling you, I'm alarmed."

"But January's always a bad month, don't forget that. And anyway, this is the first year we haven't had the January Sale. I don't know why Aunt Paula decided against it, but I think it was a mistake," India confided.

"So do I, but I can't tell her that, she's already irritated with me about my plans for the future," Linnet replied.

"Oh, drat! I so hoped she would go along with you, and with us, Evan and me as well as you, and *our* ideas. What's she objecting to?"

"Actually, she hasn't seen them all yet, the plans, I mean. I'm just finishing up my memos. But she wasn't too thrilled when I spoke to her about the spa."

"Gosh, and that's one of the best ideas you've had," India exclaimed. "I wonder how she'll react when you mention the quick food snack bars." India chuckled. "I don't think she'll be too happy, Linny."

"I know. But we have to bring this store into the new century. Listen, the reason I called you was to ask how the Leeds and Harrogate stores did last week, especially in the fashion departments."

"Very well, actually," India responded. "I was a bit surprised, to be honest. But as you know, the Leeds Fashion Floors do very well, at least in the twenty-two age-group. Those clothes have a lot of appeal, and don't forget, we have hundreds of young women studying here, at Leeds University and the technical colleges. We do record business."

Linnet had listened carefully, and now she said swiftly, "You know, we might develop clothes for this category here at the London store. I think we've neglected that age-group a bit."

"That's true," India agreed and then said in a rush, "There's another thing. Ever since Atlanta's been living with us, I've become interested in children's clothes and toys. Last week I devised a way to bring the toys and clothes departments together in adjoining areas. That's going to boost sales, I think. I'm trying some new children's clothing manufacturers as well."

"Sounds to me as if the Leeds store is a few jumps ahead of us, cousin of mine." Linnet laughed.

India laughed with her. "I'm merely trying to do the best I can."

"You go well beyond that, India. What about the Harrogate store?"

"It's doing okay. Do you want me to send you the sales sheets?"

"No. Just keep up the good work."

"I will. Any more news about the dreaded Angharad and her beau, if we can call *him* that?"

"It's the same old stuff coming across the Channel from Sarah. You know the drill: he's besotted by Angharad, et cetera. However, Gideon believes our Mr. Ainsley has met his match."

"In what sense?" India asked, puzzled.

"Gid doesn't like Angharad Hughes; he was unusually wary of her the first time he met her; he thought she reeked of evil. And he says she might well get the better of Ainsley."

"I'll be there to cheer her along," India answered drily.

"So will I. Listen, where will I find you this weekend? At Willows Hall, I presume."

"Yes, in fact I'll be staying there from tonight on. I like being with Atlanta, who's just adorable, and I've become very attached to her since she's been living with Dusty. I know it's only Thursday, but I decided to go over there later today. It's been a little lonely at Pennistone Royal with only Emsie to keep me company—and she's always doing homework. It's not the same when the rest of you are in London. Anyway, are you coming up this weekend, Linnet? If so, maybe we'll get together . . . the four of us."

"That would've been nice, but we're staying in London. Julian is going to finish the final bit of work on the memorial for his grandfather. He'll be with his father on Saturday morning, and I intend to be at the store here.

But Mummy's coming to Yorkshire with Dad. And possibly Lorne."

"Tessa hasn't been to the Harrogate store for over a week, so I decided I'd better go in there on Saturday morning, and that's where you'll find me if you need me. Or I'll be with Dusty."

After hanging up, Linnet continued to work on the memos for her mother, and when she finally had them as right as she could get them, she wrote an additional memo based on India's innovations at the Leeds store, pointing out how successful they were.

Finally, she printed out everything on her computer, put the pages in a folder, then locked the folder in a drawer in her desk. She would give them to her mother tomorrow, before Paula went to Pennistone Royal for the weekend.

Glancing at the clock on her desk, Linnet saw that it was four o'clock. Rising, she went out of her office, heading for the Fashion Floors to see what was happening in the store. It was a ritual with her, as she knew it had been with Emma Harte, the founder and her great hero. She aimed, in every way, to be the new Emma Harte. That was her ambition.

Several hundred miles north of London, India Standish was doing the identical thing at the Harte store in Leeds. India had been trained by Linnet, and so her modus operandi was almost identical to her cousin's daily regime. Do a walk-through in the morning, around noon, if possible, and another at about four o'clock. Just like their great-grandmother had done. Linnet was always reminding her of that, and also reminding her of Emma's discipline and hard work.

Thursday was usually a good day for the store, with plenty of young women and girls moving around, looking at everything, especially in Fashion. India noticed immediately that today was no exception. The clothing areas were busy, and naturally this pleased her no end.

India was intelligent and had been exceptionally well-trained, and one of the secrets of her success was that she *listened,* to everyone. However, she paid the most attention to Linnet, also endeavored to ascertain her moods; a short while ago she had detected her cousin's tenseness, and her anxiety about the sales figures. Linnet's concern had given India pause for thought, and she tended to agree that their great emporium in Knightsbridge needed an overhaul.

But, like Evan, India trembled at the thought of Paula's wrath. There was no doubt in India's mind that their lady boss would see red when she looked at Linnet's memos this weekend.

Paula's become a little set in her ways, India thought as she headed down the floor. She doesn't want change because she reveres Emma Harte. That is where the problem lies. Paula resisted Linnet's pleas to move on and into the future because she was *rooted* in the past. With Emma. Abiding by her wishes voiced long ago.

India, somewhat lost in her thoughts, did not notice the woman who had started to follow her and was edging closer. It was only when the woman grabbed hold of her arm that India was stopped in her tracks. Half turning, she exclaimed, "What are you *doing*? Let go of me! Who are you?"

And then she shriveled inside when she recognized the face. It was Melinda Caldwell. How could that be? She was in a detox clinic. No. Not anymore. And how terrible she looked: sunken eyes, face lined and tired, hair dirty and unkempt.

Struggling to get free from the woman but caught in her tenacious grip, India managed to move out of the aisle by pushing at Melinda, maneuvering her behind a rack of clothes and pinning her against a wall. Despite her appearance of pale blond fragility, India Standish was strong physically and tough mentally. Still struggling to get free but not wanting to make a scene in Designer Clothes, India leaned against Melinda and hissed, "Let go of me. *Now.* If you don't, you'll find yourself in *very serious trouble.*"

"*You're* in trouble. You and that bastard Dusty Rhodes. You've kidnapped my child," Melinda shrilled.

"Be quiet. And let me go!" India insisted. "Now, do you hear? Let me go at once." India endeavored to get free.

"I know she's at Willows Hall with him. And you. *Whore.* My mother told me where my child is. Do you think my mother wouldn't tell me?" Melinda was shouting and pushing against India, trying to move them both away from the wall.

Suddenly, India took a step back, and as Melinda moved forward, without letting go, India smashed her hand down on the other woman's arm, hard. The small signet ring on India's little finger cut into Melinda's wrist, and immediately she let go. It was obvious Melinda was frail, addled by drug use and not responding much to treatment.

One of the saleswomen was hurrying toward them, having noticed the altercation, and India called to her, "Get Security at once!" Then she turned back to Melinda, who was now backing away. It was India's turn to grab, but Melinda was swift. Darting away, she fled toward the escalator, jumped on, and rode down.

When the security officers arrived only a split second later, Melinda Caldwell had disappeared from sight. Once India had explained that she had been accosted by a crazy woman, the men took off, heading for the ground floor.

"We'll find her, don't you worry, Lady India," one of them promised before heading for the escalator.

India nodded, said nothing, but she thought: No, you won't. She's gone. She's already out in the street.

After thanking the young woman who had called Security, India went back to her office, feeling slightly shaken up. Mostly she was worried about Melinda Caldwell being out of the clinic and on the loose. She was dangerous and unpredictable.

Sitting down at her desk, she picked up the phone and dialed Dusty's private line at Willows Hall. When he answered, she told him, "Dusty, Melinda's not in the clinic. She's in Leeds."

"My God! How's that possible? How do—"

"How she got out I don't know, but she was here at Harte's," India cut in swiftly and then continued in the calmest of voices. "She accosted me, was verbally abusive, and said she knew that you had her child, that her mother had told her Atlanta was at Willows Hall."

"Good God, no!" Dusty exclaimed. "Don't tell me she visited Molly at the infirmary! This is just awful. But what happened with you, darling? She didn't hurt you, did she?" he now asked. "Are you all right, India?"

"I feel slightly shaken, but I'm all right. Unfortunately, Melinda escaped just before Security arrived. She fled down the escalator, and probably out of the store immediately. I'm sure they haven't found her, even though they were fast on her heels. I just wanted to warn you, Dusty, that she could very well be on her way to Willows Hall."

"I understand, but that won't do her any good. She can't get into the grounds, not the way Jack Figg has this place fixed up. It's tight as a drum. When are you leaving the store?"

"Very soon. I'm just waiting for the security men to come and report to me. In the meantime—"

"Just a minute, here's Paddy."

India clutched the receiver and held her breath, waiting for Dusty to come back to her. She could barely hear Paddy's voice, but she pricked up her ears when Dusty said, "This is just dreadful. Tell her to hold on a minute, please."

Suddenly Dusty was back, and he told India, "Gladys is on the other line. Melinda was seen by one of Molly's neighbors, who phoned Gladys. Apparently, Melinda was trying to get into Molly's house in Meanwood, but Molly had the locks changed recently. Smart move. I think I'd better speak to Gladys. Stay in touch, and let me know when you leave work."

"I will, Dusty. It won't be very long, and try not to worry."

"Please, India, do get a move on . . ." His voice trailed off.

"I'm safe in the store."

"Are you now?" he asked, sounding doubtful.

"*Yes.* I'll be on my way after I've seen the security officers."

Once she had hung up the phone, India cleared her desk and turned off her computer; a few moments later the two security men came into her office through the open door. "Not a sight of her, Lady India," Mack Slater said.

He was the senior of the two and had worked at Harte's for years. He continued, "She went out of the store by the front entrance and was gone by the time we hit the street. The doorman saw her running down toward City Square. He *thinks*. It might not have been her at all. Who was she, Lady India? Do you have any idea?"

India, deeming it wiser to say nothing, shook her head. "Sorry, Mack, I don't know who she was. Obviously someone a bit demented, though." India gave him a faint smile and shrugged. "The world is full of crazies these days, isn't it?"

"You're right, things aren't what they used to be, not by a long shot. Sorry we weren't able to nab her," he finished.

"You did your best, and thanks, Mack. You, too, Jerry."

The security officers took their leave, and India spent several minutes to get her things together. As soon as she had packed her carryall, she stepped over to the cupboard and took out her sheepskin coat and a woolen scarf. She had just shrugged into her coat when the phone began to ring.

Leaning over her desk, she lifted the receiver. "Hello?"

"It's me," Dusty said. "I have bad news. Molly Caldwell had a heart attack a short while ago. She's back in intensive care. Melinda's doing, I have no doubt. She went there to see her and caused this to happen."

"Oh, that poor woman, how terrible," India murmured. "Do you want me to go over to Leeds Infirmary, Dusty? Is there anything I can do?"

"No, nothing. She wouldn't even know you at the moment. She's out of it, from what I understand. The infirmary phoned five minutes ago to give me the news. They'll stay in touch with me."

"What about Gladys, what did she have to say?"

"What you know . . . that a neighbor had spotted Melinda trying to get into Molly's house but failing. Gladys had been out doing her marketing, and another neighbor said Melinda had been banging on Gladys's door as well. To no avail, obviously, since she wasn't there. Gladys is going over to Molly's now. Apparently there's a small suitcase full of papers, which Molly told her to bring to me as soon as possible when she visited her the other day."

"And is she bringing the case to you now? Is that the idea?"

"I thought it was best. Gladys is somewhat alarmed by Melinda's sudden appearance, and I don't blame her. Aside from her bringing me the suitcase, I thought it was wiser to have Gladys tucked away at Willows Hall. Don't you agree, India?"

"So that Melinda can't get at her, is that what you mean?" she asked.

"Indeed it is. Who knows what trouble Melinda might cause for Gladys."

25

Recently Jack Figg had insisted that Tessa, Linnet, India, and Evan all use discreet black town cars with ex-military men as drivers. In other words, vehicles not easy to spot and drivers who were actually bodyguards. At least during the week, when their schedules rarely varied and they were easy to track and target. His aim: to protect the women from Jonathan Ainsley's possible menace.

But India insisted on using her Aston Martin when she was in Yorkshire on the weekends, and Jack had been unable to dissuade her. He was still trying.

Now, as she sat in the black sedan which had picked her up at the store, she leaned forward and said from the back seat, "I'm sorry, Larry, I forgot to tell you that I'm not going to Pennistone Royal this afternoon. Would you take me to Willows Hall instead, please?"

"No problem, Lady India," Larry Cox answered in his polite but cheerful voice.

As she settled comfortably in the seat, India's thoughts zeroed in on Jack Figg. It occurred to her that she and Dusty urgently needed his advice, if not his help. Melinda Caldwell spelled trouble. Not only for Molly Caldwell but for them as well.

Taking out her mobile phone, India dialed Jack's number, and when he answered immediately, she said, "Jack, it's India. Hello."

"It's nice to hear your voice, India. Is everything okay?" he asked, alert as always.

"I think Dusty and I need your help."

"What's wrong? Tell me about it, take your time."

Speaking in a low voice, India explained, "Melinda Caldwell came to the store today, made a bit of a fuss. With me."

"Where are you now?"

"In the car with Larry, going to Willows Hall."

"I understand. Let me ask the questions. It's easier for you, and much more discreet." He trusted Larry, but he deemed it wise to be careful.

"I agree," India replied.

"Was this an unannounced visit, India?" Jack now asked.

"Very much so. She's supposed to be undergoing treatment. I was taken by surprise, Jack."

"Understood. So, now she's out of the clinic and floating around Leeds. That's what you're telling me, isn't it?"

"It is. This afternoon the encounter was unpleasant to say the least. And she more than likely went to see her mother as well."

"At Leeds Infirmary? Or is Mrs. Caldwell now back at home?"

"She's still in hospital. Dusty told me a short while ago that Mrs. Caldwell had another heart attack this afternoon. I think, from what Melinda said to me, she did visit her mother today."

"Oh, God, no! And too bad about Mrs. Caldwell. I hope she's going to come through this all right." Jack cleared his throat. "When was Melinda released from the detox clinic?"

"That's just it. Dusty thinks she wasn't released, that she just left of her own accord."

"I see." Jack paused, but only for a split second, then asked, "How was she? Demented? Sane? Tell me what you thought when you saw her."

"She was angry. She seemed quite sane but *very* angry. And she looks terrible."

"She's a problem, India, and a dangerous one. I think we must find her as soon as possible."

"Can we get together this evening, Jack? To go over everything. Are you in the vicinity?"

"I'm in Yorkshire but not too close. As a matter of fact, I'm in Scarborough at the moment."

"Good heavens, don't tell me you've gone off to have a winter break at Heron's Nest," India exclaimed in astonishment.

Startled by this comment, Jack answered swiftly, "Funny you should say that, but I actually went to Heron's Nest today. To see the caretaker. She thinks somebody's been using the house from time to time over the last month or so. When Paula told me the other day, I decided to look into it myself."

"And?"

"No *and*, India. As of this moment anyway. A few interesting thoughts on my part, but I can't actually target a person, at least not yet. And to be honest, nothing's been disturbed as far as I can tell, nor have any locks been forced."

"Then how does the caretaker know somebody's been going there?"

"Good question. Apparently lights have been seen there several times, and little things seem out of place, so the caretaker says."

"Who'd want to go to Heron's Nest in the dead of winter? It's icy cold in Scarborough, sitting there as it is on the North Sea, off the beaten track. None of *us* would go there right now. But perhaps somebody wanted to have an illicit rendezvous, something like that," India commented and laughed. "Heron's Nest is such a private place . . . in certain ways."

A moment ago Jack had pricked up his ears, and now he asked, "Why did you mention *rendezvous,* India? Are you suggesting that members of the family are accustomed to using Heron's Nest for assignations?"

"Do you mean my generation or my mother's? There are a lot of us . . ." After a pause she added, "From several generations."

Jack chuckled. "That I know, and I'm certainly not thinking of your grandmother or Robin. In fact, I *was* thinking about *your* generation."

"I doubt it. I mean, who of us would go *there*? *Toby*? He's about the only one who's fancy free at the moment, and in the middle of a divorce. But his wife is in Los Angeles, so he can play around in London if he wants. He doesn't have to hide." When Jack didn't respond, India asked, "Well, don't you agree?"

"Yes, I do. It's a good point."

"Why is Aunt Paula so upset that someone might have been there?" India now probed.

"I think she was worried that the house had been broken into, that there might have been a burglary."

"I see. You know, Jack, none of my generation have ever been as involved with Heron's Nest as my mother's generation. Heron's Nest was very important to them all when they were growing up. They went every summer to stay with Emma; they called it Emma's Boot Camp."

"I remember only too well. I often popped over to chat with your great-grandmother about business. Tell me something, do they still talk about those years at Heron's Nest?"

"Oh, yes. Mummy told me quite recently how much she loved the house and that Paula had often hidden her there when she was having the secret love affair with Daddy. And Linnet once explained that her parents used to meet there on the sly when Paula was trying to get a divorce from Jim Fairley."

"Now I understand why you link it to romantic doings," Jack murmured. "This is interesting information, thanks. But getting back to Melinda Caldwell, I'll put a couple of my operatives on it immediately, and I'll talk to my pals with the Leeds police, chaps in the C.I.D. I must alert them as soon as we hang up, explain that she's a drug addict and probably dangerous. I'm assuming she didn't hurt you. Or did she?"

"No, of course not. But she tried," India answered and went on. "She attempted to break into her mother's house in Meanwood today. I don't know the address, but I'll check with Dusty and call you back."

"Good. And I need a description of Melinda."

"She's about my height, blondish brown hair, striking face with high cheekbones. Actually, she doesn't look good. She's sunk very low. She was wearing black jeans and a black coat."

"Okay. I've got that. Will you ask Dusty to phone the detox clinic and talk to her doctor, please? It's important we understand her condition."

"I will. And Jack, is there any chance of seeing you this evening?"

"Why not? I'll be finished here in about an hour, so I could be at Willows Hall around seven-thirty. How's that?"

"It's great, and thank you so much. I'll be back to you shortly with the address in Meanwood."

"Thanks, India, and try not to worry. We'll soon have this in hand."

It was not long before India called Jack again with the information he required. She also told him that Dusty had already spoken to Dr. Jeffers at the detox clinic, only to confirm that Melinda Caldwell had not been discharged.

The doctor had informed Dusty that he was anxious for her to return to complete her treatment.

After thanking her, Jack clicked off and dialed two of his operatives who covered Yorkshire, as well as talked to his friends on the Leeds police force. Then he sat back and sipped his cup of tea, relaxing for a moment now that the problem of Melinda Caldwell was in competent hands. Another loose cannon was all he needed.

Jack had meandered into the Grand Hotel in Scarborough just before India had first called and had settled himself in the lounge where afternoon tea was served. He had ordered a pot of tea and a toasted tea cake, but now, as he glanced around, he thought of the times he had come here with Emma for afternoon tea. A rather grand tea it had been in those days, with a selection of finger sandwiches, scones with strawberry jam and clotted cream, and rich pastries. All too much for him now, far too fattening.

As he caught his breath after a busy day, his thoughts wandered to India's comments about Heron's Nest. He chastised himself for being so stupid; why had he focused on the younger members of the family instead of the older generation, his generation? Of course none of the kids, as he called them, would go to Heron's Nest, especially in the depth of winter. It had no special meaning for *them;* but it did have great significance for Emma's grandchildren, who had summered there with her for years. Naturally they would have a special attachment to that lovely old house by the sea.

Our salad days, he thought now, how we all remember our youth with such affection. We think of them as golden days because life seemed eternal then, and we thought we were immortal.

Rummaging around in his pocket, Jack found the small notebook he used for jotting down reminders to himself, took a pen out of his inside top pocket, and listed all of Emma's grandchildren who had come to Heron's Nest when they were young. He then added the names of Shane O'Neill and Michael Kallinski, because they, too, had been constant visitors. After scrutinizing the list, he put the small notebook away and finished his tea.

Paying his bill in cash, he nodded to the waitress and walked out to his car. Within minutes he was on his way to Harrogate, driving across the moors. Mentally, he was thanking India for pointing him in the right direction. Because of her he now had a few clues, and a possible candidate for the person who had invaded the winter solitude of Heron's Nest.

"What's in the suitcase Mrs. Caldwell sent?" India asked, hovering in the doorway of the library at Willows Hall.

Dusty was sitting at the desk sorting through the items, and he glanced up on hearing India's voice. "Her will, other papers, various things," he replied, his face lighting up at the sight of her. "You look wonderful," he added. "Come in, don't stand there, darling."

Smiling, India moved across the room, as always fluid and graceful. She was wearing a long crimson cashmere caftan, trimmed around her neck and down the front with gilt braiding, and her silvery gold hair was tied back in a ponytail. Her only pieces of jewelry were large gold hoop earrings, a watch, and her sapphire engagement ring.

Dusty jumped up and took her in his arms when she came to a standstill near the desk. He hugged her tightly to him, saying against her hair, "I'm so sorry for what happened today, India. You don't deserve any of this. Melinda Caldwell is my problem, not yours."

"Don't be daft," India exclaimed, using one of her grandmother's favorite words. "You're not responsible for her behavior. And perhaps she isn't either, poor thing. I think she could be on drugs again, don't you?"

Staring hard at her, his blue eyes narrowing, Dusty asked, "Did she seem doped up to you this afternoon?"

"No, to be honest, she didn't. But she looked dreadful. As I told Jack, she was also angry, really furious."

Dusty sighed heavily. "Unfortunately, I think Melinda's a lost cause. I hope Jack's people are able to find her, but God knows where they'd look."

"He's got the police on it as well. Apparently he knows some detectives at the Criminal Investigation Department of the Leeds police, and he told me they have lots of contacts," India explained.

Dusty nodded. "They're all good lads. I know some of the C.I.D. blokes, and I would think they'd be aware of all the places where drugs are sold . . ." His voice trailed off. "I just hope to God she doesn't start using again." He stared into India's face, his eyes clouding. He knew Melinda would do just that. Her days were numbered.

Shaking off his dour mood, Dusty said, "Molly's such a wonderful woman. She wrote me a lovely letter and put Atlanta's birth certificate and the key for the suitcase in the envelope." He gestured to the items spread out on his large Georgian desk. "There's a copy of her last will and testament, and a letter to her solicitors attached. An envelope with a thousand pounds in cash in it, a little bag of jewelry, all rather nice stuff, and the deed to her house. She owned it outright, you know. Oh, and there are two bank books for her savings accounts. Needless to say, she's left everything to Atlanta."

"Obviously she would," India remarked. "I suppose she wanted you to have all this for safekeeping, since she's in hospital."

"That's the only reason it could be." Dusty bit his lip and looked at India knowingly. "I wonder if Molly suspected that Melinda would get out of the clinic and come bothering her?"

"Who knows, Dusty. The main thing is the suitcase is safe now that you have it."

Paddy knocked on the door and came in. "Excuse me,

Mr. Rhodes, I just wanted you to know that Mr. Figg's arrived."

"Thanks, Paddy, please show him in. And I think we'll have drinks in here, it's very cozy."

"Right, sir. Mr. Figg's just freshening up. In the meantime, shall I open a bottle of white wine?"

"That sounds good," Dusty responded and looked over at India, who had gone to stand in front of the fire blazing up the chimney. "Or do you prefer something else?" he asked her.

"White wine's lovely, thanks."

Paddy nodded and left.

Dusty walked over to the fireplace, put his arm around India, and stood next to her, enjoying the warmth of the flames. "Did you tell Jack he should plan on staying the night?" Dusty asked, looking down at her.

India shook her head. "No, I guess it didn't occur to me. But it is a good idea, now that you mention it. He would have such a long drive to Robin Hood's Bay, if he were planning to go home tonight."

"I know he sometimes stays at one of the hotels in Harrogate, but I am going to offer him a bed here. It's much more comfortable."

"You're always so thoughtful, Dusty."

Bending down, he kissed her on the forehead and said, "I have a surprise for you."

"Oh. What is it?" Her eyes were pinned on his, a questioning look in them.

"My painting of you is almost finished. At long last. I hope to show it to you on Saturday."

"Oh, Dusty, how wonderful!"

"I hope you're going to like it," he murmured.

"How could I not? You're the greatest painter there is today."

"Ah, my bride to be is truly prejudiced." He laughed, his blue eyes twinkling.

At this moment Jack walked in, a smile spread across

his face. Hard on his heels came Paddy, carrying a tray of glasses and a bottle of white wine in a silver ice bucket.

"Jack, welcome!" Dusty exclaimed, moving forward, taking Jack's outstretched hand, maneuvering him over to the fireside.

"Thanks for inviting me, Dusty," Jack said, and then, turning to India, he gave her one of his bountiful smiles and hugged her to him. "It's good to see you, India."

"Hello, Jack. I do hope it wasn't too bad a drive over those windy moors."

He chuckled. "It was a bit, and I must say the moors can be hellishly treacherous in the winter. But I made it safe and sound."

"We want you to be safe and sound tonight, Jack," Dusty interjected. "And that's why we insist you stay here. You can't be driving all that way to Robin Hood's Bay."

"But I can go to a hotel," Jack began and was immediately cut off by Dusty, who exclaimed, "I won't hear of it. My home is your home. And listen, mate, it's a lot more comfortable here than at any hotel."

"Well, thank you very much," Jack responded.

"Come and sit with me here," India said, taking a seat on the sofa and patting the one next to her. "It's lovely and cozy near the fire."

Dusty said, "What would you like to drink, Jack?"

"I think I'll join you in a glass of white wine, please."

"Make it three glasses, thanks, Paddy." Dusty looked over at his house manager as he spoke and added, "Dinner in about forty-five minutes? Is that all right?"

"It's fine, sir," Paddy replied and brought the tray of drinks over to the fireplace. Each of the three of them took a glass and thanked Paddy, who smiled in return and disappeared.

After clinking glasses, Dusty moved over to the fireplace, stood with his back to it again. There was a moment of silence, and then he said, "I know it's far too early to ask if you have any news . . . but I just wanted to

say this. I'm really grateful for your help, and I'll do whatever I can to assist you. Just say the word, Jack."

"I'm not sure how you can help, unless you know any
of Melinda's haunts in Leeds, where she might go. Or
who her friends are here."

"I'm afraid I don't," Dusty answered, frowning slightly.
"You see, she hasn't actually lived here for some years. . . .
She moved to London and never came back much, except
to see Atlanta, who has lived with Molly since she was a
baby."

"I see." Jack blew out a puff of air, obviously in frustration, looked off in the distance for a split second. Then
he said, "India told me you'd been in touch with the
detox clinic. . . . Were they forthcoming about Melinda's
condition?"

"They're very open, Jack, they don't try to hide anything. I got the impression that she was clean again but
that they hadn't finished their therapy sessions. She's always called it their 'brainwashing, but I do think it
helps."

"I understand. I have one of my operatives watching
Molly's house, since Melinda might try to break in again.
And he's keeping an eye on Gladys Roebotham's house as
well. What I am hoping is that we find her in Meanwood
and not—"

"On a cold slab," Dusty cut in and lifted a dark brow
quizzically.

Jack shook his head. "I wasn't going to say that, Dusty.
However, let's do hope she doesn't end up in the morgue.
I was going to say I hope she's not found with a drug
dealer or druggies, because that would mean she's back
on heroin. It is that, isn't it?"

"Yep. And any other drug she might be able to get her
hands on. Melinda is one of those people who is addictive
by nature. It's a sickness really."

"I know that. Anyway, if anything comes up, they'll

call me." Jack patted his tweed jacket. "I've got my mobile on at all times. Now, how's Mrs. Caldwell doing?"

"She's the same. No change," Dusty said quietly.

India said, "Unless you two have anything else to discuss regarding Melinda, I'd like to change the subject, if you don't mind."

"Change away, darling," Dusty murmured, pushing a smile onto his face. "It does get dreary talking about drug addicts, not to mention rather painful when I consider the ramifications here."

Jack nodded in agreement. "All I want to say is that we are at a disadvantage, Dusty, when it comes to finding Melinda Caldwell."

"Oh, I know that, I know it only too well."

"Jack, can we talk about Heron's Nest for a moment?" India asked, turning slightly on the sofa, looking at him. "I was wondering why Mrs. Hodges thought someone had been in the house recently?"

"Dust," he responded laconically and then grinned when he saw the baffled look on India's face.

"What on earth do you mean?"

"The disturbance of dust. She told me the house quickly gets very dusty because it's so old, and several times lately she's noticed marks in the dust that accumulates in a week."

"How extraordinary!" Dusty exclaimed, looking over at Jack. "Dust, eh?" He laughed suddenly.

"Let me explain," Jack said. "If someone walks across a dusty floor, there might not be actual footprints, but the dust will be . . . disturbed. I suppose that's what she means. Anyway, Mrs. Hodges also says that upstairs one of the bathrooms has been used. Apparently this particular bathroom has a tap that drips unless it's turned off very, very hard. She found it dripping recently. She also found some black hairs on a cushion in one of the bedrooms. Quite a few little things like that have caught her attention. Then one of her neighbors reported seeing lights in the house. Well, to be completely accurate, someone saw a light bobbing around not so long ago. I think it might have been someone using a flashlight."

"Mrs. Hodges is quite the detective, isn't she, Jack?" India exclaimed. "She'll be bringing you DNA samples next."

Jack couldn't help laughing, and then he said, through his laughter, "Yes, she's a regular Miss Marple. And, she *did* bring me a DNA sample, or rather she drew my attention to the black hairs. I have them in a glassine envelope, although I must admit I have no one to match them to, India. Nor has a crime been committed."

"As far as we know," India responded somewhat pithily.

"Our own Miss Marple says nothing's been stolen from Heron's Nest," Jack pointed out.

"And there hasn't been a murder," India shot back.

"What *are* you two talking about?" Dusty asked, his attention going from one to the other.

Jack explained about Heron's Nest, and then, glancing at India, he asked, "Don't tell me you've never taken Dusty over to Scarborough to see Emma's lovely old house by the sea?"

"Not yet," India admitted; then a sheepish grin spread across her face, and, turning to Dusty she went on. "Don't you remember? Last year, after the stabbing, I said I'd love to take you to Emma's seaside house to have a few days' rest and recuperation."

"Oh, yes, now I do. And after I agreed to go, *you* changed your mind for some reason."

"Yes, because Linnet discouraged me. She said the house had been locked up all winter, and that there was only Mrs. Hodges to do a bit of dusting." She burst into laughter. "Sorry about all this play on your name . . . *Dusty.*"

He grinned at her and swallowed the last drop of his

wine, walked across the room, poured himself another glass, then said to Jack, "Would you like some wine?"

Jack followed him to the drinks table. "Why not? Since I'm not driving tonight, I can indulge a little. Thanks, Dusty."

India said, "I know it's not either my mother or my father who's having an illicit relationship and using Heron's Nest as . . . a love nest." She laughed. "Oh, nice play on words, there, Jack, eh?"

He came back to the sofa, a smile on his face, and sat down next to her. "And it can't be either Paula or Shane. Nor is it Emily or Winston. So who can it be?"

"Not Sarah Pascal, who lives in Paris and hardly ever sets foot in Yorkshire, and certainly not Amanda, who's constantly traveling, or her twin, Francesca, who's married with lots of kids."

"And Alexander is dead," Jack pointed out. "I know Michael Kallinski was one of the gang who was always there at Emma's Boot Camp. But he's divorced and can do as he wants." Jack pulled his notebook out of his jacket pocket and looked at the list of Emma's grandchildren. Glancing up, he stared at India. "That leaves only one person . . . *Jonathan Ainsley.*"

"I know! I just thought of him myself. But listen, Jack, Jonathan's single, so he can see anyone he wishes. Furthermore, he has a house of his own at Thirsk, flats in both Grosvenor Square and Paris, a farm in Provence, and a mansion on the Peak in Hong Kong. Why would he need Heron's Nest for a secret rendezvous?"

Jack shook his head, his expression one of puzzlement.

Dusty said, "Perhaps the lady lives in Yorkshire and for some reason can't travel very far. A husband? Kids? A career?"

"All possibilities, yes," India murmured.

"Jonathan's a very sophisticated man, so who would be a candidate up here in Yorkshire?" Jack wondered aloud.

"Obviously somebody we don't know," India volunteered.

Jack added, "And now he's tied up with Angharad Hughes . . ."

Listening to them, Dusty said, "Here's a thought, you two. If men or women come back to a place they knew in their youth, it's because they loved that spot, have happy memories of it. *Sentimental reasons*. That's why somebody went back to Heron's Nest, maybe to meet an old love. Someone from the past. Someone who feels the same way."

"Brilliant!" India exclaimed.

"Yes, very clever thinking indeed, Dusty," Jack added. "I must put *my* thinking cap on, go back to those days in my mind. I was frequently at the house, visiting Emma."

"Think about the things everyone *did*, Jack, that might help you to recall a forgotten face, maybe an outside person who came to stay, or just visit for the day."

"Good idea. They played tennis . . . swam . . . did the usual things young people do. Of course, Emma often invited me to tea at the Grand in Scarborough; in fact, she took everyone to tea there, and to dinner as well."

"You've jogged my memory, Jack," India cried, sitting up straight on the sofa. "Mummy told me that she and her brother Winston, with Emily in tow, used to steal out at night to go to the Grand Hotel for drinks. In the cocktail lounge, she said. They felt very grown-up. But they got caught once. Emma's summer secretary spotted them and threatened to tell Emma, unless they promised never to go there again. What about that summer secretary, she—"

"Priscilla Marney," Jack said, interrupting her, the name coming to him from out of the blue. "*Of course*. Priscilla's mother was Emma's summer secretary. They lived in Scarborough."

India was staring at him. Her face had gone pale; her eyes were wide. "Jack, Priscilla works for Paula. She does all the catering. She catered Evan and Gid's wedding. She's right in our midst."

"I know," he said, his voice somber. "I even saw her bustling around at the reception. But she's so much a part of the furniture I didn't think anything about it."

"Maybe there's nothing to think," India suggested, hoping this were true.

"That's possible. Just because she knew Jonathan years ago doesn't mean she knows him now." Jack leaned back against the velvet cushions, memories suddenly flooding back.

"I wasn't much older than any of them, you know, just eighteen and learning the ropes," he told them. "My uncle had worked for Emma for years, and I was sort of his protégé, and she made me her protégé. She took me by the hand and led me, treated me like one of the family, my uncle as well."

India said, in a worried voice, "If Priscilla Marney is seeing Jonathan Ainsley, then she's the spy Linnet's always going on about. For a long time Linny has insisted that there was someone in our midst who was involved with Jonathan. And telling him things."

"It might *not* be her," Jack murmured. "But I can assure you, I *will* find out. And very swiftly."

"Seems like he might have moved on, though," Dusty suggested. "Isn't he now caught on Angharad Hughes's hook, flailing around in gay Paree?"

"That's right," India said.

26

∽

India could see his silhouette in the moonlight. Dusty was standing at the window looking down into the gardens below, and he was utterly still, as rigid as stone. After a second or two of watching him from the bed, India slid her feet to the floor and went to him. She put her hand on his shoulder, her touch light.

He turned at once, looked down at her. In the light from the wintry full moon outside, she saw the residue of tears on his face.

Moving closer to him, she touched each cheek with her fingertips, gently wiping the dampness away. He put an arm around her, drawing her to him, holding her tightly without speaking. She understood him so well now; in the beginning, he had been difficult in some ways, refusing to meet her parents because he didn't like titles and the rich. But he was rich himself and so famous. Her parents had been amazed at his disapproval of them. But all was well now; he accepted who they were, they loved him, and he returned their love.

In the silence, she could almost hear his heart beating in unison with hers. She thought: I love him so much, I can't bear it when he's in pain.

As if reading her mind, Dusty murmured, "What a mess I've made of all this, not handling the situation with

Melinda differently. And now you have to suffer because
of it."

"That's not so, and don't beat yourself over the head,"
India replied softly. "You did what you thought was
right, did the best you could. No one can ask more than
that."

"I did try with Melinda . . ." He sighed. "I do wish I'd
looked after Molly better. I ought to have built her a small
house on the property. She and Atlanta would have been
safe here with me, with us. And I would have been
around for Atlanta whenever she needed me."

"It's not too late to do that, Dusty!" India responded,
moving her head away from his chest, looking up into his
eyes, as dark as lapis in the dim light. "I think that's a
grand idea, building a home for Molly and Atlanta here.
Let's do it."

He did not reply for a moment; there was sadness in
his voice when he said, at last, "It's too late now. I've left
it too late."

"What do you mean?" she asked, immediately struck
by the sorrow echoing.

"I don't think Molly will survive the heart attack she
had today. I didn't tell you how massive it was."

"Oh, no, don't say that. She was doing so well. And she
seems to be a strong woman. With any luck we can go
and see her tomorrow at the infirmary. We should try at
least, perhaps we can talk to her doctors. And I'll go with
you, if you wish."

He inclined his head. "Yes, let's do that . . . it will
cheer her up." His voice was lighter, more positive.

"And we can tell her about building a house for her. It
will give her a boost, be something for her to look forward to, Dusty."

"Yes, we'll do that. I hope they'll let us see her."

"They will, darling, I'm certain. Come on, come back
to bed, it's the middle of the night."

"I'm sorry. Did I wake you? I just couldn't sleep."

"No, you didn't wake me. I just know when you're not there . . . even when I'm sleeping."

Once they were back in bed, he pulled her to him, wrapping his arms around her, whispering, "Whatever would I do without you? You're always there for me, no matter what. I love you." There was a pause before he added, "You see, I can say it now."

"And I love you," she murmured against his bare chest, nestling closer. "And you'll never have to do without me, I'll be with you for the rest of my life."

"God, I hope so!" Pushing himself up onto one elbow, he looked down into her eyes, a faint smile flickering around his mouth. Then, lowering his face to hers, he kissed her deeply, and in only a few seconds his passion flared, and so did hers.

"Oh, my darling, my darling India." He brought his lips to her breasts, his hands moving over her body, touching her everywhere, his desire for her rampant.

India responded ardently, her hands fluttering over his stomach and down onto his thighs; he sighed as she began to stroke him. A moment later he was balancing himself above her, staring down at her. Wanting to become part of her, he took her to him almost roughly. She cried out as he entered her, and she cleaved to him. They began to move together rhythmically, rapturous in each other's arms and spiraling into ecstasy.

And suddenly Dusty felt all of his pain and anguish dissolve; it was as if it had never existed. What a blessed relief it was, this absence of pain. It was because of her. His love. His life.

Jack Figg had never seen anything quite like it before. The most beautiful portrait of a woman he had ever set eyes on. Yet to say it was beautiful would not do it justice, he realized that. He could not tear his eyes away from it, held as he was by the glory of the woman's face and the background spread out behind her.

Dusty had painted a landscape that was magnificent and could only be English: a canopy of dark green trees set against a pale blue sky scattered with puffy clouds, half golden, as if they were filled with sunlight. The lawns below that shimmering summer sky were lighter green, gave way to a patch of dark earth in the foreground, where the garden seat was placed. It was upon this sofalike structure that the woman reclined.

Her face was heart-shaped, with a narrow nose, high cheekbones, and finely arched brows above large, silvery eyes. The face was pale, set on a slender neck and framed by a mess of silver-gilt hair, long and silky and gleaming brightly. The face and the hair seemed to jump out at him, looked so real he wanted to lean forward and touch them.

The portrait was of India, of course, but an India Standish *he* did not know, had never seen before. There was a sensuality about her, a half-dreamy, half-knowing look in those brilliant eyes, and the red mouth, plump and half open, was positively voluptuous.

India had the look of a woman in love who had just been well loved, and naturally he did not know *this* India. She was the India known only to her lover, Russell Rhodes, who had painted this portrait of her from his very soul. The painting was a testament to that love, his adoration of her.

Her long body was stretched out on the garden sofa, which was covered with a burgundy velvet throw. She wore a filmy outfit of black chiffon, harem pants, and a draped top. This fell away from her shoulders to reveal white arms, marblelike in their perfection. Her longish feet were bare, the nails painted to match the throw.

Jack knew it was a portrait that would cause a sensation—if ever it were shown. But naturally it would be shown. Dusty wouldn't be able to resist doing so. In Jack's opinion, it was one of the most extraordinary paintings he had ever produced.

"Come on, mate, say *something*," Dusty exclaimed,

moving closer to Jack, who was still entranced in front of the easel. "Even if you don't like it, say something."

"Actually, I'm speechless," Jack said at last, turning away from the portrait to regard Dusty. "It's so breathtakingly beautiful I don't know how to express myself adequately." Jack shook his head. "Well, I suppose I can say, in all truthfulness, that it's sensational, heart-stopping, and staggering. You're a bloody marvel, Dusty. A genius. It's Classical Realism taken to utter perfection. No wonder they've always said you're the new Pietro Annigoni."

Flattered and thrilled at Jack's reaction though he was, Dusty couldn't resist teasing him. Giving him a long, hard stare, he said, "Is that all you can say, Jack? Bloody hell, that's not much of a reaction after almost a year of slog on my part."

For a moment Jack was taken aback. He blinked, and then, when he realized Dusty was pulling his leg, he began to chuckle. "I meant every word, you scoundrel. It's going to cause quite a stir when you show it."

"Yes, I know." Moving away from the easel, Dusty studied his portrait of India, and, glancing at Jack, he added, "It will look even better when it's framed. And *she's* the bloody marvel, if anybody is," he finished.

"Thanks for letting me see it." Jack stood watching Dusty throw the sheet over the painting, then asked, "When are you going to show it to India?"

"I told her she could see it on Saturday. Tomorrow, in fact. I hope she likes it."

"How can she not?"

"People have a funny knack of seeing themselves quite differently from the way others see them . . . they have a unique way of looking at themselves, as if with one eye only. They get a half-blind picture," he finished with a laugh.

"I guess they do, and that's very well said."

"Let's go and have another cup of coffee before you get off," Dusty said, leading Jack away from the painting. After locking the studio door behind them and pocketing the key, Dusty led the way to the grand Palladian house on the hill. Neither man spoke. Both were lost in their own thoughts.

After taking his leave of Dusty, Jack drove through Harrogate and took the Ripon road in the direction of Pennistone Royal. It was a lovely day, cold and crisp with a brilliant sun flung high in a pale blue sky.

Before going down to breakfast that morning, Jack had checked in with his two operatives as well as his pals at Leeds C.I.D. None of them had had any luck; there was nothing to report about Melinda Caldwell. Nor had Dusty heard from the hospital. After making a call to the nurses' station, he had explained to Jack that Molly's condition was unchanged; she was still in the ICU. The day nurse had promised to give Dusty a ring if there were any new developments.

As he drove, Jack's thoughts swung to Jonathan Ainsley and Priscilla Marney. Were those two really old lovers? Had they recently been meeting at Heron's Nest? Jack pondered this for a short while. Then it suddenly struck him that Priscilla would have been awfully young when he'd first seen her at Heron's Nest. Thirteen? Fourteen? Could she have been having sex with Jonathan then? No, too young, he decided. Kids today had sex at that age . . . but forty years ago?

Jack sighed as he drove along, wondering if he was on a wild-goose chase, going to Pennistone Royal to talk to Margaret. This trip was India's idea. Before leaving for the Leeds store earlier that morning, she had suggested he ought to go and talk to Paula's housekeeper. "There's not much she doesn't know about this family," India had pointed out. "Don't forget, her parents worked all of their lives at Pennistone Royal for Emma. Margaret grew up there, along with Paula and all the cousins. That's why she's so familiar at times. Maybe she would know if

Jonathan and Priscilla were once an item." India had laughed and added, "She's quite gossipy, you know, at times. On the other hand, maybe those two were secretive about their relationship even then, if there was one, of course."

Jack had instantly seen the sense in talking to Margaret, and before setting out he had phoned Paula at the London store. He had only one question for her: Which bedroom had been Jonathan's when they were growing up? As she had described the room, Jack knew at once it was the one which Mrs. Hodges had insisted was disturbed and where she had shown him the black hairs on the pink cushions. "New cushions," the caretaker had thought to point out to him yesterday. "Mrs. O'Neill bought 'em last summer, when she was titivating the house."

So here he was, heading to Pennistone Royal on the pretext of checking the security system. He had used this ruse to explain the reason for his visit to Margaret, realizing he might change his mind about discussing Jonathan and Priscilla with her. He had decided to feel his way on that.

It was not long before Jack reached the rear gate of the great stone house. After punching in the security code, he drove up the back drive slowly, forever cautious because of the horses that were frequently around. The drive was deserted this morning; not even Wiggs was anywhere in sight. Once he turned the bend, just before reaching the cobbled backyard, Jack spotted Wiggs poking at a bonfire blazing on a patch of dark earth.

Slowing the car, Jack rolled down the window and greeted the head gardener with a cheerful "Hello, Wiggs!"

"Morning, Mr. Jack. It's a right fine day."

"It is indeed." As he got out of the car, Jack felt a rush of nostalgia when he sniffed the smoke of the bonfire. His father had loved to garden, was forever burning twigs and leaves. It was an old, well-remembered smell, and for a moment it brought a lump to his throat.

Shaking off his past, Jack strode toward the kitchen door, knocked, and walked in, exclaiming, "Top of the morning to you, Margaret—" He broke off when he saw Priscilla Marney sitting at the table with the housekeeper. He managed to keep his face neutral as he said, "And hello, Priscilla!"

"Good morning, Jack," she answered with a faint smile.

It was Margaret who instantly jumped up, came over to him, a beaming smile lighting up her motherly face as she greeted him in a warm voice. "It's a good job you're here, Jack," she said, taking his arm, leading him to the big deal table in the middle of the spacious kitchen. "I had a real problem buzzing Prissy in twenty minutes ago. I couldn't make that there switch work. I think it's on the blink, do you know. Anyway, I had to go outside and find Wiggs, send him down to open the gate. Do you think there's a shortage or something?"

"It's possible, Margaret, and I'd say it's rather fortuitous that I decided to do a check of the system here today, and only because I was in the area."

"It's lucky for us, it is that, Jack! Now sit yourself down, luv, and how about a cup of tea?"

"I wouldn't say no." As he lowered himself into a chair directly opposite Priscilla, Jack couldn't help thinking that it was very fortuitous that *she* was here. Sometimes when things like this had happened in the past, he would tell himself: *It was meant to be.* It was as if some unseen but omnipotent hand had arranged things especially for him. And this was what he thought now. Here was the one and only Priscilla, at his disposal, so to speak, and all he had to do was think of the best way to draw her out. With a little luck, he might be able to trap her into spilling the beans. He smiled inwardly.

Pushing a big smile onto his face, he said in a friendly,

interested voice, "And how's the catering business doing, Prissy?"

"Very well, Jack, thanks. I've been extremely busy lately . . . No, I can't complain at all."

"I'm glad to hear it. You certainly catered Evan's wedding beautifully." He nodded and went on. "You grew up to be a talented lass, you really did. Why, I can remember when you were a gawky little schoolgirl in Scarborough. I often used to come across you at Heron's Nest when I went over to see Mrs. Harte."

Priscilla stared at him, taken by surprise at this mention of the past. And Heron's Nest. She simply nodded. And he wondered if he was imagining it: hadn't her face paled slightly? Wanting to breach the little gap, Jack went on. "How's your daughter? Samantha, isn't it?"

A smile struck her face now, and her dark eyes lit up. "Yes, it is, and she's terrific, Jack, thanks for asking. I'm very proud of her."

"Oh, she's a lovely girl," Margaret interjected, bringing the cup and saucer to the table, sitting down, pouring Jack's tea. "And she looks just like her father, Conner, the spitting image. God rest his soul."

Vaguely Jack remembered Margaret telling him some years ago that Priscilla's husband had been knocked down by a bus in Manchester. "Such a young man, too," Margaret had added at the time.

Now Margaret said, "Do you want something to eat, Jack?"

"No, thanks very much, though."

Sitting back in her chair, Margaret said, "Emily's going to have the christening here—" She stopped, noticing the disapproving expression on Jack's face, cleared her throat, and corrected herself quickly, saying, "Miss Emily wants to have it at Pennistone Royal because of tradition, and Miss Paula agreed. Anyway, it's a better place than Allington Hall. Prissy's doing the catering, of course."

"That's why I'm here this morning." Priscilla gave Jack

a small smile and unexpectedly confided, "I've brought the proposals over, the plans and menus for Emily and Paula to look at this weekend. Oh, and I'm doing the wedding as well."

For a moment Jack was baffled. He frowned and asked, "*Wedding?* What wedding?"

"Tessa's, of course," Margaret answered before Priscilla had a chance to respond. "Miss Paula told me last weekend that the divorce is more or less final. I believe Tessa will marry Mr. Deléon any minute now. In London, at a registry office. That's the plan. But everyone will come up here for the reception, and to spend the weekend. So we certainly need Prissy."

"But he's gone to Afghanistan. To cover the war," Jack murmured, his brows drawing together in a jagged line. "I don't think Tessa will be getting married just yet," he explained.

"Oh, but she will," Priscilla cut in. "The minute he's finished his assignment they'll be married. Paula told me that on the phone only the other day. That's why I had to draw up the second proposal. I've worked around the clock on it for the last few days. Paula wanted it by today because she's arriving later this afternoon."

Jack simply nodded.

Priscilla picked up her cup of tea, took a sip, and it was then that Jack noticed she was wearing a wedding band with a small sapphire engagement ring next to it. He now recalled that Margaret had mentioned something about Priscilla remarrying several years ago. He couldn't help wondering if she was still married; if she was, perhaps that was the reason she was meeting Jonathan at Heron's Nest. If she *was* meeting him, that is. Between her catering business, her daughter, and her marriage, she might be far too busy to meet him in London. Or anywhere else, for that matter.

Unable to resist, Jack now asked, "You *did* get married again, didn't you, Prissy?"

"Oh, yes, but I'm separated from Roger."

"Oh, I'm sorry."

"Don't be, he's not good enough to lick her boots!" Margaret announced, leaning forward, giving Jack a knowing look. "Can't hold a candle to Priscilla, that he can't."

Priscilla made a moue with her mouth and shrugged. "We all make mistakes sometimes," she remarked. "It hasn't worked out for me. Still, no harm done." Quite suddenly she smiled, and it was a brilliant smile. "You know what they say, there's more fish in the sea than ever came out of it," she said, unexpectedly looking pleased with herself.

"Hooked a good one, have you?" Jack asked before he could stop himself.

Priscilla blushed scarlet but did not answer him.

Jack decided she didn't have to. Words were not at all necessary; her face told him the whole story.

Margaret laughed. "Priscilla's got a lot of admirers, you know, Jack, and you can see why."

"Indeed I can. And I must say I'm delighted at your enormous success in business. Mind you, Priscilla, you deserve it. The food at Evan's wedding was delicious. And talking of Evan and weddings, will you be catering Jonathan's? Or isn't he getting married in Yorkshire?" As Jack asked this loaded question, his eyes did not leave Priscilla Marney's face.

Margaret exclaimed, *"What?"* Her eyes were wide in astonishment.

Priscilla said not a word. She sat staring at Jack, stunned. Her face turned a violent red, and just as quickly that brilliant color drained away and she paled, as white as bleached bone. She opened her mouth, but no words came out. There was only a strangled cry.

Margaret demanded, "What did you say, Jack? That Jonathan Ainsley's getting married? That takes the cake! Who is he marrying?"

"Evan's sister," Jack answered, his eyes still pinned on Priscilla, who was now shaking like a leaf in a high wind. "*Angharad Hughes*. You know who I mean, Margaret. The platinum blond who was one of the bridesmaids. She was—"

"Oh, God! Not *her!*" Priscilla screeched. "Not that ugly, vulgar American girl!"

"Not so ugly anymore, so I'm told. Nor so vulgar either, according to Linnet," said Jack, gazing at her.

"What are you gabbling about?" Margaret asked swiftly, glancing worriedly at Priscilla and then back at Jack, shaking her head.

He said, "I understand that Angharad and Jonathan are in Paris together. According to Linnet, who got it from . . . Paula, Angharad is now an elegant brunette dressed in couture clothes. And the expensive jewelry is also of the finest quality, at least that was what Linnet was told. I also understand they're going off to Hong Kong, so he can 'show her the sights,' to quote Linnet quoting Paula's source. Apparently he's fallen head over heels for Miss Hughes."

"But she's horrible," Priscilla spluttered, tears coming into her eyes. Her mouth began to tremble, and she could not proceed.

Jack said, "It seems her makeover, accomplished by the most talented of hairdressers, makeup artists, and couturiers, has been very successful. I'm told Angharad now looks like the young Audrey Hepburn. And let's not forget, she is only twenty-three. Nothing like young flesh to turn on an old geezer like Jonathan Ainsley."

Priscilla cried out, but her words were unintelligible. She began to groan, and then she burst into tears. Bringing her hands to her face, she sobbed as if her heart were breaking.

27

⁓

Priscilla lay on the big sofa in front of the fire in the library. After helping her into the room, Margaret had put a match to the paper and logs in the grate, covered her with a tartan blanket, and brought her a brandy, explaining that it would help her.

But Priscilla had taken only a sip, then put the glass on the coffee table. She felt nauseated, realized she wouldn't be able to keep anything inside her, least of all the Calvados. She was still in a state of extreme shock.

Jack Figg's totally unexpected announcement that Jonathan, *her Jonny,* was with that awful girl in Paris had been the most terrible blow, the worst since she had been informed her darling Conner was lying dead in the morgue in Manchester.

When Jack had said Jonathan was going to marry Evan's sister, Priscilla was so stunned and hurt and upset she had completely lost control. Now they knew she had been having an affair with him; they couldn't help but put two and two together. For a while, as she had lain here, she had been embarrassed by this, but that feeling had passed. She didn't have to explain herself to them, or to anyone else for that matter. She was a grown woman; she'd done nothing wrong.

Closing her eyes, Priscilla endeavored to relax, but this

was impossible. She was still filled with unease. And then there was the jealousy . . . how insidiously it had crept up on her, filling her with hatred for the girl, and for him.

How untrustworthy Jonathan Ainsley was, not to mention a dyed-in-the-wool liar. He had kept canceling their romantic rendezvous in Thirsk, first because he had been delayed in London on business. So he said. And then because he was in Paris. He had murmured sweet endearments to her over the phone, promising her so much, and all the time he'd held the phone, his other hand had been on the girl. Evan's little sister. Twenty-three. Delectable. *Young flesh,* Jack had called Angharad Hughes. How right he was. What man in his fifties, especially a voluptuary like Jonathan, could resist her?

Picturing them together in bed in his Paris flat sent a wave of hatred rushing through her. *Bastard.* He had promised to take her to Paris so many times, and he never had. The mere thought of him buying the girl expensive clothes and fabulous jewelry was too much for her to bear. She began to tremble. Despair, anger, hurt, and disappointment coalesced into a hard ball inside her. She began to weep uncontrollably. Pushing her face into the cushions, she sobbed until there were no tears left; then, exhausted, she lay still.

Eventually, Priscilla discovered she was calm, and her self-control slowly returned. It was then that a cold and bitter detachment settled over her, and she contemplated revenge.

Margaret sat on a small chair next to the sofa, holding Priscilla's hand. "Are you feeling better?" she asked in a kindly tone.

Swallowing hard, Priscilla nodded. "Yes, thanks, Margaret. I'll soon be back to normal." She forced a small smile. "Sorry I got so upset. You've been very kind."

"Jack says you went into shock. You did, you know, I agree with him there."

Priscilla merely nodded, said nothing.

Margaret went on slowly, "Whatever made you get involved with *him,* luvvy? Jonathan of all people. He's a bad lot."

Biting her lip, Priscilla shook her head. "I'd known him all my life . . . he sought me out at different times . . . pursued me, really. He was very flattering, even loving."

It was Margaret's turn to remain silent. She just sat holding Priscilla's hand, glad she was no longer weeping and moaning. Although she felt sorry for her in certain ways, Margaret was also silently chastising her for being such a foolish woman. But then more women fell for the bad lads than she cared to think about. She knew quite a few who'd toppled into that trap.

There was a knock, and Jack appeared in the doorway. "Do you feel better, Prissy? Can I come in for a few minutes?"

"Oh, yes, that's fine."

Closing the door behind him, Jack crossed the floor and sat down in an armchair, facing Priscilla on the sofa.

Margaret immediately got up off the stool and made to leave, deciding it was better for Jack to talk to the caterer alone.

"It's all right, Margaret." He glanced at the housekeeper. "You don't have to leave. In fact, I think it would be a good idea for you to stay."

"If you want me to, Jack," she answered and went over to the other sofa.

"Yes, I do want you here," he said. Smiling at Priscilla, his eyes filled with sympathy, Jack murmured in a warm voice, "I must apologize to you. I'm afraid I upset you greatly, blurting that out about Jonathan Ainsley the way I did. But I'd no idea you were in any way involved with him."

"Nobody knew," Priscilla informed him in a low voice.

"And why was that?" Jack gave her a keen, penetrating look.

"He wanted to keep it a secret."

"I see." He leaned forward, staring at her even more intently. After a moment, he asked, "Because you're married? Was that the reason?"

"Not really," Priscilla replied. She hesitated before adding, "He knew I was separated, and that I'm planning to divorce Roger Duffield."

"But *why* the secrecy? I don't understand."

"He didn't want the family to know about us," she answered at last. "The Hartes."

"I see." Jack now sat back, staring into space for a moment before saying, suddenly, "Did you never wonder why he insisted on keeping your relationship a secret?"

"Occasionally. But, well, I . . . well . . . I wanted to be with him, so I just accepted it. Accepted his terms."

"You've been meeting him at Heron's Nest, haven't you?"

"Yes," she responded laconically, looked down at her hands, shamefaced.

"Why there?"

"Because it meant something to him, and to me as well. You see, we'd first made . . . been together there when we were teenagers. So Heron's Nest was special to both of us. It seemed to excite him, meeting there in secret." She blushed, turned her head, gazed into the fire, wondering why she'd told him this.

Clearing his throat, Jack continued, "Presumably he had a key?"

"Oh, yes, ever since our teenage years. I believe he'd made a copy then, and Paula has never changed the locks."

Dismayed though he was about this lack of security, Jack kept his face neutral as he went on in a quiet but firm tone. "I have to tell you something very important, Priscilla. And I need your full attention."

Nodding, she said, "Yes, I'm listening, Jack, I really am."

"There's a good reason why Jonathan Ainsley wanted

to conceal your affair. He didn't want Paula to know about you and him because *he* is *her* sworn enemy, a deadly enemy of this entire family, in fact. If Paula had known how close you two were, she would not have used you as her caterer and he would have lost his informant."

Sitting up straighter on the sofa, swinging her legs to the floor, Priscilla gaped at him, her face turning extremely pale. "But I wasn't his informant!" Her eyes wide, her voice rising an octave, she added, "I *swear* I wasn't! And you're wrong, Jack, he wasn't and isn't an enemy of the family. I would have known."

"Not necessarily. Didn't it ever occur to you that he never attended any of the family functions and gatherings?"

"He always planned to come!" she cried vehemently. "He told me he was coming, but then he was suddenly called away, to Paris or Hong Kong. Or somewhere. I thought that was his life; after all, he is a big tycoon." She shook her head. "I never, ever told him anything about Paula, or the family. I didn't know anything. No one ever confided in *me*."

Jack got up, walked over to the fireplace, stood with his back to it enjoying the warmth. After a moment, he began to speak once more. "You must have told Jonathan at different times that you were about to cater a special event for Paula."

Priscilla could only nod.

"So in a way you *were* a conduit to the family, if unintentionally so. He certainly knew when the entire family would be here at Pennistone Royal, for example."

"Yes," she whispered, dismay lodging in her stomach. "That's true. But I never knew he was their enemy. He always acted as if he were on the best of terms with them. You must believe me."

"He's a clever chap, isn't he, Margaret?" Looking over at the housekeeper, Jack smiled sardonically. *"And dangerous."*

"Oh, that he is," Margaret agreed. "He'd love to kill us all off, that he would." She gave Priscilla a hard stare, hoping her words had penetrated.

"Never!" Priscilla cried, her emotions getting the better of her. "I don't believe you! That's not Jonny. You're exaggerating, I know you are."

"I'm afraid not," Jack exclaimed coldly. "Margaret is telling you the truth, as indeed am I. There's no reason for either of us to exaggerate or lie to you, Prissy. Jonathan wants to destroy Paula and the family, and that's a fact."

Priscilla sat rigid on the sofa, hardly able to take this in. But she accepted, as she looked into his eyes, now blazing with anger, that this man spoke the truth. She was aghast. How could she have been with Jonathan and not known any of these things? Not understood his evil intentions?

Nervous, even afraid, she wondered where her judgment had been. And her common sense. A fool for love, she thought disdainfully.

When she remained silent, Jack asked her, "Did you know about the problem at the church on the day of the wedding?"

"No. What do you mean?" she asked, her eyes widening.

Without answering her, he said, "But you did know the time was changed? You haven't forgotten about that, have you?"

"No. They got married in the early morning, and Margaret said it was because Evan hadn't been feeling well and everyone was worried about her condition . . . the pregnancy, the possibility of premature birth."

"Those *were* worries, but not exactly the reason the time of the wedding was changed. The family were concerned, actually, they were afraid that Jonathan might attempt to do something to harm Evan and Gideon. So Linnet devised a plan, and how right she was to do so, as it turned out," Jack said. "At two-fifteen in the afternoon, the original time of the wedding, part of the west wall of Pennistone village church blew out. Because a bomb had been planted in the church. During the night, we believe. We're sure it was Ainsley's doing, but naturally we can never prove it."

Priscilla stared at Jack, shaking her head. "I went down to London on Sunday. I didn't hear about the explosion." She felt as though she had been hit in the stomach with a cricket bat. It took her a moment to get hold of herself. "It's not possible, Jack. I *know* him, know him better than anybody. He wouldn't do anything so wicked." She was almost in tears again as she finished. "Why would he?"

"Because of his hatred." Margaret spoke up. "He's jealous and envious of Miss Paula, and of Evan, now she's in the picture."

"How do you know it was *him*?" Priscilla demanded, her eyes nervously swiveling from Margaret to Jack. "He wasn't even in Yorkshire on the day of the wedding," she protested. "So how could he put a bomb in the church?"

"You don't think he'd be foolish enough to do his own dirty work, do you?" Jack stared at her intently, his eyes narrowing. "Surely you're smarter than that, Prissy." He shook his head, his face grave. "No, no, he employs people to do his bidding, not that we would ever be able to prove that either in a court of law."

Priscilla now turned away from Jack and addressed the housekeeper. "Margaret, listen to me. You've known me most of my life, since I was a young girl. Please, talk to me straight," she pleaded. "Is all of this true?"

"Oh, yes, luv, it is. You've been involved with a monster for years, I'm afraid, and more's the pity."

"But I didn't know. I really didn't, Margaret, Jack, I never knew, I swear to God I didn't."

Margaret felt duty bound to make Priscilla understand the seriousness of all this, and she said in a stronger voice than usual, "Miss Paula's been worried for years that he would do her harm, and harm the family as well. Worried sick, she's been. After Sandy fired Jonathan Ainsley, he turned against them, all those years ago, it was. You see, earlier, just after Mrs. Harte died, he'd begun to claim he'd been cheated in her will. Wasn't true, that. *I knows.* His hatred has only grown. He *is* evil. And dangerous."

Undone by these unexpected revelations, Priscilla was also now convinced that Jack and Margaret were telling her the truth. Unable to speak, sick at heart, she sat on the sofa, her arms wrapped around herself, feeling icy cold and numb. All this was a nightmare. What a stupid fool she had been. *He had used her.*

As if he understood exactly what was going through her mind, Jack moved across the floor, sat down next to Priscilla on the sofa. "You were duped, Prissy, I'm sorry to say."

Tears came into her eyes. "I believe I was, Jack, but let me say once again, I never told him anything about the family. . . . I only ever mentioned the parties I was catering, and then because I thought that he had been invited, that he'd be there. There was nothing else I *could* tell him. I didn't know anything." When Jack was silent, she pressed, "You do believe me, don't you?"

"Yes, I do, Priscilla."

"I suppose Paula's not going to use my catering services anymore . . ." Her voice trailed off, and she looked at Jack questioningly.

He saw at once the fear in her eyes, and he understood how dependent she was on Paula for her business. For the first time, he felt a little sorry for her. "Perhaps not," he responded at last. "I'll explain everything to her. But you cannot be in contact with Jonathan ever again. You do understand that?"

"Whatever makes you think I would want to be?" she asked, her tone scornful.

He saw at once the vengeful look in her eyes.

Jack left the two women alone in the library and went off to check the main control box of the security system. He had said that this was his reason for visiting Pennistone Royal this morning, so why not make it the truth? Also, Margaret had mentioned that the switch in the pantry was on the blink. Maybe there was something wrong.

Walking through the kitchen toward the basement door, he stopped when his mobile phone rang.

"Jack Figg here," he said, leaning against the deal table.

"It's India, Jack."

"Hello! I was going to give you a ring later, tell you what a clever girl you are. I've just had a long, productive chat with Priscilla Marney, and quite by chance."

"Oh, that is good. At least I hope it is. Jack, listen to me," she rushed on. "I rang you about something else. I'm afraid Molly Caldwell died a short while ago."

"Oh, *no*. I'm so sorry. Poor lady. I'd better phone Dusty, ask if there's anything I can do to help."

"Do it later, Jack. He's rushed off to the hospital. Molly put Atlanta's name on the hospital papers as her next of kin, so he has to sort it out. Dusty wanted me to let you know that Molly passed away." There was a slight pause. "Any news of Melinda?"

"I'm afraid not. But I keep checking in with my chaps and the police. I'll ring them again when we hang up."

"Thanks. Let's speak later."

"You've got it, lovey."

They both clicked off.

Jack immediately dialed his two operatives in Leeds. There was still no news of Melinda, and when he spoke to his friends at Leeds C.I.D., they had nothing to report. "It's like looking for a needle in a haystack," Ted Fletcher explained, and Jack had to agree with him.

Although he was pleased he had been able to solve the Heron's Nest mystery, he was submerged in worry as he headed down into the basement. India and Dusty would never rest with Melinda Caldwell on the loose. He wondered if there *was* a way to find her. He doubted it.

28

Paula was crossing her bedroom at Pennistone Royal when the phone began to ring. Hurrying to the bedside table, she picked it up. "Pennistone Royal."

"Hello, Mrs. O'Neill. It's Bolton."

"Good afternoon, Bolton. Is everything all right at Lackland Priory?" she asked, wondering why Robin's butler was phoning her.

"Yes, it is. But Mr. Ainsley hasn't seemed like himself for the last few days . . ." He left the sentence unfinished.

"Perhaps you should call his doctor, Bolton, have him come over to look at him. Or would you like me to give the doctor a ring?"

"I don't think he's ill, Mrs. O'Neill—" Bolton stopped, then went on cautiously. "I think perhaps he's troubled about something, and I was wondering if you could drop in over the weekend. On the spur of the moment, so to speak. I wouldn't want him to think I'd interfered."

"Of course I'll come to see him, Bolton, that's no problem. And actually, I have a very good reason for coming, so you don't have to worry. Mrs. Marietta Hughes is our houseguest this weekend, and naturally she will want to see Mr. Ainsley."

"Thank you, Mrs. O'Neill. Should I tell Mr. Ainsley you'll be dropping by?"

"No, no, I don't think so," Paula replied swiftly. "Let's make it a surprise. We'll probably come tomorrow morning for coffee. I'll give you a ring before we set off."

"I'll be waiting, and thank you again, Mrs. O'Neill."

"Until tomorrow morning, Bolton, and I'm glad you thought to call me," Paula said and hung up. She stood with her hand resting on the phone for a moment, wondering what could be troubling Uncle Robin. He had seemed perfectly well the last time she had seen him. For a moment she thought of asking Great-Aunt Edwina if something was wrong with him. Instantly she changed her mind, cautioning herself not to stir anything up.

Walking over to her dressing table, Paula ran a comb through her short black hair, refreshed her lipstick, and then went to look at herself in the cheval mirror standing in the corner. She had left for Yorkshire directly from Harte's and was still wearing her regulation black skirt suit.

Glancing at her watch, she opened one of her closets, pulled out a wine-colored wool pantsuit, and quickly changed. A moment later she hurried toward the door leading into the upstairs parlor. Automatically, she stopped to touch the fruitwood casket on the Queen Anne chest, but of course it was no longer there. She had given it to Evan. Shaking her head, pursing her lips, she went into the adjoining room, reminding herself that the habits of a lifetime never died.

Paula positioned herself at the window, looking out at the moors, thinking of her grandmother. Emma Harte had been the fairest of people, and she prided herself on her own fairness. So why was she being so hard on Linnet?

On the way to Yorkshire, Paula had glanced at her daughter's detailed memos, and for a few moments she had been enraged by them. Since Tessa and Marietta were in the car with her, she had had to put them back in her briefcase to study over the weekend.

Staring at the bleak hills, she shook her head, dismayed with herself, and then a thought struck her. Everything Linnet was suggesting they do at the store cost money. A lot of money. And she didn't want to make that kind of outlay.

Turning away, Paula went to her desk and looked at the folders containing the memos, sighing. Then she remembered how she had wanted to make changes when she was a young woman. But she had made a very big mistake. Was that why she was fighting Linnet? Was she afraid her daughter would make similar errors? Hers had almost cost her the Harte stores . . .

There was a knock, and the door opened as Margaret came rushing in carrying the tea tray, followed by Jack Figg.

"Hello, Paula," he said, hurrying toward her, a wide smile on his face.

"Jack, it's lovely to see you!" Rising, Paula went to meet him, gave him a big hug, and then took a seat on the sofa.

Putting the tray on the coffee table, Margaret said, "Here it is, Miss Paula, and I found them there ginger biscuits you like."

"Thanks, Margaret."

As Jack sat down on the sofa opposite Paula, Margaret threw him a quick, knowing glance and said in a stage whisper, "Don't miss out a thing, tell her *everything* that happened this morning."

When the housekeeper had retreated, Paula eyed Jack in amusement, and they both began to laugh as the door closed.

"She's a card." Jack shook his head, still smiling. "She takes after her mother."

"That's true, anyway—" Paula broke off at the sound of the ringing phone and jumped up, went to her desk.

Jack glanced around, his eyes approving. He felt a sudden surge of nostalgia. How many times he had sat on this sofa, having tea with the one and only Emma, his dearest friend. He couldn't remember how many times, now that he thought about it, but the teas he had shared with her had been very special.

The upstairs parlor was full of comfort and charm; he loved its sunny yellow walls, colorful chintz fabric on the sofas, mellow Georgian antiques, and glorious paintings. The remarkable thing was that it had never changed much, and it was all Emma's work. She had had a great eye, and extraordinary taste. Paula simply refurbished it from time to time when this was required. Everyone congregated here, as they had always done. It had often struck him that the upstairs parlor was the center of this great house, around which everything flowed.

It was particularly welcoming this afternoon, with the huge fire blazing in the hearth, the silk-shaded lamps casting a soft glow . . . such lovely contrasts to the dark moors with their snowy caps, just visible through the windows. And then there were the white orchids which Paula grew in her glass houses, pots and pots of them standing around the room.

Paula came back to the fireside, sat down, and said to Jack, "That was Shane. He's delayed at the Leeds office, so he won't make it in time for tea. But he hopes you'll stay to dinner, and so do I. You will, won't you?"

"That's a nice invitation, Paula, I hope I can. I have to check several ongoing things, but hopefully I won't have to rush off to London, and thanks for asking me."

"You know you're at home here, Jack, part of the family. And by the way, Marietta's here, she came up with me and Tessa this afternoon. For the weekend. So she'll be lovely company for us all."

Jack was surprised. "Really! I thought she would be hovering around Evan at this stage of the pregnancy."

"She's rather smart, you know, not the typical fussing mother, and when I invited her she jumped at the invitation. As Marietta put it, she doesn't want to be an albatross around Evan's neck. She thinks Evan and Gideon should have plenty of time to themselves."

"Wise woman. Linnet told me she's looking for a flat in London."

Paula nodded but said nothing more about this. Her violet eyes were focused on him, and she studied him for a long moment. She wondered, suddenly, what the family would have done without him all these years. He had been devoted, their fierce defender and protector.

As Jack became aware of her scrutiny, he laughed. "Ah, Paula, I recognize that look of yours. I suppose you want to know about Heron's Nest."

"Actually, I was thinking of you . . . how wonderful you've been to us over the years. Your devotion and loyalty have been remarkable, Jack." She gave him a small smile. "But you know *me* too well. Of course I want to know about Heron's Nest. Was there a burglary?"

"No, of course not. Don't forget, there was no sign of breaking and entering, which was puzzling to me." Finishing his tea, putting down the cup, he relaxed against the plump pillows. "You should have changed the locks at Heron's Nest years ago," he admonished mildly.

"I should?" She frowned. "Oh, God, don't tell me someone got in with a key."

"Correct."

"Who was it?" she asked, looking suddenly perplexed.

"Jonathan Ainsley."

Paula stared at Jack in astonishment and then asked, "But why on earth would he want to go there in winter? Or at any time of the year?"

"It was his secret hideaway, his love nest. He was meeting someone there."

"Who?"

"Priscilla Marney."

"Good God, Jack, not Prissy!" Paula kept shaking her

head in bafflement, then exclaimed, "I'm simply astounded."

"Let me tell you the story, the one I managed to unravel this morning."

Paula simply nodded and sat back on the sofa, giving him her entire attention. As was her way, she let him speak without interrupting.

"And so," he finished ten minutes later, "that's the unfortunate tale of our Prissy and the dastardly Jonathan Ainsley. He duped her, pulled the wool over her eyes. But basically, Paula, I think she's a decent woman, honest, trustworthy, if rather stupid. And I doubt very much that she was ever any kind of conduit to you and the family. She says she never knew anything. Or did she?" he asked, staring hard at Paula, raising a brow.

"No, she didn't. Other than the dates of my various parties, dinners, and other family functions. Why would she know anything about my life?"

"India says Margaret's a bit gossipy," Jack murmured, doing a little fishing.

"Yes, she is, but it's harmless stuff, Jack. Margaret truly doesn't know anything about our lives either, except what goes on when we're at Pennistone Royal, so she couldn't tell Prissy a thing."

"I understand," Jack answered, but he thought Paula was making a misjudgment about Margaret. She knew much more than Paula realized; India had been certain of that.

Returning to the subject of Heron's Nest, Paula said in a low, saddened voice, "Poor Prissy, how foolish she's been. She certainly didn't need to become entangled with that dreadful cousin of mine. How did it happen?"

"Oh, it's been going on for years, started when they were teenagers. By the way, she's worried you're not going to use her anymore. I think she depends on *your* business to keep her catering service going."

Paula nodded. "I believe she does, actually. I'll think about keeping her on, and we'd better get the locks changed at Scarborough, although maybe it doesn't matter anymore."

"Oh, it does, it does indeed. You just never know. I'll arrange for it to be done."

"You said you told Priscilla that Jonathan Ainsley was engaged to Angharad Hughes. But is that *really* true, Jack?" Paula gave him a skeptical look.

"I'm not sure, although I'm inclined to think so. Still, there are those who might say I'm merely making an assumption."

"Tell me all about it, explain why you've come to this conclusion."

"She's been wearing a large diamond ring for a couple of days. Sarah told you that, and my Paris operative also informed me. I had a phone call from him a couple of hours ago, and since he's permanently assigned to Ainsley, he knows his every movement. Anyway, to cut to the chase, he discovered a few things which seemed to add up to a marriage in the making."

"Sarah would know if he's getting married, Jack! He's always told her everything. Well, almost everything."

"I know that, Paula. Just hear me out. My operative knows one of the women who works at Harry Winston on the Avenue Montaigne, where the ring was bought. He found out from her that Angharad was introduced by Ainsley as his fiancée, and the woman made the comment that the young mademoiselle is perfect for him. Because he wants to start a family."

"Surely that's just gossip." Paula gave him a sharp look, shook her head.

"You're right. On the other hand, I learned a couple of hours ago that Ainsley and Angharad visited a fertility clinic in Paris, a famous one. *This afternoon.*"

"Good heavens, he's thinking of *babies*!" Paula sat up with a jerk.

"Why not? He wants an heir. Obviously. And she's certainly of childbearing age at twenty-three. Perhaps that's one of the reasons he's fallen for her. Her potential for motherhood. How does that saying go? An heir and a spare."

Paula sat quite still on the sofa, staring at Jack, thinking about what he had just said. She was at a loss for words. The idea of Angharad Hughes involved with Ainsley to such an extent was deeply disturbing.

But Jack was correct, Jonathan would want an heir. Robin had once told her Jonathan thought he was sterile because he'd never made a woman pregnant. Fertility clinics were now important to him.

Jack was waiting patiently, expecting some pithy or acerbic comment, but none was forthcoming. And so he broke the growing silence between them. "Announcing to Prissy that Jonathan Ainsley was getting married so threw her off balance, she lost it completely. I knew at once it was *she* who was involved with him."

Looking at Jack intently, her eyes narrowing, Paula asked, "Why were you focused on her to begin with?"

"I'd figured it out, thanks to India. I'd asked her if any member of her generation was having assignations at Heron's Nest. She ruled that out, suggested I look at your generation. I did. Of course I knew none of you girls would have been involved with Jonathan when you were growing up, yet remember, it was Jonathan's room that Mrs. Hodges pinpointed. I suddenly wondered what outsiders had visited Heron's Nest in those days." Jack took a deep breath and finished. "I remembered Emma's summer secretary, which led me to Priscilla, the secretary's daughter."

"So it was all a matter of clues and clever deduction on your part. Well, I've always known you were exceedingly astute, and I'm glad you solved it, Jack, and—"

Paula stopped abruptly as the door flew open and Tessa burst into the room. For a split second she stood poised in the doorway. To Paula, her eldest daughter looked like a ghostly figure, dressed entirely in white and with a face as white as the clothes she was wearing.

There was no doubt in Paula's mind that something was terribly wrong, and she jumped up as Tessa came rushing toward her, exclaiming, "Mummy! It's Jean-Claude. He's vanished. In Afghanistan. I don't know what to do!"

Paula pulled Tessa into her arms and held her tightly, endeavoring to soothe her as sobs suddenly broke free. "He'll be found, Tessa, he's probably been found already. Come on, darling, come and sit down with me and tell me all about it."

Jack had risen, too, and went to the two women. Putting a hand lightly on Tessa's shoulder, he said gently, "Your mother's right, Tessa. Come to the fireside. Do you want me to get you anything, a cup of tea, water? Or maybe a brandy?"

Tessa stepped away from Paula, shook her head. In a faltering voice, she whispered, "I'm scared that . . . he's . . . been killed."

"No, no, don't even say that! I'm sure he hasn't," Paula responded in a firm tone. She took hold of Tessa's hand and drew her across to the sofa. They sat down together.

Jack threw a couple of logs onto the fire and then returned to his seat. He knew it was much wiser for him to keep quiet, to leave this to Paula. A mother was always the best person to help a daughter who was in distress, as indeed Tessa was at this moment.

Paula said, "You just found out, didn't you?"

"Yes. Philippe, Jean-Claude's son, just phoned me from Paris. I told you I'd met him at Jean-Claude's country house. Anyway, Philippe called me on my mobile, explained that ten minutes ago he'd had a call from the head of the news division at the network. The man told him that his father was missing, that he'd vanished three days ago. While he was on a special mission. After those

three days had passed without any further communica-
tion from Jean-Claude, the entire network was beginning
to worry. Then the cameraman showed up in Kabul and
phoned Paris, told the head of the news division that he'd
become separated from Jean-Claude, had no idea where
he was. The cameraman had made it back on his own."

"This is very worrying, I admit, but we mustn't think
the worst, Tessa," Paula said, reassuring her as best she
could. "Being missing doesn't mean he's been killed."

"He could have been captured," Tessa mumbled
through her tears. "If anything happens to him, I don't
know what I'll do."

Paula put her arms around her daughter again and held
her close. "And that's all Philippe was able to tell you?"

"Yes. He didn't know anything else. He'll stay in touch,
he promised." Tessa groped in her jacket pocket, pulled
out a handkerchief, patted her streaming eyes.

"When was the last time you spoke to Jean-Claude?"
Paula now thought to ask.

"On Monday. He explained he was leaving Kabul, that
he was on to something he wanted to check out. He said
not to expect a call until this weekend, but I do wish he
hadn't made that rule."

Paula, continuing to soothe her daughter, glanced
across at Jack. Her expression signaled that she wanted
him to say something.

After a moment's thought, Jack remarked quietly,
"That's understandable, Tessa. If he's on a special story,
he obviously doesn't need to be worrying about *you* worrying about *him* just because you haven't heard from him.
Telling you not to expect a call was a wise thing to do in
my opinion."

Tessa didn't say anything. Sitting up, smoothing her
hair, she looked across at Jack and nodded her understanding. "I suppose you're right. He does have to concentrate on his work, and be on the alert in such a
dangerous place."

There was a small silence.

Tessa shifted on the sofa, swiveled her head to look at her mother. Swallowing, she said in a slightly quavering voice, "I'm pregnant. I'm expecting Jean-Claude's child."

"Oh, Tessa, darling, why didn't you tell me before?" Paula exclaimed, a wide smile lighting up her face. Then it slipped slightly.

"Because I wanted to tell Jean-Claude first, and now I can't," she mumbled, and the tears started again. In a choked voice, she added, "I hope he's safe. . . . What if something's happened to him? Whatever will I do without him?"

"Listen to me, Tessa," Paula said in a strong voice. "He's a seasoned war correspondent from what you've told me. He's not going to take any chances, no chances at all. He'll call this weekend, as he promised. I can almost guarantee that."

Deciding he ought to leave Tessa and Paula alone, Jack said, "You must have faith, Tessa, and your mother is right, you know. Jean-Claude won't put himself in danger." Looking at Paula, he added, "I'll leave you two alone to talk."

"Do try to stay for dinner, Jack. We'd love it if you could."

He smiled at her and left, reminding himself that she was shockproof. As head of the family, she was used to carrying so many burdens. What a marvel she was.

29

Years ago, Emma had assigned a pleasant bedroom to Jack, and it was still his. He frequently stayed there, especially when it was too late for him to drive home to Robin Hood's Bay on the coast.

After quietly closing the parlor door behind him, Jack went upstairs to his room. He felt tired all of a sudden, needed a chance to catch his breath. He also had to phone India to ask how Dusty was doing, and put in a few calls to his operatives in the field.

Once inside the room, he glanced around, struck yet again by its lovely soft colors and its comfort. He placed his mobile on the bedside table, took off his jacket and shoes, and lay down on the bed, his hands behind his head.

Staring up at the ceiling, he thought about Tessa's announcement of a moment ago. Paula had taken it in stride, as she usually did when unexpected things happened in the family. And single women having children was not so unusual in this day and age. However, he was very much aware that if something had happened to Jean-Claude in Afghanistan, Tessa would be distraught. He couldn't help wondering where Lorne was this weekend. Was he expected? If so it would be a blessing.

The warbling of his cell phone broke the silence, and Jack reached for it. "Jack Figg here."

"Jack, it's Ted. We've got a body. At the morgue in Leeds. A young woman. She was found in a car parked in a side street, not too far from Roundhay Park. No ID on her, but she fits your description."

"Oh, Jesus," Jack said. "How did she die, Ted?"

"Medical examiner's not exactly sure yet, but more than likely it's an OD. No bruises or wounds on her. Dead since last night, around midnight, according to the coroner."

"You say there's no ID on her. Didn't she have a handbag? Anything in her pockets?" Jack asked, thinking that the lack of identification was peculiar.

"No, in answer to both your questions. Car door was unlocked, key in the ignition, but no sign of a handbag."

"And no drug paraphernalia, no needles, nothing like that?"

"Not a bloody thing, Jack. Bit of a mystery how she died. And where she died. It could have been in the car. Maybe not. Listen, Jack, what's the chance of identifying her?"

"I would if I could, but I've never met Melinda Caldwell."

"Family?"

"The sad thing is her mother passed away this morning. At Leeds Infirmary."

"Mother and daughter dying within hours of each other, that's unique," Ted exclaimed. "And I'm up a creek without a bloody paddle, that's the way it looks to me."

"Her former boyfriend, the father of her child, will identify her, I'm sure. Let me talk to him, and I'll be back to you shortly."

"I'm grateful, Jack. Thanks."

Going over to the desk, Jack sat down and dialed Dusty's number on the house phone, and when Paddy answered he said, "It's Jack Figg, Paddy. I'd like to speak to Mr. Rhodes, if he's available."

"Yes, he is, sir. I'll put you through."

A moment later Dusty was on the line. His voice was flat as he said, "Thanks for calling, Jack. India said you might. I did manage to get things sorted out all right at Leeds Infirmary."

"I'm sorry about Molly Caldwell, Dusty. I actually thought she was going to make it."

"So did I," Dusty replied, but he hadn't, not really.

"Dusty, I just had a call from Ted Fletcher of Leeds C.I.D. They've found Melinda."

"She's not all right, is she? I can tell by the sound of your voice. Is she . . . dead?"

"Yes, I'm afraid so." Clearing his throat, Jack proceeded to give Dusty all the information he had received from Ted. He finished quietly. "There's nobody else to identify her, Dusty. Will you do it?"

"There is somebody else, there's Gladys Roebotham. But Gladys is here at Willows Hall, looking after Atlanta, and I think that's what she should be doing. Yes, I'll do it, Jack. Where do I have to go?"

"Nowhere. Stay there. I'll come and get you, take you to the morgue."

"Come on, Jack, don't be silly. I'm a big boy. I can drive to Leeds by myself."

"It's a lousy experience, Dusty, having to identify someone you've known who's lying on a cold slab. Listen, I'm at Pennistone Royal. Give me a half an hour, I need to have a word with Paula before I leave."

"Jack, before you hang up, did she die of an overdose?"

"They're not sure, but it could have been an OD. And she died last night, around midnight."

There was a silence, then Dusty muttered, "I'll see you shortly, and thanks, Jack."

On Saturday morning Paula decided to go to Lackland Priory early. And she went alone. It had occurred to her that if something were troubling Robin and he needed to talk, it would be best if they were by themselves. Marietta could visit with him later over the weekend, or perhaps he would be able to come to dinner tonight.

Before leaving, she had gone to Tessa's bedroom and spoken to her for a few minutes, hoping to reassure her. But her eldest daughter had been morose, expecting to hear the worst about Jean-Claude at any moment. Nothing Paula said alleviated her anxiety, and Tessa's lack of sleep didn't help.

On the short drive to Robin's house, Paula ran the events of yesterday through her mind. It had turned out to be Black Friday in a sense or, as Shane had said at dinner, "Bad Day at Black Rock," quoting the title of one of his favorite old movies.

"Two deaths," Margaret had muttered to her as she had served the smoked salmon. "There's bound to be a third. Everything goes in threes, you know that, Miss Paula."

That a mother and daughter should die so close together had sent chills running down Paula's spine when Jack had told her about Molly and Melinda. Then he had gone to take Dusty to the morgue in Leeds, promising to be back in time for dinner at eight. And he had kept his promise.

As she drove along the main road, Paula's thoughts centered on Priscilla Marney and her unfortunate involvement with Jonathan Ainsley. How flabbergasted she had been to hear about it, and now she was faced with a decision about using Prissy's catering service. Although Prissy had only herself to blame, Paula couldn't help feeling a little sorry for her. To discover she had been so flagrantly used must have been galling for Prissy. Jack had said he believed Priscilla was decent and loyal, and so she would probably keep her on. She would talk to Shane about it later.

As she turned in to the driveway, Paula wondered what was awaiting her at Lackland Priory. Before she even switched off the ignition, the front door opened and Bolton was waiting for her on the step, greeting her cheerfully as he escorted her inside the lovely old house.

After taking her coat, the butler showed her into the morning room, where Robin was having breakfast and reading the newspapers.

"What a pleasant surprise," Robin said, getting up, kissing her on the cheek. "When Bolton said you'd be popping in, I had him set another place. Would you like breakfast?"

Sitting down opposite him, Paula shook her head. "Just coffee, thanks, Uncle Robin."

Bolton brought her the cup of coffee and quickly departed, and Paula went on. "It's such a gorgeous day, lovely and sunny and quite mild." She laughed. "As if I have to tell you that. This room's full of sunshine."

Robin smiled, too. "Where are you off to so early, Paula?"

"I'm meeting Emily in West Tanfield; we have to do a few things at Beck House. And as I knew I'd be driving right past the priory, I thought I'd come in and say hello. How have you been feeling, Uncle Robin?"

"Not bad, not bad at all. Of course I worry about Evan and the twins. I can't wait for them to be born."

"Neither can she, I'm sure of that."

"Everything's all right, isn't it?"

"Oh, yes, please don't worry. She's going to be perfectly fine." Paula took a sip of her coffee and went on. "Marietta is with us for the weekend, and I was wondering if you'd like to join us for dinner tonight."

"That sounds like a nice idea, Paula, but I'd planned to see Edwina."

"She can join us, too, unless you want to be alone with her."

Robin was silent, and then after a moment, he said, "Well, we can ask her, and I think she'd like that. We love coming to Pennistone Royal."

Leaning across the table, he now said, "Shall we take a walk in the garden? As you said, it's a gorgeous day, and I want to discuss my roses with you."

Paula was taken aback. Noting the anxious look in his eyes, she said, "Why not? But you're going to need a warm coat."

A few minutes later, both of them bundled up in coats and scarves, Robin led Paula around his garden, explaining, "I don't like to speak about private family matters when there's so much staff around."

"I understand. But you trust Bolton, don't you, Uncle Robin?"

"Of course, he's been with me for years and he's most devoted, but it doesn't hurt to be careful. The less people know, the better."

"I agree. Now, I know you didn't invite me out here to talk about the rosebushes," Paula said pithily, glancing around. "But they really do need to be in the sun, and I think those bushes over there will get too much shade in the summer."

"I know, I plan to dig 'em up when the ground's not so hard. If I'm still here."

"Oh, you will be, I've no doubt about that. So, what did you want to talk to me about?"

"Two things. First, I want you to know that I have left Evan my mews house in Belgravia. To all intents and purposes, it's Edwina's mews, but I bought it from her years ago. For Glynnis. The deeds have always remained in Edwina's name, but Anthony knows the deal, no problem there. However, I felt you should be in the picture, since you run all the family business."

"Thanks for telling me, Uncle Robin—" Paula cut herself off, biting her lip, her expression worried.

Robin said, "Don't even think about Jonathan. You see, he has always believed that the house is Edwina's, and that she simply allowed me to stay there whenever I wanted. The arrangement is that when Edwina dies, Gideon will 'buy' it as an investment."

"All right, that works for me. And thank you for filling me in, Uncle Robin. You said you had two things to discuss. What else is on your mind?"

"I have created a trust for Evan's twins. I used John Crawford, your solicitor, even though he's semiretired. I've known him donkey's years, and he is the most honorable and trustworthy of men. Again, you don't have to worry about Jonathan finding out because for years I've had a trust fund in the States. It was for Glynnis. She never touched it, and it reverted to me with her death. I was thinking of making Owen the beneficiary, but I've changed my mind. It will be for Evan's twins."

"I understand."

"You have an odd look on your face, Paula," Robin murmured, staring at her intently. "What is it?"

"Are you sure Jonathan couldn't trace it?"

"I am. You see, I created the trust for Glynnis in the nineteen fifties, with money I had invested in the States. Anyway, the twins won't inherit the trust until they are twenty-one. Believe me, Paula, John has made sure everything is absolutely watertight."

"Of course. I know how brilliant he is. But I do have a question, if that's all right."

"Fire away, Paula dear."

"Why did you change your mind about Owen Hughes?"

"He doesn't need the money. But that's not the real reason." Robin shook his head, and a sudden sadness settled on his face. "He doesn't like me, not really, Paula, and he hasn't made much of an effort toward me. I understand that. He was brought up by Richard Hughes, and Richard was his father in the best sense of that word. I think in his mind I'm just his mother's lover, and as that perhaps I don't rate too high." Robin took her arm, smiled at her warmly. "Besides, I prefer to look to the future. . . . Those twins also carry my genes . . . and they are certainly the future."

She could not move. She was lying at the bottom of the sea, unable to rise to the surface. There was a great weight on her chest, pinning her down.

Tessa struggled against the weight, endeavoring to push it away from her. Panic swamped her, and she experienced a sudden sense of death. Terror leapt through her, held her in its grip; then suddenly, unexpectedly, the weight seemed to shift, and she was floating upward. Spreading out her arms, pushing at the weight of the water, she *was* free at last . . . entering the light.

Tessa's eyes snapped open, and she blinked, glancing around. She was sitting up in bed, the bedclothes in a tangle around her. She had been having a nightmare, but one so vivid, so real, she had been truly terrified.

Pushing the bed linen away from her, she got out of bed, went into the adjoining bathroom and splashed cold water on her face, then looked at herself in the mirror. How white and strained her face was, and her eyes were filled with fear. Fear for Jean-Claude. He had vanished into thin air, and ever since Philippe had phoned her, she had been in a state of shock combined with overwhelming terror. She could only think the worst. Whatever her mother and father said, she knew that Afghanistan was a dangerous place, filled with hatred for men like Jean-Claude. There was little likelihood of him getting out alive. Tears came into her eyes, and she reached for a tissue. The thought of him being caught in their net, in mortal danger, was almost too much for her to bear. He might even be dead already.

This possibility made her reel, and she staggered back into the bedroom, lay down, and pressed her face into the pillow. She sobbed for a long time, anguish taking over as she wondered how she would ever find peace again if he was killed.

Part Four

SOLO

⁓

There shall no evil befall thee, neither shall any
plague come nigh thy dwelling.
For he shall give his angels charge over thee, to
keep thee in all thy ways.

—PSALM 91

30

To Linnet, Harte's was the most wonderful place in the world. She had been going to this great emporium in Knightsbridge almost from the day she was born. Actually, she had gone there even before she was born, because Paula had worked at the store right up to the day before her due date.

Linnet thought of it as an enchanted place, magical even, filled with thousands of items of extraordinary beauty, literally everything the heart could desire, at least when it came to material things. She knew and loved every part of the store, founded by her great-grandmother, especially the Fashion Floors, which she ran. And the magnificent Food Halls . . . Emma had been so proud of them, and Linnet felt the same way. Her mouth always watered when she passed through them, and there was nothing to compare with them in the entire world.

Harte's was for her an Aladdin's cave. It had been her childhood playground . . . and now it was her true domain.

On this Monday morning, there was no one in the store but her, except for the cleaners and security, and Linnet moved from floor to floor, taking everything in, making copious notes, and endeavoring to visualize the changes she hoped would come to fruition. Some areas received more of her attention than others, such as the Fashion Floors, the floor where the hairdressing salon was located, and the one where mattresses and beds were sold. Those definitely have to be relegated to the furniture department, she muttered under her breath, glancing at the offending mattresses before heading for the escalators.

Having arrived at the store at six o'clock, Linnet was now ready to go back to her office to review her notes and work out a strategy. She glanced at her watch as she went down on the escalator and was surprised to see it was already eight. How the time had flown. It occurred to her then that everything she had seen this morning was indelibly stamped on her brain. She was lucky she had a photographic memory and could recall things without too much effort. It often made her work easier.

Stepping off the elevator when she came to the management floor, she paused in front of the portrait of Emma Harte in its alcove in the corridor. She had been a beautiful woman, looked elegant in her pale blue dress and emeralds, but it was not the beauty that Linnet saw at this moment. Instead it was the power of Emma's face. The portrait seemed to exude that power and a special magnetism.

Stepping closer to the oil painting, Linnet whispered to it, "You've got to be with me on this, Emma. You've got to back me to the hilt." Glancing around to make sure there was no one listening, Linnet added softly, "*You promised me.*"

Leaning forward, she touched Emma's face in the painting. "I am with you all the way," she heard Emma say, as if from a distance, and she smiled at the face in the portrait and moved on.

Linnet told herself she was daft in the head the way she talked to her great-grandmother of late. The strange thing

was, Emma spoke back to her . . . at least Linnet believed
she did, was certain she heard Emma's voice. When she
had confessed this to Julian, her husband had not
laughed, had simply said, "I believe you, Linny, but don't
tell anybody else." And she hadn't; nor did she want to.
Emma was in her heart and soul, and in her head most of
the time. And she did not want to share her. How well Julian understood this, understood her, understood her
needs, her ambitions, her love of this store. But they had
been trained to be responsible, as the heirs to two great
businesses, and were always in tune.

Once Linnet was sitting behind her desk, she studied
her notes, jotted down additional thoughts, and then sat
back, contemplating her mother. Paula had agreed to see
her this morning, to discuss the memos she had taken to
Yorkshire over the weekend. But Linnet was nervous
about doing it today, having sensed over the weekend
that her mother was on edge, worried about Tessa, and
Jean-Claude's disappearance in Afghanistan. Then there
had been the trouble with Priscilla Marney, lover of
Jonathan Ainsley.

Leaning back in her chair, Linnet thought about *that* situation for a moment, a grim smile on her face. At least her
mother had had the good grace to admit to Linnet that she
had been right. She had forever insisted that there was
someone in their midst telling Jonathan about them, but
no one had believed her. "She spoke to him only about the
events she catered," Paula had pointed out. Linnet thought
her mother was being a trifle dismissive and had countered, "That's bad enough, isn't it, Mummy? *He* always
knew when we were all together in one place. He could
have dropped a bomb on us."

Her mother had protested this comment and had immediately gone on to tell her about the deaths of Molly
and Melinda Caldwell. The moment they had hung up on
Saturday afternoon, Linnet had phoned India to commis-

erate with her in general, and then she had spoken briefly to Tessa, who was so distraught it was impossible to make her feel any better.

Linnet knew that she must telephone her sister now, to ask if there was any news about Jean-Claude.

Pulling the phone closer, she dialed Pennistone Royal. It was Tessa who answered, her voice high-pitched with tension.

"It's Linnet. Have you had any news?"

"No, not a word," Tessa answered, sounding sorrowful. Linnet knew that Tessa was disappointed it wasn't Jean-Claude himself calling.

"I'm a nervous wreck. I really feel like going to Paris, being there with Philippe, but Lorne says that's a silly idea. Anyway, I'm trying to work here in the library on my laptop, and then I'm going to go to the Harrogate store this afternoon. Lorne keeps telling me I have to keep busy."

"Is he there with you?" Linnet asked.

"Yes, thank goodness. Mummy and Dad have gone to London this morning."

"How's Adele?"

Tessa's voice lifted slightly when she exclaimed, "*Wonderful.* I'm trying to spend lots of time with her. She cheers me up." There was a small pause, and Tessa dropped her voice to a whisper as she asked, "Did Mummy tell you?"

Linnet said, "About what?"

Tessa detected the puzzlement in her sister's voice and replied, "Obviously she didn't. I'm pregnant. . . . Jean-Claude and I are having a baby."

"Oh, my God! Tessa! That's great. Congratulations—" Linnet suddenly stopped. "No wonder you're so worried," she hurried on. "I mean, being pregnant makes everything even more worrisome, doesn't it? But he'll make it . . ." Her voice trailed off lamely.

"Yes," Tessa said, sounding suddenly very tired. "I've got to believe he will. That keeps me going."

"If you don't feel up to driving over to the Harrogate store today, maybe India can pop in."

"She has her hands full, wouldn't you say? What with the Leeds store and Dusty. And all his problems."

"I suppose so. On the other hand, their problems are not as troubling as yours. Let me know if I can do anything, and please phone me if you have any news. We're all anxious, Tessa."

"I will, I promise. The minute I hear."

A few seconds later Linnet was speaking to India, who was just about to leave Willows Hall for Harte's in Leeds. "I'm glad you're coping all right, India," Linnet went on. "But Tessa sounds terrible. Depressed and sad, and no wonder. I told her not to worry about the Harrogate store today, I mean going over there. Is there really any need?"

"No, and I did mention that yesterday, sure and I did, Linnet. Still, Lorne's there, and he's telling her she should keep busy. She's trying, God bless her. I'm praying for her, and for Jean-Claude. I can just imagine how she feels. Desperate. Because I'd feel the same way if Dusty were missing in a war zone."

"So would I, and how is Dusty?"

"Oh, you know him, he's like the Hartes, *tough*. And so he's coping. He's a real trouper when things go wrong. He's been really sad about Molly, though, grieving, and also troubled about the way Melinda died. But . . . well . . . he's handling things. Actually, he's planning their funerals at the moment."

"Oh, God, what an awful task he has, and by the way, India, what has he told Atlanta?"

"Nothing about her mother's death. Atlanta doesn't, I mean, didn't, know her mother well, in fact, hardly at all. It was Molly who brought her up." India sighed. "He told her that her grandmother had gone on a trip to see the angels and left it at that. Naturally she asked a lot of questions, but we've managed to appease her for the moment. And she's very fond of Gladys, who's here with us and who's turned out to be a jewel."

"I sometimes wonder about *us*, India. I mean about the family. We do seem to have more than our fair share of troubles."

"It's funny you should say that. I made the same remark to Dusty at breakfast."

"Paula says that it's because we're such a big family, and there are so many of us, with the clans, there're bound to be problems and a crisis a minute. That was the way she put it."

"I expect she's right. I've got to run, Linny, but I'll talk to you later."

Tessa's news about her pregnancy had stunned Linnet. She thought of her elder half sister as being very calculating, and clever about running her life. Especially these days. There had been the awful debacle with Mark Longden and the bitter divorce, but in the end it was Tessa who had ended up the winner, with her freedom, her child, and Mark Longden as far away as possible.

She also wanted to be the head of Harte's one day. Had she now discarded this ambition? If she asked Grandfather Bryan, Linnet knew he would laugh in her face. He had forever told her that Tessa Fairley would always be her rival. No matter what. And of course he was correct. Yet Tessa was now involved, deeply so, with a famous man who lived in another country, and she was carrying his child. Did she still want the top job? Did she mean to commute between Paris and London? Did she still think of herself as the Dauphine, her mother's rightful heir? Linnet could only wonder about that at the moment.

Opening one of the folders on her desk, she looked at the e-mails which had passed between her and Bonnadell Enloe. She had more or less worked out the deal with the

American businesswoman who had made such a big success out of her day spas, aptly called Tranquillity. There was no doubt in Linnet's mind that the day spa at Harte's would be successful.

Turning to a second folder, she went through the notes she had made when she interviewed Bobbi Snyder. Bobbi was a friend of Marietta's, from the days when Marietta had been single, an art student and living in London. Bobbi was also an American, who had stayed on in London after Marietta left. She had married an Englishman, had a daughter, and had run the Fashion Floor at Harvey Nichols for a number of years. When Marietta had learned from Evan that Linnet needed a high-powered executive to launch the bridal floor, she had recommended her old friend.

As yet Linnet had been unable to hire the admirable Bobbi, but she was hopeful that she could do so in the not-too-distant future.

The third folder on her desk was about her own Fashion Floors. As she opened it, Linnet grimaced, still feeling dismal about the low sales figures. This morning, as she had walked through Fashion, she had been even more convinced that they needed a whole new look.

The fourth folder was about opening a sumptuous shopping area for luxury goods, if her mother would agree. There was a big question mark in Linnet's mind about that. The other doubt she had, as did Evan, was her mother sanctioning a series of snack bars in the Food Halls. Closing that folder after a quick glance, Linnet suddenly wished she had never given it to Paula to look at this weekend. More than likely it would have brushed her the wrong way.

Closing her eyes, Linnet tried to envision the great emporium as she saw it, how it would look in three months' . . . in six months' time . . . a year from now. And what she saw in her mind's eye thrilled her. Somehow she had to make her mother see Harte's as she

saw the store. Not the way it was now but the way it
could be. A new look . . . modernity . . . fresh ideas . . .
flair as well as taste . . . delectable clothes from talented
young designers . . . as well as the great personal services
the store provided. Affordable real jewelry as a counter-
part to high-priced jewels . . . a floor that catered to
brides and only to brides, with services, a wedding plan-
ner, even a link to honeymoon travel . . . and the day spa
designed to pamper women of all ages.

Sitting up in the chair, Linnet exclaimed out loud, "A
shake-up. That's what Harte's needs. A shake-up and a
shove into the twenty-first century!"

I'll say *that* to my mother, Linnet now thought, antici-
pating the meeting. And I'll ask her to name me creative
director. She knew her mother would, since it had been
her father's suggestion some time ago. Her mother listened to him; she always had.

Picking up the phone, Linnet dialed Evan, who answered after a few rings.

"Are you all right?" Linnet asked. "You don't sound so
great."

"Hi, Linnet! I'm okay, I guess. I'm just so big . . . *huge*.
And I have a feeling Robin and Winston are going to pop
out any minute now."

"Oh, Evan, you've chosen the names!"

"I forgot to tell you, Gideon and I decided on them last
week. I like the sound of Robin Harte and Winston Harte
the Third, don't you?"

"I do indeed. But will your father?"

"Oh, you mean we should have used Dad's name for
one of the boys?" There was a pause, and Evan let out a
long sigh. "I can't worry about that, you know. Anyway,
Robin is actually Robin Owen, so that should pacify him.
But he hasn't been overly friendly with us, Linnet. I
haven't really told you, I guess, but he's been quite cold
to Robin, Winston, and Gideon, and I wouldn't call his
attitude warm toward me, either."

"No, you didn't say a thing, but how awful. What's wrong, do you think?" Linnet asked.

"The Hartes, that's what's wrong. I am one. I married one. I'm carrying little Hartes. I think he has quite a hatred for the family. Deep down, that is. He probably doesn't even know it. It's probably well and truly buried."

Startled, Linnet was silent for a moment.

Evan said, "Are you still there, Linny?"

"Yes. Listen, if he hates the Hartes the way you say, you don't think he would . . . betray us, go over to Angharad, do you?"

"No, of course not!" Evan exclaimed. "He doesn't have much time for her. And I know he loves me. He just has to get over this . . . jealousy he has. That's what I think it is. So does my mother. I came to London, got a job at Harte's, fell in love with a Harte, discovered I *was* a Harte. The way he sees it, according to my mother, is that he lost me to this powerful family. He forgets that he's a Harte, too."

"But he hasn't lost you, has he, Evan?"

"No. However, he is in the process of driving me away."

"Is he coming back for the christening?"

"Oh, yes, I'm sure he will. And listen, he's not really all that peculiar with me. Just a tiny bit remote. Let's move on. Are you seeing Paula today, to discuss all the new ideas?"

"Yes, I am. So keep your fingers crossed."

"Fingers crossed. And I know you'll be successful."

Brilliant sunlight, pouring into the library through the tall windows, slanted across the desk where Tessa was sitting and brought her up with a start. Blinking, she turned her head, looked out one of the stately windows, realizing that the first vestiges of spring were suddenly in evidence.

Standing up, she strolled over to the window fronting onto the moors and saw, much to her surprise, that the snow which had capped the moors over the weekend had melted. And in the gardens there was a hint of fresh green buds poking out of the ground.

She had the unexpected urge to get a breath of fresh air, to walk for while. She had been cooped up in the house for several days and had done nothing much but cry and worry, and pester Philippe in Paris. He had been so kind and thoughtful, always ready to talk to her, to soothe her shattered nerves. She had grown to like Jean-Claude's son more than ever.

They had taken to each other when they had been at Clos-Fleuri together, and now the relationship had been truly cemented in the sharing of their mutual worry. Although Philippe was not at all like his father in character or personality, he looked like him and had a similar voice. It was a comfort to speak with him, to meet such a generous reception, particularly since he sounded so much like Jean-Claude.

Jean-Claude, where are you? What has befallen you? Why don't we hear from you? These questions rumbled around in Tessa's mind, and her chest tightened at the thought that he might be already dead. There had been total silence since last Monday. A week ago exactly. No one had heard from him.

Picking up her cell phone from the desk, Tessa went to the kitchen. Pushing open the door, she said to Margaret, "I'm off for a walk, be back in ten minutes."

"Wrap yourself up well, Tessa my lass," Margaret said, her tone, as always, motherly and concerned. "I'm making ever such a nice lunch, and you're going to eat some of it, even if I have to force it down you."

Tessa actually laughed. "I'm not still four years old, you know, and you won't have to force me, I'll have something."

"Yes, you'd better, now that you're eating for two."

Tessa made no further comment, simply retreated,

took one of her mother's heavy topcoats from the hall cupboard, put it on, went out into the cobbled yard.

How on earth does she know I'm pregnant? Tessa asked herself, and then shook her head wonderingly. Margaret had always known everything that was going on in the family, and how she found out had always been a mystery. Tessa was not upset that the housekeeper was aware of her condition; in fact she didn't care who knew. At this moment all she cared about was Jean-Claude's safety.

She thought of the baby as she headed down toward the Rhododendron Walk. It had not been planned, and she had been startled when she had realized she was pregnant. But her surprise had turned to happiness; she was thrilled to be carrying Jean-Claude's child, and she knew that he would be, too, when she told him.

Now she regretted that she had not confided her happy news before he had gone off to Afghanistan. Of course he would have had to go, because he had a contract with the network; but he might not have undertaken what was probably a dangerous mission had he known he was going to become a father again.

Last night she had lain awake for hours, mostly worrying about bringing up a child by herself, if the worst happened and Jean-Claude never came back. Eventually she had fallen asleep, and on awakening this morning she had chastised herself. She was already bringing Adele up without a father and knew exactly how to do it. And she wasn't really alone; she was surrounded by a loving family, and a very large one at that.

No more negative thoughts, she admonished herself as she tramped on, her hand in her pocket, curled around the cell phone. I've got to be positive, get on with my work, attend to Adele. I must be cheerful for her, put up a good front, and I must take care of myself for the baby's sake.

Grandy did it all alone, and so can I, if that becomes necessary. After all, I'm a Harte, and the Harte women are tough. We're also competent and enterprising; we can handle anything.

With the baby coming, it was obvious now to Tessa that she would have to take time off from Harte's. For a short while? Or even permanently? And what would she do ultimately about her career? Could she commute from Paris to London? Perhaps it *was* viable. Maybe she could spend three days in London during the week and have long weekends in Paris. They had discussed all this several times, and Jean-Claude had made it clear it was her decision.

Could she be head of Harte's and a commuter? She wasn't sure. And did she really want that job after all? She had always dreamed of having it, but not every dream came true. And wasn't a happy marriage with a wonderful man and children the best dream of all?

31

~

Although she was extremely pale, Linnet thought her mother had never looked more beautiful than she did this morning. The pallor enhanced her black hair and violet eyes, made them appear all the more dramatic.

As usual, Paula was elegantly dressed, in a crisply tailored suit that was a strange but beautiful color—not quite purple, not mulberry, but a mixture of the two. With it she wore a pale pink camisole, a pink silk Chanel flower on one shoulder, and large pearl studs on her ears.

As Linnet walked to her mother's desk, Paula looked up and said, with a slight smile, "Good morning, Linnet."

"Morning, Mummy. You look gorgeous today, and so much better than last week. I thought you seemed quite worn out."

Paula nodded. "I felt it, too, but despite everything that happened this weekend, I did manage to get a little rest. Pennistone Royal has always been very restorative for me, as it was for Emma."

Sitting down, Linnet remarked, "I spoke to Tessa a short while ago. Still no news about Jean-Claude."

"I know." Paula sighed. "We must be positive, for her sake, help to keep her spirits up. My feeling is that he's alive. I hope I'm right."

Linnet wondered whether to mention Tessa's pregnancy, decided against it, and, getting down to business, she asked, "Did you get a chance to look at the memos?"

"I did, and you certainly put an enormous amount of work into them, not to mention detail. I had a lot of reading." Paula looked intently at her daughter. "A lot more detail than I required, by the way."

Linnet gazed back at Paula, thinking that her mother's face had become a little stern, even disapproving, although her voice was still mild. "I suppose you were a bit overwhelmed," she began. "I know I—"

"Not so much overwhelmed as annoyed," Paula interrupted in an unusually snippy tone. "From what I read, it seems to me you would like to revamp the *entire* store. Have you ever considered how much it would cost to do that?"

"Not the whole store, Mummy. I certainly don't want to do that! But I honestly do think Harte's needs a big shove into the twenty-first century."

Taken aback, Paula exclaimed with a hint of acerbity, "Do you really now?"

Knowing she had just said the wrong thing, Linnet leaned forward and in a conciliatory voice murmured, "Please don't be angry. I've done a great deal of research into retail marketing and merchandising, and I've also trekked around the rival stores this past week. Harvey Nichols, Harrods, and Selfridges were on my agenda. What I saw tells me that our competitors are thinking on similar lines. They're revamping, opting for a new image, a more modern look, focusing on a younger generation of women shoppers. They're also going for a whole new brigade of talented young designers, as well as established names like Chanel, Valentino, Armani, and so on. They're looking ahead, Mother."

"We're so much above those stores," Paula said in the same snippy tone. "To begin with, Harte's has become an institution over the years. We also happen to be a tourist attraction and pull a lot of foreign visitors into the store. Those things aside, we give the very best personal services in London, in fact the best of any store anywhere in the world. We can't be compared . . . we are absolutely *unique*."

"Everything you say is true, Mummy, I don't deny that. And yes, we *are* an institution, but we're starting to look just a tiny bit *staid*. We can continue to be an institution, appealing to our core, and very devoted, customer, while being more up-to-date. And yes, we *are* a tourist attraction, but that doesn't mean we sell merchandise to them. Most of the tourists just come to *look*." Linnet paused, sat staring at her mother before finishing. "And I agree with you that we give the best personal service there is. But what we need for this new world we're living in is a bit of pizzazz as well. Something a bit extra to back up everything we already are."

Paula was carefully studying her daughter, her expression reflective. After a long moment, she answered in a cold, rather remote voice. "You must pull back here, Linnet, be less extreme. I will not permit you to jump into all this revamping . . . because, very simply, I don't agree with you, and I certainly *do not* approve of it."

Linnet felt her heart plunge to her shoes, and she experienced an intense rush of disappointment.

"You mean you don't approve of anything I've suggested?" she asked, thinking of all the time and effort she had put in. But mostly she was distressed because she was certain she was right; if they did not bring a few more up-to-date ideas into the store, a year from now profits could start dwindling.

"Don't sound so down in the dumps, Linny," Paula suddenly said in a kinder tone. "I don't think I expressed myself very well a moment ago." Smiling more warmly, she went on. "What I'm trying to say is that I don't approve of this huge *overhaul* you've indicated we need. Because, very truthfully, I don't think it's necessary. However, I'm going to give you the go-ahead on several of your ideas."

Linnet sat up straighter, holding her breath and filling with immense relief.

Paula was shuffling through the memos. Looking up, she announced, "The floor devoted to brides is a great idea, and I think it will work well. God knows where you'll put Mattresses, but then, that's your problem. Anyway, to continue, you can plan the Tranquillity Day Spa as well. By the way, did you make a deal with Bonnadell yet? A tentative deal?"

Linnet nodded, regaining some of her enthusiasm, and replied, "I did make a lot of progress with her, and, most important, she's agreed we can do the remodeling of the hair salon ourselves. That'll save us money, because we'll be using Charlie Fromett's department, his carpenters and other workers, rather than her architects and designers. I said *if* you approved the spa, she could sell her products in the beauty department as well as the spa itself. That works for her and the store, gives us more profit."

"I assume her people would run the spa for us?" Paula said.

"I talked to Dad, and he thought we'd be better off using her people, who naturally are properly trained therapists and know the benefits of all the products. That's the way the spas are run in the O'Neill hotels."

Paula nodded. "He told me he'd spoken to you, and he seems to think it's a good idea for us to open a day spa."

So that's why she agreed, Linnet thought but said, "Thanks, Mummy, for letting me go ahead with the spa. I know it will pull young women into the store, and hopefully into the fashion areas afterward."

"Who's going to run the brides' floor, Linnet?" Paula now asked. "Evan's on maternity leave for some months, and you have enough to do."

"I've found the right executive to run Brides." Swiftly, Linnet told her mother about Marietta's friend Bobbi Snyder, then thought to add, "And there's another thing. We don't need to spend a lot of money to revamp the mattress department. Obviously, the walls need repainting, and we must put down new carpeting throughout, but it's a face-lift, all cosmetic."

"Yes, I realize that," Paula replied, rising and walking across the office. She stood looking down on Knightsbridge for a moment, then, turning to face her daughter, she continued. "Finally, Linnet, I want you to understand one thing. I will never, and I do mean never, endorse this idea of putting snack bars in the Food Halls. The mere idea makes me shudder; in fact, it is very offensive to me. Those Food Halls are now a legend, renowned worldwide, and I won't have them tampered with."

"But, Mummy, honestly, the snack bars could easily be fitted into a corner here and there, we could find the space."

"Please don't argue with me, Linnet. I will not have those idiotic snack bars in the Food Halls. Harte's has plenty of restaurants, the Bird Cage, Far Pavilions, London Bridge, and the coffee bar. We don't need any more. *Understood?*"

"But—"

"I said *no!*"

Her mother sounded so angry Linnet shrank back in the chair.

As Paula started to walk back to her desk, something happened to her. And she was very conscious of it happening. Her office seemed suddenly to fill with white light. It became supernaturally bright.

Continuing across the room, she felt her steps begin to falter, and she staggered toward a chair, experiencing the overwhelming need to sit down.

"Mummy, what's wrong with you?" Linnet shouted. Jumping up, she ran to her mother, helped her to sit down.

Paula could not speak for a moment. She felt sick, nauseated, and was hit by the most blinding headache. Her hands went to her head. Her neck hurt.

"Mummy, what's wrong?" Linnet cried.

"Don't know. Call nine-nine-nine. There's a terrible pain in my head. Oh, God. The pain!"

Linnet flew to the phone on her mother's desk. It was programmed to individuals, and she punched in the number two.

Jack said, "Yes, Paula—"

"It's not Mummy, it's me!" Linnet cried. "My mother's ill. Get an ambulance. It's her head. I think she might be having a stroke."

"I'm on it." Jack slammed the phone down.

Linnet punched in the number one, the direct link to Shane's office. Her father picked up after three rings. "Hello, Paula—"

"It's Linnet." Her voice wobbled as she continued. "I think Mummy's having a stroke or something, Daddy. Jack's calling an ambulance. She's complaining of pains in her head."

"I'll be there in five minutes!" Shane hung up.

Running to the door, Linnet wrenched it open, startling Jonelle, who glanced up, frowning.

"Go to my office, please. Get my coat and bag. And hurry. My mother's ill. There's an ambulance coming. I think she's having a stroke or something."

Stunned, Jonelle stared at her briefly and then ran out of the executive suite, heading toward Linnet's office.

The four of them sat in the hospital waiting room: Shane, Linnet, Emily, and Jack. Each of them looked worried as they waited for news of Paula's condition. They had been there for two hours, and after talking for part of that time, they had fallen silent, all lost in their own thoughts.

But Shane suddenly sat up in the chair where he was slumped and exclaimed, "Jack, how terribly rude I am. I forgot to thank you for suggesting to the ambulance men that they bring Paula here to King's College Hospital."

"They would have anyway," Jack replied. "In my experience, those ambulance men and paramedics know what they're doing. They were immediately telling me this was where they planned to bring her, explaining that King's is the best neurological center in London. But I think it's more than likely one of the best in England, if not *the* best. They have very advanced practices here, a great reputation."

"I'll be glad when we know what happened to Mummy this morning," Linnet murmured, her voice troubled, her expression anxious. "I feel so awful, Daddy. I'd just had an argument with her about the store, and then she fell apart, had the attack or stroke, or whatever it was. It's my fault," she whispered, sounding tearful.

"Don't be silly, darling," Shane reassured her gently, taking hold of Linnet's hand in an attempt to comfort her. His face was anguished, his dark eyes flooded with anxiety. "An argument isn't going to bring on something like this. It's a medical problem."

Emily, staring across at Shane, asked quietly, "Do you think it *was* a stroke?"

"I don't know, Emily, I don't even want to hazard a guess. I'm just praying that, whatever it is, Paula comes out of it all right."

"In my opinion, Paula's probably had a brain hemorrhage," Jack ventured.

"What leads you to that conclusion?" Shane looked at the security chief intently, his expression puzzled.

"The symptoms. Linnet told me her mother had complained of a blinding headache, of feeling nauseated. That she had terrible pains in her head. I'm not sure those are the symptoms of a stroke. Also, I noticed when they were lifting the stretcher into the ambulance that Paula's face had dropped down at one side. That's supposedly a symptom of brain damage. But I'm just making a guess that it's a hemorrhage."

At that moment the door opened and the surgeon they had seen earlier stepped into the room. "Mr. O'Neill," he said, "I have some news for you."

Shane leapt to his feet. "Please, Mr. Gilleon, come inside. Tell me what happened to my wife this morning."

"Mrs. O'Neill has suffered a subarachnoid hemorrhage," he answered in a calm voice.

"What exactly does that mean, subarachnoid?" Shane asked.

"This is a specific form of hemorrhage, caused by a weakness in the wall of the vessel which supplies blood to the brain," Gilleon explained.

"What caused it?" Shane asked.

"We don't know why it happens, we never do really. This weakness in the blood vessel wall is called an aneurysm, which is a word you might be more familiar with."

"Yes, I am," Shane answered, nodding. "I have a better understanding now."

"Anyway, the best answer I can give about this type of hemorrhage is that it happens when the pressure of the blood tears an aneurysm wall."

"And the blood goes into the brain, is that what happens?"

"Yes indeed, Mr. O'Neill. It goes into the tissues surrounding the brain. This is called the subarachnoid layer, hence the name of the hemorrhage." The surgeon put his hand on Shane's arm sympathetically. "It's such a small amount of blood, you know, just ten cc's, which in layman's terms is about a thimbleful."

"My God, so little." Shane stared at him in astonishment.

"Unfortunately, it can be disastrous."

"Is my wife going to be all right?" Shane asked now, his tone concerned.

"Mrs. O'Neill is very ill. We plan to operate tomorrow morning very early."

"Why not today?"

"We're still giving her tests, Mr. O'Neill."

"Can I see her?"

"I'm afraid not. She's undergoing tests, as I just said. We'll be in touch."

Shane nodded. "Thank you for explaining everything, and for looking after my wife, Mr. Gilleon."

The surgeon took Shane's outstretched hand, shook it, nodded to the others, and left the room as briskly as he had entered.

"So you were more or less right, Jack," Shane said, striding over to join the others. "I hope to God Paula is going to get through this—" He stopped, turned his head abruptly, then walked over to the window. His eyes had filled with tears, and he didn't want the others to see him this upset.

But Linnet was aware that her father had broken down, and she went over to him, took hold of his arm. "It's all right, Daddy," she murmured gently. "Mummy's going to be fine, I just know it. She's going to make it." Sliding her arm through his, she drew even closer and whispered, "You know what she always says, the Hartes are made of the strongest steel."

"Let's hope so," Shane muttered, brushing his eyes with his hand, then putting his arms around his daughter, holding her as if he would never let her go. Paula was his life, and he knew Linnet knew that. She had always been aware of how much her parents loved each other, and had for all of their lives.

And as he held his firstborn daughter to him, he offered up a silent prayer: Oh, God, let her live. Let my Paula live.

32

On Monday night Linnet spent part of the evening weeping in Julian's arms. Even though her husband tried to convince her that she had not been responsible for her mother's collapse, she kept blaming herself.

It was only when she had exhausted herself with crying and was quiet and still on the sofa that he finally spoke to her a little sternly. "Nobody causes anyone to have a brain hemorrhage, Linnet!" he exclaimed, giving her a long, penetrating look. "It's just as your father told you, a medical problem. And think about this, Paula hasn't looked well ever since we got back from our honeymoon in January."

"That's true," Linnet responded, sitting up straighter, her eyes pinned on his. "She kept saying she was merely tired, or had done too much, and there had been two weddings to cope with, ours and Evan's. But perhaps something else was happening . . . to her health."

"More than likely it was. And you must stop punishing yourself like this. It wasn't your fault. Remember that."

Linnet just inclined her head and, reaching out, took hold of Julian's hand. "I've come to realize, especially in the last couple of years, that Mummy's a real *worrier*. And she's done a lot of worrying lately . . . about that awful Jonathan Ainsley, and about Robin's health. I know she went to see him on Saturday, because Dad told me today that something was troubling Uncle Robin. And she apparently worried all weekend about Tessa, and Jean-Claude being missing. At least that's what Daddy was explaining after we left the hospital this afternoon."

"I don't think worrying about problems caused the brain hemorrhage either, darling. It's always a medical situation, as I just said." Julian shook his head, let out a small sigh. "I do feel sorry for Tessa. It must be hell, living on her nerves, waiting for news about Jean-Claude."

"She's pregnant," Linnet blurted out. "She told me this morning, when I spoke to her on the phone. Before Mummy collapsed."

Julian looked at Linnet, his mind racing, his deep blue eyes now focused on her intently. "Well, that changes the picture all around, doesn't it?"

"Yes, it does. She sounds happy about the baby, but I suppose she's worried that she might be bringing the child up without a father—"

"But she's already doing that," Julian cut in. "And Adele seems no worse for it. She's probably better without that loudmouthed Mark Longden around. Thank God your mother packed him off to Sydney."

"He wouldn't have gone quite so readily if Mummy hadn't given him that huge settlement."

"Money talks," Julian said, smiling at her. "But as you always say, there are many other currencies."

For the first time in hours Linnet smiled. She leaned into Julian and kissed him lightly on the mouth. "I can't imagine being married to anyone else but you, Jules."

"Don't even let that thought cross your mind," he shot back in a stern way, but she knew he was teasing her.

Linnet said, "Emily and Dad were going to phone the family, explain what happened to Mummy. Oh, God, I do hope she'll pull through." Her eyes filled, and she brought a hand to her trembling mouth.

Julian pulled her into his arms and held her close to

him, stroking that red hair he loved so much. "Stop it, darling. You must stay calm. Please don't think about her not recovering. Send out positive thoughts, good vibes. Promise me."

"I will, I promise," she murmured against his chest.

They sat like that for a while, wrapped in each other's arms on the sofa in front of the fire. They had not yet bothered to look for a larger place and were living in Julian's bachelor flat on Chester Street. It was perfectly adequate for them at the moment; they both liked the area, and the proximity to her mother's house in Belgrave Square pleased Linnet.

Julian Kallinski's thoughts were very much centered on his mother-in-law at this moment. He was putting up a good front to support Linnet, reinforce her natural courage, but deep down he was worried about Paula. By an odd coincidence his mother's sister, Ashley Preston, had died of a subarachnoid brain hemorrhage several years ago; now he remembered his mother telling him at the time that few people survived a brain injury of that nature. Almost everyone died within several days, if not sooner. He prayed to God that Paula would be one of the lucky ones. He didn't know how Shane would go on without her, or how any of the family would manage. Paula McGill Harte Amory Fairley O'Neill. My God, he thought, what a name. She had been christened Paula McGill for her grandfather Paul McGill, Harte for Emma, Amory because that was her father David's surname; Fairley came from her first marriage, to James Fairley; and O'Neill because she had married Shane, the love of her life.

He suspected that Paula was the love of his father's life. Michael Kallinski had never married after divorcing Valentine, his mother, and over the years Julian had slowly come to realize, mostly through observation, that his father was utterly devoted to Linnet's mother. Oh, Michael, Michael, he thought suddenly, you should have cured yourself years ago. Moved on, Dad. Loving Paula was a lost cause. Linnet was convinced that Jack Figg was in love with Paula also, and knowing how astute his wife was, Julian believed she was right.

But neither man had been anything but a good friend in Paula's mind, of that he was certain. She had only ever had eyes for Shane. Just as he had only ever had eyes for this bundle of contradictions in his arms. How he loved his Linnet, and all the more because of what she was, who she was. A total, dyed-in-the-wool Harte. Loyal, stubborn, loving, enterprising, strong, intelligent, and brave. It would be her bravery that would bring her through this ordeal. He had loved her since they were children growing up together, and he had never doubted her courage and her determination to overcome all odds.

He felt her stirring, and, moving away slightly, he said, "I bet you haven't eaten all day, have you?"

Sitting up, Linnet shook her head. "No, and I'm not really hungry. I don't think I could eat anything."

"I have to, I'm starving." As he spoke, Julian got up and headed for the kitchen. "Mrs. Ludlow left supper ready for us, Linny."

"What is it?" Linnet struggled to her feet and went after him, suddenly realizing she felt slightly nauseated because she, too, was hungry.

"Look," Julian murmured, lifting the lid of a pan on the stove. "Beef stew. And I know there's smoked salmon in the refrigerator, as well as salad, various cheeses, and fruit. Surely you can take a few mouthfuls of something?"

"I think I'd better, I do feel rather empty." Turning the gas ring on underneath the stew, Linnet continued, "I hope Dad's all right. He went back to his office. I should have invited him over to have supper with us."

"Knowing Emily, she took charge of him. Want to bet he's having dinner with her and Winston right at this moment?"

"I won't take the bet, because I know you're right. Of

course he's with them, they're his best friends . . . all of his life."

On Wednesday, two days after her collapse, Shane O'Neill knew at last that Paula's life had been saved by the team of doctors at King's College Hospital in South East London. Not only had her life been saved but the surgeons had informed him that there was every chance it would be a productive life. The operation on her brain had been an outstanding success, they believed.

Once he had hung up the phone in his office, Shane wept with relief. The strain of the last few days had taken its toll, and as strong and courageous as Shane was, the thought of losing Paula had crippled him. Somehow he had managed to keep a calm facade for everyone's sake, but he had been afraid and even panic-stricken at times.

With this good news in his possession, he began to call the family. He phoned his father first, because he was well aware that Bryan O'Neill was fretting over Paula, and that kind of pressure was too much for a man in his eighties to take. Then he phoned his children, who were as joyous as he was, and who promised to inform other members of the family while he called Emily and Winston.

On Saturday morning Shane was finally allowed to see Paula, and when he walked into her hospital room he was initially startled. There was no bandage on her head, even though he knew she had had a brain operation. He mentioned this to Mr. Gilleon as he was led by him into the room, and the surgeon said quietly, "New techniques, you know."

Paula was filled with relief at the sight of Shane, and after a brief word with her, Mr. Gilleon left them alone. "For just a short while," he added as he closed the door behind him.

After kissing her cheek, Shane pulled a chair up to the bed and sat down, took hold of Paula's hand. "Oh, darling, what a relief it is that you're all right. We've been worried sick."

"I can imagine . . ." A wry smile touched Paula's mouth, and she said, "I didn't remember anything, Shane. Yesterday, the surgeon explained what had happened to me, that I had had a brain injury."

Shane nodded. "Mr. Gilleon told me you've been very lucky."

"Yes, I know I have. But what happened? I remember talking to Linnet in my office on Monday morning . . . The rest is a blank."

"Linnet said you were standing at the window, looking out. Then you walked back to your desk but seemed to be faltering, staggering, and she rushed to you, got you into a chair. You asked her to call nine-nine-nine, and you told her your head hurt. The ambulance came to the store, and you were rushed here. The surgeons operated on Tuesday."

"It's funny, I don't recall any of it. The doctors told me I had classic symptoms when I came in, the right side of my face was askew, and I was terribly sensitive to light."

"And how do you feel today, Paula?" Shane searched her face, finding her remarkably unchanged in appearance.

"Tired. A little weak. Very dazed." She offered him a faint smile and settled back against the pillows. "In the family we've always said the Hartes are made of steel. Well, at least one of us now has *platinum* inside as well. *Me.*"

Shane couldn't help laughing, and he touched her cheek gently. He was full of happiness that this woman, whom he loved and who had been part of his life since his childhood, was now out of danger. "I know all about the platinum," he said. "Mr. Gilleon has told me a few things about the operation, and he explained that they use platinum coils to seal off the bleed."

"Yes, I know *that,* but I'm afraid I haven't taken in everything. I guess I'm still a bit out of it."

"Not surprising when you think about it, angel. Well,

here goes, see if you can understand what they told me. I'll try to make it simple. The surgeons find the aneurysm through the use of X-ray and radiographic techniques, by passing dye up a catheter in order to locate it precisely. Once they've found the aneurysm, they thread fine platinum wires along the catheter tube. As I understand it, Paula, the hole in the blood vessel is actually sealed by the platinum wires, which form coils. They're in place permanently in your brain and prevent any further bleeding."

"Isn't it amazing what they can do today? And thank God they can, or I wouldn't be here," Paula murmured.

"Modern miracles," Shane replied, and then, clearing his throat, he went on carefully. "Listen to me, Paula, you're doing very well, very well indeed. But many people don't, so I'm told. Some patients who survive a brain hemorrhage develop memory loss, blurred vision, or speech problems. So far so good, my darling, but you are going to have to take it easy."

"Yes, I know. But when can I come home, Shane? Have the doctors told you?"

"You do have to stay here a bit longer, darling. Just until you get your strength back. You've had a major operation, don't forget. The doctor told me it will be at the end of next week, *providing* you do as well as you have so far."

"Oh, Shane, that's such a long time . . ." Her voice trailed off. She was disappointed she wasn't leaving with him today.

"No, not long at all under the circumstances," he responded. "A week is not so very long to wait in my opinion, considering you might not have been coming home at all. I might have had to spend the rest of my life without you."

Paula squeezed his hand and murmured lovingly, "I know what you mean, darling. I can have visitors, can't I? I want to see the children. Oh, Shane, I forgot, what about Jean-Claude?"

He shook his head sadly. "No news, none at all actually. As far as seeing the children is concerned, I'm sure you can, but they mustn't tire you."

The smile on her face was beatific as he bent down to kiss her.

After examining her, Dr. Charles Addney covered Evan with the sheet and patted her shoulder. "You're fine, Mrs. Harte, just fine. But I think it's better for you to stay in hospital, now that you're already here. After all, it's the end of February."

Evan nodded. "I agree with you, Doctor. It's funny, the pains were so intense this morning at home, but they stopped the minute we reached Queen Charlotte's."

The doctor smiled. "That's not unusual, actually. But you made a wise decision to come in, since you're due any day now. Anyway, you'll be much more comfortable here." The doctor glanced across at Gideon and added, "Safer, too. I'm so glad you brought her in, Mr. Harte."

"It was Evan's decision, Doctor, and she knows best."

"That's true. I'm satisfied that everything's perfectly all right. Well, I'll be off on the rest of my rounds." He smiled down at Evan. "I'll pop in and see you again in a couple of hours. But if you need anything, the bell is there. Just ring for the nurse."

"Do you think I should stay?" Gideon asked, looking at the doctor, then peering at his watch. It was seven o'clock.

"That's up to you, of course, Mr. Harte. But I don't think it's necessary, if you want to get off to work. We'll be in touch with you if Mrs. Harte should go into labor."

Gideon nodded his understanding, bent down, and kissed Evan on the cheek. "I can be back here in twenty minutes, darling," he murmured, smiling at her.

"I know that, Gideon. So, go on, off with you." She grinned at him. "Honestly, I'm feeling great now."

After kissing her cheek once more, Gideon followed the doctor out of the room, and Evan slid down in the bed, closed her eyes, and before she knew it she was dozing. She needed the rest after her sleepless night, and she went into a deep slumber; several times the nurse looked in on her, but Evan was unaware of this.

She awakened suddenly as the most excruciating pains shot through her; gasping, half sitting up in bed, she fumbled for the bell, pushed it hard, and waited, her arms over her stomach.

Only a second or two passed before the nurse on duty came in, and when she saw Evan doubled over, she was next to the bed in an instant.

"I think the babies are coming," Evan gasped, and then she groaned as a rush of pain crippled her. She closed her eyes tightly and clenched her hands as the pain swept over her in waves.

Within minutes the two duty nurses were lifting Evan onto a gurney and pushing her down the corridor to the delivery room. But she was hardly aware of this; the pains were so intense she could barely breathe, and she was finding it hard not to scream; somehow she hung on.

Evan was in labor for two hours, and toward the end of the second hour, Dr. Addney made the decision to administer an anesthetic. The birth went without a hitch, and the two baby boys came out one after the other, screaming at the top of their lungs. As their mother dozed, they were whisked off by the nurses to be bathed and wrapped in warm blankets.

"They're the most beautiful boys, Evan, my darling," Gideon said, peering at the two babies tucked side by side next to his wife in the hospital bed. He moved the blankets slightly, and asked softly, "But which is which? They're identical, aren't they?"

Evan laughed. "Yes, they are, and it is going to be a bit of a problem, knowing which one is which. I think I'm going to have to put little bows on them, in different colors, of course."

"That's a good idea." He grinned at her. "No mistaking they're Hartes, is there?"

"Not at all, darling."

Moving the chair closer to the bed, Gideon sat down and took hold of her hand. "Dr. Addney told me you've had a bit of a rough time."

"No, it was easy," she murmured.

He shook his head. "Don't fib to me."

"I'm not."

There was a small silence, and then he said, "Thank you, Evan. Thank you for these two precious little bundles."

"Miss Paula! Whatever are you doing at that there desk? You're not supposed to be working, you're supposed to be in bed!"

"I'm not working, Margaret, I'm just sitting here." Paula grimaced, shaking her head. "I got up to make a few notes, and I can't. My brain seems unable to work the way it did. I sincerely hope that's not a permanent thing."

"Oh, it won't be, it won't be," Margaret clucked, her mother hen manner in place. Wanting to reassure Paula, she continued, "You're bound to be tired, all you've been through. I've brought you up a nice cup of tea. Where do you want it? Here or in bed?"

"I think I'd better go back to bed," Paula replied. The effort of going from the bed to the desk had exhausted her, and she, who had thought her recovery would be fast, had discovered it was quite slow. She had been out of the hospital almost two weeks now, yet even doing small, normal things seemed too much at times. Simple tasks taxed her or left her reeling.

Taking her arm, the housekeeper helped Paula across the upstairs parlor and into the adjoining bedroom. Once she was in bed, Margaret plumped the pillows, straightened the coverlet, and then hurried across the room to retrieve the tray with the cup of tea on it.

A moment later, placing the cup and saucer on the bedside table, Margaret asked, "Is there any news of Tessa's fiancé?"

"No, nothing, and it's been over four weeks now. She's distraught."

"Oh, I'm sorry. It's awful, it is that. Is she coming for the weekend?"

"Yes, Margaret, she is, and bringing Adele and Elvira. Linnet's also coming with Julian, and there's a possibility Mrs. Hughes will come, too."

"A houseful, eh?" Margaret smiled happily. "But I knows you like it that way, Miss Paula, and so do I. It's a bit lonely, this here big house is, when there's nobody else running around in it but us oldies."

"Speak for yourself!" Paula exclaimed, and, reaching for the cup, she took a sip of the tea.

"Will Tessa be doing any cooking? Or isn't she going to be up to it?" Margaret asked.

"I don't know, I didn't think to ask her."

"Shall I give Priscilla a tinkle? Or is *she* still in your bad books?"

"You know very well she's never been in my bad books! It's just that . . . Well, very frankly, Margaret, most of the family are put out with her; they think she told that nasty cousin of mine too much."

"I know very well what they think, but *I* don't *think* she's a bad woman, you knows."

"Let's find out who's coming altogether when Mr. Shane gets home tonight, then we'll make a decision. Is that all right?"

"Oh, yes, it is indeed. Well, I'll trot off to the kitchen. I'm making you a nice piece of plaice for lunch, and a baked apple. You've loved baked apples since you were a child."

"Thank you, Margaret," Paula murmured and sank back into the pillows. She was exhausted again, but then Margaret could be trying at times.

Half an hour later the phone jangling on the bedside table brought Paula out of a doze. "Hello?" she said as she picked up the receiver.

"It's Emily, Paula dear. How are you?"

"Back in bed. I felt very tired."

"Oh, I'm sorry. Have you been doing too much?"

"No. I guess this kind of sudden tiredness goes with the territory."

"I thought of popping over for lunch. I came up to Yorkshire last night. But perhaps you're not up to it?"

"Course I am, and I'd love that, Dumpling."

"You cannot possibly call a woman in her fifties Dumpling. You *must* please *stop.*"

Paula laughed. "See you soon."

"Sooner than you think."

A few minutes later Emily was gliding across the upstairs parlor and into the bedroom. Paula was taken aback. "How did you get here so quickly?"

"I called you on my cell from the terrace."

"Emily! You should have said you were here!"

"I didn't want you to feel obliged to invite me to lunch if you were exhausted."

"I'm fine—" Paula stopped as Emily's mobile, still in her hand, began to ring.

"Emily Harte here. Oh, hello, Great-Aunt Edwina! How're you?"

Walking over to a chair, Emily sat down, listened attentively, and then said, "Oh dear, I am sorry, so very sorry. How sad. Yes, yes, I'll tell her, and I'll get back to you in a few moments." Emily clicked off, looked across at Paula, and said in a saddened voice, "That was Great-Aunt Edwina, as you heard." There was a moment's pause, and then she went on softly, "Uncle Robin has just been found dead."

Paula sat bolt upright, her face turning extremely white. *"Where?"*

"At Lackland Priory. By Bolton, just a few minutes ago. Apparently he'd been out for a walk, Uncle Robin I mean, and when he came back he asked Bolton for a cup of coffee. Bolton took it to him in the library ten minutes later, and he found Uncle Robin sitting in his wing chair near the fire, stone-cold dead. Obviously Bolton is dreadfully upset, not only because Robin's dead but because of the way he found him. It was so unexpected."

"How terrible for Bolton. However, sad as I am, what a wonderful way to die. Robin never suffered an illness . . ." Paula's voice faltered and tears came into her eyes. She brushed them away, confided, "I grew to like Robin so much in these last years."

"So did I. Paula, isn't it a pity the twins haven't been born yet? He never got to see his great-grandsons, or hold them in his arms. He so wanted that."

"At least he met Evan, got to know his only grand-child, was aware that she was happy with Gideon. And he also knew he was going to have great-grandsons to carry on his line," Paula pointed out, resting her head against the pillows.

"That's true," Emily answered, and a deep sigh escaped her. "My mother is going to be grief-stricken. He was her twin."

"Poor Aunt Elizabeth, she *will* take it hard, and so will Edwina."

A small silence fell between them as they sat thinking their own thoughts about Robin's sisters.

It was Emily who suddenly exclaimed, "Paula, I've just had the most terrible thought! Does this mean that Jonathan Ainsley will be coming to Yorkshire? Will he be coming to Uncle Robin's funeral?"

"I don't know the answer to that, darling. Presumably he *will*. Robin *is* his father."

Emily said, "I'd better phone Great-Aunt Edwina back. She wants to know what to do about the funeral. When Bolton phoned her, he said he hadn't wanted to bother you with it."

"I'm just not up to dealing with this death, the funeral, Emily. I'm so sorry, but I'm not."

"I know that. I'll take over for you. Or help Edwina, whichever she wants. Shall I tell her it's her decision?"

"That's fine, but let's not forget she's ninety-five."

Emily's cell phone jangled again, and clicking it on she said, "Hello?"

"Mother, it's me."

"Hello, Gideon. Listen, I have some news—"

"Let me give you mine first," he cut in excitedly. "Evan went into labor earlier this morning. I didn't phone you because at first she thought it might be a false alarm. She's not due for a few days. Anyway, you're a grandmother! You've got two bouncing baby grandsons. And there's no mistaking they're Hartes. They both have bright auburn fluff on top of their heads."

"Oh, Gideon! *Congratulations.* How wonderful, and Evan is all right, I'm presuming?"

"She's great, Mother, but very tired."

"I'm sorry I'm here in Yorkshire, Gid. I'd come up to town, but I've a problem here."

"Don't worry, Ma. Marietta is already at the hospital, and Dad's on his way there. Listen, I've got to go—"

"Gideon, wait a minute. I started to tell you I had some news, and a problem. It's rather upsetting, I'm afraid. I'm here with Paula, and we just heard that Uncle Robin died this morning. Peacefully, at home, sitting in his chair by the fire."

"I'm so sorry, Mother. And how sad he never got to see the twins. He couldn't wait to hold them, he told me last week."

"Are you going to tell Evan?" Emily asked, suddenly sounding concerned. "I mean about Robin's death?"

"I won't, not today. I think it'll upset her too much. What do you think?"

"Keep it to yourself for twenty-four hours, Gideon. At least don't mention it to Evan today. But you'd better let your father know. Because of Robin's obituary for the papers."

33

Since I am the eldest person in this family, I think it's only appropriate that I take charge of Robin's funeral," Great-Aunt Edwina said, looking from Paula to Emily. "However, I shall certainly need your help, Emily, since I'm not as swift as I was."

"You have it," Emily responded, leaning forward, picking up the silver teapot, pouring herself another cup of tea. She couldn't help thinking that Edwina was swifter than most people she knew. "My main concern has been Jonathan Ainsley. What do we do about *him*?"

"I have all the information we need, Emily. His telephone numbers around the world, the name of his solicitors." Reaching for her handbag, Edwina opened it, took out an envelope, and handed it to Emily, who was seated next to her. She explained, "Robin gave me this several weeks ago. I have a feeling my brother knew he was going to die soon."

"It's funny you should say that, Great-Aunt Edwina. I think he did, too," Paula murmured, staring at Edwina across the coffee table. She was stretched out on the other sofa, covered with a light quilt and propped up against many pillows. "In fact, only a few weeks ago, just before I had my brain surgery, I went over to see him. We discussed various matters regarding his will."

"Oh, yes, he told me all about it," Edwina murmured, giving her a knowing look. "Now, Emily, getting back to Jonathan, I think we should just go ahead and plan the funeral without consulting him. He's never here, and he's never been here for Robin. Not only that, they were at loggerheads lately. So, where shall we have it? Here at Pennistone village church or at Fairley Church?"

"Gosh, I hadn't even thought of Fairley!" Emily exclaimed, throwing Paula a quick look.

"Grandy's buried there," Paula reminded her in answer to her questioning look. "And her brothers and her parents. As well as a lot of Fairleys."

"Oh, that doesn't matter, about the Fairleys, I mean. Robin wasn't one. Only I," Edwina pointed out, as if they didn't know. That was all she had ever talked about at one point in her life, as Paula and Emily were well aware. It had driven Emma crazy, this preoccupation with her lineage.

Paula closed her eyes, realizing that she was having trouble processing all this. Her brain was simply overloaded.

Emily announced, "If convenience is a consideration, I think Uncle Robin should be buried here, in the graveyard next to Pennistone Royal church. Do we really want to trek across the moors in February?"

"Very well put, Emily!" Edwina took a sip of tea, sat back, and straightened the skirt of her dark purple wool dress. "What time of day should the funeral be, do you think? I prefer the morning, so we can have a small gathering afterward, buffet lunch, nothing fancy, just for the family." Raising a brow, she stared at Emily intently.

"If we arrange the funeral for ten o'clock, and it's over in an hour," Emily asserted, pushing a strand of blond hair away from her face, "we could have lunch at twelve-thirty or thereabouts. Do you agree?"

"That sounds about right," Edwina replied and put a finger to her lips as she glanced at Paula.

Emily followed the direction of Edwina's gaze and nodded. Paula was dozing. "So now we should inform Jonathan Ainsley of our plans and invite him to come to his father's funeral, then let the rest of the family know the details."

"Do you think you can do that, Emily dear?" Edwina asked, then added quickly, "Speak to the rest of the family?"

"Of course, and Jonathan as well. I'll also—"

"Oh, no, no," Edwina cut in. "I wish to make that particular phone call."

"Very well. I understand. Now, Great-Aunt, when should we have the funeral? Monday, Tuesday, or Wednesday?"

"Since it's Friday today, Monday's far too soon to make all the arrangements in time. I think we had better speak to the vicar here in Pennistone today and ask which is the best for him. Tuesday or Wednesday? Probably we should aim for Wednesday, since I'm sure Anthony and Sally will come from Clonloughlin, and other family members have to travel here."

"That's true. Great-Aunt Edwina—" Emily cut herself off, staring at her mother's sister and best friend.

"What is it?" Edwina asked, noticing the odd look on her niece's face. "Is there something you want to tell me?"

Nodding. Emily said, "It's the most bizarre thing, Paula and I both agree on that. Just after you phoned me this morning, I had another call. From Gideon. Evan gave birth to the twins at about eleven o'clock. . . . Everyone's doing fine, and the boys have bright red fluff on their heads, according to their excited father. But don't you think it's a most curious coincidence?"

Edwina sat back against the pillows, shaking her head, her expression contemplative. "Well, I never. Just as Robin died, his great-grandsons were coming into this world. You're right, it is bizarre, and perhaps prophetic . . . a signal of something wonderful. Maybe they will inherit all of his talents and gifts . . . and none of his faults. But then none of us is perfect."

"Yes," Emily agreed.

"And Evan is all right, you said?" Edwina's brow lifted.

"She's doing splendidly. We'd better be in touch with her father just in case he wants to come to the funeral."

"Perhaps he won't want to come. Personally, I detest funerals. A long time ago I promised myself I would only ever go to weddings and christenings. Naturally, this funeral is a bit different, because Robin was my brother and he was always my favorite. But I never go to my friends' funerals these days. Too many of them to begin with, and, second, they go against the grain. I'm for life, Emily my dear, not death."

Emily couldn't help it, she burst out laughing.

Tessa Fairley sat in the back of the car, staring out of the window, her expression morose, her beautiful silvery eyes dull and empty. Although there were hints of spring in the countryside as they drove toward Pennistone Royal, she did not notice the change. Her thoughts were elsewhere. They went from Jean-Claude, still missing and a source of extreme worry, to her mother, deeply affected by the brain hemorrhage and the other source of constant worry.

There was nothing she could do about Jean-Claude, except pray he was safe; as far as her mother was concerned, she felt the need to protect her, cosset her, help her get well.

Whatever the others in the family thought, Tessa knew that her mother had had a traumatic few weeks. She had come home to Pennistone Royal thinking she was perfectly normal, only to discover, much to her chagrin, that she was not. Paula had quickly realized that the smallest things, which she had done automatically all her life, now took her much longer; she had also admitted to Tessa that she couldn't process things, and she became exhausted easily.

There was another troubling matter for Paula. There were no bandages on her head, because they were not needed, so most people saw the woman they had always known and didn't understand that she had had a major brain injury. "They think I'm just the same," she had complained to Tessa only a week ago. "And I'm not. It's funny, you know, if I had a cast on my leg or my arm in a sling, they'd recognize I'd been hurt."

Naturally, close members of the family—such as Shane, Linnet, Lorne, Emsie, and Desmond, and the staff at Pennistone Royal—understood everything, but Tessa had decided on the drive from London that she would remind everybody again this weekend, just to be sure.

Adele began to stir.

Tessa looked down at her daughter on the seat, and at Elvira, who was soothing Adele, stroking her hair. "I think she had a bad dream," Elvira murmured. "But we'll soon be there, and she can have—"

Elvira broke off as Tessa's mobile phone buzzed. Grabbing it from her carryall, Tessa clicked it on, said, "Hello?"

"Tessa?"

"Yes."

"It's Philippe. I have fantastic news!"

Tessa gripped the phone and held her breath. "Yes, yes, tell me!"

He seemed to fade away for a moment, and then he was back. "Did you hear me?"

"No, I didn't."

"My father is now in Kabul. With the American forces. They found him. Wounded in some makeshift hospital. He is coming home, Tessa!"

"Oh my God! Philippe, this is wonderful news," Tessa shouted, afraid of losing him. Tears were rolling down her face, and she could barely get the words out. "When is he coming back to Paris?"

"I do not know. I'll phone you as soon as I have news."

He hung up before she could tell him she would be at Pennistone Royal for the weekend, and to call her on the landline.

Looking over at Elvira, she cried excitedly, "Mr. Deléon is safe."

"That's wonderful news, Mrs. Fairley."

"Why are you crying, Mumma?" Adele asked, sitting up, touching Tessa's wet face.

"Because I'm happy, darling, very, very happy!"

Adele stared at her, looking puzzled.

A moment later the driver was pulling up outside the front of Pennistone Royal.

As Tessa opened the car door, she saw Great-Aunt Edwina and Emily on the doorstep, and she leapt out of the car, ran toward them, waving and shouting, "He's safe! Jean-Claude is safe! He's coming home."

Emily ran to meet her. They embraced, and Tessa started crying again. So did Emily. After a moment, they composed themselves and walked back to Edwina, who was beaming at them.

"Tessa, my darling Tessa, this is wonderful news. And I think we all deserve a drink. I was going home, but I think we must now go back inside and pop a cork, or at least have a lovely glass of sherry."

"What a good idea, Great-Aunt Edwina. And hopefully we can have it in the upstairs parlor with Mummy," Tessa answered.

Adele came running to Great-Aunt Edwina, a smile on her face, then said, "Mumma told me you're my great-great-great-great-aunt."

Edwina looked down at this exquisite blond child, a true Fairley if ever there was one, she thought, and said, "Not so many greats, my darling. I'm not *that* old."

"How many greats then?"

"Just *one*, Adele. . . . I'm Great-Aunt Edwina, that's what you must call me."

Adele laughed and allowed the nanny to guide her inside. Elvira took Adele to her room to freshen up, and Tessa helped Edwina climb the stairs, followed closely by Emily.

As they walked into the upstairs parlor, Paula glanced at the door and asked, "Where were you?" Then, spotting Tessa, her face lit up, and she exclaimed, "There you are, darling."

"Mummy! Wonderful news! Jean-Claude is safe." Once again Tessa began to cry, and so did Paula, as they embraced.

Emily said, "Whilst you mop yourselves up, I'm going down to the kitchen for a bottle of bubbly. We've got to toast Jean-Claude."

During the time Emily was gone, Tessa told her mother about Philippe's phone call and then explained, "I'll go back to London over the weekend, and fly to Paris on Monday. He's bound to be on his way by then."

Paula was silent for a moment, and then she said quietly, "We have news here, too, darling. Rather sad. Uncle Robin died today."

"Oh, Mummy, I'm so sorry. What happened?"

"He just died, peacefully."

Edwina said, "We're planning his funeral for Wednesday."

Tessa's face fell. "Oh, dear . . ."

She got no further. Edwina exclaimed, "But there's absolutely no reason for *you* to be there. You're better off going to Paris to look after that darling fiancé of yours. Robin won't mind if you're not there when we bury him. *He* was a true romantic, if ever there was one. Look at the way he carried on with Glynnis. And for fifty years."

Tessa stared at Paula, biting her lip.

Paula nodded. "Edwina's right, darling."

Within minutes Emily returned with a bottle of cham-

pagne in an ice bucket, followed by Margaret with a tray
of glasses. "It's luvely news, Tessa," she said. "I'm glad
he's safe and sound."

"Thanks, Margaret."

Emily poured the Pol Roger and passed the flutes
around. "Here's to Jean-Claude! And to the two new
Hartes."

Tessa gaped at Emily. "Evan's had the babies!"

"Exactly," Emily responded, smiling. "A couple of redheads, too, according to their delighted father."

"True Hartes then," Tessa said. Looking at Edwina
once again, she asked in a low voice, "Are you sure I don't
have to come to the funeral, Great-Aunt Edwina?"

"Absolutely. I've *banned* you!"

The four women laughed, and Paula thought, What a
day. And thank God I haven't had a difficult time processing all of this. Two happy events. One sad one. Somehow the balance is right.

34

~

Jack Figg stood with Linnet and Julian near the lych-gate of Pennistone Royal church, waiting for members of the family to arrive.

There was security everywhere, and there had been guards around the church for several days. Jack and his staff had also used bomb-sniffing dogs and metal detectors in the building itself, not wanting a repeat of the explosion which had happened on the day of Evan and Gideon's wedding. The wall had been skillfully repaired.

Jack had taken all these precautions because, as he knew only too well, it was impossible to predict what might happen, especially with a loose cannon like Jonathan Ainsley in the picture. And yet, deep down inside, Jack knew instinctively that Jonathan would come to the funeral of his father, and therefore nothing would happen to the church or its occupants.

As if reading his mind, Linnet suddenly turned to him and said, "I bet Ainsley comes to the funeral, so nothing's going to happen to any of us. Bad things happen to the Hartes only when he's far away."

Jack chuckled and exclaimed, "You just read my mind, Beauty."

Julian said, "Yes, she has developed a bad habit of doing that lately. I've started to think she's a witch."

"I'm glad Dad persuaded Mummy not to come, Jack, aren't you?" Linnet said, swiftly changing the subject.

"I am, yes. She's really not up to it yet." Jack lifted his eyes, glanced at the sky, pale blue and blameless, filled with early morning sunlight. "It's a grand March day, but there's a cold wind blowing down from the moors. In fact, it's going to be very nippy in the cemetery. That's why I'm pleased Evan won't be here either. And a funeral is always very draining on everyone; she's better looking after herself."

Linnet nodded. "Tessa won't be here either. You know that, don't you?"

"Your father told me," Jack replied. "I understand Great-Aunt Edwina forbade her to come, sent her packing off to Paris to wait for Jean-Claude."

"Yes, she did, she apparently *banned* her. And Edwina was right, let's face it. As Mummy said to me this morning, life is for the living. Anyway, she left Adele and Elvira at Pennistone Royal, which we all agreed was the best thing for her to do. She'll have her hands full in Paris."

"I hear she's pregnant," Jack murmured, gazing at Linnet, his eyes narrowing. "I suppose that means you're going to be the boss lady after all?"

"You bet!" Julian exclaimed.

"Only until Mummy can come back to work," Linnet immediately interjected. "She's not *retiring*. And anyway, one never knows with Tessa. She might easily decide to commute from Paris after the baby's born; she's always believed she's the Dauphine."

"Linnet will be going it alone, Jack, for the time being anyway. *Solo,* so to speak," Julian explained. "Evan's out on maternity leave, Tessa preoccupied with matters in Paris and her baby, and India's got to cope with Dusty and his problems as well as the northern stores. But I've no doubts about my girl. She'll do a fine job."

"I second that," Jack exclaimed and then asked Linnet, "When *will* your mother be well enough to go back to Harte's? Another month or so?"

"Oh, no, Jack! The neurologists have told her she has to take it really easy for at least six months. They said she can go back to living her normal life, if she's comfortable doing that, but she can't even contemplate returning to work for six to eight months, perhaps longer. Yesterday Daddy confided that he plans to take her to Villa Faviola in the summer. He thinks the South of France will do her good."

"I always trust your father's judgment," Jack remarked and pulled out a sheet of paper, looked down at it. "Emily gave me this list of names last night. Can I just read it off to you, Linnet, so you can tell me if there are any changes?"

"Of course, and I think there might be some, Jack. The phone's been ringing this morning."

Jack gave her a swift glance. "Let's start with the Hughes family. Owen, Marietta, and Elayne. They will all be here, I imagine."

"Only Marietta, unfortunately. She arrived at Pennistone Royal very late last night, and this morning at breakfast she told me that Owen and Elayne didn't come over from the States after all."

Jack raised a brow, looking askance. He exclaimed, "Really! That's surprising. She told me two days ago that Owen had agreed to come and was bringing Elayne with him."

"Obviously he changed his mind. She wasn't very forthcoming earlier, but I think she's embarrassed that Owen is staying away from his father's funeral. You know Evan can't come. She's exhausted after the birth of the twins. Also, there's some minor complication. Anyway, she's still in Queen Charlotte's, and her doctor won't permit her to leave the hospital until the end of this week."

"She's all right, though?" Jack asked, concerned.

"Oh yes, she'll be fine in a couple of days. It's just rest she needs."

"Okay," Jack muttered, crossing out more names. "Only Marietta from the Hughes family. Now to the Clonloughlin lot. Emily has a big question mark against all of these names. What do you know? Are they coming?"

"No. Edwina told them not to bother. She decided she wanted to keep the burial low-key. She thought it silly to drag Anthony and Sally and the family over from Ireland. Especially since she's planning a big memorial for Robin in London in a few months."

Jack put lines through the names of the Dunvales and their two sons and said, "So it's only India, then, representing her parents and brothers?"

"That's right," Linnet answered. "But Dusty's coming with her."

"So I see. Robin's other sisters are coming, aren't they, Linnet? Your grandmother Daisy and Elizabeth, Robin's twin."

"*Absolutely*. Grandma's staying with us, and Elizabeth is with Emily at Allington Hall. Oh, and don't forget Elizabeth's husband, Marc Deboyne. I'm sure Emily listed him, since he's her stepfather."

"She did. But Amanda and Francesca are not mentioned."

"Amanda's in China, you know she does all the buying for Harte Enterprises. Emily thought it perfectly ridiculous to pull her back here. As for her twin, Francesca is on holiday in Thailand. Again, Emily made the decision to let Francesca and her family finish their holiday in peace."

Jack nodded his understanding and went on. "As Hartes go, I have Emily, Winston, Toby, Gideon, and Natalie. I know they're all going to be here. Then there's you and Julian, your father, Grandfather Bryan, and Emsie. Your mother's not coming, but what about your brother? Desmond's not on the list."

"Dad decided not to pull him out of boarding school for a funeral of one hour, and Mummy agreed. She said it was silly. But Lorne's coming."

"My father is also definitely coming," Julian murmured. "I'm sure he's been included."

"He has indeed, Jules. Well, I guess that's it."

Linnet shivered and exclaimed, "I think it's getting colder out here, can we go up to the church?"

Julian and Jack followed Linnet up to the porch, where they stood sheltered from the wind.

Within minutes the procession of funeral cars rolled down the hill, and the family, dressed in mourning black, alighted and began to file into the church.

At last came the hearse bearing Robin Ainsley's body. His pallbearers were Winston, Toby, and Gideon Harte, Michael Kallinski, Shane O'Neill and Lorne.

After shouldering the coffin, the six men, representing the three clans, walked up the path and into the church with measured steps.

The church was filled with masses of flowers. Sunlight poured in through the stained-glass windows, and organ music soared to the rafters as the pallbearers brought Robin's coffin down the aisle to the altar steps.

As Linnet slid closer to Julian in the pew, she recognized the strains of William Blake's "Jerusalem," her own favorite hymn.

It was when the choirboys began to sing the words that a lump came into her throat and she discovered her eyes were moist. She thought of Evan and the conversation they had had yesterday. Evan had so wanted to be here, to pay her last respects to the grandfather she had known for only just over a year but had grown to love so much.

The funeral service began with prayers and hymns, and then the vicar, the Reverend Henry Thorpe, spoke beautifully about Robin Ainsley and all that he had been as a man, a politician, and a parishioner. When the vicar had finished, Robin's three sisters came to the lectern together.

It was Edwina who was the first speaker, as the eldest. Her words about her brother were eloquent, and she touched on his many kindnesses to all of his sisters, his genuine brotherly love and his enduring friendship toward each one of them until his death.

Elizabeth, Robin's twin, spoke of their closeness and then went on to enumerate in a faltering voice his many acts of courage during the Second World War. At that time he had been a fighter pilot in the RAF and very brave.

And last, Daisy, Emma's daughter by Paul McGill, talked about Robin's acts of kindness to his RAF comrades. He had brought warmth and comfort to them during the Battle of Britain, she said lovingly, by making them part of his family, bringing them home to be spoiled by his mother and his sisters. He had always been true blue, she finished.

Finally, it was Winston Harte who went up to eulogize his uncle, speaking about Robin's brilliant career as a Member of Parliament, expounding the major differences he had made in the country through the bills he had introduced, his many triumphs in the House, the things he had accomplished during his long political career.

As the service was coming to an end, Linnet turned her head and spotted Jonathan Ainsley standing at the back of the church. She grabbed Jack's arm and whispered to him, but when Jack looked, Ainsley had disappeared.

In the cemetery there was no sight of him either, but during the burial Jack suddenly noticed him standing apart, near a copse of trees.

It was only at the very end that Ainsley came closer, showed himself to the rest of the family. He did not acknowledge them in any way, nor did they acknowledge him.

Just when the vicar was intoning "Ashes to ashes, dust

to dust," he bent down, picked up a handful of earth, and threw it into the grave. And then, without a word or a glance, Jonathan Ainsley swung around and strode away, a tall, somber figure in black.

The ringing of her mobile phone brought Marietta out of a deep sleep. Sitting up in bed, slightly disoriented, she reached for the phone, pressed it on. "Hello?"

"I hope it's not too late to call, Mother," Angharad said. "I hope you're not mad."

Startled to hear from the daughter who had so nonchalantly disappeared from her life, Marietta exclaimed, "Well, yes, as a matter of fact I am. Don't you think it's kind of rude? Not being in touch with me for weeks and then calling at eleven at night."

"Oh, come on, Mom, don't stand on your high horse, I just wanted to say hi. Listen, I heard you were at that funeral today. . . . I suppose you're staying at Pennistone Royal with Paula?"

Marietta took a deep breath. "Why are you calling me, Angharad?"

"Just to say hello. How's Paula doing after her brain hemorrhage? Does she have . . . bats in the belfry as they say here?"

"Don't be so stupid!" Marietta snapped. "I'm going to hang up."

"No, don't, Mom. Listen, I'm engaged. Did you know that?"

"No, I didn't," Marietta lied.

"I am. I've got the most gorgeous diamond you've ever seen. What's that saying? A diamond as big as the Ritz. Well, mine is! I'm going to marry Jonathan, you know. He's crazy for me . . . because I drive him crazy in bed."

"I don't want to hear any of this nonsense, Angharad."

"Dad didn't come to the funeral, did he? Why is that?"

"Angharad, it's very late. I have to hang up."

"I'd like to see you, Mom. When you come back to

London, I mean. I'm not up there in Yorkshire. Jonathan is, he went to his father's funeral. He's going to be even richer, bet you didn't know that. He's getting everything. Nothing for little Evan. And how's she doing? Had the baby elephants yet?"

"Good night."

"Mom, don't cut me off. I'll be in London all week. I want you to see me, meet me for tea at the Ritz." She started to laugh, sounding shrill.

"I don't know whether I can, I'll call you."

"I'm leaving on Monday, Mom. Back to Paris we go. So call me before then, okay?"

"Very well."

"You won't recognize me. I'm very chic these days, that's what everyone says, even Jonathan." The shrill laughter echoed through the phone once more, as Angharad continued, "I'll be richer than Evan . . . much, much richer. You see, I am going to be Mrs. Ainsley."

"Good night, Angharad," Marietta said and turned the phone off.

Sleep eluded Marietta for a while, her mind preoccupied with her youngest daughter and what she had said. Thank God she had not given anything away about Paula, or the twins being born.

Should she meet her daughter for tea later this week? She wasn't sure. She would have to ask Evan what she thought and, perhaps more important, Linnet. Maybe they would want her to have tea with Angharad just to find out whatever she could.

35

~

And so it began. The most relentless, backbreaking work schedule ever conceived by anybody—except Emma Harte.

Many years before, Emma had set out to accumulate money and power, large amounts of it, and very quickly. And she had succeeded, reaching heights she herself had not dreamed of achieving. She had done it through sheer willpower, discipline, self-sacrifice, and stamina. She had been seventeen years old when she embarked upon this extraordinary journey to the top; her great-granddaughter Linnet was almost ten years older, and her aim was not to acquire money or power. What she was aiming to do was bring the great emporium Emma had founded into the twenty-first century. And faster and better than any of the rival stores could do, rivals who sought the same customers and had the same goals.

Linnet, more than any other member of the family, was blessed with those characteristics which had been Emma's stock-in-trade: that unique drive, penchant for hard work, and, most important, the sheer will to push herself beyond endurance. There was also the talent and intelligence which underscored those traits, and which Emma had bequeathed to her.

Aside from these characteristics, Linnet had been

gifted with Emma's understanding of retailing and her enormous vision. Linnet's mother, Paula, had succeeded very well over the years, never deviating very much from Emma's rules. She had been trained by the founder and revered her, and she steered the ship well.

But Paula had never had the vision which had set Emma Harte way above her competitors. Neither did Tessa, India, or Evan, Emma's great-granddaughters. It was Linnet who had inherited this very special gift.

The vision made her aware of what could go wrong as well as what could go right. Many a day, especially lately, she had muttered to herself, "I know exactly what will go right. What I need to calculate is all those things which could easily go wrong."

It was almost as if Linnet had a demon telling her things. She could sit in her office, staring into space, and see into the future, envision all those things that could bring her and Harte's tumbling down. Or fulfill her dreams to give the store a dazzling future.

Although she had free rein at the moment to run the company, Paula having made her creative director and manager, Linnet knew very well she had a board to answer to should there ever be a problem. Harte's was a public company, trading its shares on the London Stock Exchange, and even though her mother and the family owned the majority of the shares, she knew that she had to watch her p's and q's. Her father had warned her of that several days after the funeral, when he had come in to see her at the store in Knightsbridge. And so had Emily, who with Paula, Winston, and the ever-absent Amanda Linde, ran all of the Harte companies and were on the board of the stores.

And so she was watching her step, as her grandfather had instructed her to do, and at the same time going at it hammer and tongs, working around the clock, pushing forward. The Tranquillity Day Spa was finished; the bridal floor was totally revamped and decorated and was only waiting for basic merchandise; she had started to design an area for luxury goods, even though her mother had not told her she could do this. Nevertheless, Linnet knew it was essential.

In order to cover as much ground as possible in a very short time, Linnet had hired two new assistants and two new secretaries. Jonelle was holding the fort in the executive suite, and Linnet was finding her invaluable.

Although her schedule was brutal, she was managing to hold to it, mostly by sacrificing all of her social life. And also thanks to her husband. Julian Kallinski had similar responsibilities and would one day inherit the vast international conglomerate Kallinski Industries from his father, Michael, who had inherited it from his father, Sir Ronald Kallinski, who had inherited it from *his* father, David Kallinski, the founder of their clan. And so, better than any other man, Julian knew *what* she was doing and *why* she was doing it, and he applauded her for it.

Basically, Linnet wanted to bring something wonderful but just a bit old world into the future, thereby saving its life. Today, more than ever, Harte's had competition in London, not only the big department stores but boutiques, ateliers, and small shops, all of them vying for the fashion-conscious young woman, and the older, more sophisticated woman as well. Julian cheered her on, and never doubted for one moment that she would win.

And so together they formulated a plan. Every morning, Linnet leapt out of bed at four-thirty, and so did Julian. She went to the shower first; he put on the coffeepot. Within minutes he was in the shower, she was doing her makeup; he went to shave as she made the toast. Minutes later, in their robes, they sat together in the kitchen enjoying a light breakfast; then they dressed for the day and left the apartment.

Their driver dropped Linnet at the store first, then took Julian on to Kallinski House. She was behind her desk at five forty-five, he was at his office at six.

Every night, at seven o'clock, Julian picked her up at the store, and either the driver took them home for a cozy supper in front of the fire or they dropped in at a favorite restaurant for dinner.

Because Linnet needed to work Saturdays, Julian did the same. By the end of the first month, it had become a well-oiled routine; they were enjoying it because they were both, in their different ways, seeing their intense work come to fruition.

Now, on this lovely morning in May, Linnet went out onto the Fashion Floors, holding her breath and crossing her fingers. Today was the day.

The Tranquillity Day Spa would be opening its doors for the first time, and the floor now named Brides would be proudly showing off its fabulous gowns and every type of other bridal merchandise. Even the luxury goods area was finished and would open today.

Just as exciting, as far as Linnet was concerned, was her total revamping of the Fashion Floors. She had rushed to Paris for three days just after Robin's funeral, had gone on a marathon buying spree, selecting clothes from all of the prêt-à-porter lines produced by the top fashion houses. She had also bought merchandise at Valentino, Ungaro, Chanel, and some of the lesser houses, determined to bring her Fashion Floors up to par.

The handbag and shoe departments had been given the same revamp, and her new assistant Phyllis Peters had filled both boutiques with the most delectable, glamorous, and sexy merchandise she had ever seen.

Looking at her watch, Linnet realized that it was only eight; there was no one around at this hour. But as she tried the handle on the door of the spa, it opened, and she came face-to-face with Sophie Forrester, the spa's manager.

"Good morning, Linnet," Sophie said, opening the

door wider. "Do you want to come in and look around again?"

"I'd love to, Sophie."

Together the manager and Linnet toured the spa, and once more Linnet was struck by the absolute tranquillity of the space. The lighting was subdued, perfumed votive candles flickered everywhere, and there was the sound of tinkling water falling over stones. The overall decor had an Oriental flavor, with beautiful but spare floral arrangements, Japanese in style, while the treatment cubicles, small rooms actually, had the feeling of pagodas. Restfulness and peace were underscored by the gentle music playing in the background.

"I wouldn't mind lying down and having a treatment myself," Linnet said, smiling at Sophie. "And what an apt name Tranquillity is . . . *perfect*." As she left the spa, Linnet added, "Thanks for the tour, and lots of luck today."

"Thanks, Linnet," Sophie responded.

Walking across the floor, Linnet now stopped and surveyed the luxury goods corner, positioned diagonally opposite the spa for obvious reasons. She had named it Luxury Boutique, and it featured beautiful evening bags, pashminas, antique silk shawls, rare bead necklaces and earrings, exotic sandals, cashmere jackets and bathrobes, hand embroidered, and all manner of exclusive items. Fingers crossed, she muttered under her breath as she headed for the escalators.

There were no two ways about it, Brides was one of the best-designed boutiques in the store. Thanks to Bobbi Snyder, Linnet thought now as she walked through, gazing at the exquisite wedding gowns displayed on mannequins. Even her own wedding dress was on show in the boutique within Brides, which Linnet had named, very simply, Evan Harte Couture. Her own dress was there because the seamstresses had been able to finish only five gowns in the time allotted to them, and Bobbi wanted a sixth dress to make a real showing. All of the Evan Harte gowns were couture and made to measure; Evan had promised to keep on designing, even though she had now extended her maternity leave to six months.

There were beautiful veils; tiaras made of pearl or diamanté; wreaths of flowers; bridesmaid dresses; flower girl dresses; velvet and satin suits for the little page boys. Shoes and sandals, lingerie, and other decorative items were beautifully set out, and Linnet was filled with positive thoughts as she left.

There was a lovely feeling of spring on the Fashion Floors, which had always been under her aegis, and she was as thrilled now with the way the clothes were mounted and displayed as she had been yesterday. The dresses and suits were in pretty pastel colors, made of silks, chiffons, and light wools. And the banks of potted azaleas and hydrangeas furthered the sense of spring and summer everywhere.

Returning to the executive suite some twenty minutes later, Linnet felt a rush of gratitude toward the people she had hired, who had made such an effort to meet her deadline for the revamping of the various areas in Harte's.

Her mobile phone rang a few minutes later, and it was India. "I wanted to wish you lots of luck, Linny," she said. "I know the store must look beautiful."

"It does. It looks *fabulous*. There's a real springlike feeling, with all the pastel-colored clothes and the flowers, both real and artificial. The store designers have done a wonderful job on all the floors, India. Oh, and the spa is . . . *tranquil!*"

"I can't wait to see it. I'll be coming up later in the week. I have my last fitting for my wedding gown."

"Shall we have lunch or dinner?"

"Both if you can." India laughed. "I really miss you. And the store as well."

"I miss you, too, and Evan."

"Do we have any special news from Tessa?"

"Only that Jean-Claude is making very good progress. He has really bad wounds in one leg; he was shot up. But she sounded cheerful, so Mummy said."

"I spoke to Paula yesterday, and I was a bit disappointed when she said she might not be feeling well enough to come to my wedding."

"I knew you would be. Daddy mentioned it to me . . . he just thinks everything that requires real effort still exhausts her. Let's wait and see how she feels closer to the date, but you can count on me being there, with bells on."

"You'd better be, and Evan and Tessa. You're my three matrons of honor. How's Evan doing, by the way?"

"She's good, very happy, and the babies are adorable. They have auburn fluff for hair, as Gideon calls it, and green eyes. Right proper Hartes, Uncle Winston tells everyone." Linnet hesitated and then confided, "Evan's taking a longer maternity leave, India, six months altogether. I felt a bit down in the dumps about that, but it's her choice."

"God, I can imagine! I wish I could be there in Knightsbridge more often, but I've a lot to do up here, especially without Tessa." Now it was India's turn to hesitate for a moment, and then she asked, "What's Tessa going to *do* finally, do we know yet?"

"Not really, but she spends most of her time in Paris, and I doubt that's going to change."

"I agree, but listen, talking of Paris, have you heard anything more about Angharad?" India probed, curiosity getting the better of her.

"Mummy gets bits of information from Sarah. She's definitely engaged to Jonathan, well, according to Sarah. Marietta had tea with Angharad a few weeks ago, and all she did was boast about her acquisitions, according to Marietta."

"Ill-gotten gains, you mean," India shot back acidly.

Linnet laughed. "Only too true. But listen, she's seemingly keeping him occupied. What's that old saying? The devil finds work for idle hands. Perhaps he'll continue to lay off us since he's preoccupied with his fiancée."

"I hope so. My father told me that Jack's been over to Ireland, to check the security at Clonloughlin. I'm glad of that, and glad he's coming to the wedding as a guest. He's sort of . . . like my favorite uncle."

"Mine, too, India. I'd better go, I want to do another walk around the store."

It had not worked.

By the end of the week, Linnet was aware that business had been flat in all departments, and there were few bookings at the day spa.

The sales figures for Fashion were low; only two gowns had been ordered from Brides; not one item from the Luxury Boutique had been bought.

Now, on this Saturday morning, Linnet was at her wit's end and filled with gloom. Obviously she had blundered. The great emporium's new look, the latest merchandise, the extraordinary Tranquillity Day Spa—none of these innovations had made a dent, had brought in any new customers, or old ones for that matter. As far as she knew.

The Food Halls had been busy, but then they always were. She cringed when she thought of the way she had fought her mother about creating snack bars there and instantly pushed the memory of their quarrel to one side. And there was something truly weird. Mattresses, relegated to the basement, had had record sales this past week. She wondered why.

As she sat at the desk, her head in her hands, Linnet began to weep. *Failure.* That was what she was facing, something she had never really considered possible. And she had a board to answer to, as well as her mother. The mere prospect made her shiver, and she sat there for a long time, unable to think, let alone move.

The problem was she had no one to talk to, no one to

turn to for advice. India had canceled her trip to London, but even if she had been here, what could her cousin have said? Linnet knew *she* was supposed to be the smart one in the family when it came to retailing. But as far as she was concerned, at the moment she was a total failure.

"Too much chutzpah," she thought, that's what Julian would say. And she could hear her mother saying, "Pride comes before a fall." The tears suddenly spurted again, and she put her head down on the desk and wept as if her heart would break.

"Crying's not going to get you anywhere," the voice said, echoing around the large office.

Linnet sat up with a jolt, looked from side to side. Of course there was no one there. It was seven o'clock on Saturday morning, and there was hardly anyone in the store yet. Sitting back in the chair, Linnet wiped the tears from her face with her fingers and found a tissue in her pocket. After blowing her nose, she got up and went to the adjoining bathroom, stared at herself in the mirror. Her face was streaked with mascara, and she had chewed most of her lipstick off. After splashing her face with cold water and patting it dry, she went back to the desk, took out a compact, and patted her cheeks with powder, freshened her lipstick.

Walking across to the door, she went out and hurried to the long corridor, came to a standstill in front of the portrait of Emma. "It was you, wasn't it, Grandy?" Linnet said, staring at that famous face. "You were talking to me, weren't you?"

Obviously there was no answer; a portrait couldn't speak, couldn't give you advice, however much you wanted it to do so. But Linnet went on talking to the painting. "How did you do it alone?" she asked, staring into those green eyes so like her own. "How did you cope? Who guided you? Who did you turn to when things were tough?"

Linnet knew the answers to her questions, she imme-

diately understood that. Emma Harte had not had anyone to help her or guide her. She had done it all by herself.

Solo.

And *she* was solo now. Leaning closer to the portrait,
Linnet whispered, "You're right, crying won't get me anywhere. I'm not going to cry anymore. I'm going to solve
the problem. Just as you solved your problems, Emma."

As she always did, Linnet smiled at Emma's portrait,
touched her great-grandmother's face, and then hurried
back to her mother's office, which she had used off and
on these last few months.

Linnet was aware that everyone would think her fanciful if they knew she believed Emma Harte spoke to her,
and that was why Julian had always warned her not to tell
anyone. Certainly they would think she was crazy if they
knew she was actually talking to the portrait.

Fanciful or crazy, what did it matter? Linnet felt better
when she sat down behind the desk, picked up a pen,
and began to make notes. She had attended to all the
right things, she was sure of that. She had done plenty of
clever advertising in the newspapers, so customers knew
about the day spa and fashion innovations; she had hired
new window dressers and designers, and had even
brought Perry Jones over from the New York store to lend
a creative hand. Advertising and windows had been taken
care of. So what had she missed? What had escaped her?
Bad weather? It had rained during the week . . .

Impatient, Linnet thought, the word popping into her
head. I haven't given it enough time. . . . Yes, perhaps
that's it. . . . She remained at the desk making notes until
eleven o'clock; then she went down to the ground floor
and outside to look at the windows.

Staring at them as objectively as possible, Linnet began to realize they were too busy. It was true she had
asked the designers to create a spring–summer feeling,

but wasn't there just too much decor and not enough fashion here?

As she went around to the side street, to look at the window containing new handbags, she heard two women talking. One of them said, "You can't see the wood for the trees here. But there's the Cholly Chello bag, the one I told you about. Do you see it, that red one? It's the only bag in the world that every woman wants. I wish I could afford it."

The woman was right, there were too many bags in the window, Linnet recognized this at once. But what struck her most was that phrase about the Cholly Chello being the only bag in the world, and she dashed back to her office, her mind working overtime.

The side window of Harte's was now stark; it had a plain cream backdrop. On a simple wooden packing crate stood the red Cholly Chello handbag, and, to one side of the crate, a large yellow board hung down from the ceiling. Written in bold black letters were the words THE ONLY BAG IN THE WORLD THAT EVERY WOMAN WANTS.

"It's perfect, Perry," Linnet said to the American window designer. "You'll see, it's going to do the trick."

"From your mouth to God's ears," Perry answered, and, taking hold of Linnet's arm, he led her to the windows facing Knightsbridge. "Now, what do you think? We finished them about half an hour ago, and I sincerely hope they do the trick, too."

The large front windows were as stark as the one on the side street, and Linnet could see the clothes, no longer felt overwhelmed by the decor. "Oh, Perry, they're great! You've done a terrific job!" she exclaimed, her eyes now focused on the pale blue sky filled with puffy white clouds. The sky and a white picket fence with three yellow daisies growing next to it composed the backdrop for the clothes. And only two dresses were displayed in each window, so that they had breathing space.

"Less is more," Linnet murmured. "And thank you for working such long hours to redo the windows, Perry. I really appreciate it."

"It's my pleasure, and by the way, that was a great slogan you came up with about the bag. Actually, I've never heard of the Cholly Chello."

"Neither had I," Linnet admitted with a laugh. "But my handbag buyer says it's the up-and-coming item for the fashionistas."

Perry laughed with her as they went back into Harte's, the greatest emporium in the world.

"It's the Cholly Chello that's bringing them into the store in droves," Linnet said to India two weeks later. "We can't keep it in stock, and the manufacturer can't make it fast enough. They've never had such success with a bag. *Ever.*"

"It's strange," India answered, giving Linnet an odd look. "I'd never heard of it before, had you?"

"No. Still, it *is* a big hit."

"You know what, it's the slogan you thought up," India suddenly asserted, pushing the fish around on her plate. "You created a market for the bag with your slogan."

"Oh, really, India, come on, I'm not that clever."

"Listen, Hermès did it with the Kelly and the Birkin. They cleverly created a market by not producing so many. These days people have to put their names on a waiting list to get either bag, and they wait years."

Linnet chuckled. "We've got waiting lists, too, for the Cholly Chello. And when these smart young women are putting their names on our list for the bag, they notice the Tranquillity Day Spa and wander in, become entranced. And they're also very taken with my Luxury Boutique, not to mention the Fashion Floors. But I've got to admit, this upswing in traffic in the store is happening because of that darn bag."

The two cousins were sitting in the Bird Cage having

lunch and catching up, and it was a relief for Linnet to have someone to talk to about work. Evan was preoccupied with the twins, Tessa was in Paris, and her father still did not want Paula disturbed. During the hour they were together, Linnet went over her plans for the store with India, and they agreed that she would come to London more often. The Leeds and Harrogate stores were now running well, and Dusty's problems regarding the Caldwells and Molly's will were in the past.

"What he has to look forward to now is our wedding in Ireland," India murmured as they left the restaurant. "As you know, Atlanta is going to be a flower girl along with Adele, and she's very excited about that."

"I'm so happy for you, India, and thankful that everything worked out for you and Dusty in the end. And I can't wait to come to Clonloughlin in June for your wedding."

36

She had come here to Ireland as a young bride over seventy years ago, the wife of Jeremy Standish, Earl of Dunvale, and it had all been like a dream. Here in this beautiful Georgian house in Clonloughlin she had spent the happiest days of her life.

She wished that he was here today to see this other bride of Clonloughlin, their exquisite granddaughter, India Standish, only daughter of their son Anthony. She's a mixture of all that's best and bright, Edwina thought, part Dunvale, part Harte, part Fairley. Oh yes, India has inherited a lot in *her* genes.

Edwina sat at a table in the ballroom of Clonloughlin House on a glorious Saturday in the middle of June, and she was, as was her way, surveying the assemblage. The guests were mostly family, but there were a few friends present, about fifty people in all. The house had been a whirl of activity for several weeks, but the wedding was not the splashy event it had been meant to be, and for a number of reasons—good taste, death, and security. Bowing to what they deemed her better judgment, Anthony and Sally had agreed to her suggestion of keeping it simple. And so had India and Dusty, who were totally on her side. Robin had died only a few months earlier, and before that there had been the upsetting deaths of

Molly Caldwell and her daughter. "Such bad form to have a big, fancy affair," Edwina had intoned. "Let's be proper about this."

The deaths aside, there was the matter of security, plus the specter of Jonathan Ainsley. He and Anthony had quarreled badly. Since then, Ainsley had been vindictive and threatening, especially after Anthony took Paula's side in the great debacle some years before.

It was a lovely gathering nonetheless.

Edwina had caught her breath in delight and pride when India walked down the aisle in the little church on the estate, holding on to the arm of her father.

Edwina looked across at her now, standing with her parents, talking to Winston, her mother's brother. What a gorgeous young woman, she thought, there's no other word to use. The pale ivory taffeta wedding gown, designed by Evan, had big puff sleeves, a scooped-out neckline, and a huge crinoline skirt that floated around her like a cloud. She had removed her veil, but the antique diamond tiara was back in place on her shining silver-gilt hair. Adele Fairley's tiara, Edwina mused, inwardly smiling, thinking of their lineage, India's and hers.

India was a dreamlike creature on this, her wedding day; she looked out of this world. And suddenly the bridegroom was standing there, darkly handsome and so proud of his wife. It showed on his face, that pride. A genuine man, honest and true, a dependable man, and, oh, what a talent he possessed.

She would never forget the look on Dusty's face as India had glided toward him and his best man, Gideon, who were waiting at the altar. It had been one of pure love, pure joy.

After the marriage vows, they had all come back here to Clonloughlin House for cocktails in the main drawing room, where many photographs had been taken by the professional photographer. Two hours later, at six-thirty, they had settled in the large formal dining room for supper. All of the antique Georgian furniture had been removed, the room filled with circular skirted tables partnered with gilded ballroom chairs. Edwina had been pleased with the effect. Almost everything was white, from the organza tablecloths to the flower arrangements. The women in their lovely gowns introduced a splash of color, and, as she had looked around, she couldn't help admiring the glittering Waterford crystal chandeliers she had chosen years before, which hung from the high-flung ceiling.

After the supper, at which many speeches were given, many toasts made, they had moved in here to dance and enjoy the rest of the evening. There was a trio at one end of the room, and now, much to her pleasure, came the bride and groom. They walked onto the dance floor for their first dance together as man and wife. When the strains of "True Love" filled the air, Dusty took India in his arms and led her into the middle of the floor.

"Are you all right, Great-Aunt Edwina?" Linnet asked, sitting down with her.

"I'm in great form, Linnet, great form." Peering at her intently, Edwina continued in a low but vibrant voice, "My goodness, in your pale blue gown and those emerald earrings, you have such a look tonight, the look of my mother."

"So Grandfather Bryan said earlier." Staring at the couple on the dance floor, Linnet exclaimed, "Oh, Great-Aunt Edwina, isn't India the most perfect bride you've ever seen?"

"She is indeed, but you three girls look wonderful, too. Everyone does in fact, the women in all their elegance, the men in their morning suits. It's just sad for me that Paula and Shane aren't here."

"Daddy is very protective of Mummy. He thought the strain of travel, the excitement of the wedding would be too much."

"But she's looking so well, I thought."

"She gets mixed up a lot, and can't always fathom things out the way she used to," Linnet explained.

"But she isn't ill?" Edwina pressed, giving Linnet a keen look.

"No, no, she's not. It's all part of the recovery, so I understand."

"And you're holding the fort, so to speak?" Edwina asked.

Linnet smiled a little wryly. "Trying to, and I must admit, it's tough at times, especially without India, Tessa, and Evan. I'm lonely."

"It *is* lonely at the top. Always. I know what my mother went through."

"Can I ask you something, Edwina?"

"Anything you wish, my dear."

"Once, you said you heard your mother's voice talking to you. Did you mean really *heard* it, or was it simply an echo from the past in your head?"

"An echo mostly, I'm sure," Edwina responded carefully. "But sometimes I thought I did really hear her. Perhaps I was simply remembering . . . it could have been memories coming back to me. Why do you ask?"

"Because I hear her voice . . . hear her telling me things. Do you think I'm daft in the head?"

"No. *Imaginative.*"

Linnet was silent, studying her great-aunt.

Edwina leaned forward, pinning her eyes on Linnet. "You've been programmed all of your life, been told you look like her, sound like her, act like her. You've grown up believing you've inherited her strength, stamina, intelligence, and business acumen. She's been all around you since the day you were born. She is part of you, just as you are part of her, and you *do* have her genes. So when you're stressed and worried and feel utterly *alone,* you think she comes to your aid."

"Yes, yes, I do, that's true!"

"It's all in your head, in your mind, Linnet. Don't fret

about it, my dear, because if it helps you, so what? No harm done. However, don't tell anyone else."

Linnet smiled, and, leaning closer to Edwina, she whispered, "That's what Julian says. I suppose he's worried people will think I'm crazy."

"Perhaps they would. On the other hand, why should you care what the world thinks of you? You are your own woman, and that's what you must always be, Linnet. Then you really will be the new Emma Harte."

India and Dusty were suddenly standing at the table, beaming at Linnet and Edwina.

"May I have the honor of this dance, Edwina?" Dusty asked, bowing slightly.

"It will be my pleasure, Dusty. And did I say it before today? Welcome to my family."

"You did say it, but you can keep repeating it as much as you want," Dusty responded, leading her onto the dance floor with a show of gallantry.

India put her arm through Linnet's and murmured sadly, "I miss Paula and Shane."

"So do I, but it's better Mummy stays quiet."

"Is she getting back to normal, though?" India asked softly.

"Yes." Linnet nodded.

"So when is she coming back to the store?"

"I don't know. Dad's taking her to Villa Faviola for July and August. Also, Tessa told her the other day that she and Jean-Claude want to get married the first week of September. In Yorkshire. So there'll be another wedding."

"I'm happy for her," India remarked, meaning every word, and glanced around. "Look at her, Linnet, over there, she's so in love with her lovely Frenchman."

"I know. What a difference there is between him and the horrible Mark Longden!"

"Has Tessa mentioned what she'll do after she's married?"

"I don't think she'll work in London, India. Still,

Mummy gave me the impression that Tessa wants to keep her hand in by doing our fashion buying in Paris."

"That might work out well for us all," India said, throwing Linnet a knowing glance.

"I hope so. India, just look at your grandmother and Dusty! She's having a rare old time out there, a regular Ginger Rogers."

"And she's a rare old bird, don't you think?"

"There's no one like her. She's the jewel in the crown."

The two of them sat watching Edwina waltzing past with Dusty. Regal and elegant in purple chiffon and diamonds, and truly a miracle at ninety-five.

A short while later, Dusty brought Edwina back to the table and danced off with India; then Julian came to claim Linnet. Suddenly Edwina was alone, watching the festivities, a smile on her face. Within seconds, Gideon and Evan joined her, followed by Grandfather Bryan, Emsie, and Desmond. A moment later Jean-Claude and Tessa arrived and sat down with them, and so did Lorne. Edwina was surrounded by those she loved, and this pleased her enormously.

Touching her arm, Grandfather Bryan remarked, "Well, well, just look over there, Edwina. Marietta Hughes dancing with Jack Figg. They make a grand couple, mavourneen, don't you agree?"

"Sure I do, Bryan, my lad," Edwina said, adopting a soft Irish lilt. "I'm all for romance."

Bryan laughed, and so did the rest of the table.

Edwina glanced around. Her wise old eyes settled on each one of them, and she thought: Most of them are the progeny of Emma Harte. And they are absolutely . . . the very best. Emma would be so proud of them all, because they do her proud every day of their lives. And Edwina's heart was full. She felt so glad to have witnessed this day.

A week later Linnet was working late at the Harte's in Knightsbridge, and she glanced up when her mobile phone rang. Picking it up, she said, "Hello? Linnet O'Neill."

"It's India," her cousin said.

"Hi, darling, how's the honeymoon going? Is Dusty enjoying being at Clonloughlin?"

"Oh yes, he's fallen in love with the place. Linnet?"

"Yes, what is it? You sound odd."

"Grandma died."

"Oh, no, not Edwina!" Linnet cried, her eyes filling up. Her throat instantly became tight, but she managed to say, "I can't believe it, she was going strong at your wedding."

"She was ninety-five, you know."

"Everyone thought she'd live to be a hundred, that was her goal, she told me. Oh, India, it's just awful that she's gone. The whole family's going to miss her terribly." Linnet reached for a tissue, wiped her eyes.

India began to cry. Through her tears she managed to say, "I found her, Linnet. I thought she was dozing on the sofa in her bedroom, but she was gone. And in her hands she had a photograph of herself and Emma when she was a little girl, and she was clinging to her mother's hand. She must have been thinking of Emma when she died."

"I have to put the phone down a minute," Linnet said, tears rolling down her face.

"It's all right." India was still weeping herself.

A moment later, after blowing her nose and endeavoring to get hold of her swimming senses, Linnet finally said, "When is the funeral, India?"

"We've buried her," India replied, also sounding less tearful. "This morning, actually, in the cemetery on the estate. That's the way she wanted it. She told my father recently that her funeral should be totally private, that she didn't want the whole family dragging themselves over to Ireland." India paused, took a deep breath. "She said she didn't believe in funerals, only weddings and christenings."

"I would have liked to have been there," Linnet remarked. "And I bet *everyone* would have come."

"You'd all just left, after the wedding. Dad thought it wiser to abide by his mother's wishes." There was a pause, and India began to laugh through her tears. "Grandma did say she wanted a memorial service, though. A big one."

After India had hung up, Linnet sat for a while staring into the distance, thinking of Edwina and all that she had been as a woman. How odd that she had been holding a picture of Emma and herself when she was small. But no, perhaps it wasn't. After all, she had loved her mother.

For a split second Linnet thought of going down the corridor to tell the portrait of Emma that her firstborn child was dead. But she didn't.

Instead she wrote a letter to Anthony, telling her uncle what a remarkable woman his mother had been, speaking of her own sorrow at this loss, and sending him her condolences.

It seemed to Linnet later, when she looked back, that the summer had just slid by.

She and Julian kept to their routine, working hard at their jobs. Much to her relief, the innovations she had made at Harte's in Knightsbridge had proved successful. There was heavy traffic all through June, July, and August, with customers flocking to the Tranquillity Day Spa, invading the Fashion Floors, and making the Luxury Boutique their favorite place to buy the most expensive merchandise in the store. Brides had finally taken off, and bridal gowns designed by Evan Harte were the pick of the season.

Every day Linnet prayed that her luck would hold. And it did. The store acquired a lot of new, younger customers and provided better choices to the old core customers who had patronized Harte's for years. And everyone remarked on the fresh look, the updated merchandise, and the spectacular displays.

Linnet knew she had managed to pull Harte's of Knightsbridge into the twenty-first century; she was also aware that her work had only just begun. She had to keep improving on everything, launching new ideas to titillate the taste buds of the customers while making sure that her rivals didn't outsmart her.

India came up to London twice a month, and the two cousins enjoyed being together. Linnet was fully aware how much she needed India running the northern stores; many a time she asked herself how her great-grandmother had run all three stores when it took her all of her time to cope with just one.

If there were occasions when she panicked, felt alone, stressed out, and even a little afraid, there were many more times when she experienced the thrill of satisfaction, knowing she had pulled off yet another little coup. This might be the new Cholly Chello bag, called Cholly Baby, a smart little evening bag that had not walked, but run, out of the stores in London, Leeds, and Harrogate. Or it might be success with a beauty product or a spa treatment.

And so the days went by.

What started as a soft, drizzling rain had turned into a thunderstorm. Lightning flashed across the sky, thunder echoed like cannon in the distance, and the rain fell in a heavy stream. Jonathan Ainsley cursed under his breath, accepting that he would arrive late in Annecy. He wondered whether he ought to call Angharad in Paris, ask her to speak to her friend Bill Tremoyes. He decided against it. Tremoyes would wait for him; it was to his advantage to do so. Tremoyes wanted connections in China that only Jonathan had.

As Jonathan drove, he contemplated the American financier and tycoon, whom Angharad knew from Connecticut, a man to whom she had apparently sold many priceless antiques. Before embarking on this trip,

Jonathan had checked him out, and he was genuine enough. But what could Tremoyes know about the Hartes that would be to *his* advantage? Angharad had set this meeting up, had sworn to him that she did not know what it was Tremoyes had on the family, or a member of the family. What she did know was that it would be ruinous to them. Tremoyes had confided at least this to her.

So here he was, sitting in his Bentley Continental, driving to the Haute-Savoie in a bloody thunderstorm. And suddenly asking himself why he had listened to Angharad. Did she have an ulterior motive, sending him on this journey? Certainly she was duplicitous, he knew that now. But what motive could she have, except to help him? He knew she was enamored of him, in love with him, actually.

The rain slowly began to lessen, and Jonathan pressed his foot down hard on the accelerator, wanting to arrive as soon as possible, have the meeting with the American, and return to Paris early tomorrow. He pushed on, glad to have the empty road in front of him. He increased his speed considerably, turning up the stereo set in the dashboard, enjoying the soaring orchestra, the pianist pouring his very soul into the last movement of Rachmaninoff's Piano Concerto no. 2 in C minor.

Surging forward, enjoying the speed, the smooth ride, humming to himself, Jonathan Ainsley was unaware of the huge refrigeration truck barreling along the road behind him.

And in the relentless rain, the driver of the truck did not spot the Bentley immediately in front of him until it was too late. The truck rammed the Bentley, pushing it forward at such great speed it went into a tailspin.

Jonathan Ainsley felt the impact from behind and clutched at the wheel, pressed his foot down hard on the brake as the car rode on into a terrifying skid. The Bentley slid across the road, spun around, slid backward, and went off the road onto a bank, rolling over and over as it fell into a deep ravine.

The driver of the humongous truck braked, jumped out, and ran to the edge of the ravine. He looked down, heard the music playing for a split second before the car exploded, the night sky illuminated by the flames. He pulled out his cellular phone to call for an ambulance.

Late one afternoon toward the end of August, Jack Figg buzzed her. "It's me, Beauty," he announced when she answered her private line. "Do you have a minute? Can I come up and see you?"

"Of course. Is there a problem, Jack?"

"No. I wouldn't call it that. Be there in a jiffy."

Linnet stood up when Jonelle showed him in a few minutes later, and she went around the desk to embrace him. Then she led him to a circular table at one end of her mother's office and indicated the chairs. "Let's sit here, Jack, I much prefer it to those dumpy sofas."

He laughed. "So do I."

"Do you want a cup of tea?"

"Why not? But only if you are," he replied, sitting down.

Nodding, Linnet went to the phone, spoke to Jonelle on the intercom, and returned to the table, took a chair opposite Jack.

"How's your mother?" he asked.

"Great. The South of France has done her good, according to Dad. Julian and I have been trying to get down there off and on for ages, but we're just too busy right now."

"I know your routine. It's twenty-four seven these days, isn't it, Linny?"

She laughed and looked at the door as Jonelle came in carrying a tea tray. "It's good over here, please," Linnet told her, smiling.

Once they were alone again, Linnet poured the tea and asked, "So, Jack, if it's not a problem, what is it? Why did you want to see me?"

After taking a sip of his tea, Jack put the cup back in

the saucer and said, "Emma used to say to me that everyone got their just rewards in life, got what they deserved
in the end. And your great-grandmother was right."

"Do you mean we all reap what we sow?"

"Sort of, yes . . ." Settling back in the chair, Jack gave
her a long look through narrowed eyes. "One of my operatives in France just gave me some extraordinary news.
About Jonathan Ainsley."

"What is it?" Linnet asked, staring back at him with
great intensity. "You sound enigmatic, and solemn."

"Ainsley has been in a car crash. Outside Paris, so I
understand. He's in the American Hospital in Paris, has
sustained horrific injuries, according to my chap."

"He's not dead then?" Linnet asked.

"No. But he's not expected to live."

"What happened? Do you know?"

"A crash with a lorry."

"What about Angharad? Was she with him?"

"It seems she was not in the car." Jack's mobile war-
bled, and he took it out of his pocket. "Jack Figg here."
He listened attentively, and after a few seconds, he said,
"Keep in touch. And thanks, Pierre." Clicking off the
phone, he went on. "My operative who's at the hospital
told me that Jonathan Ainsley is not expected to live."

"Oh, my God! I can't believe it!" Linnet shouted, grabbing Jack's arms. "We're free of him at last! Free of his evil
and wickedness!"

"Just rewards, as Emma always said," Jack murmured.
"Jonathan Ainsley got his just rewards."

"I can't wait to tell everybody," Linnet cried. "There's
going to be a celebration throughout the family."

And there was.

Late one morning at the end of that week, Linnet had a
surprise visitor. She was studying the overall sales figures
for the previous month when a soft voice said, "Hello,
darling."

Swinging her head, a look of astonishment crossing her face, Linnet saw her mother standing in the doorway.

"Mummy!" she cried, rushing to her. "I didn't know you were back from the South of France."

"We got back last night," Paula responded, embracing her daughter, holding her close. "I've missed you, Linny."

"And I've missed you, Mummy. Come on, come and sit down. Better still, come and sit at the desk. It's yours, you know, I've only been borrowing it."

"No, no, I haven't come to work," Paula answered, and, spotting the circular table, she headed over to it, saying, "This is a good idea. Better than those awful sofas."

Linnet laughed, following her mother, thrilled to see her and looking so well. "You're your old self, Mums."

"Not quite, not yet, but I'm getting there."

Sitting down with her mother, Linnet asked, "Do you want a cup of coffee or tea? Anything?"

"No, not really, darling, but thank you. The store looks beautiful," Paula began and paused. Reaching out, she patted Linnet's hand. "You've done a wonderful job. And you've certainly introduced a fresh, modern look without destroying all of those traditional things our customers love. Your innovations have been successful. . . . *Congratulations*."

"Thanks, Mummy. It was a bit tough at times, and I never stopped wanting to ring you up, but Daddy was adamant, he didn't want me to bother you. He told me to do the best I could."

"Oh, yes, he told me all about that, Linny, and I longed to talk to *you*, too. I kept worrying about you, knowing how tough it is here sometimes. But I restrained myself."

"Let me sink or swim, was that it?" she asked, her green eyes sparkling.

"Sort of, darling."

"Anyway, Mummy, welcome back. It's wonderful to see you. I'll clean my stuff out of the office this afternoon. I never moved very much in, actually."

"No, no, you don't have to do that, Linnet."

"What do you mean?"

"This is your office."

Again Linnet looked baffled. "I don't understand."

"I'm not coming back to work." Paula sat back in the chair and gazed at her daughter for the longest moment, and then in a strong, steady voice, she explained, "Long ago, my grandmother told me that there comes a time in everybody's life when it's appropriate to step aside, to permit younger voices to be heard, greater visions to be perceived. This was said when she was eighty years old. It was at the birthday party we gave for her. She wasn't saying those words only to me, Linnet, ·she was saying them to everyone, and especially my generation, her grandchildren. It was the night she retired."

Linnet gazed back at her mother, transfixed. "Mummy, I don't understand . . ."

"I'm retiring, Linnet. It's your turn now, your turn to run the Harte stores, to be the boss lady, as you've always called me."

"But—"

"No buts," Paula cut in firmly. "All those years ago, Emma said this to me: 'I charge you to hold my dream.' And I did. Linnet, I charge you to hold Emma's dream and my dream. All this . . . it's yours now. I know you love the stores as she did, as I do. I know our dreams are safe in your small but very capable hands."

Epilogue

ZURICH, 2002

The woman was tall, slender, and elegantly dressed. She stood by the window in the dimly lit room, looking out at the mountains, snowcapped, glittering in the bright after-noon sunshine. She liked Zurich, it was a beautiful place. She hoped she would be living here. She swung around as the door opened and the man walked in, holding out his hand.

Hurrying toward him, she shook his outstretched hand and looked at him intently. "What are the results?" she asked in a low, well-modulated voice.

"I am happy to say that the X-rays told us a great deal more than we expected. The problem is not as terrible as you have been led to believe. You were right to come to us, and yes, we can help you. There will be recovery, I am certain of that. It will be slow. But in the end it is worth-while, is it not? If everything can be restored to normal? As, in fact, we believe it can."

"Yes, you're right, it *is* worth the time and effort. And money. I am going to trust you. I will put myself in your hands."

The man inclined his head graciously.

"Please give me a moment, and then I will come to your office to go over the details."

"Of course, madam," he said and slipped out of the room.

The woman walked over to the corner, looked down at the bandaged head and face, the almost lifeless body which was prone on the narrow bed.

She reached out, put her hand on one shoulder. "It's going to be all right," she whispered. "You'll be all right."

There was no response, no sound, no movement. Nothing.

She knew he was alive. The doctors here had confirmed that. And now she knew they would get him back for her. The director of the clinic had just told her so.

Bending down, she kissed the bandaged cheek and stepped away. She did not want to leave him, but she knew she must. "You'll get better, darling," she murmured and walked across the room to the door.

He had to get better. She was carrying his child, that longed-for child. And he would be called Jonathan Ainsley, just as his father was. Angharad Hughes Ainsley smiled to herself.

They would win in the end. Because they were winners. Jonathan had told her *that* the day he married her.

READ ON for an excerpt from
Barbara Taylor Bradford's next book

THE RAVENSCAR DYNASTY

Coming soon in hardcover from St. Martin's Press

YORKSHIRE 1904

Edward Deravenel galloped ahead at great speed, leaving his brothers behind, rapidly gaining the advantage. He urged his white stallion forward, oblivious to the icy weather, the lash of the wind on his face.

At one moment, half-turning in the saddle, glancing behind him, Edward laughed out loud, his hilarity filling the air as he waved to his brothers: George, endeavoring to catch up, his face grim in its determination . . . Richard, struggling even farther behind, yet laughing and waving back. But then Richard was the youngest, and much less competitive, the baby of the family, and Edward's particular favorite.

For a split second, Edward considered slowing down and allowing Richard to win this impromptu race, which had come about so spontaneously a short while before, then instantly changed his mind.

George would inevitably contrive to finish first, by pushing Richard out of the way in his overriding desire to be the winner. Somehow he always managed to do this, whenever he had the opportunity, no matter what the circumstances. And this Edward could not permit. Not ever. He strived to make certain Richard was never humiliated, never diminished by George, who was older than Richard by three years. In consequence of this, George frequently endeavored to lord it over the younger boy.

Edward continued at a gentler pace along the narrow path, glancing down to his left as he did. The plunging cliffs fell steeply to the rocks and the beach; six hundred feet below him the North Sea roared under the gusting wind, resembling polished steel in the winter sunlight.

The surging waves frothed and churned against the jagged rock formations, while above him kittiwakes, graceful and buoyant in flight, squawked stridently as they wheeled and turned against the pale sky. Hundreds of these beautiful white gulls with black-tipped wings made their homes on projecting ledges of rock on the cliff faces, and as a child he had watched them nesting through his binoculars.

He shivered involuntarily as the sudden remembrance of a tragedy of long ago hit him most forcibly. A man in his father's employ, who had been birdwatching, had plunged to his death from this very spot. Now, instinctively, Edward veered away from the precarious cliffs, headed in the direction of the dirt road which led across the moors and was much safer terrain.

This morning the moorland was dun-colored and patched with slabs of frozen snow, and there was no question in Edward's mind that he much preferred riding up here in the warmer months. At that time of year, the weather was more benign, the air even balmy and filled with the scent of wild flowers, and the northern summer light was dazzling.

Edward mentally chastised himself for taking his brothers out on this January day. He had realized, rather late, that it was far too bitter, especially for Richard, who tended to catch colds so easily. He dared not contemplate his mother's ire if the boy fell sick because of this ill-conceived outing on the cliffs.

Swinging his head, he saw that the boys had again slowed and were lagging behind, obviously even more fatigued than ever by the long ride. He must spur them on, encourage them to move forward with swiftness, get them home without delay and into the warmth of the house.

Beckoning to them, he shouted, "Come on, chaps! Let's get a move on!" And he set off at a brisk canter, hoping they would follow suit.

Once or twice he glanced behind him, pleased that they had heeded his words and were cantering hard on his heels. Within minutes, much to his profound relief, their ancestral home was in his direct line of vision and he couldn't wait to arrive there.

Ravenscar, the beautiful old manor house where the Deravanels had lived for centuries, stood on high ground, set back from the sea, and it dominated the surrounding landscape. Dark green trees, ancient, tall and stately, formed a semicircle around it on three sides, and these in turn were backed by high stone walls; the fourth wall was a natural one— the North Sea. This stretched into infinity below the tiered gardens and sloping lawns that ended at the edge of the precipitous cliffs.

As Edward drew closer, he could easily make out the crenellation along the line of the roof, smoke curling up from the chimneys, and the many mullioned windows glittering in the sunlight. Within seconds he was bringing his horse to a slow trot, riding through the black iron gates and up the long, tree-lined drive. This ended with some abruptness in a small, circular courtyard covered with gravel and with a sundial in its center.

The house was built of a local, pale-colored stone that had mellowed to a soft golden beige with the passing of the centuries. An Elizabethan house, it typified Tudor architecture with its recesses and bays, gables and battlements, and many windows of differing sizes. Ravenscar was one of those grand houses from the past, and it was utterly unique, and had a lovely symmetry and charm all of its own. To Edward, there was a sense of timelessness about it, a quality of serenity and peace dwelling in its gently flowing facade, and he understood why his forebears had always cherished and cared for this treasure.

The Deravenels had lived in their house by the sea since 1578, the year it was finished. Before then, for many centuries, the family had occupied the fortified castle that had stood at the bottom of the gardens on the edge of the cliffs; a ruin now, it was nonetheless a well maintained ruin. This stronghold had been built in 1070 by the founding father of the dynasty, one Guy de Ravenel, a young knight from Falaise, liegeman of William, Duke of Normandy.

Duke William had invaded England in 1066, claiming his right to the English throne through his cousin, the deceased monarch Edward the Confessor, who had promised him that the throne would be his one day. But for political convenience, Edward the Confessor had reneged on that promise and passed over William in favor of his wife's brother, Harold, bequeathing the throne to the man who became, briefly, Harold III.

Believing his claim to be absolutely legitimate, William had crossed the English Channel with the six knights who were his trusted childhood friends and a large army. He defeated Harold III at the Battle of Hastings, was proclaimed William the Conqueror, and crowned on Christmas Day of 1066.

Some time later, William had despatched Guy de Ravenel to the north to act as his marshall. Based in

Yorkshire, Guy had followed William's orders, had kept the peace, by force when necessary, built defenses and forts, and ensured the north's loyalty to his friend the Norman king. And Guy had been enriched by William because of his staunch loyalty and unparalleled success.

Ever since that time, some eight hundred and thirty-five years ago, descendants of Guy de Ravenel had lived on this long stretch of coastline high above the North Sea known as Ravenscar. Nearby was the ancient seaport and spa of Scarborough; a little farther along the expansive stretch of coast was a picturesque fishing village with the quaint name of Robin Hood's Bay. Both dated back to Roman times.

Moving forward, Edward rode out of the courtyard and around to the back of the house, heading for the stable block. He clattered into the cobbled stable yard, his brothers following behind him, and jumped off his horse with his usual vitality and energy. As he hurried over to his youngest brother, he greeted the stable lads cheerfully; a moment later he was reaching up for the eight-year-old Richard, exclaiming, "Let me help you down, Dick!"

Richard shook his head vehemently. "I can manage, Ned. I truly can," the boy protested, stealing a surreptitious look at George through the corner of his eye. He knew only too well that George would tease him unmercifully if Ned helped him to dismount.

But Ned paid not the slightest attention to

Richard; he put his strong arms around him, obviously determined to lift him out of the saddle. Richard sighed, swallowing another protest that had sprung to his lips. Accepting that he now had no other choice, he slipped his riding boots out of the stirrups and reluctantly slid into his brother's enfolding arms.

For a split second, Edward held Richard close to his chest, hugging him tightly, and then he put him down on the cobblestones, noting, as he did, that the youngster's narrow face was pinched with cold and drained of all color. My fault, he chided himself, regretting more than ever his thoughtlessness earlier that morning.

"Thank you, Ned," Richard murmured, staring up into Edward's face through his steady, slate-gray eyes. His eldest brother was six feet four, broad of chest, very strong and athletic. His brilliant eyes were as blue as the speedwells that grew in the summer meadows, and his thick hair was a stunning burnished red-gold. To Richard, and every woman who met him, Edward Deravenel was the handsomest man alive, plus he had a warm, outgoing and endearing personality. He was affable, inordinately friendly, and blessed with a beguiling natural charm that captivated everyone. Richard loved him more than anyone else in the family, was completely devoted to him, and he would be all of Edward's life, and even after that.

"Inside the house as fast as you can," Edward cried, giving Richard an affectionate push toward the side door, which led to the mud room. "And you, too, George, my lad. No dawdling around this morning."

The two boys did his bidding, and as Edward followed them at a quick pace, he called out to one of the stable lads, "The horses have been ridden hard this morning, Ernie. They need your very best rubdown, and put the heavy wool blankets on them before you give them water and feed."

"Aye, Master Edward," Ernie shouted back, glancing at him. He and the other stable lad took the reins of the three horses and led them across the yard in the direction of the stables and the sheltered stalls where the tack room was also located.

Once Edward and his brothers entered the mud room, they felt the warmth of the house surrounding them. Shedding their black-and-white checked caps and thick woolen Inverness capes and hanging them up, they scraped their riding boots free of dirt. A moment later, they all went down the corridor at the back of the house, heading toward the Long Hall at its center.

"I shall ask Cook to make us a small snack and hot tea," Edward informed them, an arm on each of their shoulders. "Perhaps she'll be able to rustle up some of those delicious Cornish pasties of hers."

"Oooh, I hope so," George exclaimed, added, "And sausage rolls as well. I'm very hungry."

"And what about you?" Edward asked, glancing down at Richard. "Aren't *you* ravenous?"

"I will enjoy the hot tea," Richard answered, smiling up at his brother. "But I'm not really very hungry, Ned."

"We'll see about that when you smell some of Cook's tidbits. You know how they make your mouth water," Edward said and shepherded his brothers into the Morning Room.

The boys raced over to the huge fire roaring in the grate, stood warming their hands, glad at last to be thawing out. After doing exactly the same thing, Edward swung around and went back to the door, explaining, "I'm going to have a word with Cook. I'll be back in a few minutes." Closing the door behind him, he left them to their own devices. Edward hoped George wouldn't tease Richard; he so often did. He was a bit of a bully, and Richard had not yet learned how to go into verbal combat.

Mrs. Latham, the cook at Ravenscar, glanced up expectantly when the door to her kitchen opened. Instantly her mouth broke into laughter. "Why, good mornin', Master Edward!" Her surprise and pleasure were most evident.

"Hello, Mrs. Latham," he responded in his usual

polite manner, giving her one of his most beguiling smiles. "I've come to beg a small favor. I know how busy you are on Tuesdays, but would it be possible for you to make a large pot of tea and something to eat for us? The boys are famished after their ride on the cliffs."

"By gum, I bet they are!" She wiped her big, capable hands on a tea towel and strode across to the long oak table standing in the middle of the huge kitchen. "I've just been baking a few things—" She broke off, waved a hand in front of her morning's work and added, "Pork pies, fishcakes, Cornish pasties, sausage rolls and savory tarts. Take a look, and take your pick, Master Edward."

"How splendid," he said, grinning at her. "A veritable feast, Cook. But then you're the best in the world, no one has your remarkable skill in the kitchen, no one."

"Oh, get along with yer, sir. It's a real flatterer yer are." This was said with a hint of pride at his compliment. Straightening her back, she added, "I knows yer all like the Cornish pasties, and Master George is ever so fond of my sausage rolls. I'll get a tray ready for yer, sir, and send young Polly with it in a tick, once I've made the pot of tea. Does that suit, Master Edward?"

"It does indeed, Cook, and I can't wait to sample some of this fare, it smells delicious. Thank you so much, I do appreciate it." Once more he gave her the benefit of his warm smile and inclined his head.

"My pleasure," she called after him, watching him walk over to the door.

Swinging his head, he grinned at her, waved and was gone.

Mrs. Latham stared at the door for a moment, her eyes filled with admiration for him. Edward Deravenel was blessed with the most pleasant nature as well as those staggering good looks. She couldn't help wondering how many hearts he would break in his lifetime. Scores, no doubt. At eighteen he already had women falling at his feet. Spoil him, that they will, she thought, clucking to herself, turning to the ovens. Aye, they'll all spoil him rotten, give him whatever he wants, and that's not always a good thing for a man. No, it's not. I've seen many a toff like him ruined by women, more's the pity.

She swung around as the door opened again and muttered, "There yer are, young Polly. I was just wondering where yer'd got to—" Cook broke off and clucked again. "Bump in ter Master Edward, did yer, lass?"

The parlor maid nodded and blushed. "He's ever so nice ter me, Cook."

Mrs. Latham shook her head and sighed, but made no further reference to Edward. Instead she continued, "Set a large tray, please, Polly. I'm preparing a mornin' snack for Master Edward and his brothers. When it's ready, yer can take it ter the Morning Room."

"Yes, Cook."

After crossing the Long Hall, Edward made his way back to the Morning Room where he had left his brothers. He was lost in thought, contemplating his return to university. Today was Tuesday, January the fifth; in two days he would travel to London and go up to Oxford that weekend. He was looking forward to returning and especially pleased that he would be reunited with his best friend and boon companion of many years, Will Hasling, who was also an undergraduate.

His attention suddenly focused on the end of the corridor. He had just caught a fleeting glimpse of a dark skirt and jacket, a froth of white at the neck, a well-coiffed blonde head. And then there had been the click of a door closing.

He hurried forward, passing the Morning Room, not stopping until he reached the last room at the end of the corridor. Pausing at the door which had just closed, he listened intently. There were no voices, only the sound of someone moving around, the rustle of papers. Tapping lightly on the door, he did not wait to be summoned inside. He simply walked in.

The woman in the room stared at him, obviously startled.

Edward closed the door, leaned against it. "Hello, Alice."

The woman took a deep breath, then exhaled. After a moment she inclined her head, stared at him, but said not one word.

Stepping forward he took hold of her arm just as she started to move around the desk, wanting to put it between them.

Holding her arm, pulling her closer, he leaned forward and murmured, "Alice, my dear, you didn't come to see me last night. I was devastated . . ."

"Please," she whispered, "let go of me. Your mother might walk in at any moment. Please, Master Edward."

"Not *Master Edward*. Surely you mean Ned . . . that's what you whispered to me in the dark last week."

She looked up into the handsome face, was momentarily blinded by the vivid blue eyes, and closed her own.

Edward was instantly alarmed. "What is it, Alice?" he asked in concern. "Are you ill?"

She opened her eyes, shook her head. "No, no, I am not ill. But I can't see you anymore. I'm afraid of . . . what might happen to me if we were to continue our . . . intimacy."

"Oh, Alice, darling, don't be frightened—"

"And then there's your mother to consider," she cut in peremptorily, her eyes darting to the door. "She would be furious if she found out about our liaison. You know she would dismiss me at once. And I do need this position . . ." Her voice trailed off, and she swallowed hard.

Looking down into her pretty face, Edward saw the tears glistening in her hazel eyes, and he now noticed the fear and anxiety gripping her. He nodded. "Yes, I'm afraid you are correct, Alice." He studied her for a moment. If she had been from the working class, or even a woman of his own class, he would have pressed his suit, certain that there would be no serious repercussions. But Alice Morgan was from the middle class, and also very vulnerable, and because of that he knew he must show consideration to her. She was the widow of a local doctor with a small child to support, and she did indeed need this position as his mother's secretary. And so because he was a compassionate young man and had a kind heart, he let go of her arm and stepped back.

A rueful smile touched his lips and he let out a small sigh. "I won't trouble you any further, Alice," he said in a very low voice. "You are perfectly right, everything you have said is true. And I don't wish to be a nuisance to you or cause you any difficulties."

Leaning forward, she touched his cheek with one finger, and then she swiftly edged around the end of the desk, where she stood looking at him.

"Thank you," she said in a voice as low as his had been. "Thank you for being such a gentleman."

He left without glancing at her again, and as he closed the door behind him he did not hear her say, "It's not because I don't want you . . . I do. But I know you're the kind of man who can't help but break a woman's heart."